WITH
FROM THE CO
SACRAMENTO P
SACR
S
D0404028

stand by me

PAT SIMMONS

sourcebooks casablanca

Copyright © 2021 by Pat Simmons
Cover and internal design © 2021 by Sourcebooks
Cover design by Elsie Lyons

Sourcebooks and the colophon are registered trademarks of Sourcebooks.

All rights reserved. No part of this book may be reproduced in any form or by any electronic or mechanical means including information storage and retrieval systems—except in the case of brief quotations embodied in critical articles or reviews—without permission in writing from its publisher, Sourcebooks.

The characters and events portrayed in this book are fictitious or are used fictitiously. Any similarity to real persons, living or dead, is purely coincidental and not intended by the author.

All brand names and product names used in this book are trademarks, registered trademarks, or trade names of their respective holders. Sourcebooks is not associated with any product or vendor in this book.

Published by Sourcebooks Casablanca, an imprint of Sourcebooks
P.O. Box 4410, Naperville, Illinois 60567-4410
(630) 961-3900
sourcebooks.com

Library of Congress Cataloging-in-Publication Data

Names: Simmons, Pat, author.
Title: Stand by me / Pat Simmons.
Description: Naperville, Illinois : Sourcebooks Casablanca, [2021] | Series: Family is forever ; 3
Identifiers: LCCN 2021023691 (print) | LCCN 2021023692 (ebook) | (trade paperback) | (epub)
Subjects: GSAFD: Love stories. | Christian fiction. | LCGFT: Domestic fiction.
Classification: LCC PS3619.I56125 S73 2021 (print) | LCC PS3619.I56125 (ebook) | DDC 813/.6--dc23
LC record available at https://lccn.loc.gov/2021023691
LC ebook record available at https://lccn.loc.gov/2021023692

Printed and bound in the United States of America.
KP 10 9 8 7 6 5 4 3 2 1

Caring for a loved one or friend may seem like a thankless job, but take heart. My grandmother, Jessie Atkins, was diagnosed with dementia symptoms in the mid-1990s. She couldn't remember my name or how we were related, but one morning, she made a profound statement that I still carry close to my heart today.
"I want to thank you for what you're doing. You never know whose hand is going to give you that last piece of bread."

And let us not be weary in well doing: for in due season we shall reap, if we faint not.

—Galatians 6:9 (KJV)

Chapter 1

"Excuse me. You look familiar." A deep, unfamiliar voice pulled Kym Knicely from her musings. A man stood in front of her, invading her personal space. His presence interrupted her from flipping through magazine pages as she waited at St. Louis's Lambert airport to board her flight back home to Baltimore. He could use a fresh pickup line.

Kym raised an arched brow as she lifted her head and almost gasped for breath. Trying not to ogle the intruder, she could only stare. Kym would have definitely remembered meeting this good-looking man who evidently cared about his appearance even when he traveled. While some dressed for comfort—like her, in fashionable jeans and a simple top, with comfy flats on her feet—he, on the other hand, was meticulously coordinated in a sweater, slacks, a blazer, and dress shoes.

"Sorry, we haven't met." She *wished* there were something familiar about him, but there wasn't, so Kym dismissed the handsome stranger, found her breath, and continued reading.

At thirty-six years old, she gave the illusion of contentment in her single state. Behind closed doors, she suffered through the loneliness. Keeping a busy lifestyle was merely a cover-up. She wanted what her sisters had: husbands who loved them unconditionally.

Not that Kym hadn't attracted her share of attention from some notable eligible bachelors. Attraction didn't equal love. Plus, something always seemed amiss about them. She wanted a man to be more than intelligent, confident, and a gentleman beyond measure. Since handsomeness was in the eye of the beholder, good-looking had to be in the top five assets. But the man who snagged her had to possess a selflessness about him.

Maybe she needed a cupid. Kym's aunt had passed away two years prior. Even in Aunt Tweet's sickness, she somehow had played matchmaker for Kym's two younger sisters, Tabitha and Rachel. *Where are you, Aunt Tweet, to track down Mr. Right One for Me?* she mused.

While in St. Louis, Kym had mixed her business with pleasure and attended a three-day conference on leadership in higher education. She found the seminars informative, and they'd reconfirmed she was on the right path with her dissertation to target children in grade and middle schools. It was the seed to nourishing their desire to graduate from high school, but the hand-holding couldn't stop there. It was up to administrators and the community to lift up teenagers to apply to college, then help them to finish the course.

Afterward, she couldn't wait to smother her first and only nephew, Marcus Brownlee Whittington, with hugs and smooches. It was a perfect way to end her trip—a visit with Tabitha and her family—despite also using the time to tweak material for the upcoming week of October midterms.

Marcus wasn't a *junior*. Her sister and brother-in-law had bestowed the middle name in honor of their late relative Priscilla "Aunt Tweet" Brownlee. She had impacted her three great-nieces' lives as children and adults.

Tit for tat, Rachel, her other sister, expected a visit too. And Kym would oblige. She had already made travel plans to fly to Nashville around Christmas to be with her baby sister, who was a breast cancer survivor.

It was the prayers and God's will that her illness remained in remission for almost two years. Nicholas, Rachel's hubby, spoiled her rotten. Kym suspected it had nothing to do with the cancer but that he was deeply in love with his wife for better or worse.

As the oldest, Kym refused to relinquish her right to check on her sisters, so: *Husbands, beware. Sister chats took precedence.*

Tabitha Knicely Whittington had returned to their childhood home in St. Louis, the Gateway City; Rachel Knicely Adams loved her life in Nashville, Music City; and Kym wouldn't dream of living anywhere other than Charm City, with Baltimore's Inner Harbor.

Home. Maybe she and her best friend, Judith, could enjoy an evening cruise to relax after the exhausting week.

A while later, the gentleman returned. "Is this seat taken?"

He didn't wait for her to answer as he claimed the chair as if it were assigned to him. Handsome but rude—a bad combination. Best to ignore him, although it was a challenge as his faint cologne tickled her nose.

"Hi again. I'm Chaz Banks." He extended his hand.

His persistence bordered on annoyance. She accepted his gentle grasp—strong hands—and nodded without giving her name.

From the corner of her eye, she saw him study her. He bobbed his head and bit his bottom lip as if he had come to a decision.

"I saw you in the audience at LLU's presidential speaker series. You were stunning in that white pantsuit."

"Excuse me?" Was he a stalker? Had the man followed her from Baltimore? Her heart raced as she considered her options: call for security, which could cause the airport to be locked down, or pray for her safety. She chose the latter.

"I didn't mean to cause you alarm." Chaz frowned. "I live in Baltimore, and I'm an alumnus of Lewis Latimer University."

Okay. Breathe. That explained him being on campus, but that event had been more than a month ago. Kym remembered stepping out in that two-piece pantsuit with gold heels and jewelry. She had garnered many compliments that evening from colleagues and students. A few days after that seminar, Kym had retired her "wear anything white" streak, which had consumed her fashion sense for weeks. "An alum?"

"Yep." He nodded. "Proud LLU Lion. BA in finance, master's in public health."

Tilting her head, Kym discreetly scrutinized him. She was doubly impressed. There was a lot to be said for a man who valued education, and his field of choice said something about his commitment in life.

A lazy grin spread across his smooth face, clean shaven except for a black mustache sprinkled with gray strands. Nice smile. White teeth. "I'm Kym Knicely."

His eyes twinkled. "Honored to meet you, Kym. What about you? What's your connection to Lewis Latimer University? You're an alumna?"

"Only for grad school. I earned my BA from Temple in Philly, then I worked in the private sector for a couple of years, trying to find my purpose."

"Did you?" He seemed interested in her answer.

"I did. After a few substitute teaching assignments at grade schools, I accepted my calling to mentor. When I shared my concerns about my students lagging behind in reading and math, my aunt encouraged me to make a difference for their future and seek a graduate degree."

Kym caught herself rambling and stopped. Why was she opening up to this stranger, even if they had exchanged names? Identity theft was real. She was giving out pertinent info that could be password hints.

"So you're not a native?" Chaz made himself comfortable. "What attracted you to my city?"

The softness in his voice encouraged her not to retreat. "No, I'm a St. Louisan. Go Cards," she said the city's baseball fans' cheer. "I had visited Baltimore a couple of times and was wowed by the historical landmarks and its unique museums."

His attention was intense. Not once did his eyes stray to the activity around them. She liked that.

"It offered more than those physical attractions. My great-aunt, who we affectionately called Aunt Tweet, attended Storer College, one of the earliest Black colleges. Education was a big deal for Blacks back then, and my aunt made it her business to instill in us that education opened doors. Enslaved Africans sought learning to read, while slaveholders withheld the opportunity."

"I think back in the day, every Black had a schoolteacher in the family," he said, adding to their conversation.

"Right. There was no way any of the Knicely girls were not going to attend college. Only my youngest sister attended a historically Black college and university—Fisk in Nashville. Since prestigious Lewis Latimer University was an HBCU, hands down, Baltimore was a winner."

As Chaz rubbed his chin, she glanced at his ring finger for the first time. Kym wondered at his status. He could be married and not displaying his commitment, or married and with no regards for his vows, or single and satisfied, enjoying the lifestyle of no entanglements. She chided herself for questioning. *Focus on a professional conversation.*

"What were your majors?"

He stayed on topic. She liked that. "Since I couldn't decide on a concentration, I pursued a bachelor's in liberal arts. Being well-rounded has its advantages to explore different fields. I was still indecisive when I applied to LLU's impressive grad school."

He shook his head and squinted. "You don't strike me as a woman who doesn't know what she wants."

How am I supposed to take that—as a pickup line, or is he perceptive? There was something about him that made her comfortable to talk. Clearly, she was overthinking it. "Because of my love of fine arts and history, I was torn between a master's in museum studies and historical preservation..."

He leaned closer, and she caught a whiff of his subtle cologne or aftershave. His dark brown skin was flawless—not a razor mishap in sight. His features were sculptured with care.

"What was your other choice?"

Kym found herself blushing from this man's attention. "African American studies."

"So which one was the winner?" His eyes sparkled.

"Neither." She laughed at herself. "I prayed and asked for direction. God reminded me of the students when I was their substitute teacher. I chose curriculum and instruction as my concentration for my master's. That allowed me to research the coursework in the local public school system, then I compared it to the national curriculum of districts that showed improvements." She paused. "Sorry, when I talk shop, I get carried away."

"I'm not complaining, and I'm following you every step of the way." He shifted in his seat and exhaled as if he had sucked in a breath of fresh air. "Please continue."

A willing audience to pass the time until her flight. "Well, after my aunt's death, I applied to the doctoral program in urban education. I've worked on my project for four years. Finally, I plan to graduate next spring. If only my aunt were alive to see my achievement because of her gentle guidance." Kym swallowed back the sentimental moment.

Chaz gave her soft applause. "I'd be honored to stand in the gap for her, Professor Knicely," he stated with a surprising conviction as the ticket agent instructed everyone to line up in their designated boarding numbers under the A section.

"Not yet." Kym blinked as she stood to gather her bags. "That's more than six months away."

"I'll remember." Chaz got to his feet too.

Sure you will. Either he was mocking her or committing himself without much thought. She wasn't holding her breath. She nodded her goodbye and got in line to board Southwest Flight 5070 to Baltimore.

Oh no. Not again. Chaz had allowed Kym to vanish the day of the speaker series before he could introduce himself. Not today as he admired Kym's strut that had a slight bounce down the ramp.

Who would have thought, at a random airport, his virtual reality would become an actuality as he watched her check in for her flight. His heart rate sped up at the mirage. He'd blinked and studied the image. Of all places, it was here in St. Louis, dressed in a shade of blue, which made her stand out just like the white outfit she wore on the day of the lecture.

If he couldn't find a seat next to her or bribe another passenger, he would sit as close as possible. Chaz twitched his mustache, a habit he had developed when in deep thought since forever. Yep, he had a plan.

Once on board, he thanked God for the small blessings to see her adjacent seat vacant. Kym was glancing out the window. Another gentleman hugged the aisle spot. That didn't deter Chaz, although he would rather sit in the back rows or near the engine than squeeze his six-two, solid bulk into a space meant for a petite teenager. But if he was going to seize the moment, Chaz needed to make an exception.

"Are you saving this seat, Professor Knicely?" He waited for her permission to insinuate himself.

Kym glanced up, and unlike the first time, mirth danced in her eyes, while the man in her row didn't look happy for the intrusion, as if he had intentions of his own. *Sorry, buddy*, Chaz mused.

"I'm not."

Permission granted, so Chaz lifted his carry-on overhead and held up the line, forcing the gentleman to stand and allow him entry.

Surprisingly, he fit into the middle seat, adjusted his weight, and displayed a smug grin as he clicked his seat belt.

"Kinda tight fit, don't you think?" Kym chuckled at his distress. He surrendered his façade and laughed with her.

"What's a little discomfort to be in the presence of one of the loveliest and most intriguing women I've met in a long, long time?" He attempted to stretch his legs, but his movement was thwarted by the constraint of the seat in front of him.

Chaz eyed Kym as she faced the window, attempting to hide her amusement. *Perfect*, he thought as he admired her features. She had dark, silky hair that was thick and long, but her curls appeared to be as soft as her skin. Her complexion was unblemished. She was a beauty. There was no rock on her ring finger. What was wrong with the men who saw her?

He was content watching her as others boarded the plane. When she turned and caught him staring, he didn't blink. She lifted a brow as if challenging him to look away—he didn't.

She squinted. "Do you have family in St. Louis?"

"I do." He nodded, glad their conversation had turned from professional to personal. "My older son, his wife, and my granddaughter—the apple of Grandpa's eye," he boasted as he unsnapped his phone from his belt, unlocked it, and scrolled through party pictures, plus a recent family portrait of the Banks clan. "I was in town for her fourth birthday." He pointed to Chauncy.

"They're beautiful. Your son looks like you."

"I agree with both compliments." He didn't hide his grin. "You still have family in the Lou?" He noticed her eyes lit up when she talked about something she was passionate about.

"Yes, my sister, brother-in-law, and my little nephew, who has Auntie wrapped around his finger." She beamed, unlocking her phone and scanning through her photo gallery.

Although her sister was as pretty as Kym, the woman sitting next to him was a standout. "No husband or children?"

"No wife?" she countered without answering his question, and he liked her boldness.

"Not anymore." Chaz shook his head. "I married at eighteen, was a father at nineteen—she wasn't pregnant beforehand—and divorced by thirty-three. Instead of growing together, we grew apart." He thought he was as confident as any other man, but this was one area in his life where he had failed—as a husband.

She must have picked up on his sullen mood because she touched his arm. Not a caress, more like a tap. It was enough for the hair on his arms to rise and pull him back to the present.

Kym pointed to the front. "They've asked for everyone's attention."

He grunted. "I can probably recite their instructions in my sleep. Can't you?"

"Maybe, but I'm an instructor. I always pay attention."

Noted. She had put him in his place. "Good to know."

During the flight, Chaz took his cues from Kym. When she became silent, he didn't interrupt her quiet time. Anyway, short nap was a premium after an exhausting visit.

To say that he had a special bond with Chauncy, his namesake, was an understatement. At forty-two, some of his female colleagues said he looked way too young to be a grandpa, but Chaz was proud to hold that title ever since his first grandchild made her entrance into the world four years ago. Chauncy Lauren Banks even had those bluish Banks eyes at birth that had yet to transition to brown, retaining their bluish-gray color.

For the first two years of Chauncy's life, she had developed according to the milestone checklist; then without warning, she had digressed and her chatter stopped. After extensive testing, his granddaughter had been diagnosed with autism. Everyone was devastated. What did that even mean?

From working in the public health sector, Chaz knew the basics: boys were four times more likely to have autism than girls—so why had his sweet little princess been affected? Babies born to older parents could be at a higher risk. Gee and Lana were young, so why his Chauncy? The facts didn't add up. His granddaughter's young life would be filled with therapies: speech, occupational, applied behavior, and on and on. The doctors had tried to encourage the family, but it was prayers that gave them all peace and acceptance to support Chauncy.

When Kym's head tilted to the side and indicated she was asleep, he grimaced from being restrained in his seat and closed his eyes, hoping to drift into darkness too.

Chapter 2

Kym had been played—or she had created a fantasy. In her mind, Chaz Banks had pursued her, wooed her, and cut her loose within a two-hour plane ride. His presence had been overpowering, his conversation engaging, and his wit entertaining. Not to mention the man was mesmerizing. Yep, he was all that. It didn't happen often, but Kym *was* flattered by a man's attention—his.

That flattery fizzled to humiliation as they parted ways at baggage claim. Actually, it was after they made pit stops at the restrooms before retrieving their luggage. What had happened? Chaz had waved goodbye without asking for her number or showing a desire to see her again. Reality check: all the personal interest she thought he had was wishful thinking on her part.

She returned his wave as another round of passengers circled the carousel to retrieve their bags. Kym gripped her luggage, held her head high, and hurried toward the exit, swallowing the disappointment.

There hadn't been any commitments or emotional investment, just friendly chat to pass the time. She was tired of the games men played, and Chaz was toying with her, right? She was wasting too many brain cells on deciphering his actions.

Waiting for her at curbside was her best friend and colleague Judith Berry. After putting her carry-on in the back of Judith's car, Kym settled in her seat and looked ahead, deep in thought. The whole thing seemed silly—to be smitten by a stranger in a short span of time—so she blamed her quietness on a long trip. Judith accepted it.

Once behind closed doors at her home in Baltimore's historic neighborhood of Mount Vernon, she had to repent. She lied to herself and Judith. They were both of the same status: outgoing professionals and committed churchgoers who, despite a sometimes exhausting social calendar, remained single. Judith was convinced the good ones were either married or in a nursing facility. On the other hand, Kym held out hope love would find her, not the other way around, where she had to go on the hunt.

"I've used enough brainpower for one day," she mumbled and prepared for bed after showering and reading her Bible. She had to keep hope alive that God had someone for her. Besides, she had enough to keep her focused this week, with giving midterm exams and grading them.

The next morning, Kym had regained her "no cares in the world" attitude as she sashayed across LLU's campus. She was a doctoral candidate and loving life, she reminded herself as she nodded to colleagues and greeted random students.

In her office, Kym overrode the silent protests in her mind to let Chaz fade away. Instead, she convinced herself it was okay to search through the *Alumni News Magazine*'s online archives to verify Chaz's story and see if there were any random photos of him that might have been taken at the presidential speaker series talk—there weren't.

Why do I care? she thought. She had students in her urban education class nervously waiting for her to administer their tests, which meant she needed to head out. Yet her body wouldn't move until she checked one more place—the sidebar under *ON THE MOVE*, which highlighted news about alumni's promotions, appointments, and retirements. She was about to give up when there was a short mention under class notes:

Charles "Chaz" Banks ('01, '10) has a new role as community public health liaison at Johns Hopkins Bloomberg School of Public Health. Banks previously worked as a health planner with the government of Maryland.

"So you are legit." She peered closer to admire his slight smirk in the photo.

"Who?" Judith wore an odd expression, appearing in the doorway with her laptop.

Kym jumped and stood behind her desk. She signed off her computer. "Nobody important."

"Good. Come on. I'm sure our students are ready to be done with their midterms." Judith smiled. Her friend was a whiz when it came to numbers and taught college algebra, trigonometry, and calculus. She also tutored, so it wasn't unusual for Judith to hold those sessions in her office, library, and sometimes in a conference room for groups. Judith and Kym were kindred spirits as teachers. They were both committed to excellence.

Once Kym was in her classroom, she gave her students instructions and the code for them to download their tests. Some questions were multiple choice, but the bulk of the exams were essay questions. Kym liked to read how her students deduced their opinions.

While she waited, her mind drifted back to Chaz. What had happened in his marriage that resulted in a divorce? Was he cheating? Maybe she was biased, but when it came to failed marriages, it was, most times, the man's fault. She sighed. But Kym had heard of some wives walking away too.

Forty-five minutes later, her students had completed their exams and begun to trickle out. After the last one left, Kym stood, stretched, and exited the classroom herself. She had a few hours before she had to administer the afternoon exam. In the interim, she would either start to grade tests or review the introduction on her dissertation outline to have a solid oral defense on mobile tutoring.

Kym and a fellow grad student had coauthored a study to receive a grant from the Annie E. Casey Foundation for a one-year pilot program. The model had gotten the attention of Baltimore's media outlets, including *The Afro,* noted as the longest-running African American family-owned newspaper in the nation.

At the time, it had been too early to call the project a success, because the students' educational performances had to be followed for several years. To further expand the program and make it permanent, they needed more funding. That was where the stats and the limited results had to justify the six-figure funding request from another foundation.

Kym's mind was in the research zone when she blinked and almost broke a heel to keep from stumbling. Chaz Banks was on campus and posted outside her door? When he saw her, he stood. One couldn't help but admire his larger-than-life presence and his lazy swagger toward her, meeting her halfway. He cast her a warm smile while his eyes appeared to dance.

Her heart fluttered at the surprise. She was sure they had gone their separate ways at the airport. *Act cool*, she coaxed herself. Clutching her laptop against her chest, she nodded and switched to her professional mode. "Why, hello, Chaz. Can I help you with something?"

His eyes twinkled as if he wasn't buying her aloofness. He lifted a bag. "I brought you crab cakes. Please tell me you aren't allergic to fish or seafood."

Chaz shows ups unexpectedly and wants to have a meal with her? Strange, I'll bite. "I'm not…" She tried not to inhale the aroma from Jimmy's Famous Seafood and remain all business, especially with a few onlookers in the background. It wasn't every day that a handsome man showed up at her office. "But you don't have an appointment. We're in the middle of midterms…"

He stepped closer, less than a foot from her breathing space. "I need a moment of your time to apologize."

Suspicious, Kym squinted. "For what?" *Capturing my thoughts?*

"I have a bribe gift. If you invite me into your office where I can speak freely, I'll explain."

Although the man appeared confident on the outside, she sensed a vulnerability and suspected his request was a masked plea. "I think you just invited yourself with those crab cakes." She lifted the bag from his hand. Laughing, he matched her steps. After she unlocked her door, Kym moved back so he could enter. As she glanced over her shoulder, she locked eyes with Judith.

The expression on her friend's face was priceless as her jaw dropped. "Wow."

Right? Kym mouthed before turning back and offering Chaz a chair in front of her desk, then taking hers behind it as if he were a student. Folding her hands, she studied him; he appeared to be fascinated by her recognitions and other plaques on the walls. Again, the man was unexplainable.

When he met her eyes, he smiled again. "I hope you plan to share those." He nodded toward the bag.

"I'm thinking about it." She chuckled, then sobered. Kym wasn't a game player, so she didn't understand his motive. "I didn't expect to see you again except in passing at some university events."

She tapped her finger against her desk, expecting an answer. If he wanted a crumb of a crab cake, he'd better start explaining, because they were best served hot. Plus, she had another midterm to give in a couple of hours. Learning from the best, Kym gave him one of her mother's no-nonsense expressions that made him look sheepish. *Good.* That would give her time to control her nervousness.

"I waved at you—"

"And I waved back." She shrugged as if it was no big deal.

"Yes, then you left"—his tone was accusatory—"before I could grab my suitcase and ask for your number."

Oh. Her heart soared at his admission. So he did want to see her again.

"When I came out of the men's room, I waited a few minutes across from the women's because I know how you ladies take extra time. When you didn't reappear, I assumed you had gone ahead to the baggage area. That's where I last saw you, and I waved. I didn't expect you to be gone in a flash as I wormed my way over to where you were standing."

Kym remained silent; just because he confessed didn't mean she felt obliged to come clean and reveal her disappointment too.

"So I'm here today for your number that you cheated me out of getting yesterday." His lips curled, but his expression became intense, and he didn't blink. "Now that I have a name to go with your gorgeous face, I don't want to hope for another chance meeting. I came with a peace offering and to invite you out to lunch or dinner." He lifted a finger as if she were about to speak. "Whichever comes first. If you're not seeing anyone."

"I'm not, and I'll think about dinner." She unwrapped his delivery. With a cake in hand, Kym bowed her head and gave thanks. As she sampled it, Kym consented to dinner. "Next week would be nice."

Chaz frowned. "I was hoping you would say in the next few days."

She stopped chewing. Huh? His assertiveness charmed her. There was something about Chaz Banks that made her want to concede. "I have midterms to grade in between going over my dissertation."

He leaned forward and reached for the bag, which she inched closer to her in a cat-and-mouse game. "Aren't you at least a bit curious about me, as I am about you?"

"I am, which was why I looked you up in the alumni news." Kym dabbed at her lips.

He puffed out his chest at her admission.

"I'll pencil it in this week, but only for a few hours."

Chaz pumped a fist in the air as if the Ravens had scored a touchdown against their archnemeses, the Pittsburgh Steelers.

"If you're up for an adventure"—his eyes sparkled with mischief—"how about this Thursday evening at seven?"

Dating is an adventure, she mused. Depending on how the night played out, this dinner could possibly lead to another. "Where should I meet you?" She offered him a cake.

"Thanks." He indulged in a hearty bite and shrugged. "Ah, not sure yet."

He didn't think ahead in case she said yes? Maybe she *should* pass. Chaz must have sensed she was about to back out.

"I thought about the Secret Supper thing. I've heard a few people in my office mention it. Sounds like an adventure I would like to try with you—if you're game." Chaz wiggled a brow in a challenge.

She frowned. "Hmm, that's the event sponsored by the *Baltimore Sun*, right?"

Chaz nodded, dusted his hands on his pants, and stood. "I hope you haven't attended one." He waited for her to confirm she hadn't. "Say yes, and I'll book us tickets."

"Yes." Kym smiled.

"I am so looking forward to this exploration." He turned to leave, then pivoted. "Wait. Your number please."

There was no hesitation as Kym gave it to him. If she didn't, he would probably show up at her office repeatedly, until she had campus police escort him out. He punched in her digits, and her phone rang.

"Lock my number in. I plan to use it—a lot." Chaz opened her door and strolled out, leaving behind a tease of his cologne.

Chapter 3

Two days later, Chaz was shaving in preparation for his dinner date. He wanted to stand out from her previous suitors. The concept of taking a woman to a restaurant that he hadn't personally vetted could turn out to be a bust, despite its positive reviews. But he wanted to chance something different—hopefully memorable, not disastrous.

When he had checked his email this morning from Baltimore's Secret Supper, Chaz was pleased to learn that he and Kym would dine at the Bygone on top of the Four Seasons Hotel Baltimore.

The place was in the Harbor East area, where upscale hotels had replaced abandoned warehouses. He clicked on the link and viewed the pictures. The decor was an elegant throwback to social clubs of the 1920s. To heighten the ambiance, the restaurant boasted a sky-high view of the harbor.

The Secret Supper tickets were for an all-inclusive four-course meal, specialty cocktail, and wine pairings, including tax and gratuity. He wasn't a drinker because of his faith. As a matter of fact, his Christian lifestyle steered him away from indulging in sex outside marriage and other self-destructive activities.

When he called Kym to tell her about passing on the drink option, she wasn't fazed, explaining she was also a practicing Christian who attended Abundant Life Church, a sister church to his Solid Rock Church.

Chaz guessed her to be ten years younger than his forty-two years, but her mature personality put her on par with him. Age was never a hindrance whenever he asked a woman out. Forty was the new thirty. He didn't feel a day over thirty-five years old, and he believed his grooming backed him up.

Kym Knicely. His curiosity was piqued at LLU the moment a flash of white caused him to look in that direction to see her engaged in a conversation with other alumni.

From that moment on, his eyes had clocked Kym's every movement, even as she posed for pictures with the Honorable Loretta Lynch. If he had moved faster, he could have made his presence known under the guise of shaking hands with the first African American woman to be confirmed as attorney general of the United States. Kym had been a vision of beauty and appeared as confident as the former U.S. attorney general.

He had taken a chance when he left his office on Monday for the twenty-minute drive in the opposite direction from the LLU campus for the crab cakes.

"It paid off, my brotha." He grinned at his reflection in the mirror, applying his cologne. Chaz strolled into his bedroom closet as his cell chimed his son's ringtone.

"Hey, Pop," Gee, his oldest son, greeted him when Chaz answered.

"How's my favorite son doin'?" He tapped the speaker and laid the phone nearby so he could sift through his shirts for his black sweater.

"I know you tell Drake the same thing," Gee joked. "So you busy?"

"Never too busy for you. What's up?" Chaz spied the time. He didn't want to keep Kym waiting. She had been adamant about driving herself, but he wanted to arrive first. He continued chatting while he finished dressing, then double-checked his appearance.

Scooping up his keys off the counter, Chaz didn't miss a beat as he continued his stroll out the front door, excited about what the night would bring. Once he was behind the wheel of his car, the chime alerted him that he hadn't snapped his seat belt.

"Oh, were you going somewhere?"

"Yep. Out to dinner. So is everything all right?" His family was his heart.

"Alone?" His son avoided Chaz's question to bait him.

After checking the rearview mirror, Chaz pulled out into the street. "Son, we've been on the phone for at least ten minutes. What's going on?"

"I needed some advice…wondering what you thought about me changing jobs, because I applied at Centene. The position offers more money, which we could use with Chauncy's expenses, but I'll have to travel once or twice a month, maybe more. That could throw her schedule off. She looks for me after her favorite television program ends. I try to stick to a routine for our daughter-daddy time before bedtime. I've thrown that off a little working overtime."

Chaz was proud of his son's dedication as a family man. "Gee, you seldom ask for my help, but I offer it freely. There's no reason for you to struggle." Geoffrey earned a good salary as a plant manager and was wise with his money, yet doctor expenses were always stretching the budget.

Even with Gee's frugality, neither he nor Lana had anticipated their child would have special needs that could run up tens of thousands of dollars in medical bills yearly after the insurance. During his drive, Chaz interrogated his son about the pros and cons of his present job versus the other one. When he arrived at the hotel, he ended their chat with a prayer for guidance. "Talk it over with Lana. You have to do what's best for your family."

"Yeah. Thank, Pops, for listening. Now back to you going out to dinner in the middle of a work week… What's her name, how does she look, any children, and what does she see in my old man?" He laughed, and Chaz chuckled along with him.

"You want to go there? All you're getting out of me is I'm dining with another alum."

"Of course you are. You should be the chancellor of LLU the way you stay involved. Okay, answer me this: Is she pretty?"

Chaz smirked. "No, she's beautiful. I'm not saying anything else. Kiss your wife and my grandbaby, and we'll talk later—but not later tonight."

As Chaz waited for the valet to park his car, he glanced around, hoping Kym hadn't beaten him there. That wouldn't be good. As he handed over his keys, he asked, "I'm meeting my dining companion here. Has a beautiful woman arrived within the past ten or fifteen minutes?"

"You mean her?" The young man gawked, then grinned.

Chaz glanced over his shoulder and zoomed in on the beauty.

Another valet held the door open as Kym stepped out of her vehicle a few cars behind his. The wind stirred just enough for loose strands of her hair to flirt with him. He mumbled his thanks and made a beeline to her. The woman was a knockout in another royal-blue outfit.

"Whew. I was hoping I didn't keep you waiting. You look stunning." He inhaled and her perfume tickled his nostrils.

Kym blushed. "Thank you."

Touching her elbow, he guided her to the entrance, where a doorman opened the door for them. "We're here for the Secret Supper."

"Yes." The older gentleman instructed them where the bank of the elevators were and what floor to push. Another couple stepped into the elevator with him.

"Are you here for the Secret Supper? This is our third one. We love it!" The young woman chatted without taking a pause.

Chaz pegged her to be midtwenties. Both of them wore their hair in long locks and had on matching hunter-green outfits. They reminded Chaz of Geoffrey and Lana, who often dressed alike when going out, more so when Chauncy was with them. They were the picture-perfect family.

"Yes, it's our first. I hope my date and I will enjoy it."

"No," the woman's companion said in a baritone voice, "you'll love it and be hooked on these events. Surprise is part of the adventure."

Adventure—that was what he wanted with Kym. Chaz eyed her and winked.

The bell announced the top floor, and Chaz waited for them to step off, then followed Kym. A hostess greeted them before steering them toward a table in a dimly lit restaurant.

"Ooh, nice place," Kym said in a low voice as they trailed the woman.

"I guess I did good."

"I think so."

There was something about Kym that threw Chaz off balance, but he wasn't a teenager, controlled by hormones. He was a forty-two-year-old practicing Christian who wanted more in a relationship than what only the eyes could behold.

Once they were settled across from each other, Chaz smiled. "Thank you for coming."

"Thanks for inviting me." Kym lowered her lashes, which appeared to be natural, not the artificial ones that were so long they could fan a forehead. She looked up and returned his smile.

Their server appeared and recited the meal selection for the Secret Supper. Kym gave the young man her undivided attention while Chaz watched her. Kym had said on the plane she was focused, so she was a good listener. When their server left, she tilted her head and studied him.

"You're quiet."

"I'm not sure where to begin." Chaz exhaled and shook his head. "There is so much I want to know about you."

"I'm intrigued too." She rested her elbows on the table and crossed her arms, displaying slender fingers with polished nails.

"Good. I'm glad this isn't one-sided." Folding his hands, he leaned forward. "I see blue is your favorite color."

"This week." She grinned. "I'm known to go on color binges."

Chaz made note of that tidbit. "A man isn't supposed to ask a woman her age, so I won't. I'll tell you mine." She lifted one of her delicate eyebrows and waited. "I turned forty-two back in January."

"You're six years older than me, so there, you didn't ask."

He bit his bottom lip, enjoying their friendly banter. "You definitely don't look your age."

"Neither do you. The gentleman gets a brownie point."

"Am I up to three? The crab cakes, dinner, and bad guessing?" They chuckled together. "I hadn't planned to talk shop, but I like the way your face lights up whenever you mention something you're passionate about, so tell me about your dissertation?"

That earned him a smile. "Like I said, my interest in education started when I was a substitute teacher. Of course, there is a correlation between homework completion and classroom preparedness. Teachers would have students do homework in class to make sure it was done and provide help. There was also after-school tutoring. My concern was students' study habits at home—minorities specifically. If their parents aren't able to help them, for example, because they're working second jobs, then the child will lag behind whites when it comes to test scores."

In her element, Chaz listened to Kym's every word. "Your goal was for them not to get lost in the system."

"Exactly." She bobbed her head. "But walking door-to-door through neighborhoods wasn't feasible. I kept hearing the term *pop-up* where businesses, mainly on the East Coast, would show up around the holidays and bring the merchandise to customers instead of the customers going to them."

She lifted her shoulder in a shrug. "So I thought why not offer a pop-up tutoring service in neighborhoods where the students struggle academically because they can't stay after school for tutoring due to lack of transportation, whether it was a ride home or a bus ride. Without accessibility to one-on-one tutoring, they couldn't thrive and achieve life's goals."

She stopped and blushed. "Sorry, I know I'm rambling."

"No, you're educating me," Chaz said, assuring her.

Kym graced him with a smile that he would always remember as she continued, "When I enrolled in LLU's master's program, I explained the concept of these pop-up stores to my mentor in the doctoral program. Why couldn't STEM tutors do the same thing with an ice-cream-truck concept? We could drive to predetermined neighborhoods and offer on-the-spot tutoring. The bus would be outfitted with computers, tabletop desks—three stations on each side—and books. I was advised to write a grant. I did, and the rest is history." She lifted her arms in conclusion.

Chaz applauded. "You're fascinating." This woman was an innovator. He could definitely see the influence of Black American inventor Lewis H. Latimer's ideology on Kym and her thinking of an outside-the-box approach to solving problems and altering situations. "What's been the outcome?"

"This is my fourth year monitoring a set number of students' performances in the doctoral program, plus the two in the master's program. Since tracking them, all their teachers report their study skills have improved and so has their classroom participation. The pop-up tutoring concept is making inroads." She beamed.

Chaz lifted his hand for a high five, and when she patted her hand against his, he clutched it. Her expression gave nothing away. Did she feel the spark too? He lowered their hands as the server returned with their meals.

"This looks delicious," she said. Had the moment been lost on her?

"And it is," the waiter assured them.

Once he left, Chaz reached for her hand again. "Mind if I ask for blessings?"

"Please." Kym bowed her head.

"Lord, thank You for the fellowship and the food. Sanctify it and remove impurities. I ask that You bless the hands that prepared it, and help us to remember those who are hungry. In Jesus's name. Amen."

"Amen," she whispered.

He waited for her to sample her steak first.

"This is good. I'm surprised I've never eaten here before." After a few more bites, she asked, "So what's your passion?"

"Family first, the public's health and well-being second." That earned him a warm smile from her.

"Why public health?" She rested her elbows on the table, seemingly making herself comfortable as he answered.

"Most people think of infectious diseases like TB, influenza, or coronavirus when it comes to public health or safety, and they are part of that, but gun violence is also on the radar. So are traffic fatalities. Anything that is a threat to the community's health is our concentration."

"I admire your caring attitude," she said, complimenting him. "I'm sure it's a quality that started in the home."

"You're right. Very astute. You've already seen a picture of my eldest and his family. My other son is twenty-two and lives here… I don't see Drake as much as I would like." *Don't show your disappointment*, he coaxed himself. "He's in medical school at Johns Hopkins."

"You have to be proud."

"I am." Chaz took a sip of his beverage and grinned. By the end of the evening, his cheeks would probably ache from smiling so much.

"Speaking of Johns Hopkins, I was at their Turner Auditorium last month to hear Dr. Griffin Rodgers and meet the Lacks family. Imagine how the human cell of a poor Black woman changed medical research for decades without her or her family's consent. Who would have thought her cancer cells would be the origin of cures…and the money."

"Just imagine people who are driven to work tirelessly to become pioneers during their lifetime, but Henrietta Lacks became one without consent in her death." Chaz reflected on how America benefited from the free labor of enslaved people and how great institutions were built by them, like the White House, or sold to pay debt for Georgetown, St. Louis University, and other Jesuit colleges. "At least descendants of Henrietta Lacks have a say now about the HeLa cell. I was in that packed auditorium too."

"Knowledge is wisdom. I'm glad we both appreciate seminars and lectures."

Before Chaz could say more, a familiar presence at his table interrupted his thought—to his delight.

"Well, well, well, if it isn't my old man on a date."

Chaz's heart swelled with pride. He stood and pumped Drake's hand before engulfing him in a hug. Both were tall. However, his son had him by pounds. How long had it been since he had seen his youngest? Too long. "Who you calling an old man?" Chaz joked and faced Kym. "This is my son Drake. This is Professor Dr. Kym Knicely."

"I'm a PhD candidate," she corrected. "Nice to meet you." She extended her hand, and Drake glanced at Chaz with an amused expression before he accepted it.

"Good taste, Dad." He linked his fingers through the woman's beside him. "This is Patrice."

Typical Drake, he was always seen with a pretty lady, but never twice, as far as Chaz knew. He wished his son would find the right one. Maybe Patrice was the one if Drake had put down a hundred bucks for dinner tickets. Any other time, Chaz would be interested in hearing more about Patrice. Not tonight. He was fascinated by Kym.

Patrice blinked before her eyes sparkled. "Wow, your father looks as young as you. Hi, Mr. Banks."

After a few more pleasantries, Chaz nodded. "Call your old man sometime. Maybe we can go fishing or take a day trip to the railroad museums…or whatever you want to do."

Drake bobbed his head. "Sounds like a plan. Enjoy your evening."

Chaz accepted his son's noncommittal response and retook his seat and exhaled. Why couldn't he bond with Drake, who lived close by, like he did with Gee, who was hundreds of miles away?

"Hey." Kym's soft voice and pat on his hand rescued him from his sullen thoughts. "He loves you. Something tells me he'll call soon."

He studied her. "It would be pointless for me to ask what you mean, so I won't. I thought I mastered my poker face, yet you saw through me."

Kym shrugged. "I've never been married, divorced, or a parent, so I don't have any sixth sense going on. I have no words of wisdom, but I see the longing of a father and the adoration of a son. I'm sure he can read you too."

Her morsel of encouragement gave Chaz a jolt, and he returned to the present. For the remainder of the evening, they talked about his love of antique trains and her interest in sailing. It didn't take long for the subject of family to surface.

"My sisters and I have always been close, even growing up. After our parents died, we clung to our great-aunt, the matriarch. She was ninety when she passed a couple of years ago, but honestly, we thought she would be around forever. When the doctors diagnosed Aunt Tweet with advanced-stage dementia, we agreed on a caregivers' pact, where we took turns caring for her six months at a time.

"In hindsight, moving her from city to city was a bad idea, but my sisters and I made the best out of it." Her eyes watered over, and this time, Chaz reached across the table and rested his hand over hers and gave her time to gather her thoughts. "It was hard to let her go. Next, my baby sister was diagnosed with breast cancer. Whew." Kym shook her head, then rubbed her temples as if she was trying to erase the memory. "The Bible says in Jude to build up our holy faith. We all had to find our faith for that trial."

"How's your sister now?" Chaz was hesitant about asking but hoped the outcome was victory.

Kym exhaled and beamed. "Living her life to the fullest with her husband. That period brought us all to a place where we had to know who God is for ourselves. Tabitha, my sister under me, and I stayed at Rachel's side too. Friends come and go…"

"Sometimes spouses too," he added, "but family is forever."

"Exactly." They exchanged a high five.

There was nothing about Kym that Chaz didn't like, and something told him there never would be. Her conviction was endearing. "I haven't met a woman in a long time with whom I've felt I have so much in common. It's as if we share some DNA." Kym excited him. He could talk to her all night, but they had to work in the morning. "This night has been refreshing. I hope you enjoyed the food, ambiance, and my company enough to agree to go out again soon."

Her eyes sparkled as she lifted her chin. "Sure. Sunday morning, church service," she stated without hesitation.

"I accept." His lips curled into a smile. "And brunch afterward?"

"Yes. This time, I'll pick the place." She stood, and Chaz retrieved her wrap.

As he placed it around her shoulders, he glanced across the room at his son's table. The couple were absorbed with each other. What mattered to Chaz most was that his sons find happiness. Gee had Lana. Would Drake be next?

Chaz and his ex-wife, Valerie, had been young and in lust, not love. They never developed a friendship. They added two sons into the equation, thinking parenthood would solve their relationship woes. It didn't. The blame didn't weigh solely on her. Chaz stopped caring too. Suddenly, they had been incompatible, their interests had changed, and their affections had numbed. They had become uncomfortable roommates.

Six months after their divorce was final, Valerie announced she had found the love of her life. Now, his ex and her new husband were coming up on ten years of marriage. Chaz wished them the best and hoped they surpassed the fourteen-year milestone he and Valerie barely reached.

Chaz had never had a desire to tie the knot. Kym shifted his mindset at the seminar, and the longing had reignited the day at the airport. The professor had triggered an emotion he thought was dormant—a yearning for companionship. He was excited about the future and what it might bring with Kym.

With her by his side, Chaz made a detour before leaving. He nodded at Drake. "Love you, Son. Hope we can see each other again real soon. Nice to meet you, Patrice."

Drake got to his feet, hugged Chaz, and patted him on the back. "Yes, sir."

Once they were outside, Kym handed her parking stub to the valet, and Chaz asked, "Will you call me when you arrive home?"

"Yes," she whispered as it started to rain, and then the unexpected happened: she stepped from under the awning into the rain.

"They have umbrellas for this type of weather." Chaz frowned in confusion.

"Nah. I like the feel of raindrops. Reminds me of showers of God's blessings."

"Well, if you put it that way…" Chaz joined her, laughing. "You're a fascinating woman, and I look forward to our next adventure."

She giggled when he took the liberty of spinning her under his arm at the amazement of the valets. "Most women wouldn't dare get their hair wet."

"Black women have options. Unless I want to wear it naturally curly, that is what flat irons are for."

The fun ended when her Mercedes SUV arrived, and she slid into her leather seat as he held her door open. He couldn't wait to jump inside his car and blast the heat. "Good night."

"Night." Her eyes sparkled.

Chapter 4

KYM WOKE THE NEXT MORNING GIGGLING AS SHE STRETCHED IN HER bed. Had last night been a dream, or did she have dinner with a distinguished, caring, and engaging man? His eyes, an unusual shade of brown, were mesmerizing.

Sliding out of bed to her knees, she gave the Lord thanks for another day and praised God for a wonderful evening with Chaz.

As she went through her morning ritual, she hummed a chorus to one of her favorite gospel songs. She even changed her current color obsession from blue to shades of red.

Kym was high on happiness when she hurried from the parking lot to the educational building, named after Ramona Edelin, who founded a program to assist Black teachers in their quest to educate minority youths in the United States.

"You're glowing so bright it almost blinded me." Judith scrunched her eyes as they crossed paths in the main corridor. "After we give our last midterms, I want details about last night's dinner."

If there was anyone in Kym's corner as deserving of a happily ever after, it was Judith. Her friend believed it was past time for the right one to come along for both of them. "Not all of them I hope," Kym teased.

"Ooh. Yep, every morsel of the goodies!" Judith gave her the side-eye.

"You'll have to wait. I'm administering makeup tests to those who missed their scheduled midterms, then I have a meeting."

"Ooh. I have nothing but time to get into your business." Judith beamed, walking backward out of the office until she spun around to resume her trek to her classroom.

Kym chuckled to herself. She was as excited as Judith to give a recap of the previous night. An hour or so later, she returned to her office to grab some things before her appointment with her mentor. She spied a box outside her door. After the crab cakes, she suspected Chaz was the culprit.

Behind closed doors, she forgot about her meeting and ripped open the box. Kym sucked in her breath as she gently lifted a magnificent crystal paperweight out of the tissue. In awe, she admired the red rose in full bloom encased inside. The note read:

You're one of a kind. Unique. Special. Beautiful. Call me when you have free time. See you Sunday. Don't be late for service! Chaz.

Kym barked out a laugh. The man would soon learn she believed in punctuality.

Before she could relish the private moment, Judith tapped on her door, peeped in, and stepped inside. "Caught ya."

"Leaving. I'll call you when my meeting with Tina is over." Kym placed the paperweight back in the box, grabbed her file and laptop, then ushered her friend out the door.

"Hmm. An after-the-date gift… I guess flowers just wouldn't do. You've got a lot of explaining to do." Judith bobbed her head and wagged a finger.

"Bye, girl."

Minutes later, Kym knocked on Dr. Tina Massey's door and entered her office. Tina had backed Kym's research on the mobile tutoring concept from day one. "Thanks for seeing me." Kym was winded as she slid into the chair around a small table in the corner of her office.

"I want to see your Teachers on Wheels project a permanent solution for underachieving students." Tina perched her reading glasses on her long, narrow nose. "Your research and results show promise. How's your tracking of the eighteen students who have received extra help from it?" Teachers on Wheels was the original name of the pilot program while Kym was working on her master's. Tina still referred to it as TOW from time to time.

"I plan to visit the students at home this evening and their teachers next week. Even though we had midterms, my assistants continued with their two-hour sessions."

"At our last meeting, you mentioned TOW had a wait list. Although you've tapped into a need, what a shame students have to be turned away. What's your recommendation? That's the question you must answer," Tina said, grilling her.

Kym nodded. "I know. Based on mobile tutoring's marginal success, the public school system should adopt the program. Funding can come from the government, private donations, or nonprofits to serve all children in urban or low-income areas. More teachers and wheels are needed to keep the program going. It shouldn't cease when my research ends."

Tina had a way of egging Kym on to come up with her own answers before offering advice, because Kym would be on her own when she faced the board to present her findings and offer solutions. "Let's look at your data charts again."

She waited while Kym accessed the files on her computer. "This is one student's progress report from the first year. The second year, her grades improved, and she held B averages throughout the third year. So far this year, others in the program are straight-A students."

"Bravo." Tina folded her arms, then leaned back in her chair.

"Adrian Davis entered high school this year, so I checked in with him. He's on track to make the honor roll." Kym outlined the success of most students and pointed out the few where the tutoring hadn't made a significant change in grades or study habits. "Other factors prohibited intellectual growth. When I learned that Jason was hungry, I factored in some nutritional snacks for energy. But I also learned his adult environment wasn't supportive. His mother works long hours, and there is no father in the home."

Their brainstorming session continued for another hour before Kym packed up and headed back to her office. The doctoral program was intense. Every high and low had to be documented and explained. She couldn't afford to leave any holes in her presentation.

She was a firm believer every child deserved a chance to make it to the finish line. Society owed them a quality education in order for them to thrive and be productive. Whenever Kym became a mother, she would be supportive of her children and drive home the importance of learning, like her parents and Aunt Tweet had done.

Interacting with the youngsters made her reflect on motherhood. She thought about her sister Tabitha, who currently had the only baby in the family. Little Marcus resembled his father. Kym wondered if she had a son, would he be a mirror image of his dad? Chaz's face materialized. Whoa. She shrugged it off. It was too early—way too premature—to think long-term.

I guess it's only natural I'd think of him because of our dinner date, she reasoned with herself, but where would they end up in six months: cordial alumni, acknowledging each other at events, or in a committed relationship? Kym wished she had an answer as she strolled into her office. One date didn't mean permanent, no matter how alluring the guy was. It would be best if she remembered that.

Kym's door opened, and Judith stepped inside. Kym chuckled at her friend's persistence. "Come in, why don't you?"

"Thanks for the invite." Judith snickered and wiggled herself in a chair. "Tell me everything you don't want me to know." She didn't hide her eagerness as she sat erect and intertwined her hands like an attentive student.

Anchoring her elbows on her desk, Kym rested her chin on her folded hands. She closed her eyes and smiled as she conjured up the memories. "The evening was perfect, from the location to the food and conversation. Chaz is an excellent conversationalist and a great listener as I opened up and shared things about myself. He did the same. I met his son and his son's girlfriend. We capped off the night with an impromptu dance in the rain."

"Ahhh. Sounds romantic, but I'm not sure about the last part." Judith grinned from ear to ear. "That explains why you're flaunting your natural curls today. Now, back to the date." She pouted. "I want a man like him! I'd be jealous, but I've gone on more dates this year than you."

Judith patted her short do, which framed her pretty face, and batted her eyelashes. Judith could be bald, and she would have pulled it off and still grabbed a man's attention. "You've held out for the right one."

"I don't know," Kym admitted in disbelief. "We did seem to connect. The sparks between us were exciting rather than uneasy. More importantly, I admired his honesty, and there was no pretentiousness." She strained her mind. "It doesn't seem like we met less than a week ago. It's mind-boggling my level of comfort around him." She giggled, then covered her mouth before leaning forward. "He had a clever way of asking my age."

Judith shook her head. "Something tells me nothing Chaz does will be status quo. I like him!"

"Well"—Kym glanced at the paperweight, then back at Judith—"despite all the things we have in common, he's a grandfather, and I haven't made it to the altar to become a wife and a mother yet."

"Blending families are part of today's relationships." Judith didn't hide her disappointment. "Honestly, I'm not sure if I'd be a good fit in those types of relationships." She picked up the paperweight, scrutinized it, and placed it back. "Consider me your protégé. If you can master being stepmom material, I'll follow your lead if the right man comes along."

Kym laughed, entertained by her friend's sense of humor. Judith had no problem going on blind dates. That was how she racked up more dates, where Kym preferred to scrutinize a person's mannerism and personality. So far, Chaz Banks had passed her inspection.

"I've never been in a blended family relationship, so this is new to me too," she admitted to Judith, who was three years younger. Kym considered Judith her away-from-home little sister.

"Unless his sons are living in his house and he claims them on his W-2, I doubt they would interfere. Enough juicy details for one day. I'm heading out." Judith stood. "If you ever want to double date, please ask him to bring a carbon copy for me."

"I heard your dinner date is gorgeous—'bout time. That's my pops," Gee said during a Saturday morning phone call.

That she was. "Your brother has a big mouth." He was glad his sons remained close despite living in different cities. Chaz didn't mind, but he usually kept his random dinner dates out of chats. However, there was nothing casual about Kym. He wanted a next time and another time too.

"Better than that." Gee tee-heed. "Amazing how the newest iPhone can capture clear images of you with your *alum*. Very nice, and from the way you were laughing and holding her hand, I'd say you had a good time with your *alum*," he said, teasing. Chaz wasn't going to take the bait, so Gee pressed. "Is there anything you want to tell me? Are you giving Chauncy a grandma?"

"You're way ahead of me, Son, with your assumptions. She already has a grandmother." Chaz switched subjects. He wanted things to develop more between him and Kym before her name became a standard inquiry in family discussions. "Speaking of my grandbaby, how's she doing?"

"Her home therapy is coming along, and she's saying more words. Lana rewarded her with stars, and they walked to McDonald's for playtime… There was a scene in the playground area."

"Uh-oh." Chaz cringed. Gee and Lana had been working on Chauncy's social interactions.

"Yep. Two little girls asked Chauncy her name. When she didn't respond, they tried to hug her. Chauncy pushed them away, and they fell."

"The rest is history," Chaz finished. His granddaughter needed patience when interacting. Something most children lacked. Socially withdrawn, Chauncy required extra time to respond. Plus, she only allowed familiar people to touch her. He had read an article about how some children with autism could have a hypersensitivity to touch, so hugging could come off as suffocating.

His heart ached. "She'll be okay, Son. One therapy at a time." Chaz tried to encourage him.

"This is so hard, Pops," Gee admitted. "Lana and I want her to make friends. Lana gets so humiliated in public because of Chauncy's unpredictability, so she'd rather stay at home, which makes her feel isolated.

"Years ago, Lana and I caught a glimpse of the reality show featuring Holly Robinson Peete's family. Her son, RJ, has autism. Aside from his flat-affect expression, he's leading a typical life with a job. That is our prayer for Chauncy—a happy, healthy life."

"We'll have to keep hoping and praying for her progress." Chaz reassured Gee he and Lana weren't in this alone. When they ended the call, Chaz went for a jog to clear his head.

Later that night, his close friend Ezekiel "Zeke" Cumming called him. They were brothers in Christ and colleagues. Zeke worked in another department at Johns Hopkins.

"Hey, I came by your office late Friday but missed you. I'm calling to remind you about the function following morning worship tomorrow."

Chaz scratched his head. The brotherhood fellowship had slipped his mind. "Oops. I've been invited to Abundant Life tomorrow, so I won't be at Solid Rock Church."

"Really? What's going on over there that's got you skipping out on a Sunday? Unless you're out of town, you're like clockwork warming your seat."

"True, but one of my alum invited me to a sister church, so I accepted."

"Hmm. The same *alum* you mentioned you were taking to dinner but have yet to share any details about? I would say you two are hitting it off if you're playing hooky from your own church."

"Sorry, buddy. I do need to fill you in on that, don't I?" Chaz grinned. He had forgotten that he had mentioned it to Zeke in the first place. The two just happened to cross paths when Chaz was returning from LLU after the crab cake delivery.

"I guess I need to keep an eye on you and your calendar. A long lunch break across town, a midweek date, and now tagging along to church service?" Zeke whistled. "Because you, my dear friend, are over your head." Zeke released a roar of laughter.

"Stay out of my business." Chaz feigned a warning. "You're exaggerating things."

"Nope. You've finally got some business, and I can't wait to see how this plays out."

Me either, Chaz thought as they ended the call.

Chapter 5

"YOU'RE LATE." CHAZ GREETED KYM WHEN SHE ENTERED THE foyer of her own church, Abundant Life.

"No, you're early." Kym flirted back, happy that he had accepted her invitation as he held open the door for her.

Chaz stood out. Not because he was a visitor but his persona was one to notice. Were all his clothes custom fit? She had yet to see him look less than polished. The deep red tie complemented his dark gray suit with faint red pinstripes. She smiled to herself.

Inspired by the euphoria she experienced on their dinner date, Kym was now rocking an "anything red" trend. They were matching without exchanging a memo. Yet it was his smile that held her captive as he complimented her hair.

Kym fingered a few strands and grinned. "Yeah, I don't think there are any rainstorms in the forecast."

He snapped his fingers. "And I was looking forward to that next dance." He winked.

"Rain check." She nudged his shoulder. "Come on. I'll show you where I like to sit." It seemed surreal that he was there. In the past, she had invited other acquaintances, and they came, but it seemed just for show. After one visit, they had excuses why they weren't available to attend church.

How many times had she envisioned a relationship with a man who put God first? She made introductions to familiar faces along their path, then they entered a sanctuary that could hold up to a thousand easily.

Once inside, their actions were in sync as they knelt to pray, then stood to join others in praise songs. It wasn't long before Kym closed her eyes and blotted out her surroundings to escape to the hidden place with God to worship Him. Too soon, the service transitioned to the next phrase.

Pastor Harrison approached the podium and greeted visitors, whom he asked to stand. Next, he opened his Bible and gave the congregation a hint of his sermon. "We live in a sophisticated and intelligent society today. Yet the world lacks wisdom. Turn to Proverbs 3:6: 'In all thy ways acknowledge him, and he shall direct thy paths.'"

For the next half hour, he preached on the consequences of making bad decisions. "God is our Counselor, so don't be afraid to go to Him from the smallest matter to the greatest decision, whether it's about a relationship or a major purchase. Listen and let Jesus guide you."

Kym sucked in her breath and wondered what Chaz heard from God. One sermon could carry multiple messages, tailored to each person in the congregation. What was Chaz's purpose in her life? Would they remain in a friendship, or would it lead to something more? *More is good*, she mused. *Lord, give me the wisdom to know what You want for me*, Kym prayed.

Chaz was grateful for the refresher sermon on wisdom. Even though he was a practicing Christian, sometimes he made decisions without weighing all the options.

Attraction had led him to Kym, not lust. He had no regrets in his pursuit. They were meant to be something more, but he had to use wisdom not to charge ahead of God's plan.

After the altar call, offering, and the benediction, Kym asked how he liked the service. She had a radiance about her. He lifted his Bible off the pew and hers and smiled. "I won't wait for another invitation to come back."

His answer seemed to make Kym's eyes sparkle. "They say the doors to church are always open."

There was a sense of contentment for him with Kym. "Although I received a Word from the message, I surrendered my thoughts and cares before the Lord during the worship service."

"A man after my own heart," she mumbled as she gently scooted him out of the row. "Do you always give the right answers?"

Chaz released a respectful laugh in the sanctuary. "Woman, what you see is what you get. Where to for brunch? You pick the place and surprise me." They walked across the parking lot, greeting others who were leaving too. Looking up into the sky, he shielded his eyes from the sun and sighed heavily. "Too bad. Not a cloud in the sky for a chance at rain."

"Nope." Kym retrieved her Bible from his arm and veered to the right, and he followed. "My car is this way."

Chaz stopped in his tracks and gave her a reserved, disappointed pout. "I was expecting to be a gentleman and drive. I'll bring you back for your car."

Kym was silent as she studied him as if she was coming to a decision. "Chaz, I like you, but I don't trust easily, so please don't be offended personally. If we keep seeing each other, that will change."

His nostrils flared in amusement as he snickered. "You do realize you gave me a green light to continue pursuing you, which I'm thoroughly enjoying?" Chaz grinned and resumed his steps. "I'll trail you."

He drove behind her as she weaved in and out of traffic, going in the direction of his job near the Johns Hopkins University campus. Kym chose Gertrude's for brunch, located inside the Baltimore Museum of Art. Not only did that suit her passion, but it also made Chaz like her style.

They both indulged in crab omelets. They discussed their thoughts on the sermon and their jobs. He made sure to ask about her progress on her dissertation.

Tilting her head, she rested her fork beside her plate. "Thank you for wanting to know."

Chaz leaned forward. "This is important to you, so I'm listening."

"Wow." She bowed and shook her head, then met his eyes. "Chaz, I'm not used to this."

He had overwhelmed her. "Hey." He placed one hand over her soft one. "The only way to know things about you is to ask."

Thank you, she mouthed, then resumed her meal. Chaz was in no hurry to leave her company, and he would prolong it as long as she allowed. He dabbed his mouth with his napkin. "So what do you recommend for dessert?"

"The mango cheesecake." Kym's eyes lit, and he chuckled.

Women and their cheesecakes. He was a chocolate ice cream sundae or apple pie man himself. "Want to share? Promise I won't take big bites."

He signaled their server when she agreed. Their dessert arrived five minutes later, and the battle began with their forks. At times, their forks clashed as if they were fencing. "So what do your Sunday afternoons look like? Stroll on Inner Harbor, movies, shopping, or visit one of the plethora of museums..." He paused for her to fill in the blanks.

She shrugged. "Since Sunday is my downtime, I normally don't make too many plans. One routine is my video chat with my sisters. We had set up the weekly schedule to stay up-to-date on our great-aunt's health issues. When she passed away, we kept the tradition going, because we all live in different cities.

"Plus, with my youngest sister as a breast cancer survivor, we like to see her for ourselves to make sure she's healthy, but with a husband like Nicholas, Rachel is in good hands." She smiled. "What about you? I sensed you and your younger son don't keep in touch regularly."

"You're observant, Professor, but it's not from my lack of reaching out. Gee and I have a closer relationship."

"The one in St. Louis?"

"Correct. When my ex-wife and I divorced, she couldn't leave here fast enough. There was a good-paying job in the Midwest that eventually took her to St. Louis. The boys would spend the summers with me, and during those three months, they were my sole focus. I was determined for them to know that whatever problems their mother and I had didn't change how much we loved them."

"I admire you for not bad-mouthing their mother," Kym interrupted.

At times I want to strangle her. Chaz kept the thought to himself and quietly accepted the compliment. "Drake earned several academic scholarships at top schools, including Howard University. HBCU won out," he said about the historically Black college. "I had hoped because he was only an hour away, we would do more things together, but our schedules never aligned. A few times, I took a quick trip to DC to surprise him, but twice Drake told me he had other plans and I should've given him a heads-up—and he was right." He shrugged. "An old man can't compete with the excitement of the college lifestyle.

"Now he's doing his residency at Johns Hopkins. The other night was the first time I had seen him in almost a month." He swallowed and glanced out the window. Drumming his fingers on the table, he tried to keep his emotions in check. If she wanted a man whose armor didn't have weak spots, he wouldn't be the one for her, and she could make her exit after brunch.

He didn't lack confidence in other areas in his life, but when it came to his younger son, Chaz had insecurities. Kym had no idea how much he wanted to be his son's best friend. Chaz had been Gee's best man at his son's nuptials. He hoped for the same honor at Drake's whenever that happened.

"Hey." Her voice was soft. "Family will always need family. Don't ever forget that." She covered his hand with hers. The gesture was comforting…and filling a void, something he didn't realize he'd craved.

Chaz snapped out of it. "You're right." He shook himself free of the longing and opened his eyes to the possibilities with his charming date sitting across from him.

"Sorry for getting sidetracked." He sucked in his breath as he admired her beauty. There was nothing about her not to like. Her facial features were exquisite. Chaz rubbed his chin. "You're stunning, intelligent, and a good listener, so why aren't you married?" He watched with intensity as her expression changed. When Kym lifted a brow, Chaz wondered what he had said wrong.

"I'm sure you're aware that men outnumber women in Charm City. The big question is why a man like you is divorced. You're handsome, astute, and compassionate. Plus, you hold no hostility against your ex-wife." She exhaled with a guarded expression as if she was unsure that she wanted to hear his answer.

Chaz shrugged. It took two to be cordial, and he and Valerie had called a truce for the sake of their sons. "In a nutshell, I don't have an excuse. I should have fought for our marriage, but I wasn't a practicing Christian back then, so I didn't take my vows seriously. Neither of us knew how to mature into a loving couple aside from being parents. In hindsight, we married out of lust, not deep-rooted love."

"Wow." She seemed surprised. "I wasn't expecting such honesty."

"Usually I'm tight-lipped about my past regrets, but with you, I don't want you to feel there might be secrets for you to uncover."

Kym blinked and became tongue-tied, so he changed the subject.

"So when you talk to your sisters, are you going to tell them about us?" Chaz pointed from himself to Kym.

She opened her mouth but didn't say anything right away. "I'll need more crab cakes for there to be something to tell."

Chaz grinned. "You're so easy to please. You've got that and more things for us to share, so much so that there will be a lot to tell." Chaz nodded for the waiter to bring the check. He had only just begun to woo the pretty professor.

Chapter 6

Kym inhaled the moist air from the Inner Harbor. The carefree stroll with Chaz was surreal. The day was perfect. A few times, she thought Chaz was about to reach for her hand, especially as they entered the historic Lexington Market. He didn't. Oh well, it was too soon for hand-holding anyway, but that didn't stop her from being disappointed. Why did she want to pout like a toddler at his restraint?

Opening for business in 1782, Lexington Market was known for its eclectic selection of local raw and cooked food, from shrimp to various types of roast. It was considered a landmark in Inner Harbor.

Kym patted her stomach. Their walk hadn't burned up enough calories for her to be hungry, so they detoured to the merchandise aisles. Chaz seemed content to let her take the lead. When she glanced at him, he graced her with a smile and a twinkle in his eyes.

Euphoria engulfed her. Giddiness was bottled up inside her; she wanted to explode and tell her sisters all about this weekend during their video chat, but Kym didn't dare get her hopes up, or theirs, in case the sparks between her and Chaz fizzled.

A pop of color from a small boutique grabbed Kym's attention. She crossed the aisle for a closer perusal of the scarves at Choice Gifts and Accessories. She fingered the silkiness of the oversized scarf. It was a paisley of blues, golds, and reds. Sold. Before she could unzip her handbag for her wallet to pay for it, Chaz beat her to it.

When she was about to protest, Chaz's eyes softened. "Let me treat. If you were mine, I'd pamper you, no exceptions. Will you let me?" He convinced her as the merchant seemed amused.

Taken by surprise at his declaration and his tone more than the gift, Kym swallowed, then blushed, speechless. Was he talking about buying her the scarf or letting him pamper her in a relationship? *I'm overthinking this.*

She had turned the tables on him when he asked why she wasn't married by asking her own question about his divorce. Kym desired to be in a Christian relationship. However, before she could invest emotionally, she had to know the godly man was interested in her beyond the outward appearance.

If only Aunt Tweet were here to guide her through matters of the heart. She was beginning to really like Chaz and looked forward to their dates. "Okay."

Chaz appeared pleased by her consent.

Too soon, she had to leave for her scheduled videoconference. "When will I see you again?" he asked as he escorted her to her vehicle.

Tomorrow, her heart was ready to shout until her mind took the reins. "I-I have classes during the day, then I'm out in the field for two afternoons."

"Since I have a day job too, I meant which evening." Chaz snickered.

"Oh." Where was her head? She knew that.

He watched her. The determination she saw in his eyes conveyed he wouldn't be deterred, even when she hadn't given him an answer. "LLU's Founders' Day is this week. Since I know the faculty will be in attendance, I'll take off for a few hours to be there." He squinted. "I'll find you, even in a crowd."

Kym chuckled. "You already did."

He bit his bottom lip and stared into her eyes. "I'd like to think God was turning my head in your direction." This time, he didn't hesitate to reach for her hand. His gentle squeeze was more of a massage that left her hand tingling as she slipped behind the wheel of her SUV and drove away under his watchful eye until she couldn't see him anymore in her rearview mirror. "Whew." She exhaled. That man was making her hope for things, but she didn't know if they were even possible or God's will.

Once home, she dropped her keys and purse on the counter and lifted the scarf out of the bag and wrapped it around her neck and shoulders. Walking into her bathroom, she admired the gold undertone that highlighted her skin.

Suddenly, she felt inspired to go on another fashion binge. She raided her closet, searching for anything with a hint of mustard gold. Kym counted three garments. It was time for a shopping spree—and she would get Judith to tag along. The two knew exactly what fashions worked and didn't work on each other. With that settled, she texted Chaz.

Thank you for the gift. It's so beautiful.

He responded immediately.

Thank you for accepting, beautiful. I'm looking forward to seeing you again and the time after that.

Kym didn't lack confidence in her brainpower or appearance, but to know he thought she was beautiful made her feel…well, beautiful. Although she wanted to engage him more, Kym resisted the temptation. She had to tackle grading the last two classes' midterms and post the grades. Pushing aside all thoughts of Chaz, Kym refocused and got busy.

At exactly seven thirty on the East Coast, she accepted Tabitha's video call, and soon, Rachel joined in. Their faces revealed the contentment of happy wives. *One day*, she always reminded herself.

"Hey, Big Sis. What are you up to?" Rachel, the youngest, asked first.

"Busy. It's hectic on campus with midterms and, of course, gathering my research."

"How's that going? Let me know if you need any help. You know I'm the data guru," Tabitha chimed in.

"We know." Kym snickered. "You're the mommy guru now."

"True." Tabitha looked bashful. "But in all your researching, research where you can meet someone extraordinary."

"Sounds like you're borrowing that from a certain Scripture. Must have been the message this morning at church."

"Yep." Tabitha grinned. "You know what they say, use it or lose it, so I'm trying to apply Proverbs 4:7 to everything."

"That's a good practice." Rachel grabbed her Bible. "Hold on, let me look up that Scripture before I forget. 'Wisdom is the principal thing; therefore get wisdom: and with all thy getting get understanding.'"

"I need that Scripture myself." Kym thought about Chaz. She definitely needed an understanding about what kind of relationship would develop between them.

"How's the research going?" Tabitha asked.

Glad for the subject change, she rocked her head from side to side. "To be honest, frustrating. The demand is greater than I could have ever imagined when I initiated the pop-up tutoring concept. I have six tutors this semester, and usually I get eight or nine a semester. That means we're helping two to three students each during the two-hour time frame I allotted on the project, but we're also turning away others.

"We don't want the children outside the bus waiting until their turn comes to step inside, so we have to stay on schedule. It's not safe for them to be out after it gets dark in their neighborhoods. Plus, the school bus is equipped with computers and other materials, so if we're vandalized, there goes our grant money and the project."

Kym had another grant in the pipeline. The additional funding would mean she could target more neighborhoods for participation, and more students could have access to after-school help. Educators from cities across the country were monitoring the long-term success of her innovative approach to urban education.

"I believe God will watch over you while you're helping the children. Plus, the educational community took notice after you published years of research in that journal," Rachel said. "I think if you ask for more help, you'll get it."

Kym beamed. "Yes, it was impressive to see the results on mobile urban education in the *American Educational Research Journal*." Copies of the article were framed in her office and at home.

"Now, back to your love life," Rachel almost whined. "There's got to be a colleague, church member, or stranger you passed on the sidewalk who is a perfect match for you."

Tabitha and Kym laughed and asked in unison. "A stranger?"

"Really? You think I'm that desperate? I do go out to dinner from time to time." Kym hid her smile as she thought about meeting someone special. In a sense, Chaz had fulfilled all three categories. On the surface, the man was perfect, but was he really the one? "I don't have Aunt Tweet here to play matchmaker," she joked, wanting to tell them she had a prospect but not knowing if the spark would still be there in a month, so she held off.

"I believe of all the men in the world, God has molded a one-of-a-kind man just for you," Rachel said with conviction. Her husband, Nicholas Adams, was a godsend before their aunt passed away. He ministered to Rachel's spiritual deficiency and stayed by her side throughout her cancer treatment. As a matter of fact, his prayers gave the sisters peace in the middle of the stormy unknowns.

"Because I have lunch or dinner with a guy doesn't mean he's dating material. When I know without a doubt I've snagged the one, he'll be up for discussion before the sisterhood board."

"You better," Rachel warned as Kym scrutinized her baby sister.

As usual, Rachel's makeup was flawless. "So how ya feeling, Sis? I see your hair is growing like a fertilized zoysia lawn."

Rachel shook her head, and her mass of hair bounced from side to side. Her hair had grown past her shoulders and was thick. Unless someone personally knew about her bout with cancer, there was no hint of Rachel's battle.

When her chemo treatments ended, Rachel decided to let her new hair grow naturally without adding heat or chemicals to straighten it. She could turn heads before her illness, but now, Rachel was stunning, as if she were taking beauty steroids.

"I'm happy—with Jesus, in my marriage, and with my health. Every morning, Nicholas and I thank the Lord for new mercies and His faithfulness. Just like in Lamentations 3:23—it's our golden text."

"Girl, you and your minister husband. Y'all are hot!" Kym mimicked as though sweat were dripping from her forehead.

Next, she turned her attention to Tabitha and her favorite nephew, to which Tabitha replied, "Little Marcus is your only nephew for now."

"Hopefully, the Lord will change that soon," Rachel added. She and

Nicholas had been biding their time until Rachel got the all-clear from her doctor to start a family.

After about a half hour of small talk, they ended with a brief group prayer led by her brother-in-law Minister Nicholas Adams and promises of videoconferencing again next week if it was the Lord's will.

Monday, Kym fell back into her structured routine. Although Chaz wasn't around, he was never out of sight or far from her thoughts. This morning, he'd sent her an inspiring Scripture. In her head, he was the real deal, but she wasn't going to move too hastily just because he was touching the right buttons in her heart.

Later that afternoon, Kym was about to lock her office door and leave with her grad students for a pop-up tutoring session when a deliveryman intercepted her steps. She smiled at the meticulously gift-wrapped box. This wasn't a standard delivery. She untied the ribbon and pulled out the card:

Because you are in my thoughts and prayers, I'm counting the days until I see you again. I hope this treat is as sweet as you. Chaz.

Enclosed were two jumbo cookies from Vaccaro's Italian Pastry.

Her students eyed her with snickers.

"We already know you're not going to share those, are you, Instructor Knicely?"

"You've got that right, Tammi Cole." Kym chuckled. "Let's go."

Minutes later, the group climbed into the bus branded with the LLU logo. On warm days, the teachers set up portable desks outside the bus. Some students liked the open atmosphere, while others preferred the feel of the makeshift mini classroom. Their targeted area was Monument Street.

It wasn't the worst neighborhood in Baltimore, but it was a far cry from the safest, with the low property values, underemployed residents, and high unemployment rate. The other area she focused on was Park Heights. The neighborhoods were a gold mine for her research. She wanted to prove that zip codes didn't tell the entire story on a child's intellect.

A lot was riding on Kym's shoulders. It had been an overwhelming task in the past, but with Chaz in her life, she felt that the load was bearable because he was there to give her a boost of encouragement. He believed in her. Kym smiled. Was it possible she had a man she could lean on? Time would tell.

In his office, Chaz checked his emails and scanned a few health blogs. The World Health Organization declared obesity the number one preventable health threat to societies, and the condition triggered other costly ailments.

Weight gain affected all the organs, yet there wasn't one solution to combat it all—diet and exercise weren't enough. Plus, those goals weren't easily achievable in some sectors of the population.

Since his appointment as community public health liaison at Johns Hopkins Bloomberg School of Public Health, he kept tabs on the research, the trials, and the victories. The increase of gun violence was fast becoming a health concern, not only for the nation but also in his hometown of Baltimore.

Researchers with the Bloomberg School of Public Health had worked on a published report with the Centers for Disease Control about autism. The results were disappointing for Chaz.

After a three-year study, there was a 15 percent rate increase of children diagnosed with the disorder. Yet the public couldn't identify a nonverbal autistic child's agonizing full-blown meltdown versus that of an age-related temper tantrum.

Chaz had learned a lot about autism over the years. A therapeutic assistant at the Kennedy Krieger Institute Center for Autism and Related Disorders kept him informed. On more than one occasion, he and Debra had met for lunch or coffee as she shared literature to better help him understand Chauncy's diagnosis.

Another time, they had talked all night at a restaurant, Debra in her element and Chaz soaking up her every word. When she stopped by his office a couple of times after that, Zeke had cautioned him not to send the woman the wrong message.

That was absurd. Their relationship was strictly professional. Still, Chaz kept his friend's advice at the forefront every time they conversed. However, in reality, Chaz needed Debra's expertise to guide him through the autism maze.

One thing his colleagues could agree upon: more analysis was needed to pinpoint the genetic contributing factors that caused autism, which meant Chaz followed the research, articles, blogs, or conferences that dealt with the topic.

Chauncy's condition wouldn't lessen, so her symptoms would have to be monitored and managed. His heart ached for her. That little girl was his next generation, and he would do everything within his power for her to thrive. He smiled, thinking about the time they sat in her backyard and watched two robins flying from tree to tree. The moment had been tranquil.

Although he had a meeting in a half hour, he picked up the phone to call his daughter-in-law to check on Chauncy. He liked how Kym stayed in touch with her sisters weekly via videoconferencing. He could suggest that to Gee.

It might do Chauncy good. Like many children on the spectrum, her autism made it difficult for her to maintain eye contact whenever someone talked to her, which frustrated his ex-wife and tested her patience.

Valerie didn't understand their granddaughter wasn't being rude or misbehaving. Chauncy had her own way of communicating, which could be a struggle for outsiders to understand. Chaz suspected it was more like that for Kenneth, Valerie's current husband, who had low tolerance for children period. As long as the man wasn't rude and didn't mistreat his granddaughter, Chaz would stay on the sidelines and let Valerie handle her husband.

"Hey, Pops," Lana answered the phone.

Prior to Chauncy's birth, Lana had a high-paying salary at a tech firm. Once her daughter was diagnosed, Lana had to cut back her hours. But juggling the numerous doctor appointments and her work and home schedule caused Gee and Lana to do some soul-searching. Lana willingly made the decision to be a stay-at-home mother and pour all her attention into her baby.

The outpatient care, the meds, and the therapies added a strain to their household budget by forty thousand plus dollars a year, so Chaz had started a payroll deduction to send funds directly to their account to use for whatever they needed.

Plus, he was committed to sharing in the cost of their deductibles and copays. Despite living in different cities, he was in it with them for the long run—emotionally, physically, financially. Whatever they needed, he planned to fill in the gap, whether they asked for help or not.

"Good morning to you, Daughter." They chatted a few minutes before he asked, "How's my grandbaby doing today?"

"We've had a good day. Baked cookies as we worked with her on verbal skills while teaching her a few sign language words…then something was off. Whenever I tried to touch her or anything she was playing with, Chauncy kept pointing to my fingers and pushing my hands away." She sighed. "She worked herself into a frenzy, and I couldn't figure out why."

"Hmm. Could it be new hand lotion or something you were wearing?" He racked his brain as he heard the dejection in her voice. When Lana thought she had a routine with Chauncy, one slight variation could disrupt the entire day's schedule.

"No new lotion, but I tried this neon green nail polish for fun. It's a process of elimination. We know she doesn't like most vegetables, especially green—like most children. When Chauncy uses crayons and breaks the green ones—go figure. And she's fussy when we're picking out her clothes; anything green, she refuses to wear. I thought it had something to do with the texture. Now, I'm wondering if it's the color. Of course, your son—my husband"—she lifted her voice in irritation—"thinks I'm making a big deal out of nothing."

Chaz listened to her frustration while watching the time. As it got closer to his meeting, he coaxed her to take a deep breath, and he said a brief prayer for her mental strength. Marriages were tested when there was a child with special needs. When it came to outside intervention, a caregiver trained in autism was a must for Chauncy.

"Baby, I've got to run. Put Chauncy on the line." Not that his granddaughter would carry on a conversation with him, but whatever she had to say was important to him. Plus, she had an uncanny ability to store conversation infinitely until she saw him again. Once, she had drawn a picture about something he had said a while back that he had forgotten about, so Chaz exercised caution with what subject he brought up. "How's my favorite little girl?"

"PawPaw," she responded after a long silence.

He blew kisses over the phone as Zeke walked in with a raised brow. His office was in the other building, which housed the accounting department where he was the senior manager. Whenever Zeke had a meeting in Chaz's building, which was often, he stopped by.

"Well, well. Judging from the goofy expression on your face and the kisses I suspect you'd rather give in person, you've found a winner." His friend's expression was anything but innocent.

Chaz quickly said his goodbye and waited for Lana to end the call. "One woman at a time. That was my heart, Chauncy."

"Then I feel sorry for the other woman." Zeke snickered but Chaz didn't.

"There is no 'other' woman," Chaz argued. "There's room for Chauncy and Kym." He grunted. After yesterday, she hadn't been far from his thoughts, so when he arrived at the office, he'd sent her the cookies. Standing from behind his desk, Chaz grabbed his tablet, then led Zeke out. "I'm deeply attracted to Kym. After one week, I won't deny that."

"Ha!" Zeke shook his head. "That woman's been in your head for months." He pushed the elevator to go down while Chaz tapped the up arrow.

"You got me. I'm looking forward to seeing her again."

"Does that mean you'll be taking her out to breakfast, lunch, and dinner? Look out, Professor. Chaz is on the hunt!"

The elevator going up stopped, its doors opening. Chaz stepped inside, which saved him from telling Zeke he was right.

Chapter 7

Kym shifted in her seat in the auditorium of the Mitchell-Jackson Building, which was named after two families vaunted as civil rights pioneers. Chaz reminded her that he would attend the Founders' Day program in his inspiring morning text she had grown accustomed to. Numbers 6:24 was a short and sweet blessing: The Lord bless you and keep you. He sent a second text: I won't leave until I look into your eyes and tell you how beautiful you are.

So now, as she sat in the front row along with her colleagues, waiting for the program to begin, Kym shivered, knowing Chaz was there.

"You're cold?" Judith fanned her face and glanced around, clearly not expecting Kym to answer. "I think it's warm in here."

Glancing over her shoulder, Kym scanned the sections from left to right. She could feel his eyes watching her but had yet to spot him in this crowd of students and faculty. She gave up and turned around.

Moments later, she felt his presence before he made his appearance. When their eyes connected, the buzz around her seemed to fade.

Chaz reached out his hands, and she rested hers in his palms. The touch was so magnetic that it was hard for her to pull away. She exhaled in contentment.

"You're more dazzling than I ever imagined in that scarf." His voice was low and husky.

Knowing Judith had bionic ears caused Kym to blush at his compliment. Chaz had no idea his gift had sparked another color-scheme fixation. She had been wearing gold and yellows for a week now.

"I have to get back to the office, but you know I couldn't miss my alma mater's Founders' Day. Can we sit together?"

You have no idea how much I want to. "Sorry, the faculty has to be seen in the front." She feigned a pout for good measure.

"Understandable, but know I'll be admiring you while the speaker is talking. I can multitask." His eyes narrowed on her before he strolled away to find himself a seat.

"Mm-hmm," Judith mumbled. "Eye candy."

The convocation opened with a prayer from a prominent local minister. The board chairman followed with his remarks. "Continuing the legacy left by inventor Lewis Howard Latimer, it's no accident that Lewis Latimer University has graduated many successful Black entrepreneurs over the course of the school's one hundred and fifty years. To nurture those ideas, we have to ensure everyone has access to higher education, especially Blacks and other people of color. Our urban education department is leading the way on how to reach and empower young minds..."

Talk about pressure—Kym knew President Harold Cummings was referring to the mobile tutoring program she'd initiated.

"LLU is more than a public HBCU. We're the largest historically Black college and university in the state. We're a member of Thurgood Marshall College Fund..."

Kym's mind wandered as the president recited information most staff members and students already knew. Founders' Day served as a refresher to the veterans of the school and to inform freshmen and newcomers about the proud history and the accomplishments of their HBCU.

Her mind drifted to Chaz and the excitement of knowing he was nearby. It was too soon for her to be this mentally invested in a man. Labeled as the cautious sister, Kym wondered if she was really throwing caution to the wind to be with Chaz.

The school president pulled her attention back to the program when he yielded the stage to the Lewis Latimer Choir for a selection. As expected, the speaker came with a profound message to encourage students and faculty to remain vigilant in the pursuit of knowledge and truth.

When the audience released hearty applause, Kym exhaled. Although she prided herself on paying attention when she attended seminars and lectures, she had slipped up on this one. Kym couldn't wait for the conclusion so she could see Chaz. As the crowd thinned, he was nowhere in sight. Her shoulders slumped in disappointment as she slowed her steps.

Seconds later, she heard Chaz call her name. He was feet away. Her heart blossomed to a rose in full bloom. As he approached, his steps seemed to move in slow motion. First, he stared at her before his lips curled upward into an alluring smile. His nostrils flared as he lifted a brow. "Whoever gave you that scarf has good taste, because it complements your skin tone."

Okay, so he wanted to play. She had a few minutes to do that. Kym teasingly scrunched her nose at him. "It was a gift from an admirer."

"A big admirer indeed." Chaz shook his head. "Woman, you're a skilled chess player. I enjoy our skirmishes."

"Me too." She smiled. "I thought I had missed you."

He reached for her hands again. His touch was strong but gentle. "Did you think I would leave without saying goodbye?"

"I had hoped not." There was something about this man that didn't make her hesitate about being transparent.

"We have to do something about taking scheduled breaks. Please find some downtime this weekend. If that's not possible, I volunteer to be the teacher's assistant or fellow researcher." His eyes sparkled.

"Oh, and for the record, I'm comfortable fellowshipping at Abundant Life again this Sunday." Chaz glanced at the huge wall clock near the stage. "Think about what I said. I've got to go." After one more squeeze, he released her hand and swaggered toward the door.

"Nice view." Judith came up behind Kym.

Kym twirled around, patting her chest. "Did you have to scare me like that?"

"I called your name twice." Judith gave a peace sign, then folded her arms. "A man like that can hold my hand anytime."

After inhaling, then exhaling, Kym nudged Judith to steer her toward the exit that led to the courtyard and the path back to their offices. "I want to take things slow, but my heart keeps galloping forward."

"I could see *him* being a problem."

Alarmed, Kym stopped in her tracks and tugged her friend out of the path of others onto the lawn. "You do? Why?" She wasn't going to budge until Judith shared what was on her mind.

"I don't gamble, but I'm betting your homemade Belgian waffles he's the one. If that's the case, you're not going to be able to smother love. Come on."

Smother? Kym welcomed it—if Chaz was the one. On autopilot, they continued striding to their offices without another word. There was no denying that her attraction to Chaz was strong and thinking about him coaxed a smile out of her. She prayed it wasn't lust, because Kym was looking for the real thing. *God, I'm going to need Your help on this. The Bible says* guard my heart. *How can I when he's so gentle with it?*

Chapter 8

The woman had messed with Chaz's head. The sight of Kym could give him high blood pressure. He respected her work boundaries because he believed in her mission. But the absence was hard on a brotha.

As he parked his car in the garage near the building where he worked, he was already compiling the message he was about to send her. He stepped off the elevator to his floor on a mission as he texted while walking. You are breathtaking. Hoping for a standby status to make your list of "to do's" this weekend. You make the call.

She texted back: A brief distraction is good. :) How about a trip to the museum? I live near the Walters Art Museum.

You really do like museums. Chaz smirked. Does that mean I get to pick you up like a real date? He lifted a brow and waited for her reply.

She responded: It will be a real date. I'll meet you there. It's in my neighborhood.

Chaz grunted out his disappointment. The woman knew how to temper his excitement. Didn't matter. They were still in the "getting to know you" phase, and Chaz was a determined man. She would see that his intentions were honorable. It was comical almost. He never had to work so hard to be a gentleman.

Kym pushed herself on her dissertation to free up time on Saturday. She didn't care what Judith said about her and Chaz. She didn't care that her heart fluttered when he texted, called, or was nearby. Kym didn't care that he seemed to be everything she wanted in a man who professed to be a practicing Christian. She had to slow it down and take her time to see if their feelings were genuine or if it was hormones on overdrive. She was scared to pray that what she was feeling wasn't lust.

At noon, she slid her arms into a denim duster, which matched her jeans. A mustard-colored turtleneck made the ensemble pop. She scrutinized her appearance from her riding boots to the cap over her head—casual but classy. The look she was going for.

She drove the short distance from her home to West Mount Vernon Place, which now housed the Walters Art Museum. Chaz was there outside, strolling through the courtyard. He always appeared calm and confident, but today his body language revealed impatience. Once he recognized her SUV, he stopped in his tracks and waved. His strides were long toward her as she parked curbside.

Chaz opened her door to assist her out. "One day, you're going to have to give me permission to pick you up for a date. I don't like the idea of us meeting at places, denying me the pleasure of displaying my chivalry."

Kym giggled.

"Oh, this is not funny. Either you don't trust me, or you don't enjoy my company as I had assumed."

Was he challenging her? Now she frowned. "It's neither."

"I don't know what bum mistreated you in the past, but I'm not him." Chaz's expression was endearing, as was his tone soft. The man seemed offended.

"We've only been seeing each other a couple of weeks. Patience is a virtue. Do you need me to find that Scripture?" She thought he looked comical with a slight pout.

"I know it well. James 1:4 says, 'But let patience have her perfect work, that ye may be perfect and entire, wanting nothing.'" He sighed. "It's a tug-of-war with you. It seems like you've been in my life longer than that. At the same time, I'm eager to know everything about you at an accelerated pace."

Aww. She wanted to wrap her arms around him and smack a big kiss on his lips. But that would truly send a mixed message. "Baby steps."

"Okay." He agreed as they walked toward the entrance, then he held the door for her to enter into the massive foyer of the nineteenth-century mansion. "I feel a tad guilty about taking you away from your project, so let me know if I become too demanding. I sense the passion you've poured into your work."

"Don't, Chaz. If I feel like I'm falling behind, I'll say no. My dissertation has consumed me because I let it. I meant what I said about welcoming the distraction."

"Whew. My guilt trip is gone." A wide grin stretched across his face. "I still feel I should share the responsibility of helping you reach your goals."

"I like the way you think." Kym's heart fluttered as she studied his expression for sincerity. *Lord, Chaz has to be the right one for me. It has to be him.* She felt comfortable that she didn't have to explain her priorities. What mattered to her seemed to matter to him.

"So"—Chaz glanced around as he removed his jacket, then helped her out of hers—"be my tour guide. What makes the museum so endearing to you?" He slipped her arm through his and patted her hand as if they were about to enter a ballroom or go for a stroll back in the Harlem Renaissance era.

That gesture sparked something within that made her feel faint, but she knew Chaz wouldn't let her fall. "Ooh, I'm so glad you asked. What's really impressive here is their visual and manuscript collection from ancient times, more than five thousand years, possibly before Christ throughout biblical times." She nodded at his surprised expression. "I know, amazing, isn't it? Plus, the museum's collections include thousands of artifacts from around the world, French to Ethiopian art images."

Chaz glanced around. "I guess this is the place to be for an art lesson."

"And history. Check this out." She steered him toward what once was the mansion's dining room. "Here's a letter written by the original owners who enslaved cook Sybby Grant. History that never made it to classrooms."

Next, at an elegant marble winding staircase, Chaz guided her steps as if he feared she would fall. Yeah, chivalry definitely had its benefits.

"On this floor, there's an impressive ceramic collection and even a studio for community artists to create their own masterpieces." She laughed at his feigned scary look. "Don't worry. We don't have time today for an impromptu class."

"Yes!" He pumped his fist in the air. "Although I appreciate artists and their contributions to the world, I'm not one."

"How about this tidbit—Roberto Lugo out of Pennsylvania. He's an artist of Color who got discovered from his graffiti, then he mastered pottery to become an acclaimed ceramicist. Impressive, huh?" Kym smiled.

"Wow. I guess God takes an individual's talent and creates masterpieces. You are the best tour guide I've had the pleasure of being with." He exhaled and faced her. "Your passion is the reason why I can't come between you and your dissertation. You have so much to offer, and I want to do whatever I can to help you get there. I believe in you."

Kym's lips formed *wow*, but the word caught in her throat. She blinked to keep her eyes from watering. "You have no idea how much that means to me."

He patted his chest. "It came from my heart. I really do want you to do well and complete the project, I'm a little selfish too, so you'll have more time for me." He grinned.

A laugh escaped, and Kym had to cap her mouth with her hand. "You, Mr. Chaz Banks, are one of a kind."

"A keeper?" He lifted his brow.

"Most definitely!" As they retraced their steps downstairs, Kym experienced mixed emotions. She had to get back home, but she wouldn't object to playing hooky with Chaz. Common sense won out as he escorted her to her vehicle.

"Kym, a date doesn't have to be a planned activity to see you. It could simply be spending time with you." He closed her door. "Think about that."

She drove off with more than the dissertation on her mind.

Chapter 9

Despite Chaz's distraction caused by his attraction to Kym, his thoughts never ventured far from his family. Some of the Knicely habits had even started to rub off on him. Chaz tried to incorporate weekly videoconferencing with Gee and his family.

Drake was a hit-and-miss with a regular phone call, and his responses to texts were slow. Chaz didn't hold out much hope that adding a request for another form of communication would be effective. To his surprise, Chaz was able to catch a few minutes with his son through a video chat. He had been grateful for that.

Days later after work, he decided to check on Chauncy. He knew instantly something wasn't right when his daughter-in-law answered.

"Sounds like you're having a not-so-good day."

First came Lana's sigh, followed by silence before her reply. "Correct. Since it was a nice fall day, I decided to take Chauncy to the park. It went downhill from there when some other toddlers wanted to climb the slide. Chauncy screamed and yelled at them until those children cried. The parents chewed me out about raising a bully."

She groaned. "My child isn't a bully! She's the sweetest little girl who is trying to assimilate in a world that can't relate to her inappropriate responses to situations and is aggressive sometimes when she interacts with others, but she's trying. Her therapist says she's improving, but there will be relapses." She mumbled something Chaz couldn't make out.

"We have to remember most people don't know the difference between autism and a brat." His tone was meant to be soothing.

"And it's my fault people make judgment calls?" she snapped. "Sorry, Pops, I'm so tired of apologizing for something I can't control. At the end of the day, Chauncy is my baby I carried for nine months. She's perfect.

We do all the things a little girl likes to do—dress up, baking…but I will go Momma Grizzly too, like any mother. It's exhausting being a parent of a child with special needs in and outside home."

Chaz's heart ached for her.

"There should be more public service campaigns. I saw somewhere on the news where an officer used a Taser on a teenager because he was rocking back and forth and the policeman thought he was on drugs!"

"Stimming," Chaz said, referring to the repetitiveness of the rhythmic movement that often soothes them.

"Doesn't anybody watch *Sesame Street* anymore! They even have a Muppet, Julia, who's a little girl with autism."

"I understand your frustration," Chaz said.

Awareness was slow going despite the public service announcements in schools, on YouTube, and in pediatricians' offices. There were no words or stats about the success of the campaigns that would comfort his daughter-in-law at the moment.

"Once we returned home, I tried to calm her down with her favorite chocolate milk. By that time, she was having a meltdown. It took me more than an hour to calm her for a nap. When she woke, Chauncy picked up where she left off—upset."

"I'm so sorry, baby."

"Then Gee called and said he would be late because he is going to stop by and see his mother. I hung up the phone. I'm tired, Pops. I'm tired."

Chaz exhaled. *Lord*, he began to silently pray, *give me the words to say that she would hear and be comforted.* "You two need a getaway, even for a few hours."

Lana grunted. "No, I need a getaway from everybody for twenty-four hours. Can you make that happen?"

His daughter-in-law wasn't bluffing. "I'm going to have a talk with that husband of yours." Chaz was irked, learning his son planned a detour before going home. What was more important than getting to his wife and daughter?

Plus, his ex-wife, Valerie, should step up and give Gee and Lana some respite, but Chaz held his tongue. If only he were there… It had crossed Chaz's mind to move to St. Louis to help out. He even considered applying for a couple of positions there to be closer, but at the end of the day, Baltimore was home. Valerie and the boys were the ones who had moved away.

Lana began to sob. "I feel alone."

"But you're not. I'm a phone call away, and I'll continue to pray for Chauncy's development and your peace."

She whimpered. "Thank you."

"The house is quiet. Where's Chauncy?"

"Sitting across the room in the corner, turning the pages of a coloring book."

Chaz imagined Chauncy either staring at the pages or turning them as if she were reading text. When she did pick up a crayon, it was blue. No other color.

His stomach growled, reminding him he had skipped lunch at work and had yet to prepare something for dinner. Once Lana had calmed down, he reluctantly said his goodbye. As soon as he ended the call, he texted Gee: Send your wife flowers—NOW!

His phone rang immediately. "What's wrong, Pops? Why?"

"Never let another man tell you what's wrong with your own wife. She was having a bad day when I called. She needs a day off—to herself—or she's going to lose it, Son."

"Dad." Gee's frustration was apparent in that one word. "We've tried to get a sitter who is capable of handling Chauncy's special needs. As you know, it hasn't been easy, even with those who specialize in children with autism."

"We're all Lana has." Chaz wasn't accepting any excuses. "If only her parents were alive to provide an extended support system, but they aren't. I do my best by calling to check on her, but you should speak to your mother about caring for her grandchild more often. Valerie boasts constantly that Chauncy resembles her," he pointed out.

"I've tried. I had planned to stop by there on the way home today. Mom says she understands that I need to recharge before I get home."

Chaz gritted his teeth in aggravation with his ex-wife. Knowing Valerie, she would probably prepare food to keep Gee there for a couple of hours. She might send a plate home with him for Lana, if she cooked enough servings. Valerie wasn't a bad person; she was disappointed by her first grandchild's lack of interaction with her.

"Take care of your wife. She needs you. Lana wants a getaway, and I'm sending money as we speak." Chaz tapped the app to send cash to his son and Lana's bank account. "If I were you, I'd let her go somewhere quiet. She deserves it."

They ended the call with Chaz feeling just as worked up as Lana. He recalled Kym's jest about patience being a virtue. James 1:4 had to be the mission statement for everyone who cared for loved ones. *God, give us a double dose of patience*. "Amen."

Chapter 10

Kym smiled to herself. After reviewing Baltimore schools' test scores, she tapped away on her keyboard.

"Hey." Judith popped her head into Kym's office. "I'm about to head out." She stepped inside.

"Go on. I'm tweaking my pros and cons before I meet with Dr. Massey this week. It's already November, and if I want to walk in May, I have to stay on schedule to defend my research by end of March—and that's pushing it."

Judith folded her arms and smirked. "Mm-hmm. God help you with Sir Chaz on the scene. He would be a distraction for any woman."

Kym chuckled. "That he is, but I took him up on his offer of a 'do nothing' date at the library. Chaz has served as a sounding board on ideas a couple of times. A well-read man is sexy." She grinned, thinking about the many compliments he bestowed on her, but one shone above the rest.

Not only are you incredibly smart but also passionate, he had once said.

"Pulling him into your work isn't dating. You need a refresher course on Dating 101." Judith laughed and backed out of Kym's office. "Don't let a good one get away. Remember, men are babies. They want all the attention."

Kym disagreed. Chaz wasn't one of those men. He was the one giving her all the attention, and she had no complaints as she returned to her computer.

Chaz couldn't keep the grin off his face as he met Zeke for lunch. "Kym and I have been seeing each other for weeks, and I have no complaints."

"After so many years of knowing you, Chaz Banks, I've never seen you this smitten." Zeke laughed so hard that others in the Abbey Burger Bistro shot them curious stares.

Chaz sat back in his chair. His friend was right. "Dating a woman has never felt so natural."

"I don't care what you say. If I met a date at the library, you wouldn't have to worry about me being quiet, because I would be asleep." Zeke snickered.

"You have so much to learn about life, son." Chaz tsked, teasing his friend, who was nine years younger than him, even though they interacted more as brothers.

"Ha. If we're keeping score on bona fide dates, then I have more checks on my board than you. It's a split between sisters at church and acquaintances. Trust me, dinner better be on the agenda." He swirled a fry in ketchup before devouring it in one bite.

"Oh, we do dine out, but there're also movies and a few Saturday outings, one that included a trip to DC to visit the African American museum." What they'd expected to be a morning excursion had turned into a day trip. They hadn't gotten back to Maryland until late that evening. They'd basically stayed until they shut the museum down. "We have a lot in common. We chose careers to help others, we love family, and we both walk with Christ."

"It's the last part that is the most impressive."

"I know." Chaz agreed.

"I have to meet this woman."

"That can be arranged, but this Saturday, we're going to another museum." Chaz felt smug as Zeke groaned in disbelief.

"Come on, man. I know Charm City has its share of attractions, but let me make some suggestions like—"

Chaz held up his hand. "No need. This time, we're going to the B&O Railroad."

Zeke shook his head. "Poor woman. That's an all-day adventure."

"That gives me an idea." Chaz stood and gathered his trash. "Come on. Time's a-wastin'."

Kym felt safe around Chaz, so she had given him her address to pick her up for their day date.

In his element, Chaz reminded her of her love for history and art museums as they walked the grounds of the historic B&O Railroad Museum.

"This is where the history of railroad began, where the first rail tracks were laid… The trains are more than a graveyard of days gone by."

Chaz became a walking Wikipedia of information, recalling incredible tidbits about history as he intertwined his fingers with hers. Their connection was strong, yet his hold was gentle.

The museum had life-size replicas of Black porters. "I'm glad the museum included them." She pointed. "That was one position Blacks weren't denied. The darker a Black man's skin, the more the image of servitude lived on."

"Yes, the Pullman Porters." Chaz talked about the discrimination, disrespect, and racism they suffered to get the coveted jobs. "In the 1920s, a social activist formed the Brotherhood of Sleeping Porters to fight for better pay, working conditions, and respect." His eyes twinkled. "My dear enchanting museum enthusiast, Chicago has a fascinating museum honoring his legacy, the National A. Philip Randolph Pullman Porter Museum."

Kym's heart swelled with pride. Chaz's knowledge about the history of Blacks and the railroad was impressive. He continued pointing out facts until they strolled inside the terminal museum, where displays were in glass encasements, but there were plenty of other railcars that were a playground for young minds to learn about the history of transportation, with a few stagecoaches in the mix. At first sight, most of the railcars looked similar until Chaz's trained eye pointed out the intricate details and features.

Without Kym realizing it, their tour lasted a couple of hours. She was enjoying the information and his company. They retraced their steps outside to watch a display of a model train set with six cars and a caboose climb the green hills of a small village, then jerk around tracks to disappear inside a tunnel, all the while blowing the whistle as it charged ahead. No wonder little boys wanted train sets for Christmas when Kym was growing up.

"This was fascinating, Chaz. It slipped my mind that trains were the first motor transportation that enabled the great Black migration from the South."

Her comments seemed to make his day. "Whew. I was worried you wouldn't like it."

She wiggled her nose at him. "What's not to like? It's American history. I really enjoyed this. Despite advances in travel, the metro train can be the fastest way to get places when there is traffic congestion. I guess trains are to little boys what dolls are to girls."

"When my boys were small, it was bonding time to put together the train tracks and build a town around it." Chaz paused as if he were contemplating whether to salute the train about to loop around the tracks. "When my sons were teenagers and stayed with me during the summers, I purchased other pieces to add to the collection."

Kym nodded. "If my brother-in-law hasn't already thought of a train collection for Little Marcus, maybe I'll introduce my nephew to something this nostalgic. Come on." She pivoted on her heel to head back inside to the gift shop, for Chaz to recommend the perfect gift for Little Marcus.

Before leaving the museum, he surprised her with a picnic lunch. "This is so thoughtful. Thank you."

"I want bragging rights to this being the best day date ever, but honestly, I haven't had one bad date with you." Chaz took a swig from the bottled water and gave a tender smile. "I'm aiming for a perfect score."

Kym blushed. "I guess it depends on how long you plan to stick around."

He reached for her hand and didn't let go as jolts of electricity raced through her veins. She had to exhale slowly to mask the shivering that he sparked from his gentle touch. "I'll be the first to admit your beauty captured my attention, but now there's an emotional, spiritual connection. I'm not going anywhere."

"Good to know." That was exactly what she wanted to hear. "Me either."

Their date officially ended that night on her porch. Chaz stared into her eyes as he leaned closer to her lips and stopped. Was he asking her permission to kiss her? This was the type of man she could fall for—or maybe she had. Kym closed her eyes and welcomed the soft brush of his lips against hers. The moment was brief but unforgettable, as he placed one more peck against her lips.

When he pulled back, they both opened their eyes at the same time. "Just what I thought—a perfect kiss." His nostrils flared as he whispered, "Good night." He swaggered away and never looked back as he climbed into his car.

Chapter 11

Four weeks and counting. Chaz had been attending the praise and worship at Kym's church. Yes, he had been missing in action at his own, but he was hearing the gospel preached. It had become a Sunday tradition for both of them. Some of the members at her church even greeted him by name.

This past Wednesday, Kym showed up at his church's Bible class. What a surprise. Chaz had sensed her presence before she slid in the pew next to him. He never felt happier. She had often missed her own church's early midweek Bible class because of her field work. His church's evening Bible class started an hour later.

Chaz swallowed back the emotion of contentment, knowing the time she sacrificed to be with him when she had so much on her plate. Their relationship wasn't one-sided, with him always giving and her always taking. They both shared their affections.

"Thank you for being you," she whispered as he tugged her closer until they were shoulder to shoulder. With Kym beside him, Chaz felt she had come home. He held his breath at the realization he was falling in love with her. His heart froze at the thought, then recharged and skipped a beat at the possibility. He glanced at her. She looked up and smiled. She had no idea of the depth of his feelings. *Whew.* Chaz was coming to terms with his increased emotions, and he needed to slow his heart rate.

"Pastor's teaching on the fruit of the Spirit from Galatians, chapter five." He pointed to verses twenty-two and twenty-three, which he had highlighted on his tablet. "We can share—"

"Pay attention." She nudged him. "I'm going to take my own notes." She pulled her phone out of her purse to do that.

She was right. If he didn't, he would have to reread the lesson plan because his mind was still processing an emotion that he had found a woman who seemed to complete him. This was going too fast.

The hour class ran over about fifteen minutes because of questions from members. Before he and Kym could say amen to the benediction, Chaz saw Zeke making a beeline for them.

He leaned into Kym and mumbled a warning. "Here comes my buddy. Brace for trouble." Zeke approached from behind Kym and gave him a thumbs-up. Amused, Chaz shook his head and made the introductions.

He smirked at Zeke's tongue-tied expression. Yep, Kym had that *wow* effect.

"I see why my friend has been missing Sunday morning services here."

Kym blushed. "Sorry about that, but he's getting a healthy dose of the Word at Abundant Life."

"Mm-hmm." Zeke exchanged a knowing look with Chaz. "To be frank, I hope you two keep it going strong. I like seeing this guy happy." Zeke motioned toward Chaz.

Chaz grunted. If he didn't step in, the man would tell all Chaz's secrets. "Remind me again why we're friends."

All three laughed, and Zeke took the cue to say goodbye. Kym turned to Chaz. "It's good to hear I make you happy, considering I feel like I'm not giving a hundred percent."

He gathered their things off the pew. "I can't wait to experience your hundred percent." His eyes brightened, then he winked.

"Since words are powerful, Mr. Banks, it's still good to know and hear it." She lowered her voice. "You make me happy too. I wasn't expecting that."

"What were you expecting?" he asked, pressing her for an answer.

She shook her head, and a few curls bounced from side to side. "Honestly, I had no expectations."

"Good—I guess." He grinned. "Then I've exceeded them," he said as they crossed the parking lot to her car and he watched her drive off.

"A good-night kiss would have been nice," he mumbled as he headed to his own vehicle.

—

It was mid-November, and Chaz was treating Kym to a Saturday matinee to celebrate her mentor's approval of her dissertation progress.

While driving, Chaz snuck peeks at Kym whenever he stopped. "Thanksgiving is coming up. I'd like to invite you to dinner at my house. I'm roasting the turkey and fixing the dressing. Usually I have a few friends over, and they bring the sides. Since the Ravens have the best record in the NFL this season, I'm sure Drake will make an appearance to watch the game, along with Patrice."

"Oh, I'm sorry I won't be able make it." She pouted. "I'm going home to St. Louis. Rachel and her husband are coming too. I can't wait to see her. But I hope you enjoy your holiday anyway."

"Won't if you're not there." He grunted. "And I won't hesitate to cancel my Thanksgiving plans and go with you." Chaz wasn't bluffing. Let someone else cook the dinner.

No doubt he would feel the emptiness from not sharing the holiday with her. If she was going to St. Louis, he would make a special trip there to see his grandbaby. Granted his ex-wife reserved Thanksgiving with Gee's family, and Christmas was Chaz's time. That had been the agreement in the divorce decree decades ago, and somehow, the routine had stuck.

"How about some company?" he asked.

The look of bewilderment on Kym's face was priceless. "Huh? You just said you were hosting Thanksgiving dinner and…" She swallowed.

"And I said I won't think twice about canceling it. You won't be there, so humor me. I don't want us to spend the holidays in separate cities," he admitted, to his own surprise. He had wanted to mask his feelings longer to see if she felt the same way. They hadn't been dating two months. "I'll visit with my family while you visit yours."

"So would your plans include us meeting each other's family? Because I'm not sure if I'm ready for that this soon."

In reality, he agreed with her. If he introduced Kym to Gee and Lana, they would offer to pick out her engagement ring. Although he loved her, which was premature, she didn't know that—yet. They needed time to nurture their relationship. "I'm going along for the ride. Nothing more, babe." He covered her hand and held it as he drove off after the stop sign.

"You've never called me that before." Kym blushed.

"It came naturally, and I meant the endearment." He looked at her with love in his heart. Maybe she could see it.

"If you're sure, I welcome your company." Her eyes seemed to dance as her lips curved up.

Soon they were at Cinemark Egyptian 24 in Arundel Mills. They munched on junk food from the concession area and attempted to figure out the suspense flick's plot. They never did.

By the time Chaz returned home, he was more determined to back out of hosting Thanksgiving dinner. It wasn't like he had family there—except Drake. He paused to consider whether making the split decision was worth it. He came to the conclusion that the close relationship he wanted with Drake had to be more than one holiday out of the year.

With a decision made, he pulled out his phone and scanned the flights to St. Louis. At this late date, his chances of getting on the same plane with Kym were slim, and it would cost him—big time. No sweat.

What made him rethink this brainy idea was the normal two-hour trip would take half the morning. Not only did he have to endure a short layover in Atlanta, but he had to leave two hours earlier to coordinate his arrival within twenty minutes of hers.

Rubbing his eyes, Chaz had to slow down. This was the part where he asked himself: Was this really worth it? As he considered the answer, Kym's smile seemed to flash before his eyes. Chaz bit his lip, grinning. He paid the price. She was worth it.

Next he called Drake to give him the change of plans, expecting to get his voicemail. His son answered on the second ring.

"Hey, Dad. What's up?" He sounded upbeat, and judging from the noise in the background, his son wasn't home.

Chaz felt a twinge of guilt. "Son, I think this year I'd rather skip the cooking and spend Thanksgiving in St. Louis. Are you okay with that?" If Drake put up a big enough fuss, he would back out on Kym.

"Oh, yeah. Works for me. I was going to call you anyway. Patrice's family invited me to have dinner with them. You know, something different."

Why did Drake's words sting when Chaz had made the same decision to be with Kym? Of course, his son didn't know that. "Okay, Son. Enjoy yourself. Remember, your old man loves you."

"I know, Dad. Same here."

After their call ended, Chaz called Gee, who was surprised by his father's unexpected holiday plans. "Does this mean you're not coming for Christmas?" he asked.

"Oh no. I plan to still come." Chaz chuckled at the concern in his son's voice. "If Valerie and Kenneth have a problem with me inviting myself to their house, I'll respect their boundaries. Plus, consider this a bonus trip to see my grandbaby."

"Actually, this works out great, Pops. Lana wants to attempt hosting Thanksgiving dinner this year, so it will be at our house instead of Mom's."

Chaz was surprised by Lana volunteering to host the holiday dinner, considering his daughter-in-law had recently been so stressed. "Are you helping her?"

"You know it. I did some soul-searching after our last talk, Pops. I love Lana, and I know Chauncy's care is a team effort. I've been paying closer attention to her stress level. We have some downtime when Chauncy is asleep, and we reaffirmed our vows to each other by watching our wedding DVD again."

"You make a father proud," Chaz barely choked out.

"I have a great dad."

His change of plans seemed to work out for everybody. He could thank Kym for that.

Chapter 12

A week later, Chaz groaned and struggled to wake up. He had to get to the airport two hours early for his 6:45 a.m. flight. More than once, he had to remind himself that the purpose of taking a layover in Atlanta instead of a nonstop flight was to beat Kym's nonstop plane to St. Louis.

By the time Chaz arrived at Lambert airport, he wondered how he could have jet lag with a one-hour time change. Forcing his eyes not to cross, Chaz double-checked the board for Kym's arrival time and strolled to her gate to wait. When she appeared, the weariness he suffered was worth it.

Although they had seen each other days earlier, it felt like forever. It took all his restraint not to prolong their embrace. When they stepped back, Chaz studied her attire. Kym had been on a purple color binge for weeks now. He lifted a brow and she giggled. "What's so funny?"

"I'm ashamed to say I was more excited knowing you would be waiting for me than seeing my family." Kym blushed, which was not only attractive but alluring.

"I couldn't think of you coming here without me. This very airport is where it all began for us." He paused and chuckled. "Can't believe I got up at three thirty in the morning to catch my 6:45 flight to beat you here."

"There's never been a dull moment with us." Her eyes twinkled with mischief. "So how are we going to pull this off? If we walk out together talking, my sisters and brothers-in-law will be suspicious. What about your family?"

Chaz adjusted his carry-on. "I usually rent a car, so they don't have to bother coming to get me. Sometimes—not all the time—Chauncy doesn't do well in crowds."

Kym nodded as if she understood, but he doubted she really did. Chaz hadn't at first either. Since Chauncy's diagnosis, he and his family had God to lean on for her development. In the interim, the Bankses would do all they could to help her grow into a well-adjusted person. He reined in his thoughts.

"I'll be steps behind you, babe." She stopped, and he watched her eyes light up when she heard the endearment. "At least we'll fly back on the same flight. I'll meet you at the gate."

She took a deep breath, then feigned a pout. "I guess this is goodbye."

Shaking his head, Chaz didn't like the sound of that as he traced the outline of her lips with his finger. "Keep looking at me like that and your family is going to think you missed your flight because I'll kiss you and hold you hostage."

"Okay, okay." Kym tried to muster a straight face. "I'll behave—maybe. Enjoy your family, and happy Thanksgiving. I have to get my checked bag."

He snickered.

"What?"

"We're here for less than a week, and you packed a suitcase?"

"Yep." She lifted her delicate chin in a challenge. "I needed my makeup, shoes, and extra clothes in case the weather changes. I never know what I might need."

Chaz chuckled. "You don't need much for perfection."

He reached out and squeezed her hand, then, reluctantly, let her go and walk ahead of him.

Whew. Why did Kym have mixed feelings about her and Chaz going their separate ways? They both had family to visit. Even though she was enamored by Chaz, she wasn't ready for the Knicely clan to meet him.

Their relationship was too new, surreal, and hopeful. She didn't want her sisters cheering them on, only to be let down like with some of her other short-term dates.

Judith knew about Chaz by default. If Kym needed a sounding board, she had her best friend. Still, Kym would miss him, because whenever they were together, happiness filled her being.

Knowing Chaz was tracking her every movement, Kym felt electricity run through her veins. Glancing over her shoulder, she admired Chaz's slow swagger. He winked, and she tried not to blush. Oh, how she loved that man. *What?* She caught herself from stumbling before Chaz would race to her aid.

Love? She kept moving, but her heart was stuck in neutral. *Love?* She whispered, "God, I'm scared." Was what she felt for Chaz that once-in-a-lifetime, forever, happily-ever-after love?

What if he didn't love her back? The devastation would crush her. What if his love didn't align with hers? Couples could date for years and years without ever making a commitment. That wasn't what she wanted. Whew. *Take your time, hold your tongue, and save yourself from disappointment*, the rational side of her warned.

All thoughts of Chaz were put on hold when she exited the terminal. Her family was off to the side, holding flowers, balloons, and a sign that read *Welcome Home* as if she were a returning servicewoman.

It was useless to complain they were making too much fuss for a routine holiday trip. Her protests in the past had been ignored, so Kym accepted their affection with love and now would probably have a fit if they didn't greet with her the hoopla.

Tabitha and Rachel met her halfway and engulfed her in hugs, then they looped their arms through hers, almost dragging her to the spot where Marcus and Nicholas waited. Taking turns, the men opened their arms for hugs—Nicholas first, then she reached to take her nephew out of Marcus's arms. After a few attempts to get over his shyness, Little Marcus went willingly into her arms, where Kym smothered him with kisses.

Her brother-in-law Marcus walked between his wife and Kym, keeping a steady hold on their arms as they descended the stairs. Nicholas linked hands with his wife and trailed them. At the baggage carousel, Rachel nudged her. "Hey, Sis, some fine brotha is staring you down."

"Where?" Kym turned her head from left to right.

"Be discreet, would you," Rachel said in a hushed tone. "To your left. Tall, built, he's taking fine to a whole new level. He's in a brown cashmere coat."

Rachel's description of Chaz was on point. Kym had thought he would be gone by now. Feigning a clueless expression, she played the game and turned in the opposite direction before meeting Chaz's eyes for the briefest moment as her luggage appeared. She pointed to it, and Marcus stepped forward to grab it.

Kym looked in Chaz's direction again. Gone, like the first time they met, only this time a misunderstanding didn't stand between them. The more she protested against falling for this man, the harder she sank. How long could she keep Chaz and her love for him a secret from her sisters?

Long enough for me to figure out if he's the one, she coaxed herself. Was two months too short to have a serious talk about the long term?

Chapter 13

Early Thanksgiving morning, Kym, along with her family, attended the holiday service at Bethesda Temple Church. Before the choir's selection and pastor's sermon, the congregation had their traditional testimony segment where anyone—members or visitors—could give thanks to the Lord Jesus for His blessings throughout the year.

There were testimonies about how the Lord made a way to pay bills when there was no income; others received job offers despite their lack of experience or not even applying.

Some cried happy tears as they recounted situations where God's protection kept them safe from violence. All the testimonies were moving and a reminder that the Lord was not only a God of miracles but a Provider and Healer despite the doctors' diagnoses.

Since Nicholas, Rachel's husband, was a minister, the pastor invited all visiting clergy to join him on the pulpit. That left Rachel squeezed between Kym and Tabitha on a pew. When Rachel stood to testify, Nicholas gave his wife his full attention as if he were unaware of the praise she was about to declare.

"I'm thankful this morning for being here. Period." Rachel lifted her arms in the air and shouted, "Each day, I'm a cancer survivor. Each morning, His mercies are new, and I surrender to God's will in my life, whether it's life or death, so while I have an opportunity to live, I will forever give the Lord praise for giving me breath in my body…" Rachel continued for a few more minutes, then quoted Psalm 107:8 as her favorite Scripture: "'Oh that men would praise the Lord for his goodness, and for his wonderful works to the children of men.'" Then she sat again.

Kym reached for her left hand as Tabitha took Rachel's right. The cancer scare had tested their faith in God. Kym couldn't fathom losing her baby sister, especially during the same time the three of them were still mourning Aunt Tweet's death.

The pastor ended his sermon with an uplifting message on thanks, citing 1 Thessalonians 5:18–23: "In everything give thanks..." Instead of a prayer for the benediction, the choir and band ushered people out the door with their rendition of "Thank You."

Back at the Whittingtons' house, Marcus's parents and brother showed up. Under the watchful eye of Tabitha's mother-in-law, the sisters had mastered her pecan and sweet potato pie recipe. The combination was mouthwatering.

Aroma from turkey, dressing, rolls, and desserts filled the house. The sides were already prepared. Kym's stomach grumbled in anticipation. Throughout the teasing, laughs, and fussing over Little Marcus, Kym wondered about Chaz. She hoped he was enjoying his family as much.

Once everyone was gathered around the table, Nicholas gave thanks for their meals and asked for the Lord's blessings. Seconds after the amens, lips smacked and forks clattered while the toddler took center stage with his antics.

As expected, Kym's single status became the topic of discussion around the dinner table. Her brothers-in-law offered to introduce her to some great candidates, but she would have to relocate back to St. Louis or Nashville.

"That ain't happening. My big sister is too picky for the men in Baltimore or any city." Rachel playfully stuck out her tongue.

"It's called selective, and I have been going out." Kym corrected her with a slight lift of her chin. Then she dropped the subject, not ready to reveal her situation, especially since she thought she had fallen in love.

Kym noted Rachel's hopeful expression as she watched their nephew. Rachel was following her doctor's precautions about adhering to a waiting period to ensure all the chemo drugs were out of her system and the cancer wouldn't return within the first couple of years. Of course, everyone was praying for a complete Godly healing, just like He had done for those who shared their testimonies at church earlier.

"Remember, Christmas in Nashville. I can't wait for everyone to see our new house." Rachel didn't contain her excitement. "Plus, we're counting down the months before we can start our own family, so I want to get all my practice in with Little Marcus."

Rachel leaned over and peppered their nephew with kisses. Her husband competed with her to garner the toddler's attention. Nicholas didn't hide the longing on his face too.

Lord, please restore my sister's health so she can bear children, Kym silently prayed in Jesus's name as everyone witnessed the touching scene.

"Okay, everyone. I feel left out," Kym announced.

Tabitha lifted her brows. "You want a baby too? You need a hubby first, Sis." She chuckled, and the others joined her.

"You're partially right about wanting a husband, then a child, but I was referring to a designated holiday for my sisters and brothers-in-law to come visit me. Tab, you and Marcus have Thanksgiving, and now we celebrate Christmas in Nashville with Nicholas and Rachel." Kym pointed out.

"Hmm." Tabitha tilted her head and playfully scrunched her nose at her big sister. She nodded at her husband. "We should put a stipulation on it. Get me another brother-in-law, and we'll be there."

Kym couldn't wait to tell them about Chaz. Only there was no guarantee he would become her husband or be around six months from now. Willing that for herself didn't mean the Lord Jesus was on the same page.

Chaz had experienced parts of life that she hadn't yet. As a divorcé, would he want a second chance at love? A second family? How deep were his feelings for her?

What would her family say about her dating a grandfather? The six-year difference didn't faze Kym.They might think he was twenty-plus years older than her or joke he was probably a kingpin.

Rachel reached across the table for Kym's hand. "Sis," she interrupted Kym's faraway thoughts, "there are some good guys out there. Why settle for random dates when the right one could walk into your life any moment?"

"I know." *I've met one*. Kym needed to change the subject, or she just might slip about Chaz. "I'm serious about a designated holiday for me to play host in Charm City. Why not put Baltimore on the holiday-gathering rotation?" she said in her big-sister, no-nonsense tone. "I'm thinking July, in honor of Aunt Tweet's birthday?"

Tabitha was the first on board. "Yes, let's make it the Fourth of July weekend celebration."

It was unanimous, to Kym's delight. If she and Chaz were still together, Kym would no longer be the odd man out.

Chapter 14

"Charles! I'm surprised to see you in town," Valerie said in her drawn-out voice when she strolled inside Gee's house with her current husband by her side.

"Nice to see you too," Chaz responded cordially, then shook hands with Kenneth.

Valerie air-kissed her son's cheeks, then her daughter-in-law before allowing Kenneth to remove her coat. She stepped farther into the room, craning her neck. Her eyes lit when she spotted Chauncy in the corner, occupied, playing with her favorite pair of craft sticks. She didn't make eye contact when Valerie walked to her and squatted. "Chauncy, aren't you going to give your Gran-ma-ma a hug?"

The child darted her eyes around the room, stood, and scrambled away.

Valerie also stood and placed her fists on her hips. "She acted like I was some monster. I'm not going to chase after her." Chaz saw a glimpse of a wounded expression before Valerie recovered and tsked in a concerned voice. "I wish that girl would talk. She won't even give me a hug. We've come to visit, and she prefers to be by herself."

"Mom," Lana said respectfully, "she can hear you."

Chaz curbed his urge to inform Valerie he had been rewarded with a hug upon his arrival, plus a few kisses on the cheek. Instead, he took pity. "Perhaps she doesn't like the feel of your sweater, perfume, makeup—anything could be making her withdraw."

Everyone eyed her attire.

"Chauncy doesn't like stuffed animals that are furry either," Lana added.

"That's ridiculous. I've worn this sweater jacket before around her."

She huffed and removed it to reveal a crisp white blouse. Valerie glanced in the room where her granddaughter had run off to. She squinted for a moment as if she was debating whether to give it another try.

Chaz hoped she would. While some children with autism had heightened sensory issues with taste, touch, and smell, for Chauncy, noise was the real villain. His ex needed to keep trying. *We all should never give up.*

Valerie huffed again and walked toward the room with her heels clicking across the wood floor.

"Mom," Lana called out, "please. Loud noises could trigger a meltdown, so do you mind walking softer?"

Kenneth stuffed his hands into his pants pockets. "This is so ridiculous. When will she grow out of this?"

Although Chaz coaxed himself to be a fly on the wall because this was Valerie's holiday time, he didn't like the man's tone. "They don't grow out of it. With therapy, they learn to manage it."

"Thanks, Pops. Can you imagine being trapped in a body that won't do what you want it to do? She communicates the best way she can." Gee added. "Plus, she's only four—a child."

"Okay." Kenneth bobbed his head. "I stand corrected, but I still don't like to see my wife upset like this." He flopped in a chair and watched Valerie.

That was the problem with Kenneth. He had been "corrected" more than once about his snide remarks. Chaz held his peace and let his son handle the man.

After slipping out of her heels, Valerie padded barefoot across the room. Chauncy made random eye contact before she reached out and rubbed Valerie's sleeve, then slid off her chair. Their granddaughter rested her head on Valerie's chest as if she were listening for her heartbeat. It was an endearing moment, because Chauncy gave the best hugs.

When Kenneth clapped, Lana shushed him. "This isn't a performance."

"Come on. Let's eat," Gee said with an edge, and everyone followed him into the dining room.

Although Chauncy was still in Valerie's arms, Valerie asked Lana if she needed any help.

"Sure, Mom."

Gee took his daughter and situated her at the table. He used any downtime to interact, like counting, using her fingers. On a functional level of autism, Chauncy's progress was considered level two out of three. He was determined to keep working with her to reach the top level, which signified baby steps.

How is Kym faring with her family? Chaz wondered.

Valerie complimented Lana on the setting as she carried dishes out to the table. Once that task was done and everyone was seated, they held hands while Gee gave thanks and asked for the Lord to bless their meal. Next, everyone served themselves. When Chaz slid the dressing in his mouth, he could taste the spices. "Daughter, this is delicious," he complimented.

Lana grinned widely. "Thanks, Pops. Gee and I found the recipe online."

Valerie dabbed her lips. "Online? You could've called and asked me. But everything is good."

Gee spoke up. "We wanted to do this ourselves."

"I don't see how you could manage and watch after Chauncy." She shook her head in pity.

Chaz glanced at his granddaughter's expressionless face. Chauncy could hear and feel their negativity. As her understanding advanced, she would be able to decipher the emotion behind Valerie's thoughtless remarks.

He used the remainder of the evening to observe his son and Lana. They were one of many young couples doing the right things for their child. But it drained them mentally and strained their marriage.

That concerned Chaz. He didn't want them to become a statistic of dissolved marriages. He had already done that. Chaz would intervene to remind Gee to be attentive when Lana was reaching her breaking point and needed a respite, even if that meant from her own husband.

"So, Pops, are you going to tell us about the 'alum' you're seeing?" Gee winked.

"Nope." Chaz was tight-lipped.

"Oh, come on, Charles." Valerie perked up. "We want to hear all about your new love interest."

"Nothing to tell." Chaz maintained his poker face. He and Kym had a plan. When the time was right, their families would meet one another on the same trip. Until then, he wasn't sayin' nothin'.

Later that night, while lying awake in bed, Chaz smiled as his thoughts drifted to Kym. He yearned to hear her voice but had no idea if her sisters were nearby. Chaz didn't want to intrude or cause speculation about who was texting her when she wasn't ready to introduce him to her family. He got that. Still, it would have been nice to have been coupled off with her for the evening and have her meet his family, to see how she would respond to Chauncy and vice versa.

Kym's text the next morning woke him. Miss you. Enjoy your family. Jesus loves us.

Assuming she was alone, he chanced texting her back. Miss you!!! Loving my family. But Missing You! He pulled up his Daily Scripture app and copied it to his message: Philippians 4:4–8: Rejoice in the Lord always: and again I say, Rejoice…

After reflecting on verse eight—Finally, brethren, whatsoever things are true, whatsoever things are honest, whatsoever things are just, whatsoever things are pure, whatsoever things are lovely, whatsoever things are of good report; if there be any virtue, and if there be any praise, think on these things—Chaz prayed, showered, and dressed. That verse never seemed more alive than now, since he had started dating Kym.

Downstairs, Gee invited him to tag along on their outing. "We plan to go skating while the masses take over the malls for Black Friday deals."

"I definitely like the alternative." What would be the odds he would cross paths with Kym?

He doubted it would be at a skating rink. Chaz couldn't remember the last time he had been on skates. He chuckled to himself. "My granddaughter and I might be going the same speed."

After a while at Steinberg Skating Rink, Valerie and Kenneth suggested taking Chauncy to the zoo since they were in Forest Park. They did.

By the time everyone returned home, Chaz was exhausted, but it had been a good day for Chauncy. She had one-on-one attention with each grandparent in addition to her parents. Since he was in town, Chaz offered to babysit if Gee and Lana wanted to go out. "I could read to Chauncy from some of her books."

Excitement seemed to replace tiredness around Lana's eyes at his suggestion.

"Thanks, Pops." Gee gave his father a fist bump.

"Always, Son." Chaz sprawled on the sofa with Chauncy balled up on the other end, fighting sleep. He felt his age today as he had watched younger skaters spin, curve, and slide backward while he stayed out of their way and used his granddaughter as the cause of him taking baby steps before Valerie and Kenneth had taken Chauncy to the nearby zoo.

Gee was the first to shower and dress. He returned to the living room looking refreshed and happy and favoring Chaz when he was that age. Almost thirty minutes later, Lana graced the stairs. Gee happened to look over his shoulder, and his jaw dropped as his eyes lit at the sight of his wife.

The expression on his son's face was amusing. Happiness had engulfed Lana as she modeled a colorful outfit. Plus, she had taken the time to curl her straight hair. The pair made a stunning couple.

Chaz had made a good decision in traveling with Kym. His presence in St. Louis was needed to give Gee and Lana some "them" time. Plus, he was no different from other grandparents. Chaz wanted to spend time and engage his granddaughter.

Not long after they left, Chauncy stirred. Ignoring Chaz, she climbed off the sofa and went into the playroom, where she rummaged through the toy crate and pulled out a wooden puzzle. Instead of bringing it to Chaz to play with her, she was content to stay in the room and play by herself.

Back in Baltimore, his friend who provided therapy to children under the age of six with autism spectrum disorder said a child's interactions had to be encouraged, not forced, so he got up and followed Chauncy into the room. He pulled out a children's book and settled in a chair and began to read in hopes it would draw Chauncy to him.

Halfway through the story, Chaz was disappointed his granddaughter still hadn't taken the bait. When he switched his thoughts to Kym, Chaz couldn't stop smiling. He wondered if she was having a good time. As soon as he closed the book, Chauncy stood, ran over, snatched it, and retreated to her corner. Chaz didn't react but prayed that her local therapist would make inroads with his grandbaby's social skills.

Saturday morning, Chaz woke early and made a big breakfast. He could tell his granddaughter liked his eggs, because that was all she ate on her plate.

Once again, he was content to babysit while Gee took his wife shopping. They were gone most of the day, then decided to eat out and take in a movie. When the couple returned home later that night, he and Chauncy had already turned in for the night.

On Sunday, Chaz was packed and ready to return the rental car to the airport. Since arriving in St. Louis, Chaz felt like he was in solitary confinement not getting to see Kym or hear her voice. He prayed the short respite he gave Gee and Lana would recharge their energy so they'd have an extra dose of patience with Chauncy.

"I'll be back next month, but in the interim, if you need anything, and I do mean anything, don't hesitate to ask. You know I'll be on a plane in a minute."

At the airport, Chaz looked forward to getting back to his life in Baltimore. This weekend had been an eye-opener. He didn't like not being able to see or talk to Kym. He paced the terminal, waiting for her to clear the security checkpoint line. Once she did, he reached for her carry-on. "Let's go home."

Kym liked the sound of *home*. It conjured up permanency. He pulled her into his arms, and their hug lingered. She felt cherished.

"I missed you, lady," he mumbled over and over.

"Missed you too, PawPaw." She giggled. Growing up, both her grandfathers were elderly and in bad health. They had passed away before she was a teenager. It was hard for Kym to picture Chaz as a grandfather.

He was incredibly handsome, full of life, and patient to a fault—no one could accuse him of being a stereotypical cranky old man. "But I've talked to you in my dreams." She smiled as he scrutinized her. It was a perfect ending to the weekend.

Chaz lifted a brow and twisted his mouth. "Not the same. Next time, call me in the flesh." He hugged her again, and she melted into his arms. She sighed, enjoying the moment.

He looped her arm through his as they strolled to the terminal. "By the way, what did we talk about in the dreams?"

"Maybe one day I'll share." Kym remembered it clearly. Chaz had asked her to marry him. She had said yes, and they'd ridden away on a white horse.

After they settled in their seats to await boarding, Kym noted Chaz hadn't let go of her hand as he stretched his legs. With his touch, it was as if they had never parted. For her, Chaz was home.

"So shall we do this again next month for Christmas?" Chaz's eyes twinkled with mischief, and he squeezed their intertwined fingers.

Kym wanted to ask what would happen after December but didn't. "I'm spending Christmas in Nashville with Nicholas and Rachel."

He didn't look happy. As a matter of fact, she could feel his disappointment seeping from his pores. "Sorry, that's been my travel itinerary for those holidays. However, during this trip, I demanded to be put on the holiday rotation, so now I'll host the Fourth of July celebration in Baltimore."

Chaz mustered a smile, but it didn't reach his eyes. He said nothing.

His silence was deafening. She wanted to ask him if he planned to stick around for the summer barbecue. Was he thinking long-term?

Finally, Chaz lifted her hand and brought it to his lips. "It's no one's fault. I'm just getting accustomed to us doing things together."

"I like there being an us." Kym stared into those brown eyes.

Once they were aboard the plane, Kym snuggled closer and rested her head on his shoulder. Before she dozed off, she felt his soft lips brush a kiss on her forehead. A perfect way to end her trip.

Chapter 15

A WEEK LATER, ON MONDAY MORNING, KYM SAT BEHIND HER DESK. She sent emails to schedule appointments with her six grad assistants to discuss their findings for her dissertation.

With Christmas fast approaching and the semester ending, she had to snag them when she could, especially those who were due to fly home for the holidays.

Kym had already recorded the progress of ten students. She still had to contact the parents and teachers of the remaining eight.

As she headed out of her office, she spied Judith chatting on her phone. Kym got her attention and mouthed, *Lunch?*

Judith nodded.

Since their classes ended about the same time, they trekked across campus to a café. They ordered crab wraps and fries and found a seat at a table near a window that overlooked the campus.

After giving thanks for their meals, Judith grinned. "You never told me about your weekend getaway with Chaz."

"There wasn't a weekend rendezvous like you make it sound." Kym rolled her eyes. "We went to the same destination on different flights. Once we landed, we didn't see each other again until we returned home on the same flight."

"Mm-hmm. Sounds covert. I'm loving this!" Judith wiggled in her seat as if she were a child waiting for the conclusion of her favorite bedtime story.

"I think I'm in love with Chaz," Kym blurted out.

Her friend smirked and waggled her finger. "You are. I knew he was the one when I first saw him. I'm so glad you let your guard down…"

"Me too." Kym looked out the window and fingered her napkin. "I know he cares for me, but I don't know where we're going."

"I believe Nelson Coleman Jewelers is on East Joppa Road in Towson." Judith blinked. "After that, personally I think you should go big, with a Jill Andrews gown, or go home."

"What, no referrals on caterers or invitations?" Kym mocked. "Judith, I'm serious. I'm having some insecurity issues. I love the man," she screamed with her inside voice, closing her eyes and holding up her hands. "The timing couldn't be worse."

"I'd always imagined falling in love makes the timing perfect." Judith twisted her lips in amusement.

Balling up a napkin, Kym aimed, then threw it across the table at her friend. "I need a sounding board. If you're not up to the task, I'll call one of my sis—"

"Hold it!" Judith raised a hand while straightening in her seat. "I'm your girl."

"One"—Kym started to count off her fingers—"Chaz may love me, but that doesn't mean he wants to get remarried. Two, he's a grandpa." She shivered. "That sounds odd to even say it, which would make me a grand—"

"Grandma," Judith finished.

Kym frowned. "Remind me to take you off the guest list to my wedding—if there is one."

"Okay, okay. I'm just having a good time seeing you so flustered. It must be love, so I don't understand the problem." Her friend shrugged.

"Does he want to start another family? If not, what does he want out of this relationship?"

Judith rested her elbows on the table and folded her arms. "Talk to Chaz about your feelings and hesitations, but I think he's the real deal."

"I don't know." Kym gritted her teeth in thought. "Men are scared of commitment, and he might be twice shy when it comes to marriage. If he even knew I was thinking these thoughts, he might retreat. I'm used to being alone, but I'm not used to having a broken heart, and if anyone can break it, it would be Chaz Banks."

—

Chaz wasn't happy. He hoped once he and Kym were back in Baltimore, they would have some downtime together—a movie, dinner, even shopping. The most they'd shared were morning Scriptures, a cup of coffee near the campus, and brief phone calls, because she was wrapping up her research. He respected that, just didn't like it.

"It's crunch time. As soon as I can breathe from my commitments, I'm hoping we can check out the Christmas lights displays around town, shop, and make some holiday memories."

"We can do that," he'd replied, looking forward to taking her to Hampden neighborhood's *Miracle on 34th Street* Christmas lights and the must-see parade of fifty-plus boats decorated with Christmas lights at Inner Harbor.

That mesmerizing date had come and gone. Now Kym was consumed with her dissertation preparation and final exams.

Chaz didn't like feeling his relationship with Kym was on hold when he wanted to accelerate their dating. And shame on him. He knew how challenging it was when he had been in his master's program. She was a doctoral candidate, which was even more demanding.

It also had been a long time since he was in a relationship that squeezed past a month. Although he and Kym had been going strong for three months, the craving hadn't ceased, as he wanted more of her time.

His musing was interrupted when he got a memo about the latest news on what the public health institute was tracking: *E. coli* clusters in prepackaged salads, weekend violence that resulted in four Baltimore deaths, and although the smoking rate was down, the cases associated with vaping injuries among high schoolers were on the rise.

Zeke tapped on Chaz's open door. "Hey, on my way to a seminar on the top floor. I've been meaning to ask, how was your trip to see your family?"

Chaz nodded. "Trip was good. Family is fine. Saw my ex-wife and flew back home with Kym."

"Hold up." Zeke invited himself into Chaz's office, took a seat, and eyed Chaz with suspicion. "Let's backtrack in thirty seconds or less. Crossing paths with Valerie isn't out of the norm, but traveling with Kym is. What's that all about?"

"I gave you a recap." Chaz laughed. "Let me explain. You know I rarely plan a trip to St. Louis or anywhere, if I can help it, around Thanksgiving because of the crowds. I braved the masses to be with Kym as she flew to St. Louis. Remember, she has family there."

Zeke crossed an ankle over a knee and bobbed his head. "So you met her family?"

"I wouldn't say that. At the airport, she went her way and I went mine, to Gee's house. After the holidays, we took the same flight home. Now, she's under pressure to meet her deadlines."

"Sometimes, you've got to take a back seat," Zeke reasoned with a shrug.

"Doesn't mean I have to like it. I miss her." Chaz rocked back in his chair and patted his chest. "She fits here. It's more than a physical attraction."

"That woman is Miss America, Miss USA, Miss Teen USA, Miss Universe, Miss World, Miss Everything all rolled up in a gorgeous package presented to you, my friend."

"Yes, and tied with a red bow." Chaz grinned and played along. "Plus, we share our strong faith in the Lord and a commitment to our Christian walk."

"So…" Zeke gave his friend a pointed stare. "The question is, is she the marrying kind?"

Chaz rubbed the back of his neck and huffed. "That's complicated."

"This isn't a Facebook status. It's a yes or no answer." His friend pressed him.

"Is she the marrying kind? Oh, yeah."

"But?" Zeke leaned forward with an odd expression.

"After my divorce, I've had no desire to marry again—Kym is making me rethink that. So many emotions are playing in my head."

"I think you protest too loudly. While you're playing the unsure tune in your head, don't give Kym the wrong signal that she walks away. See how you'd like that."

Frustrated, Chaz pounded a fist on his desk. "No one's talking about walking away—" He paused when a visitor appeared in his doorway. He tucked his personal life back into his mental pocket and waved Debra inside. "Hey there. How's it going?"

"Hey, Chaz." She nodded at Zeke. "I didn't mean to interrupt. I was in the building and thought I'd stop by and see how your little princess is doing."

"If you've got a minute, I want to give you an update on my grandbaby." His friend didn't budge, so Chaz cleared his throat. "Talk to you later, Zeke."

"Oh, we will. I've got to get to my meeting anyway." His friend got to his feet and waved goodbye.

Debra snagged the vacated seat. "So what's going on with Chauncy?"

Chaz shrugged. "Since I'm not around her constantly, I can't tell if the therapies are helping. She's saying more words, but her social skills aren't helping her make friends."

"Hmm. Too bad I can't do my own assessment." Debra shook her head. "I have some new literature I can drop off, or if you have time to meet for lunch, I can bring it with me."

"I'll swing by your building and pick it up." He noticed a hint of a crestfallen expression cross her face.

On Tuesday morning, after a long weekend without speaking much to Kym, he sent a fruit basket to her office with a note: *It's flu season. Here's a healthy start to your day. BTW, not too late to get your flu shot.*

"Aww, the gift was sweet." Her melodious voice, filled with laughter, came in a midmorning call. "Thank you, Chaz, for thinking of me. Sorry I had to cancel plans this weekend. Some of my grad students could only meet with me Saturday and Sunday before they took off for the Christmas break…and by the way, I always get a flu shot."

"Great. Just what the doctor ordered. You're forgiven. To be honest, I miss you like crazy, lady. It's torture not seeing you through the week or on Saturday. If it weren't for Sundays…"

"Which I missed this week too." She didn't hide her frustration. "Chaz, your understanding means so much to me. This morning's Scripture you texted encouraged me."

"I'm glad. When I read John three, verse two—'Beloved, I wish above all things that thou may prosper and be in health, even as thy soul prospers'—I immediately thought about you."

She chuckled. "So you're the self-appointed gatekeeper of my spiritual and physical health, huh?"

"Unless I have competition, I'm the one."

"There are no Chaz Banks imitations out there. Let me make it up to you next weekend. You can sample my home cooking. I'll invite Judith, and you can bring a guest too."

His friend came to mind. He was single. If Zeke wasn't free, he was going to have to give somebody else a rain check, because Chaz wanted him to tag along. "We'll be there. Bon appétit." Chaz's spirits were lifted after speaking with her.

Somehow, Kym had come to fill the gap in his life. Whatever he needed to do to ensure that she could breeze through her doctoral program, he would assist.

Zeke taunted him about letting Kym walk away.

Chaz had no plans on that happening—at all. How without a wedding ring? His answer wasn't a simple yes or no. Marriage could be overrated. It didn't always bring happily ever after.

Chapter 16

Kym missed Chaz more than she thought humanly possible. The dinner was perfect for a respite from the demands of her career goals. Throughout the week, she took short breaks to decorate her house with garland, bows, and beautiful black angels she had collected over the years. She strung lights in her windows, where she also placed red candles.

Weeks before Christmas, she and Judith took a day trip up to the nation's capital to admire the White House decorations. Kym always made a choice to celebrate the reason for the season over the commercial Christmas "magic."

The one thing she couldn't resist the urge to splurge on was an eye-catching door wreath to greet guests to her home. There was no denying something special was in the air. Too bad she couldn't enjoy the holidays with Chaz.

Knicely tradition meant Kym hopping on a plane to Nashville to spend Christmas with her sisters and their families. Otherwise, without a family to call her own, Chaz had filled voids in her life with his companionship.

The next day at work, the minute Kym had a window of free time, she made a beeline to Judith's office to include her in the plan. "Want a free meal?"

Judith's head popped up. "You know me, I'm always game. What happened to dining out with Chaz? Don't tell me you're replacing my replacement?" she teased.

"Never." Kym tsked. "You were never replaced. I invited Chaz to dinner at my house and…"

"You need a buffer not to tempt your Christian walk. I get it and don't blame you." Judith added, "Mr. Banks is a walking temptation. Sure, count me in."

Thank you, Kym mouthed. The few times Chaz had been to her house, it had been to pick her up for a date, and he never stepped farther than her foyer. It was as if he understood her boundaries too.

"Am I getting paid to babysit, or will there be someone I can talk to?" Judith playfully scrunched her nose.

"I've already asked Chaz to bring a friend."

"Mm-hmm." She twisted her lips. "All I've got to say is his mystery guest better be old enough to drive and not too old to collect social security."

"Noted." Kym laughed and returned to her office. She glanced at her phone, at the Scripture Chaz had sent this morning, which began: Be careful for nothing; but in every thing by prayer and supplication with thanksgiving let your requests be made known unto God.

Philippians 4:6–9. Yep, she definitely planned to have good thoughts throughout the day.

Then her to-do list became more challenging as she prepared for final examinations and to interview parents and teachers of the students. She had already reviewed the assessment reports from her grad students and entered their findings on her spreadsheet.

An hour later, she was en route to conduct follow-up interviews with two teachers in the Harford school district. When Kym arrived at Midtown Academy, Mrs. Abernathy was waiting for her in the fifth-grade classroom.

"Sorry for my tardiness. Traffic was the culprit," Kym apologized, feeling like a naughty student.

"You're here now, so let's get started." The woman pointed to a desk in the front row that Kym squeezed into. She powered up her laptop and located the list of students in the university's mobile tutoring program.

"Three years ago, Shante Gipson stopped at the university's bus out of curiosity rather than to seek help. The next time we parked on her street, she showed us her failing grade on a math test. We gave her an assessment test and noted her reading level was below average, which affected her comprehensive skills to solve math problems. I reviewed the survey you completed, given by one of my grad students. I want to discuss the child's confidence, character building, and if she has improved enough to be released from our program."

"No." The teacher's eyes widened in horror. "I mean, she has improved, but please allow her to stay enrolled. The extra one-on-one has made a difference not only in math but her eagerness to learn. Her reading has slightly improved almost to her grade level, where she's catching up with the students who do stay after school for extra help."

"Good to know." Kym's mission to balance the playing field for struggling minorities was working.

When the thirty-minute interview had concluded, Kym somehow was able to wiggle her hips out of the miniature furniture to stand. She shook hands with Mrs. Abernathy and prepared to speak with the next teacher.

"Miss Knicely, I hope you get additional funding. This is our next generation of educators, doctors, lawyers, and presidents."

"I know." Kym agreed. Mrs. Abernathy's comments would be included in her research. She turned down the hall to the classroom for Mr. Green, where Kym repeated the process.

By Saturday, Kym was exhausted from the week's projects, but her excitement about the gathering at her house overruled the weariness. Dinner was at six, but Chaz arrived early with Zeke.

She remembered him from Bible class. Chaz's friend was well-groomed with a low cut. Zeke wore wire-frame glasses and had a killer smile. He was tall, about an inch or two shorter than her beau. Like Chaz, his personality could probably command an audience. Yep, a good choice for Judith.

Minutes later, her friend rushed in after Kym opened the door. "Sorry, I was running late..." She stopped in her tracks when she saw the two guests. Judith exchanged glances with Kym, then Chaz.

Zeke seemed just as taken. Kym had never seen a shy side of Judith in front of the opposite sex. It was comical, and Kym would tease her about it later. Kym excused herself to head into the kitchen. Chaz followed and assisted with the finishing touches on dinner.

It felt surreal to work alongside Chaz in the kitchen. She didn't want a make-believe scenario. She craved the real thing—the ring, house, forget the car, but she wanted the children. What was the possibility of that happening?

"I've missed us doing things together," Chaz admitted before she could profess the same thing.

"I'm sorry—"

"Don't be." He placed a finger on her lips, and she shivered from the touch. Their stares lingered, and Kym longed to feel his arms wrapped around her. The passion between them was a steady climb. That was why Judith and Zeke were there: to tame the intimacy between them.

Chaz smiled first. "You know I want to kiss you, don't you?"

"Yes." She returned his smile. "And you know I want to be kissed." Didn't every woman want their fairy tales to come true?

Kym exhaled and stepped back. She turned and glanced over her shoulder for Judith. Her friend was occupied. Some watchdog. She chuckled. Kym turned back to Chaz.

"You think those two hit it off?"

Standing beside her in the doorway between the kitchen and living room, Chaz wrapped his arm around her waist and squeezed her close. "I'd say they have potential for what we have. He works in accounting, and you mentioned Judith teaches math. I'd say they have something in common."

"Most definitely! Ooh." Kym jumped. "The rolls." She hurried to the stove, slipped on her mitts, and opened the oven door. "I can't show off my cooking by burning the food."

"I'd eat it anyway. So how long will you be in Nashville?"

"Usually, I stay about three weeks. I need the downtime after a rigorous semester. How long do you plan to be in St. Louis?"

"Not three weeks." Chaz whistled and twisted his lips in a sulk. "One week, tops. Before we leave, let's have some us time."

How could she say no to his request? She didn't answer as she wrapped her arms around his waist. His strong arms trapped her in a warm embrace.

"Break it up, you two. You have impressionable adults in the room," Judith called out and tee-heed.

Zeke laughed while Kym blushed from embarrassment. "Dinner is served anyway."

Judith stood. "I'll help set the table."

"I got this." Chaz took Kym's hand. "Come on, babe." His eyes were tender.

At the dinner table, Chaz gave thanks for their food with joined hands. Seconds later, the serving bowls were passed from one to the other.

"This mac and cheese is melting in my mouth." Chaz closed his eyes and shook his head.

"She's a keeper, my friend," Zeke stated.

Chaz opened his eyes and stared into hers instead of at his friend. "Yes, she is."

Judith cleared her throat and mumbled, "Mm-hmm."

Without saying more about their relationship, the energy was still charged between her and Chaz. Her heart soared with love. She wanted to hear him say those three words so badly, but her mind reminded her of the Scripture in the first chapter in James, to let patience have her perfect work.

Patience. How did a woman have patience for the man she loved to catch up with her feelings? After the compliments, Chaz stood and gathered the discarded dishes and whispered in her ear, "You cooked. Let me take these."

She hoped Chaz could see the love she had for him as she whispered her thanks.

Once he was in the kitchen loading the dishwasher, she glanced at her other two guests. They both had silly grins on their faces. What did Zeke know? While waiting for Chaz, they moved to the living room and gathered near the fire. The gas fireplace wasn't so much for warmth but for the ambiance.

The night ended with Chaz's sweet kiss. The dreams she had that night were filled with promises.

Monday morning, Judith glided into Kym's office with much fanfare and took a seat. Kym had never seen her friend this happy. Lifting a brow, she asked, "Okay, I'll bite. What can't you wait to tell me?"

Judith jutted her chin as if she were posing for a camera shoot. "Since you asked."

Kym chuckled. "I don't think you gave me much choice."

"Well, Zeke and I exchanged numbers, and we stayed on the phone late into the night talking about family, friends, hobbies, favorite food, and movies…" She took a deep breath. "Did you know he's a senior manager in accounting? Ooh. A man who loves numbers. Sunday, we had a late lunch after church." She rambled on.

Kym's head was spinning as she tried to keep up. That was so unlike Judith's character to give out her number so freely and to lose sleep getting to know a guy.

"I like him. We connected," her friend stated. "I'm learning a lot about him. I mean, he's not bringing me flowers and crab cakes, but I enjoy his company. Thanks for the invite."

"You're welcome." Kym snickered. "All those blind dates you had in the past and yet you might have found a winner at my house."

"And what better introduction than from the man of my best friend? I'll thank Chaz when I see him."

"You do that." Kym smiled and texted Chaz about Zeke and Judith's budding friendship.

"I already know," he said when he called her back later and they shared notes about the couple. "He was all smiles when I passed him in the hall. Without saying a word, he gave me a high five and kept moving."

They laughed and chatted a few more minutes before they had to say their goodbyes.

The bustle and cares of the holiday sped by until it was time for Kym to leave. The moment was sentimental between her and Chaz. His presence tempted her to stay, but he was leaving too.

Chaz arrived at her house to take her to the airport. Standing right there in her foyer, he handed her a slender box wrapped in gold foil paper. It was decorated meticulously. "I wanted to give you your Christmas gift."

How long had it been since a significant other had given her a gift? It didn't matter what was inside. "I thought we agreed to exchange gifts when we got back? Hold on. Let me get yours." She hurried to her bedroom and grabbed the small box.

Kym returned and handed it to him. One glance at the tie and handkerchief set in a boutique's window, and she immediately imagined Chaz commanding a suit with it. "I hope you like this."

"I love it already because it's from you." He winked.

Oh, to hear him utter those words to her, not about a gift. She sighed and would have to wait. Kym opened her present and gasped. "Chaz… Chaz…" Her heart pounded. "This is beautiful."

"It sparkles like you." He pulled the necklace from the box and twirled Kym around under his arm as if they were dancing in the rain. When he gently steadied her, Kym waited as Chaz draped it gently around her neck.

She fingered the rose gold chain. "I love it. Your turn."

Chaz opened her gift. When his eyes lit, Kym knew she had made the right choice.

She met him halfway for a kiss, and it was like an explosion when their lips touched before she heard Chaz whisper Genesis 31:49, a Scripture used to dismiss the congregation at the end of services. "Now, may the Lord watch between me and thee…" Kym joined him, "while we're absent one from another. This we ask in Jesus's name."

Kym's lashes fluttered as she stepped back and rested her forehead on his. She didn't open her eyes right away, relishing the moment. She admired his thoughtfulness and the intensity of the simple prayer before he grabbed her suitcase, and they left for the airport.

Chapter 17

Chaz believed there was nothing better than spending Christmas Day with the family. However, this holiday, he wasn't feeling it as he yearned for the presence of the woman he loved—yes, he loved Kym and probably had from the minute he saw her. Love at first sight.

He chuckled to himself, prompting others to follow, which snapped Chaz out of his reverie to watch Chauncy examine each present.

"Can you imagine if she had a hundred gifts? We would be here until next year," Gee said.

"Not funny, Hubby." Lana appeared in the doorway.

Chaz frowned and studied his granddaughter. "Has Chauncy developed allergies? She's scratching herself a lot."

Lana huffed and shook her head. "I have taken her to an allergist, pediatrician, dermatologist, and therapist. It may be something in her diet, and you know how limited that is, but she's getting tested. But I've been applying some anti-itching cream until we can pinpoint it." She walked away, looking defeated.

"Hmm" was all Chaz could respond. When he returned home, he would ask Debra at the institute if allergies were more prominent in children with autism. Sometimes, it was easier to ask her than to overload himself with Google searches. Plus, Chaz wasn't one hundred percent on board with Chauncy's current therapist's assessments.

When Lana left, he asked Gee in a low voice, "How's your wife doing? Are you helping her? I can't stress that enough, Son."

Gee rubbed his face as his frustration surfaced. "I'm doing the best I can as a daddy, husband, and breadwinner. Plus—"

Lana returned. "Will you apply this to Chauncy's welts while I take the ham out of the oven?"

Gee stood to do his wife's bidding. Later, while they were feasting on the delicious meal, the couple dropped a bombshell. "Dad, Pops," Gee and Lana spoke at the same time, "we're going to have another baby."

Stunned, Chaz heard himself saying, "Congratulations!" while his mind shouted, *uh-oh*. He grinned despite his mixed emotions.

Suddenly, Lana burst out crying. Gee was at his wife's side and engulfed her in his arms. Chauncy didn't react to the crisis around her.

Chaz attempted to reassure Lana she was indeed a great mother. "I'm here for you two. Does your mother know?" he asked Gee.

"Yes, and she wasn't exactly thrilled," his son replied. "Honestly, I don't know if we're happy or scared."

"Everything will work out." Chaz recited Romans 8:28: "'And we know that all things work together for good to them that love God, to them who are the called according to his purpose.'" He had to believe it for himself before he could encourage them. *Lord, help us all.* "So…" He regrouped and asked, "When is my next grandbaby due?"

"Mid-June." Lana exhaled and mustered a smile that clearly she wasn't feeling. "Pops…you've done so much for us, and we can't thank you enough. If only you lived here." She got a boost of energy. "What about transferring? I know Wash U has a renowned school of public health."

Chaz chuckled. "It's not that simple, sweetie, but we'll work something out before the baby comes."

"I love you, Pops." Lana left the safety of her husband's embrace and planted a kiss on Chaz's forehead. "If someone will watch Chauncy, I think I'm going to take a nap."

If Chaz had a daughter, he would have wanted one as sweet as Lana. Chaz helped his son clean up while spying Chauncy scratching her leg again. *Lord, what more can I do to help my family?*

Later that evening, he called his ex-wife. "Hello, Valerie, this is Chaz."

"Yes, I know your voice, Charles," she responded, monotone.

"I'm calling about our second grandbaby coming. They're going to need our help more so than before."

Valerie didn't speak right away. "I hope the baby is okay. I don't know if I have what it takes for two special needs children."

That remark hit a nerve with Chaz. "Valerie, Chauncy needs help, more so than other children, but she isn't in a grouping labeled special needs anything. She simply needs extra attention."

"Half the time, Chauncy acts as if I'm not around, and when she does acknowledge me, she barely interacts with me." Valerie tsked.

"She's only four. Try some type of play therapy. We have to be patient in building a relationship with her." He tried to keep his annoyance out of his voice. "I'm calling because, as grandparents, we can help relieve the load. I can help financially and try to visit once a month—"

Valerie cut him off again. "Charles, I know you have made a judgment call about how I respond to Chauncy, but I wasn't expecting my first grandchild to have a disability. She's such a pretty little girl and looks normal, but her meltdowns make me not want to take her out in public. It's embarrassing to have to explain her behavior."

She failed to mention sweet, kind, precious, and so on. Chaz did his best *not* to judge Valerie. It had taken him some time to digest the diagnosis himself. After many initial sleepless nights, Chaz had decided to take the time to invest in knowing what the Bankses were up against. "Everyone's 'normal,'" Chaz did air quotes with his fingers, "isn't the same."

"Okay. Maybe when she gets older, I can handle her better," she admitted. "I get too frustrated trying to play with her like normal little girls. And Kenneth doesn't like to see me get upset."

Kenneth wasn't supportive, period. Chaz gritted his teeth to keep from saying anything bad about her second husband, who came off as a man who wanted the wife but not anything extra. Unless the Lord breathed into his grandbaby's body, her progress would always be delayed. "I see. Sorry to bother you. I was hoping we could double our efforts…"

"If you want to band together for grandparents' duties, I suggest you move here, so we can share babysitting duties, doctor appointments, or grocery runs for formula while our son works, then we could coordinate a schedule. Goodbye, Charles."

Chaz sighed, bowed his head, and prayed for his family's strength and the unborn baby, making Chauncy a big sister. She would have an instant playmate.

Kym fought back the urge to show off her necklace and removed the treasure from around her neck in the airport bathroom before she left the terminal. She wasn't ready for her sisters' interrogation on her budding relationship with Chaz.

She needed to hold off any suspicions for a few more weeks—a month tops. She didn't need that additional pressure while she was preparing her dissertation.

As the oldest, she was expected to lead by example. Kym missed that mark when Tabitha, then Rachel, beat her to the altar. She had to save face to show she indeed knew how not to be gullible in a relationship. But she had failed, because their big sister had fallen blindly in love with a man who might not want the same thing as her—a path to marriage.

Days later, Kym joined her family to watch the Nashville Ballet, which had become a holiday tradition for the sisters and spouses. She'd have rather shared the moment with Chaz. Her heart shouted, *I want to go home*, just like Judy Garland in the iconic scene from *The Wizard of Oz*, but her mind overruled and autocorrected.

Family time was priceless, and she needed to remember that. Aunt Tweet was gone, and only by the grace of God, Rachel was a cancer survivor. Her sisters—and now brothers-in-law—were all Kym had. Family was forever.

Barring emergencies, Kym wouldn't see her family after this until her Fourth of July barbecue. *Sorry, Chaz*, she mused as she tucked her memories of him in a hidden compartment of her heart until later.

Soon enough, the sisters enjoyed another tradition—an all-day after Christmas shopping spree. The hubbies laughed when the ladies returned and collapsed on the sofas in Rachel's new home. Thanks to their generous inheritance from Aunt Tweet, the sisters could shop to their hearts' content.

"You need to move," Rachel said out of nowhere.

"Excuse me?" Kym turned her head and squinted at her sister.

"Why?" Tabitha glanced at Rachel too.

"Because there aren't any eligible men in Baltimore, and our dear big sister needs to find the right one. I vote she relocates to Nashville after she gets her degree." Rachel lifted her chin. "She has a plethora of college and university picks in Music City."

"Oh, no." Tabitha shook her head. "If Kym is moving, St. Louis is home. Plus, I'm the one who could use a babysitter."

"Hold up." Kym waved her hands in the air to speak. "I'm right here while you two are plotting my future. I'm all for babysitting my adorable nephew, but Baltimore is home, and I have no plans to leave."

"*Hmph*," Rachel grunted. "Without a husband, you've got no reasons to stay." Both her sisters exchanged discouraged expressions.

Kym chuckled. "Am I supposed to be looking? Because the Bible says—"

"I know. I know. 'He who finds a wife finds a good thing, and obtains favor of the Lord,'" Rachel quoted Proverbs 18:22. "How can a man find you when you're buried under your research and only come out to eat and for church?"

Tabitha waved her ring hand in the air. "Mind you, I didn't want to be found when I was Aunt Tweet's caregiver. Praise God Mr. Whittington found me, or more like Aunt Tweet found him for me." She grinned.

"God knows how to inscribe my name on the right man's heart for him to find me. That way, the man will know I'm not the one to let get away," Kym said.

They gave her high fives before getting up to eat some leftovers, famished from their bargain hunts.

If Chaz didn't consider her "the one," maybe Kym should consider moving closer to her sisters, because there would be nothing to lose except a broken heart.

Chapter 18

Chaz got Luther Vandross's old-school song "A House Is Not a Home." The words played in his head as he flew back to Baltimore after his spending the week with Gee and his family. Kym wouldn't return for another ten days, so Charm City wouldn't feel quite like home until she was back.

At least this time around, while they were apart, their communication was late-night texts before Kym fell asleep. He could tell she was enjoying herself, despite the many times she texted him I miss you. Ha! *Traitor*, he chuckled to himself.

During her absence, Chaz planned to meet with Debra at the Kennedy Krieger Institute. The literature she had given him not long ago was stored in his memory bank, but he wondered how a new baby would change things.

The burden weighed heavy on his heart one day at work. The bright spot came as he was leaving his office for home. His younger son's call lifted Chaz's spirit. "Hey, I haven't spoken to you since last year."

"Ha-ha, Dad," Drake said. "Did you forget I called you at midnight, so that counts for the New Year? Anyway, I have two tickets for this Sunday's Ravens game. It's been a while since we've hung out...you know, with me in medical school. Want to go?"

"Are you kidding me?" Chaz hooted. "With Lamar Jackson as their quarterback, they're smokin'. And I get to enjoy it with my favorite son—"

Drake laughed. "I've never known a father who has two favorite sons."

"You're talking to him." He patted his chest. "I'm excited about watching a game with my boy." Chaz grinned. "Come to church with me on Sunday.

We can go right after morning worship." He had to throw that in. Chaz never pressured his sons to accept Christ's salvation, but he believed in reminding them that he walked with God as the best example he could give them.

Drake was slow to agree, but he committed. "The hospital rounds are draining me, but I'd like that. Are you still seeing that pretty professor?"

"Nice of you to remember, Son. I am, but she's out of town."

"Good. I need to talk to you about something—man to man."

Chaz froze. "Is everything okay?"

"Yeah. It's good. Just wanted to have a heart-to-heart. See you on Sunday. I'll meet you at your church."

"Great place to start." Chaz was proud Drake reached out to him. At times, Chaz felt invisible to his youngest even though they lived in the same city. Actually, the invitation had choked him up. He wanted a closer relationship with Drake. A parent could never be too busy for his children's attention, even as adults. His family came first.

Kym's plane landed home Sunday midafternoon. It was like old times, with Judith waiting outside instead of Chaz, who would have come inside for her. After one trip together, Chaz had Kym spoiled. Traveling would never be the same.

She couldn't begrudge him for going to a Ravens game with Drake after hearing the excitement in his voice and asking if she was okay with Judith picking her up. "I'm more than okay," she had told him. Chaz appeared to be a good father who yearned to bond more with Drake.

Kym wanted that for him too and told him as much when she texted him. Home. Enjoy the game. Call me when you get a chance.

At curbside, Kym hugged Judith. "Thanks for coming to get me." She slid into the passenger seat of her friend's car.

"I thought my Uber days were over when Mr. Banks arrived on the scene." Judith grinned and hit the accelerator to get in the exit lane.

"Don't take this the wrong way, but it would have been nice to see Chaz." Kym batted her lashes.

"I tell ya, best friends are underrated and underpaid," Judith joked.

"But never replaced. So how was your holiday? Did you spend it with anyone special…like Chaz's friend?" she teased.

"Zeke and I went to the movies, and believe it or not, we tried a Secret Supper." Judith giggled. "I'm having so much fun getting to know him. The night was adventurous and telling."

Judith cleared her throat. "Rumor has it from a source close to Mr. Banks that you are the one." She winked, then looked at the road as if she hadn't said something so profound.

The one? Really? Kym's heart leaped in the air like a ballerina, then she fanned herself. "Whew." Now she needed to hear it from Chaz. "You've made my day even brighter."

At home, Kym was too exhausted to unpack. She crashed on the sofa for a power nap. Her phone's chime stirred her from her sleep.

"Welcome back, baby," Chaz's deep voice greeted her. "I wanted to meet you—"

Kym yawned, then shushed him. "No need for an apology. It was important that you spent time with your son, and I want to hear all about it—later."

He chuckled. "All I'm going to say is the Ravens gave the Rams a beatdown. It felt good watching a home game with Drake. So how would you like us to kick off our New Year?"

"Surprise me." If she was truly the one, Kym would never have to worry if he would be a good father to their children. He had proven it during their months of dating. "Do you ever think about having any more children?" It was a test question.

His silence was deafening and telling. If the Lord allowed her to be able to have children, she wanted them. It was a deal breaker before she married any man—*any* man. The silence was becoming awkward.

"I always wanted to have a daddy's little girl. The closest I've gotten is my sweet granddaughter."

Okay. Kym couldn't read between those lines. As far as she was concerned, it was a yes-or-no question. She cleared her throat.

"Oh, speaking of grands, Gee and Lana are expecting again!" Chaz's pride came through in his voice.

"Congratulations!" Kym had yet to have one child, and here this man she was in love with was about to experience his *second* grandchild. Maybe they weren't compatible at all.

"I didn't mean to disturb you, but I wanted to welcome you home and invite you to dinner this week or to the symphony next weekend—or both."

Her doctoral degree had to be her focus this year, because she might need it to prove she had achieved some milestones in life if she parted ways with Chaz over her deal breaker—or her mind was playing games with her emotions. Maybe it was just her imagination trying to plant doubt in her heart and mind.

Kym needed to let patience do its perfect work. She regrouped, and in the most pleasant voice, she picked the Baltimore Symphony Orchestra.

"Good choice. Good night, babe." And he was gone.

Babe? Kym closed her eyes. His endearment always moved her.

"Life sure is funny." Chaz reflected on the time he'd spent with his son. After the game, they had grabbed a bite to eat at a nearby sports pub. It was as if the parent-child roles were reversed. Instead of the boy being eager to spend time with his dad, it was Chaz pumped about being with his son.

"Dad," Drake drummed his fingers on the table. "When do you know a woman is the right one? I mean, you and Mom married and looked what happen." His son's question was honest, not accusatory.

Chaz took his time answering. "I think a person could be the one, but that doesn't keep couples from having problems. In the case of your mother and me, we didn't know what love was."

He shrugged. "True love bears all things and is patient. In hindsight, to be truthful and not disrespectful to your mother, we weren't a good match. So to answer your question, I thought Valerie was the one I couldn't let get away, but there was more attraction and less love." Chaz held up his hand. "Again, no disrespect to your mother."

Drake bobbed his head. "I get that, Dad… So what about Kym?"

"I can't let her get away. From the moment I saw her, it was love at first sight."

"But I'm hearing you say your judgment was cloudy because you equated attraction with love." Confusion plagued his face. "My old man is falling in love—again."

That didn't sound good. Was honesty overrated?

Never, he heard the Voice of God reply.

"Your mother seems to have found her happiness. Maybe I'm due that too." Chaz paused when their waiter brought their check. "Enough about me. I want to hear about Patrice. How do you feel about her?"

His son grinned. "I love her. She's quiet, pretty, smart, and kind, but I don't want to hurt her by getting married and then discovering she's not the one I can celebrate those yearly anniversaries with, all the way up to our silver." He frowned, revealing his frustration. "It's important to me that I get it right the first time."

Where Gee resembled Chaz, Drake's expressions were all Valerie. He favored his ex-wife's side of the family more than Chaz's.

"Son, I've learned a lot of things in my forty-two years. Be honest. Tell her how you feel, but take it real slow. If your heart aches when she's not near, maybe it's a sign she completes you. Again, take it slow."

Drake smirked and bobbed his head. "I can do honesty. Can't promise the last part."

Chaz chuckled. "Has your brother told you Lana's expecting again?"

"Yep." Rubbing the back of his neck, Drake whistled. "I'm proud of my big bro."

Too soon, their time together ended. Drake had to get to his apartment to catch a nap before starting his sixteen-hour shift, but he gave his dad a promise that they would hang out more.

Chaz was honored that Drake wanted his dad's take on relationships, marriage, and love. Drake had no idea how much that had meant. His son's request was proof Chaz hadn't lost his status as a role model. That day made Chaz crave more time with his son.

Saturday evening, Kym dressed in a gold, shimmery dress and slipped on the necklace that Chaz gave her for Christmas. She styled her hair up and felt like a princess. "Lord, please let Chaz be the one for me—if it's Your will." She had to remember to tag that to her prayer requests. Kym didn't want anything God didn't want her to have.

Half an hour later, Chaz stood on her doorstep with a gift box in one hand and flowers in the other. Her prince for the evening. "Hi." She stepped back to welcome him inside. She accepted the flowers and sniffed and thanked him.

"The sparkle in your eyes outshines what you're wearing. You look gorgeous." He leaned in for a soft kiss. "I see the Lord has watched over me and thee while we were absent."

"Yes, Jesus did." She couldn't read that Scripture in Genesis 31 without thinking about Chaz, the kiss, and the Lord's protection while they were away from each other. Knowing he cared about her beyond the physical and had tapped into her spiritual health too encouraged Kym to be patient.

She hurried into the kitchen for the vase she had used many times for flowers she had purchased for herself. In the past, they had boosted her mood while she waited for her prince who had finally arrived.

Chapter 19

While Kym manned the tutoring bus, she asked Lizzy, a student who struggled in math, about famous Blacks' contributions to history as the annual Dr. Martin Luther King Jr. birthday celebration approached.

Most of the time when Kym randomly quizzed students about famous Blacks in American history, she would receive generic answers like George Washington Carver, Charles Drew, or Garrett Morgan. In addition to the academic assistance, Kym wanted to instill confidence, self-assurance, and cultural knowledge in Black children who might not receive nurturing in their classrooms with non-Black teachers.

If she could stir their curiosity outside the classrooms and help them be proud of the Black roots planted in local history as well as the state, her mission would be accomplished.

In school, Kym had learned about the famous enslaved man Dred Scott, who argued his case for freedom on the steps of the Old Courthouse in downtown St. Louis. Some of his descendants still resided in the Gateway City.

"What is Baltimore known for?" Kym asked as she checked Lizzy's work.

Her brown eyes widened as she raised her hand as if she were in the classroom. "The show *The Wire* was taped here."

That wasn't the answer Kym was going for. "Yes, but how about way back to the mid-1800s, and Frederick Douglass? Why was he famous?"

Tilting her head, Lizzy frowned for a second. "He was an abolist."

"An abolitionist." Kym corrected her with a smile. "He was born in slavery and escaped the bondage to help free others."

"Like Harriet Tubman?"

"Exactly." Kym nodded. "Check out the National Great Blacks in

Wax Museum. They have some cool stuff. They have…probably more than a hundred replicas by now." She realized it had been a while since she had visited the wax museum herself.

Kym mentioned a museum visit to Chaz since his office was closed for the MLK holiday.

That Monday after LLU's Black History celebration, the wax museum was their destination.

Chaz parked the car and helped her out. "I didn't think it would be this crowded. It's packed."

"Coming from a teacher's viewpoint, that's a good thing." Kym looped her arm through his. "You know, I'm glad Dr. MLK's birthday is a national holiday, and I'm not saying that to get an extra day off work."

"I agree." Chaz slowed his steps to match hers. "The day gives folks pause to reflect on Dr. King's vision of unity."

Inside the building, Kym noted the diversity of parents and children, then she spotted Lizzy in the distance with some friends.

Kym sighed in contentment. The power of suggestion.

Chaz was in a good place in his life until he got the bittersweet news: Gee and Lana were expecting twins. Although the couple was looking forward to the addition to their family, there were unspoken concerns.

The worry had eaten at him until he picked up the phone. "You're going to bill me soon." Chaz was partially serious. Debra's words carried a lot of weight with him. "My son and daughter-in-law are expecting twins." He inhaled and released his breath. "What are the twins' chances of having autism?"

"There's a slight chance, between an eleven to fifteen percent increase if there is an older sibling…"

His heart dropped. That would devastate his family. Before his thoughts ran away, Debra pulled him back.

"Chaz, you're a man of faith. How many times have you told me that God is in control? So believe it. I also believe that God gives professionals the knowledge to help patients."

Her soothing tone brought calm to his spirit. How many times had Chaz wished Debra were Chauncy's therapist? The woman was the best. He released his anxiety through an audible sigh.

"Thanks."

"Because of Chauncy's autism, the doctors should monitor their developments more closely. I believe everything happens the way it's supposed to."

"You're right. Needed that pep talk." He bobbed his head in agreement. "If you ever think about relocating, St. Louis would be a great place, and my son and daughter-in-law would be the first ones to book an appointment." Debra's hearty laugh caused Chaz to chuckle.

"I'll remember that. Say, want to grab a bite to eat after work and I can answer more of your concerns? My next appointment is here, but you know I'll always make time for you," Debra said.

"Friend, I'm good. I had that quick question. Thanks again." Chaz ended the call. Kym had his heart, and he didn't want to give another woman the impression he was interested when he wasn't.

Chaz didn't move from his desk. Overwhelmed, he had to accept the heavy burden the Banks family had to endure. He choked to keep his emotions in check. Chaz looked up to the heavens as his vision blurred. "Lord, we need Your mercy."

Debra had given him a pep talk, but he needed more. He and Kym prayed together at church services, at night, and whenever they were separated for a trip. There was a myth women liked men who showed their vulnerability—not today. Chaz had to get a grip before he called Kym. He needed to show her he had great faith in God.

He didn't like the chances for his unborn grandchildren. Chaz didn't care how slight. He stood and crossed the room to shut his door. Lifting his arms toward heaven, he silently cried out to the Lord as tears rolled down his cheeks.

Great faith meant yielding to God's divine will, and Chaz wasn't sure he wanted to know if more precious babies being born with a brain development disorder was part of God's plan. As he wrestled with his heartache, Chaz became thirsty—not physically but a spiritual thirst for his soul.

He thought about Kym's pastor, whose dynamic preaching style and biblical revelation left him feeling spiritually satisfied each Sunday. If only he could hear one of the sermons now, he yearned. Since that wasn't possible, he reached for his tablet in the drawer to retrieve a passage on his Bible app, but a loud knock interrupted him. Taking a deep breath, he wiped his eyes and cleared his throat. Chaz stood and walked across his office to open the door.

"I've been tapping on your door and was about to give up on you being inside…" Zeke rambled while squinting. "What's up? Everything okay with you and Kym?"

"It's not Kym." Chaz exhaled. "I found out that Lana is having twins."

"Wow." His friend flopped in a chair and crossed his ankle over his knee. "Three rug rats. A day care."

"Yep." Chaz didn't want to burden his friend with his worries. Then he heard God's soft whisper to cast the burdens on Him according to 1 Peter 5:7.

"Hey, the reason why I stopped by was to invite you and Kym on a double date with me and Judith." Zeke grinned.

Chaz found himself smiling despite his concerns about the babies. "I think I was supposed to invite you and Judith."

"Clearly, you're moving too slow, so I guess that's a yes."

"Definitely." Chaz studied his friend. "You really like her, huh?"

"My feelings are taking root. Who knows? You and I could have a double ceremony." He held up his hands like a holdup. "Just kidding, man, on the double ceremony part."

Chaz's jaw dropped anyway. "You're talking about marriage…so soon?"

"No, I'm *thinking* about who and what I want in life. I'm not scared." Zeke tilted his head. "Don't tell me you are."

"Scared? No." Chaz smirked at the absurdity of the statement. He considered himself a fearless individual.

"Doubts?" Zeke gave him the side-eye.

Shaking his head, Chaz defended his statement. "No doubts. I love Kym, and I feel she loves me back, so I guess it's time for us to have a talk about what we both want for the future."

"Whew. You had me wondering if you might get scared and think about walking."

Chaz folded his hands and shook his head. "When it comes to Kym, I'd rather fight than flee."

"I'm excited about our double date tonight," Kym said as she stepped into Judith's office.

"I know. When is the last time we did that?" Judith frowned, racking her brain, then shrugged. "Doesn't matter. This time, we both have the perfect dates."

"Amen to that." Kym couldn't be happier. "So do you know where they're taking us?"

"Zeke wouldn't tell me."

"Chaz either." Kym lifted a brow. "Says it's a surprise. Whatever they are masterminding, I'm sure we won't be disappointed. Chaz is one of the most romantic men I've ever met." She closed her eyes, then opened them. "Well, I'm heading to my last class so I can get out of here."

Hours later, when Chaz stood outside her door, Kym could feel an overpowering sense of happiness with just one look from him. He reached for her hand, since she already had her wrap in her arm. "Ready?"

"Always with you," she whispered as he graced her with a kiss before escorting her to his car. "Is dinner still a surprise?"

"Yep."

It didn't take long for Kym to guess they were heading to one of the many eateries near the harbor. She wasn't expecting dining on a sailing boat though until they pulled into the Harbor Court Garage minutes before Zeke and Judith drove up. "Chaz?" She turned to him all smiles.

"You mentioned you liked sailing, so I thought a dinner cruise would be nice."

"I love it!" Kym unlocked her seat belt to reach over and hug him tight, almost strangling him. "Thank you."

He cleared his throat. "Baby, you're welcome. Come on. Zeke and Judith are already out of their car."

Kym stepped out and did a happy dance with Judith. Many weekends in the past, the two friends had set sail from the harbor for relaxation in prep for an upcoming workweek.

"Ah, ladies, didn't you two see each other today at work?" Zeke and Chaz laughed in agreement.

"True, but we haven't double dated in…" Kym looked to Judith to fill in the blanks.

"Forever!" The bliss on Judith's face was undeniable.

Now, Kym could see the mirror image of the emotions she felt with Chaz. And Kym liked the look. They boarded the *Spirit of Baltimore* and set sail for a three-hour cruise on the Patapsco River.

Chaz had reserved window tables so they could view the city's skyline and several landmark attractions while indulging in selections from the buffet. "Enjoying yourself?" He rested his arm on the back of Kym's chair, and she scooted closer to melt into his embrace.

"Yes. Who suggested this double date?" Kym asked.

"We did." Judith waved from the other side of the table.

"Judith, I'm glad Zeke has someone to keep him in line," Chaz joked.

Judith looked into her date's eyes. "I think I like him just the way he is."

Kym felt the same way, and so for the rest of the evening, the couples were caught up in their own worlds.

Chapter 20

Chaz planned to take Zeke's advice and talk to Kym about their future.

Tonight was all about pampering her. For Valentine's Day, he had hired a driver so they could relax and admire the scenery. In the past, Chaz had avoided dinner dates on the "lovefest day of the year" because some women read too much into it. As if love was tangible, he could sense it as he showered, shaved, then dressed. The moment Kym opened her door, the energy around her was so thick he could have reached for it, but like a cloud, he couldn't grasp it.

Her eyes sparkled more than the necklace draped around her neck. Both seemed to wink for his attention. Kym's face glowed as if he was seeing an angelic vision. She had put aside her latest brown color trend for a shimmery silver dress. "Hi, beautiful."

Kym blushed as she lowered her lashes. "Hi, very handsome." Her voice was as soft as a whisper. Instead of waiting for him to make the first move, she stepped closer and wrapped her arms around his waist. She gently rested her head on his chest. His heartbeat had to have been deafening.

The moment was unrushed. When she slowly stepped back, Chaz gazed into her eyes. The love staring back at him matched what he was feeling. They had skirted around the L word as if they both were waiting for the other to profess it first. Chaz planned to be bold about his love tonight. "Ready?" When she nodded, he placed her evening wrap around her shoulders.

Once outside her front door, Kym sucked in her breath when she spied their transportation.

Chaz whispered close to her ear, "I want us to remember this night."

She twirled around and faced him. "I'm with you. How can it be a bust?"

"You're putting pressure on a brotha." He laughed and escorted her down the steps and into the waiting vehicle. Before releasing her, he twirled Kym under his arm to her delight. How could he not love this woman?

Inside the limo, the ride was slow as they cuddled. Chaz inhaled the subtle fragrance of her perfume. When he glanced at her, Kym's eyes were closed. A faint smile hinted at her contented state.

When their driver parked in front of the Charleston Restaurant, Chaz waved off the chauffeur and the valet to open Kym's door—he wanted that honor. He stepped out first. She accepted his outstretched hand. Before they took the steps to the restaurant, he twirled her under his arm again. "See? We don't need raindrops to go dancing."

Throwing her head back, Kym's body arched like a ballerina's and she laughed. "And we don't need any music either."

Once they were inside and seated at their table, Chaz reached for her hand. He didn't want to lose their connection. "Thank you…and before you ask for what, for coming into my life."

When her eyes teared up, Chaz thought she might cry, and he didn't want that to happen. She blinked away any moisture, tilted her head, and studied him. "I'm happy."

"I'm deliriously so. We've been seeing each other for about six months—"

Kym shook her head and corrected him: "Five."

"I see you're better at accounting than me." Chaz snickered but wasn't embarrassed about his miscalculation. "I'm looking forward to six. Meeting you has been life-changing for me. You're in my head and my heart." He rubbed his chest as his nostrils flared. He tried to regulate his breathing. "I love you, lady, more than I thought possible." He leaned across the table to seal his declaration with a kiss, and she met him halfway.

"I love you too, Chaz Banks," she mumbled against his lips.

"I know. Your eyes gave your secret away a long time ago." He wiggled his brows as she blushed.

With her hands securely in his, Chaz sat back as the waitress appeared at their table to take their orders. Once they were alone again, he continued, "I know we've talked about a lot of things—hobbies, family, our walk with Christ—but I want us to have an honest discussion about what you want from me and our relationship—and in life beyond the doctoral degree."

Kym took a deep breath, then exhaled. "In terms of worldly possessions, I've got it all—money, the house, and the car. Spiritually, I grow stronger in the Lord every day by abiding in His Word, and us praying together…" She smiled. "That's a bonus. When you called and said you needed a prayer partner about the situation with the twins, I was touched."

"It had to be you to have my back, Kym—no one else."

"And you have mine. The missing piece in my life is the next level: a husband who loves the Lord and me, children—four is my max and two is my minimum."

Four? Yikes. Chaz did his best to display a poker face as he swallowed slowly while his heart rate accelerated. What woman wanted that today? Was he too old to start a second family? He envisioned a companion—a wife—to travel with and to attend countless social gatherings and enjoy his grandchildren.

"I don't feel another man will cherish me the way you do." She shrugged. "I know you've had a jump start in life experiences. You've been to places and done certain things I haven't, but that isn't stopping me from still wanting those things in our relationship." This time, the light dimmed in her eyes. "If you don't want the same things, Chaz Banks, walk away. Please spare my heart," she pleaded at the same time as his heart took a hit.

"I can't walk away, Kym," he choked out. "I want to make you happy. True, I know what it's like to be a husband, father, and PawPaw, but I haven't experienced those things with you. I'm bringing to the table an existing family with a set of issues. You want children, and I want you to have them, but are you comfortable becoming a grandmother before you're a mother?"

He wanted her to be okay with being an instant grandparent. In the end, they had to make it work, because he wasn't going to let her get away.

She didn't blink. "Honestly, I don't know." When Kym shook her head, her curls bounced with each turn as moisture filled her eyes. This conversation was torturing her.

Chaz knew they had to have the talk, but he didn't think it would be this difficult, yet they had to have an understanding of each other's expectations. "I don't want you to have any doubts. We're going for until death do us part, and I'm praying for good health and a long life with the woman I love."

Kym exhaled without saying a word. She looked away, and he wondered at her thoughts that seemed to zone her out.

"Are we good, Kym?" His expression was deadpan as she turned to meet his eyes. "This topic was long overdue, but I want you to know I'm not going anywhere."

"Good. I don't want you to go."

There. They had the talk. They both knew the other's expectations. He still wasn't sure what was agreed upon. One thing was for sure: he wasn't going to ruin a good evening on any more deep discussion.

After dinner, their driver cruised to Inner Harbor. The first stop was dessert at Charm City Cakes. "I love this place."

"I thought it would be a memorable way to fuse your love of art with the decorative treats." Pleased with himself, Chaz rocked on his heels.

"You're a keeper, Chaz Banks." Kym sampled the mini cake shaped like a toy helicopter. He watched as she closed her eyes to savor the flavor, then opened them with a twinkle. He snickered. "That good, huh? I was hoping you would share."

"I guess so." She laughed and guided a piece to his mouth. "They have cake classes. We should take one."

He lifted his brows. "Did you forget you're under deadline for your dissertation?"

She pouted. "I guess I did for a moment."

Chaz coaxed her lips closer for a kiss. "That's why you have me to help you remember."

They left the bakery and strolled along the Inner Harbor while their driver waited patiently for them to return. There was no more discussion about the talk.

Whew. Kym had never been so close to a marriage proposal as she had been last night; she could almost taste the wedding cake. Not that Chaz had actually said the four words; it was the hint that it was coming that made her swoon. When they had sampled the cake, she imagined it as their wedding cake.

She could only hope to be a good mother, but Chaz was asking her to skip a generation to be a grandmother first. He didn't know Kym had thought about that scenario off and on but never lingered on it since he had never brought it up.

After last night, they both had some soul-searching to do. It was easy to be swept up in the moment and say yes, then possibly regret it later. Now that the topic was on the table, Kym had no choice but to think about her answer. She just didn't know how long it would take.

The next day at the university, Kym and Judith carved out enough free time to have lunch and compare notes about their Valentine's Day dinners before their next scheduled classes.

"Ooh." Judith bobbed her head. "Chaz definitely upped Zeke with the chauffeur, but we still enjoyed a good dinner and a movie. He got no pressure from me on wanting more. We're only talking about six weeks and counting. If he makes it to the three-month mark, I'll think differently."

Judith blushed. "You and Chaz are what, five or six months invested in your relationship? Girl, you better practice your yes. You know"—Judith became animated—"whether you want to have an ugly cry, sniff, or be pretty before answering when he asks. Keep your nails manicured."

Amused, Kym rolled her eyes and rested her chin in the palm of her hand. She exhaled. "You sound like some of our students. I love that man, but love can't make me say things I'm unsure about. I don't want to be the last Knicely sister to get married and the first one to get divorced. Chaz wants us to keep praying about our relationship."

"That advice alone makes him a winner."

"I know, right?" She stared at her nails. They didn't look bad, but a manicure wouldn't hurt.

Since that night, Chaz seemed to mean business that they should seek God's will on their relationship. Their morning exchanges now included, "Let's pray about us."

For the next couple of weeks, they had heart-to-heart discussions about children in general and those who required extra attention. "What are your thoughts about inheriting a blended family?" he had asked one night over the phone.

"I'm thirty-six. Blended families are normal with women my age and older—sometimes even younger." She thought about Rachel and Tabitha, who started off fresh and would experience firsts with their husbands: first baby, first and only marriage, first grandchildren. Kym withheld her sigh as she continued. "I feel as if I woke in the middle of a chapter instead of at the beginning, and I need to be brought up to speed so I can get to the end of the chapter with everyone else, if that makes sense. Chaz, I don't want to feel pressured or uncomfortable as I try to catch up."

"Baby, I'm your protector. If, God forbid, I hurt you, I will apologize and make it up to you." He shook his head. "I'll set the rules, and God help me and the offender if someone breaks them."

Kym didn't respond as she listened to his no-nonsense tone. She smiled, feeling cherished. Since their talk, she had been thinking more about a role as a surrogate grandmother before motherhood. *It's part of the package,* she convinced herself.

Sometimes, Chaz showed up with a meal or took over her kitchen and prepared dinner to make sure she got her nourishment as she worked on her dissertation. If he cooked, he would eat with her, clean the kitchen, and leave her to concentrate. How could she focus knowing the man from her childhood and teenage dreams had become a reality?

One night as Chaz stood at her front door about to leave, he made a confession. "I struggled with the thought of having a second set of children, but the more we talk and spend time in prayer, I know they will be a blessing. Otherwise, God wouldn't have put you in my life." He wiggled two fingers before her eyes. "But can we compromise at two children, unless they're boys? I'm willing to try for two more to get a daddy's girl."

"Thank you. That…that has always been a deal breaker for me." Kym couldn't stop the tears from falling.

Chaz looked scared and pulled her in his arms. "What did I say? I'm sorry if I said the wrong thing…"

Hiccupping, she sniffed and found her voice as she looked at him through her teary vision, then closed her eyes and kissed him. "You said everything I needed to hear."

A few weekends later, with the clock ticking, Kym was three-fourths complete with her oral defense draft. Two hundred plus pages were no joke. Her progress gave her confidence to play hooky with Chaz. Knowing her commitment, he still timed their dates in order to have her back home at an appointed time to resume her task.

When Chaz arrived at her house, he wrapped his arm around her shoulders and held her tight. "How does it feel to know I love you no matter what? With you, I feel complete. Now, we've kept each other a secret from our families—well, actually yours.

"Gee knows of you, Drake has seen you, but neither know the depth of my feelings. I'm ready to introduce you to my family. I want you to meet Chauncy." He held her attention. "Are you ready to introduce me to your family?"

"Yes." Kym nodded. "It's past time. I want to show you off to my sisters, and they'll see how happy you make me." She had made a good decision in holding off until she had no doubts Chaz was the one.

"How about I book us round-trip tickets for an upcoming weekend visit?"

"I would like that." Even though the dissertation was in the forefront of her agenda, Chaz wouldn't let her stray too much from her doctoral commitment.

"But before we get on that plane, there's one thing we need to take care of." He grinned.

"What?"

"You'll see." Chaz linked his fingers through hers and tugged her toward the door to leave, not saying another word.

Chapter 21

Gee called minutes before Chaz was about to book his and Kym's flights to St. Louis. "Hey, Pops."

"Hi, Dad," Lana said, chiming in on speakerphone with her husband.

Double teamed? Alert warnings rang in Chaz's head. If they were both calling, something was up. His heart raced as he held his breath. "What's going on? Is everybody okay?"

There was silence on the line before Gee sighed, then answered. "The obstetrician is putting Lana on partial bed rest because she has some bleeding. No cleaning and no cooking, and...no lifting Chauncy. Any exertion could cause more problems."

"Seems like everything is getting worse." Lana weeped. "We're struggling—I don't mean money-wise, because you've been there to pick up the slack, Pops, but I feel like I'm about to lose my mind."

Not good. "I'm so sorry you're having a rough time with my grandbabies." Chaz closed his eyes and silently screamed, *Lord, help us, please!*

"Dad, we don't know what to do. I can take family leave for three months, but I can't afford to go without my full pay, and I don't want to ask you to cover our bills that long." Gee sighed. "I feel like a failure as a husband, father, and man."

Oh no—he didn't like the sound of the sound of their defeat. "Gee, you're a strong, confident Black man who loves his family. You're doing your best." Closing his eyes, he tried to recall Scriptures of comfort and encouragement, but he was drawing a blank. One thing was for sure: his money wouldn't help this time. "How long is Lana supposed to be on bed rest?"

"For six to eight weeks," Gee said.

Yikes. Chaz gritted his teeth. Something had to be done, so he made a decision. "I'm coming to get Chauncy and will bring her back with me until Lana delivers the twins."

"Huh?" Gee stuttered.

Lana gasped, then became quiet.

Chaz allowed his solution to sink in, then he reasoned with them.

"The only way you can take care of the twins is to allow someone else to take care of Chauncy. I've reared two sons; you don't think I can take care of my grandbaby?"

"I don't know, Dad. That means I won't see my baby for weeks." Gee's voice was shaky.

"Pops, you're not a retired stay-at-home grandpa," Lana argued.

"Sweetie, we don't have many options." The wheels in Chaz's head were spinning at full speed. "Baltimore has social agencies too, to help with her therapies. Plus, I have a friend at the therapeutic day program for autism. I think most of her clients are under six, so I'll drop Chauncy off before work and pick her up after. It will be the perfect setup, since Johns Hopkins is partnered with the Kennedy Krieger Institute. The sooner I can get her on a routine, the faster she'll adjust. See, problem solved." Chaz had impressed himself with his fast thinking.

"You make it sound easy, Pops, but there's nothing routine about Chauncy not seeing her mommy and daddy."

They were right. "I have no perfect plan, just a plan," Chaz told them. It took some convincing, but finally Gee and Lana conceded there was no plan B. Valerie had offered no alternatives for help when the couple called her first.

"All right," Gee said. "Maybe Mom can come and stay with Lana a couple of hours a day while I'm at work."

"That would be helpful." His ex-wife needed to be involved too. "I was about to book a flight there so you two can officially meet Kym. We'll put that on hold. I'll pack my bags tonight and be there tomorrow."

"Thanks, Dad." Gee sounded relieved.

"No problem, Son." Chaz ended the call but didn't move from the spot where he was standing in the kitchen. In a matter of hours, his world—their world—had changed. He closed his eyes to gather strength.

He was about to become a full-time babysitter for two months. "God help me."

Next, he checked the time before calling Kym. There were certain times he didn't disturb her so she could concentrate. Unfortunately, he felt he had to interrupt.

"It's not quite break time, Mr. Banks," Kym answered, forgoing the standard hello.

"Hey, baby, sorry to—"

"What's wrong?" The panic in Kym's voice boomed in his ears.

Chaz took a deep breath and gave her a recap. He felt bad for upsetting her while she was in her dissertation zone.

"Oh, Chaz, I'm so sorry to hear that. Poor Lana. You're doing the right thing," she assured him, and that made him love her more.

"So are you okay with a rain check to meet the family? I mean, maybe we can do it when I take her back."

"That's longer than I wanted to wait, but I understand. I'm here for you. Breathe," she coaxed him.

He did, as if she could see him. "Of course you are. You're my prayer partner. I feel better hearing your voice. Now, you're still on the clock, Professor. Get back to your work. I'll talk to you in the morning."

She nearly pierced his eardrum when she smacked kisses over the phone. For the first time since getting the news about Lana, Chaz smiled.

Kym hadn't slept well the night before. She was concerned she might oversleep because she insisted on taking him to the airport for an early flight before heading to the university. Her heart ached for Gee and Lana. She knew Chaz wouldn't be able to take care of Chauncy solo, so despite her schedule, she would do as much as she could whenever she could.

One thing for sure, Chaz had no idea what he was up against as a caregiver, especially for a beloved relative. She and her sisters hadn't either when Aunt Tweet was diagnosed with dementia symptoms.

In hindsight, they would have done some things differently. There were so many trials and errors as a caregiver, and without "burning bread" on Chaz's situation, he would soon find out what worked and what didn't.

"I can't wait to meet Chauncy," she said, double-parking at the curbside in front of the airport's Departures entrances.

Chaz's eyes twinkled. "Me too. I love you." He fingered a curl.

He pulled her closer for a kiss, and before their lips touched, Kym whispered, "Now, may the Lord watch between me and thee," she began, and he joined in, "while we're absent. This I ask in Jesus's name. Amen."

She closed her eyes and welcomed the soft brush of his lips against hers before he stepped out and disappeared through the double doors. She sighed as he took a piece of her heart with him. "This is going to be a long day," she mumbled.

Her mind was still on Chaz and Chauncy when she got to her office. Kym would offer to go shopping when they returned, to get whatever the little girl needed. How much time could she invest in getting to know his granddaughter?

Kym blinked and noticed Judith standing in the doorway. She had been distracted since the phone call from Chaz the previous evening. His crisis was now hers.

Judith gave her a bewildered expression. Her laptop was pressed against her chest, an indication she was headed to teach her class. Judith didn't wait for an invite as she walked into Kym's office, closed the door, and dropped in a chair. "What's wrong?"

"Chaz is on his way to St. Louis." Kym frowned and gnawed on her bottom lip.

"Today?" Judith squinted. "I thought you two were going in a week or so to do the big reveal to your families? What happened?"

"Gee's son and daughter-in-law are expecting twins, and they already have a little girl with special needs as you know…the doctor is putting his daughter-in-law on bed rest, and…"

"How does that affect you and Chaz?" Judith frowned.

"He's going to get Chauncy and bring her here for a couple of months until Lana has her babies. I offered to help."

Judith stood. "Wow. And how are you going to do that?"

"I have no idea." Kym rubbed her head. "But I will, because he can't do it by himself. I don't want him to."

That evening at home, Kym was stressed. She definitely had bit off more than she could chew. In all honesty, the countdown had begun to finish her dissertation. If she wanted to walk in the spring ceremony, she had three weeks to compile all her work and practice her oral defense.

There could be no room for cracks in her defense presentation. The committee that would grant her the doctoral degree had to be convinced her research was solid and the program was needed.

Although closing the educational gap between minority and white students wasn't the primary focus of the mobile tutoring program, the benefits would achieve that.

When she freed her mind of her dissertation, Chaz flashed before her. He would soon learn he needed backup. She hoped she could fulfill the role.

Chapter 22

Chaz had mixed emotions as his plane touched down in St. Louis. The flight had been smooth, but he couldn't be sure about the return trip with Chauncy in tow. "Hold it together, Banks. This is your precious granddaughter. You can handle it." He gave himself a pep talk as he slid behind the wheel of his rental car, on a mission to his son's house. The plan was to spend the night and leave with Chauncy the next morning.

Mentally, he had downplayed his one-on-one grandpa duty for a couple of months as doable. A prolonged babysitting stint wasn't the same as being a caregiver, right?

Soon, he parked and got out of the car. Taking a deep breath, Chaz knocked and waited.

The door opened, and a barrage of expressions played across Gee's face—relief, anguish, regret, fear—when he opened the door. "Thanks, Pops, for coming." He latched on to his father in a bear hug with no hint of letting go.

"How's Lana?"

"She says she's resting, but I'm sure Chauncy's leaving is stressing her. Both of us." Gee sighed, then grabbed Chaz's overnight bag and ushered him inside. "I may have more gray hair than you, Pops, after the twins arrive."

Chaz spied Chauncy in the corner, rearranging two craft sticks. She never looked up. "I can imagine no mother wants to part with their child."

Gee nodded. "Or daddy either, but Lana knows she needs her strength for the babies she's carrying."

Chaz squeezed his elder son's shoulder to reassure him they were making the best decision under the circumstances. The arrangements weren't ideal, but the options were limited, so when family needed him, Chaz never hesitated to help. Nothing else took priority in his life—until he met Kym Knicely.

Later that evening, they kept Lana company as she propped herself in the bed, eating ice cream and watching cartoons while Chauncy slept beside her. All of a sudden, Lana's shoulders shook as she muffled her cries of agony. Gee rushed to her side to provide comfort as Chaz sat, silently praying, as he witnessed his daughter-in-law's emotional breakdown.

"Maybe she shouldn't go. I can try to be careful," she said as her lips trembled and tears filled her eyes. "I don't want my baby to think we're giving her away or abandoning her. She's made improvements with her therapies, and I don't want her to have any relapses."

"You know that's not the case, babe. Once the twins arrive, Dad will bring Chauncy back home."

Lana sniffed.

"The time will fly by, because she'll be having fun with her PawPaw," Chaz said, chiming in. He hadn't counted on Lana having this magnitude of separation issues for a couple of months—if that long. Babies sometimes came early, right? "Lana, Chauncy is in good hands. I need you to take care of the little ones." He glanced at her swollen belly. "She needs attention that you can't give her right now."

She gave him a pointed look. "How does your girlfriend feel about all these sudden changes?"

Chaz smiled, thinking about her. "Kym supports me and understands my decision." He recalled her telling him how she had put her life on hold to be her great-aunt's caregiver, then again when her younger sister was diagnosed with cancer. She was on standby to leave at a moment's notice. When it came to a family in crisis, he and Kym were on the same page.

Nobody but God knew Chaz was beginning to feel overwhelmed, and he and Chauncy hadn't left yet. He was accustomed to interacting with boys as children. He knew next to nothing about the nuances of little girls. He hoped there was a YouTube channel. Chauncy would be his responsibility, but so was Kym. Chaz still owed it to Kym to make sure she stayed on task with her dissertation. Yep, the next couple of months were going to be a balancing act.

The next morning, Lana had dressed Chauncy in a red cap and matching red coat. Her long hair was combed in cornrows instead of the twin thick braids she normally wore. Chaz exhaled. At least he wouldn't have to fuss with her hair every morning, but he dreaded it when the time came.

"Dad, the cornrows should stay neat until she comes back. All you have to do is tie a scarf around her hair at night, and wash it once a week. Make sure it's dry to prevent it from matting, and lightly oil her scalp. Easy."

Who said? Chaz played off his confidence level with a nod. "Check."

"I've packed some clothes in here"—she lifted a tote bag—"her favorite snacks: bread, cheese, and apple slices. Here's her favorite blanket if she gets cold, and headsets, so she won't get startled by the noise." There was more in a long checklist sent via text. Since Chauncy wasn't a fan of stuffed animals, she had her two craft sticks. Chaz hugged his son goodbye, then Lana, who whispered in his ear, "Please take good care of my baby."

"I promise you. Me and Jesus." God knew Chaz was going to need all the help he could get.

Gee lifted Chauncy into his arms so Lana could hug her with little strain. If their daughter sensed her routine was about to change, her poker face gave nothing away, as usual.

"We'd better head out. I don't know how much time we'll need to board." Chaz picked up Chauncy's suitcases. Gee trailed him outside with an adjustable car seat while Lana watched out the window from her spot on the sofa, waving a tearful goodbye.

At the airport, Chaz had to remind himself why he was enduring a mixture of sympathetic stares and annoying glares as he tried to get a handle on Chauncy's energy at the gate waiting area. *My daughter-in-law is on indefinite bed rest.*

Finally, Chauncy sat quietly next to him, clutching her blanket in one hand and the craft sticks in the other. Chaz's mind drifted to Kym. He couldn't be inside this airport without thinking about her. He unfastened his phone from his case and texted her. On my way home with Chauncy. So far so good.

She texted back seconds later. I'm praying for a smooth flight in Jesus's name. Amen.

Amen. Thank you, he texted back.

Chaz. I'm here if you need me. Sure you don't want me to pick you up?

Before Chaz could respond, an announcement came over the intercom, startling Chauncy. She covered her ears and shrieked like she had lost her sticks. It garnered unwanted attention.

No, no, no. A meltdown? Between Debra's quick checklist for distinguishing a meltdown from a temper tantrum and Lana's refresher course on how to respond, Chaz's mind kicked into overdrive.

"Identify the source of the sensory stimulation and remove the child from the offending environment," he mumbled as he dug into her tote bag for her kiddie headset, hoping that would muffle whatever sound was triggering her discomfort.

Next, he lifted her in his arms and gathered their things. He kissed her cheek as he searched for a quiet place. He saw the sign for the family assist bathroom ahead. Debra had said meltdowns were overactive nerves that needed time to rest.

Rubbing her back, Chaz had to wait it out and hope they didn't miss their plane. One thing for sure, if Lana knew about this episode, she would get behind the wheel and drive to the airport for Chauncy.

Chaz exhaled. Now they had to get on the plane and make it to Baltimore. *Lord, wrap my precious grandbaby in Your arms and let her have a peaceful flight. In Jesus's name. Amen.* The headset wasn't coming off until they landed.

They stayed in the restroom until it was almost time to board their section. When he reemerged, Chauncy was resting her head on his chest with her blanket balled into her fists. Everything was all right in her world again.

Chapter 23

Two days. Two days since Chaz's return, and Kym hadn't seen him or Chauncy. Her frustration with Chaz had been building. She was feeling dumped and wanted to be petty about it.

Chaz had returned to Baltimore flustered. She could tell he was in over his head when she called him this morning. He sounded as if he were in a drug-induced deep sleep. His words were barely recognizable. There was no way he would make it to their church service on time.

Poor baby. Kym would call him again after her video chat with her sisters. Kym doubted Chaz would remember their brief—very brief—conversation anyway. Maybe it was time to face the music with her sisters and fess up. Five minutes into the chat, Kym blurted out, "I met someone." They all blinked in surprise, including her.

"Well, it's 'bout time," Tabitha Whittington yelped, then grinned, halting Kym's mind from drifting. "I was hoping I wouldn't be on my third child by the time you decided to commit." She jumped up and did a happy dance in front of the monitor.

"Silly. You don't have two yet. Give Nicholas and me time to catch up. It's a new year. The doctors say we're almost cleared for takeoff." Rachel beamed. Her face glowed with happiness as if she were already expecting.

Tabitha squinted and tempered her celebration. "Ah, wait. Kym, why don't you look happy about it?"

"Because I don't know if I should be concerned, mad, or…" She gritted her teeth. "Aggravated."

Rachel frowned at the screen. "I'm confused. Start from the beginning."

Kym stalled as she toyed with a piece of mail on her desk before looking at the monitor. "His name is Chaz Banks." She smiled. "He's passionate, charismatic, distinguishable in a crowd, and a practicing Christian. Perfect for me."

"Why do you not look happy?" Rachel squinted. "I don't like him already."

"Trust me, you will, because I'm in love with this man." Kym closed her eyes briefly and exhaled. She fanned her face to keep her emotions in check. "Having a moment, so I wanted my sisters to hear me out."

"Who are you, and what have you done with my big sister? You are too critical of men to let someone discombobulate you." Tabitha paused as Little Marcus climbed up on her lap and started to tap on the keyword. His eyes widened in delight when he recognized his aunties on the screen. He bounced and showed them an adorable grin as he drooled. "Honey! Come get your son," she yelled for her husband.

Seconds later, Kym's brother-in-law appeared in the background and reached for the toddler. "Hey, sisters-in-law."

"Hi, Marcus," Kym and Rachel said in a singsong manner.

Once they were alone again, Rachel ordered Kym to talk.

After taking a deep breath, Kym squirmed in her seat. "Well, six months ago—"

"Six months!" Tabitha shrieked and shook her head. "Wow… Who keeps a man hidden for six months unless… Are you the mistress?"

"I'm not desperate or backslidden." Kym shrugged. "I wanted to be sure as I protected my heart."

"Mm-hmm. And that's the story you're sticking with," Rachel said. "And to think you kept a straight face every week for twenty-four weeks! That's Thanksgiving, Christmas, New Year's, my birthday. You missed your calling in theater and—"

"Hush," Tabitha said. "So we can hear all the details *we* haven't been privy to."

"Okay." Kym took a deep breath. "Here goes. While at the St. Louis airport waiting to fly back home after that conference last fall, minding my own business, this very handsome, distinguished man approached me…" She told them his opening line. "We carried on a conversation when I learned we're both LLU alums. He has family in St. Louis like me, so we've even flown back to St. Louis together," she rambled.

"Hold up. You what? How come we've never seen or met him?" Tabitha asked. Now she had an attitude to match Rachel's.

"You've seen him—once." She closed her eyes and summoned up the memories as she recalled everything about Chaz Banks. "So now you know the full story. He's stressed and I want to pick up the slack, but I don't see how. I'm this close to defending my dissertation." She demonstrated the distance with her thumb and forefinger.

"Tab?" Rachel looked in her sister's direction on the screen. "I'm so ready to book our flights this minute."

Tabitha pouted. "I would be on the next flight out of here too, sisters to the rescue, but I'm a mommy now. There are logistics I have to plan before going to the grocery store—diapers, toys, snacks. The best I can do is Friday. That way, Marcus won't be solo for too long."

"Who said I want both of you to come?" In all honesty, Kym did need her sisters ASAP. She regretted keeping them out of the loop, but they had their own lives now. Before, whenever one of them had a crisis, they would drop whatever they were doing and come running.

"We're a sisterhood. We're supposed to be here for each other. Our husbands understand our bond and have the same with their siblings, but don't think because we're holding our tongues on your whole secret love connection thing that you won't hear it when we get there." Tabitha wagged her finger. Within minutes, they had all signed off.

Kym took a deep breath and stared at her computer. She didn't have brain cells to waste. There were five parts to her dissertation. She had written three, but there was so much more work left to do. Yet Chaz had always been there to keep her on task. It was time to check up on him.

Chapter 24

CHAZ'S SNORING STARTLED HIM FOR THE THIRD TIME THROUGHOUT the day. This morning, he had woken exhausted and disoriented. Now he blinked. Where was he? What day was it, and why did he hear the patter of little feet in the other room? Suddenly, his situation came flooding into view. Chauncy was there with him.

Had he slept the day away? He groaned, threw the covers back, and stepped out of bed as the doorbell rang. It was after seven. Drake had promised to stop by to see his niece.

Yawning, Chaz checked on Chauncy, who seemed to be building a structure from some books she had pulled from his shelf. He took note of that. Although he liked to read to her, hands-on activities suited her better. The doorbell rang again, and he hurried to open it.

Expecting Drake, he was happier to see Kym and rubbed his head. "Oh, baby, I'm sorry I forgot to call you back. Come on in."

"Yep, you forgot to call me back, wash your face, and put on decent clothes." She mustered a chuckle, but her expression meant she was serious. "Chaz, please take this personally. I've never seen you so… disheveled."

Suddenly, Chaz became aware of his appearance. "Make yourself at home. Give me fifteen minutes to make myself presentable. Chauncy is…" He looked over his shoulder, and his little munchkin had disappeared from view. "She's around here somewhere. I'll find her after I take a quick shower." He dashed down the hall.

"Bless him, Lord," Kym mumbled as she scanned the room for his granddaughter. In the few times she had been in his home, nothing was out of order. It was the exact opposite at the moment. Toys were tossed in two separate corners of the room. She caught sight of motion from her peripheral vision. Chauncy peeked out from a doorway, then scrambled away.

Classic hide-and-seek. "Chauncy," Kym called out. Debating whether she should play, Kym decided to hold off until Chaz returned from the shower. When, after a few minutes, Chauncy hadn't reappeared, Kym powered up her tablet.

Chaz's cologne permeated the room, breaking her concentration.

"Baby, I'm sorry."

"For not calling me back?" She saved her work and stood to welcome his hug.

"Thought I had and we had a long talk. Wow." He rubbed his neck. "Maybe I was dreaming."

"You were. I got worried when I didn't hear from you. I know you are adjusting, but I had hope you would have reached out to me."

Chaz nodded and squeezed his lips before responding. "I should have. When I brought Chauncy home, she became frenetic and kept opening doors and searching the house as if she had a warrant, looking for her parents. That frustration caused another meltdown. Not knowing what to do, I called my son and daughter-in-law. Big mistake. Lana was ready to get on a plane.

"Needless to say, it took hours to calm her down. Today, I woke up about four in the morning to use the bathroom and noticed Chauncy was sitting at the kitchen table ready to eat. I turned on the light, and she stared at me with those beautiful Banks eyes. 'Eat, PawPaw,' she said patiently.

"I prepared her toast and rice with a pinch of sugar—per Lana's list. She doesn't like meat, so any crispy bacon is all mine." He yawned. "This is just the beginning of PawPaw's babysitting stint. I've got to get this right."

"You will. You're her grandfather who loves her. You'll do fine, and I'm here to do what I can." Kym rubbed his arm.

"I knew you would be, but I have to arrange some home visits for her therapies. Plus, I didn't want to bother you and take you away from what's important to—"

Her finger shushed him. "Both of you are important to me. When I hadn't heard from you, I thought you were shutting me out. I'm glad I came over instead of letting my imagination take over more than it had. I came clean with my sisters during our video call this evening. They weren't happy to be kept out of the loop. Both are coming next weekend. They want to see the man who has done the impossible—according to them."

"Which is what?" His lips curled up into an amused smirk.

"I'll never tell," she said, teasing him as he softly tickled her.

"Tell me, my beautiful woman." His voice was husky.

"You captured my heart." Kym was breathless when she stared into his eyes. But it wasn't about them anymore; there was a third person she had yet to meet. She stepped back and cleared her throat. Focus. This visit was about Chauncy. "Listen, I can't be here daily, but I do plan to check on you two as much as I can. When my sisters get here, I know they're going to want to meet you…and Chauncy."

Chaz cupped her face in his hands. "First of all, know this: I'll never push you away. Never. I need you, but I have to admit, I'm trying to figure out how to adjust to Chauncy and make sure you stay on task with that dissertation. Can I get a rain check on meeting your sisters?" Chaz reached for her hand to follow him. "Hopefully, they'll forgive us. Sorry, babe, again for making you feel like I was ignoring you. Let's find my grandbaby."

Even with all that was going on, he was still worried about her. Kym smiled. "Hey, I think I see her." She pointed to the cracked door to the bathroom.

"Chauncy," he called and walked in that direction. Seconds later, he reappeared with a beautiful little girl clutching his shirt and a blanket. How precious. Kudos to her mother who had thought ahead about hair care. Chauncy's braids were adorned with colorful beads.

Chaz sat on the sofa with Chauncy in his lap, but she didn't make eye contact with Kym. He held the girl in his arms and kissed her forehead.

Not sure of what to do next, Kym looked to Chaz for guidance. He seemed as clueless as she was.

"She's overwhelmed with the new surroundings. Grab your tablet." He nodded to where she left it. "Get some work done while you're here as we follow Chauncy's lead until she grows accustomed to you."

"I'd like that." She kissed Chaz's forehead and chanced a kiss on Chauncy's cheek. The child didn't respond.

For the next few hours, the only sound in the room was Kym tapping on the keyboard and mumbling to herself. She would glance at Chauncy periodically because she thought she had fallen asleep. She hadn't. When Kym yawned, she called it a night.

Chaz placed Chauncy on the sofa and walked Kym to the door. He was the first to speak. "I love you. Thanks for checking on this old man."

Kym smirked. "Old man nothing. I don't date men older than forty-two." She winked as his breathing deepened and his nostrils flared.

"I'm glad I made the cut." He leaned forward and kissed her softly.

"Me too." She rubbed his cheeks that felt rough, needing attention from a razor.

"I'll stop by in a few days, but I'll call you like before. Next time you dream of talking to me, Mr. Banks, pinch yourself, and do it."

He grinned. "Will do." He kissed her again, and she left a happy woman. Yep, Chaz needed backup, and she was going to do her best to give it to him.

There were no words to describe how Kym's surprise visit had lifted Chaz's spirit. To say he was overwhelmed in less than two days was an understatement.

One thing Lana had drilled into his head on the list sent via text message was consistency with sleep, eating, activities, and therapies. "Create a schedule and stick with it," he mumbled. Chaz had overslept and missed the mark on today's routine. Monday morning would be better. His therapist friend had also given him a paper with a list of activities to start at home that she would reinforce at the institute.

After seeing Kym off, Chaz walked back to the sofa and lifted Chauncy in his arms. "You've got a snack coming, then it's bedtime, little sweetheart." Lana had noted that Chauncy's favorite fruits were sliced red apples and red grapes. Hopefully, Chaz would be able to expand her choices by the time she went back home. He had high hopes about a lot of things for his grandbaby before she returned to St. Louis, and he was looking to Debra's expertise as a therapist to make that happen.

Monday morning, first things first, Chaz had to freshen up Chauncy and get her dressed. Reading her favorite book last night only caused him to doze. When he stirred and looked at her, Chauncy was wide awake. Lana had warned him about her irregular sleep patterns. *Work on consistency*, Chaz could hear her voice in his head.

Funny how he never gave a second thought to mindless tasks. Actually, when Chaz visited them in St. Louis, Chauncy was either dressed already in her play clothes or still in her pajamas.

Lana had said Chauncy liked to pick out her clothes, so she would lay them out on the bed each morning. His daughter-in-law stressed that although Chauncy needed instruction to perform tasks, he should allow her the independence to implement them while timing her for mastering certain things. So many rules for a four-year-old. But his daughter-in-law emphasized rules and rewards went hand in hand.

While he waited, he texted Kym. Morning, my sunshine. Miss you.

Miss you too. Love you so much. Your prayer partner is praying for you to have a good day bonding with your adorable grandbaby. Meditate on James 1:3.

He smiled. Thanks, partner. Praying for completing your dissertation with perfection, Genesis 31:49: The LORD watch between me and thee, when we are absent one from another.

Chaz spied his Chauncy again. If his granddaughter didn't pick out an outfit soon, he would choose for her. She studied her clothes and rearranged them as if she were performing the classic cup and ball trick game where a ball was placed under a cup, then shuffled with others. The spectator had to guess which cup hid the ball.

Finally, Chauncy made a decision with a little prompting from him. She donned a skirt, T-shirt, and tights. She slipped her feet in her tennis shoes. "PawPaw." She waited for him to tie them.

He grabbed his computer bag and her backpack, making sure it contained her blue craft sticks, then they left for Kennedy Krieger Institute.

With her arms folded, Debra greeted Chaz without a hello as they strolled into her office. "You're late—twenty-five minutes. Punctuality is key," she said, then squatted to Chauncy's eye level. "Hi, it's nice to meet you." She stood when Chauncy didn't respond. "Let me do her assessment. When do you return to work?"

"Tomorrow." Chaz needed the respite. Being PawPaw was much easier when he visited. *I'm too old for daddy duty, even temporarily*, he thought.

"I need you to have her here at nine sharp. Remember, you're the adult, so you're going to have to adjust your schedule to get Chauncy on a schedule. Would it be possible for you to take a noon lunch and eat with us? Then pick her up by four p.m.?" His friend acted like a drill sergeant. The schedule Debra set up was doable because his boss knew Chauncy was in his care, and Justin preferred Chaz to be in the office with reduced hours than be out on family leave for two months.

According to Debra, no two children with autism were the same; their levels of required support would be different. Some excelled at mimicking, while others struggled, so Chaz observed from the sideline as Debra made gestures to see whether Chauncy would follow, then jotted her notes.

An hour later, Debra introduced Chauncy into a group of children where a puppet show was underway. Some children sat silently. A few were twirling in circles. One thing he did notice, all but one had a parent or guardian doing the exercises with their children.

Chaz closed his eyes. He was exhausted after the first day. This was day two, and he was operating on even less sleep. At this moment, eight, nine, ten—whatever weeks—seemed years away. It was worth it if Lana got her needed rest and Chauncy made a lot of progress. He didn't regret his decision to take his granddaughter. He knew it would be challenging, but he'd had no idea what he'd signed up for. Visiting was one thing, but actually being a parent again… Yikes. He swallowed. Wasn't that the expectation that Kym had discussed with him? He wondered if that topic was up for renegotiation.

At two the next morning, Chauncy was awake and asking for her mother. He braced himself for the fallout, because he refused to wake his daughter-in-law at that hour. Chaz considered himself a late riser at 7:06—it was a mental thing. That gave him plenty of time for prayer, shower, and breakfast and still get out the door by 8:37.

By the third day, Chaz surrendered. His morning routine had crashed. Getting Chauncy dressed was no small task. If she didn't like the feel of the fabric, she would yank her hand back as if she had been burnt, or maybe she wasn't feeling the color. How was that even possible? They were her clothes from home that Lana had packed.

"PawPaw." Chauncy signed with her hand as if she were scooping up soup to signal she was hungry. Sometimes she said the word, and sometimes she signed what she wanted. Chaz hoped Debra could get his granddaughter on a consistent routine.

Chapter 25

Kym knew firsthand caregiving wasn't easy, but for a child—a little girl too—Chaz needed a lot of prayers going up on his behalf to keep his sanity. According to her sisters, their experiences as caregivers had tried their patience. Not for Kym. Aunt Tweet had been nothing less than easygoing, heartwarming, and memorable during her stay. She would cherish their time together for a lifetime.

Her thoughts drifted to Chaz again. Despite the stress on her with the dissertation, Kym missed him. She couldn't wait to get back to Chaz and Chauncy. Yet she had to recalibrate. Kym had been in college off and on for eight years, chasing the dream of reaching the top of the educational ladder.

At home, she tapped on her keyboard. The components of the introduction to her dissertation were preliminary background info—check; the precise focus of her study—check; value, aim, and objective of her research… Kym hovered on those sections and gritted her teeth. "A work in progress." That was the meat of her project. She had to be so passionate and compelling that her conclusion would generate meaningful questions and discussions. Kym yawned and craved iced tea in her favorite tall clear glass with the illusion of sand at the base. She stood and stretched, then padded across her living room to the kitchen.

Leaning on the counter, Kym took a sip and stared out the window into the well-lit street. "God, please don't let me fall short with my years of research," she prayed in Jesus's name and returned to her computer. Before she resumed, Kym came up with a brainy idea—another distraction, despite her resolve and prayers—and called her friend. "You up for a quick shopping spree tomorrow afternoon?"

"Aye aye, ma'am," Judith mocked. "My last class ends at one."

"Mine begins at one thirty. Be ready to go at three."

"And what are we shopping for?" Judith asked.

"Chauncy. I don't want to go back to Chaz's without bearing gifts." Kym was hyped. Little girls were meant to be spoiled, pampered, and anything else that made them feel special.

Judith giggled. "Bribing a kid. I love it! Maybe I'll see something I like for Zeke."

Kym snickered. "We're going to have to catch up on you and Zeke."

"Of course. He is my favorite subject." Her friend laughed and ended the call. Without giving in to any more distractions, Kym refocused and tackled loopholes in her paper.

The next afternoon, the two friends were on a mission as they entered Children's Place, where she had planned to buy a cute outfit for Chauncy.

"What do you know about what she likes?" Judith asked, tapping her cheek in thought.

Kym froze in her heels and twisted her lips, thinking. "Hmm. No idea, and I don't want to ask Chaz because I want it to be a surprise."

"Hey, don't worry. Let's skip the clothes." Judith waved her hand.

"Man, I was hoping to doll her up with a cute outfit and matching purse. Never too early to start diva training."

"Another time, girl." Judith laughed. "Only you. Let's stick to toys, games, dolls, or a stuffed animal. Come on. I think there is a Build-A-Bear Workshop here."

"Sounds like a plan." Kym grinned as they speed walked across the Towson Town Center mall to jump-start their shopping spree.

By the time they finished, she and Judith were lugging bags that would overflow the basket Kym had purchased to hold the toys. "I want to make a good second impression."

Judith eyed Kym's purchases. "I think you've accomplished that. Chauncy should love all those goodies."

"I hope so, because I won't be able to spend too much time there. It's crunch time for me."

"How is the dissertation going?" Judith asked as she climbed into the passenger seat of Kym's SUV.

"I'm meeting with a few committee members for a test run on the third part. But I'm nervous, so for a diversion, I'm going to Chaz's house for a couple of hours before I jump back on the project."

For the impromptu visit, she had donned a green flowing dress, since all shades of the color were her favorites in her closet right now. Her hair had been freshly done the other day, and her makeup was meticulously reapplied with Chaz in mind. Lifting up the basket, which had to weigh more than thirty pounds considering all the things she had stuffed inside, Kym left, giddy with excitement.

Soon, she parked in front of Chaz's home. The neat and clean exterior reflected the man inside. She missed him, his thoughtfulness, hugs, whispers of love, and surprises, like the times he had shown up on campus with gifts. This time, she had a surprise for Chauncy.

Kym rested the basket at her feet and rang the doorbell. Chaz opened the door, and his eyes did a slow assessment of her. An odd expression flashed on his face before a slow grin stretched across it. What a mixed signal. Before she could question him, she got lost in the intensity of his stare. The monstrosity of a basket stood between them, and he reached for it as if it were as light as a loaf of bread and set it inside on the floor without taking his eyes off her. "How long has it been since I've seen you?" he said in a husky voice.

She giggled. "Four days."

"Definitely too long." He guided Kym inside, then twirled her under his arm.

Ahh. She missed these moments with him.

When he closed the door, she pointed to the basket. "For Chauncy." She grinned. "I hope she likes it."

He barely looked. "Woman, did you leave anything on the shelves?" Chaz gazed into her eyes and shook his head. "If I didn't say 'wow' before, an oversight. You smell good, look good, and feel good." He wiggled his brows.

"You say the right things." She playfully scrunched her nose as he intertwined his fingers with hers, tugging her toward the sofa.

"Where is she?" She craned her neck to peep down the hall while sensing his eyes admiring her.

He sighed and collapsed on the sofa and pulled her down next to him. "Asleep."

"At six o'clock?" Kym blinked. "That's awfully early for bedtime."

"Trust me, she'll be up soon." Chaz exhaled and patted her hand. "Sometimes, it seems she can operate on four hours of sleep, be awake for an hour or so, then knocked out for eight hours. This is just the first week, so I'm taking it easy on her, but Debra and Lana said—"

Kym interrupted. "Who's Debra?"

"The therapist at the institute," he explained. "She said to adhere to Chauncy's schedule as I take small steps, but eventually I'm going to have to be the grown-up and take control."

They shared a laugh, but Kym noticed the tiredness around his eyes. While he massaged her fingers, she leaned forward. "Tell me about her sessions."

"I'd rather talk about us." His lips curved upward. "But okay. Chauncy's in a small group setting with other children her age. Debra works with them on communication and social, emotional, and behavioral development." She nodded when he paused. "I've seen some, and I mean *some* minor changes." He inched his lips closer to hers. "May I?"

"I granted you permission to kiss me a long time ago," she whispered and closed her eyes to receive his sweet offering. As her heart surrendered from the softness of his lips, he pulled away. Kym didn't want to open her eyes, but Chaz coaxed her to by squeezing her hands, and she pouted.

"How's the dissertation going?" he asked, seemingly amused by her rebellion.

What a mood killer. Kym was trying to take a break from it, not think about it. "It's getting close. I sat in on a few open presentations this week, which made me nervous."

"I believe in you, babe."

Kym blushed as her heart soared. Those very words were the reason why she loved this man and wanted to weather the storms and dance in the rain with him. "I hope Chauncy wakes up soon. I want to get to know her as much as I can with my limited schedule."

Chaz chuckled. "I've got mixed feelings about that one. Yes, I want you to see her again, but God knows I enjoy those long naps. Some days, I feel too old to be her playmate."

Kym held her breath. Did Chaz misspeak, or was he dropping a hint? Did he mean his age or life experiences? They had already had this discussion.

They heard some noise, and Chaz looked up and so did Kym. Chauncy. She didn't make eye contact with them as she slowly scooted around the perimeter of the room against the wall before coming to stand at Chaz's side. She wore an adorable pink polka-dot top and pink pants set. Her facial expression was blank as she tapped Chaz's thigh.

"PawPaw."

"Yes, sweetheart?" His tone was gentle.

The child repeated her endearment three times before Chaz seemed tired of the cat-and-mouse game and made the introduction as he lifted her on his lap. "This is my friend Miss Knicely."

The girl had her grandfather's eyes. She was adorable with her chubby cheeks and made Kym yearn for a sweet little girl. "Hi, Chauncy. How are you?" Kym leaned forward as she nudged the gift basket laden with treats and toys toward the child.

Instead of the curiosity Kym had hoped for, the girl slipped off Chaz's lap, ran across the room, and dropped to her bottom. She pulled her legs to her chest and rested her forehead on her knees, looking the other way.

Kym had expected excitement, thanks, or a smile to indicate they were on a path to friendship. Instead… *What just happened?* Kym's heart dropped, and she felt cut deeply. "That didn't go as I had hoped."

Chaz let out an audible sigh rubbed his face. "Oh, man. I forget to mention—"

"Mention what?" She stared at him, waiting.

"For some reason, Chauncy has an aversion to the color green."

"What? Everything green?" Kym gasped. "Chaz! A memo would have been nice. You're making me not win brownie points with your granddaughter." She squeezed her lips to stop herself from saying more. Talk about slamming into a brick wall.

"I'm sorry, babe. I don't know what she's associating with green, but she won't touch, taste, or play with anything green. Forgive me?" The puppy dog face didn't faze her.

"Let me think about it." Kym kept a straight face. She was striking out.

He blinked. "You're really serious, aren't you?"

"Yes, my feelings are hurt." She nodded and folded her arms. "I'm being sabotaged."

He disentangled her arms and pulled Kym into his. "Baby, I'm so sorry. When I first opened the door, you distracted me. I was in such awe, nothing else mattered. Forgive me."

"This time, but if I'm going to make friends with her, I need to know these things," she said in a scolding tone, but being mindful that Chauncy was still in the room. Kym didn't want to send off the wrong vibes where the girl would build a defensive wall around her.

"Noted." He stood and reached for Kym's hand. "Let's eat." Walking over to Chauncy, he helped her to her feet, and they continued to the kitchen. Chauncy broke free and climbed into a chair. "I guess she's hungry. I'll tell you what I've learned. Children are picky eaters, so I try to encourage healthy snacks. The only problem with Chauncy is she doesn't like many vegetables, but Debra has been experimenting."

Debra again. One fire at a time, Kym thought as she shuddered in her outfit. "Ah, Chaz, do you have a shirt, jacket, or sweater I can put over this to hide the color?"

"Sure, babe." He went into his bedroom and returned with a denim long-sleeved shirt. He helped her slip it on and stood back and admired his handiwork with a smirk.

"What?"

He chuckled and shook his head. "Some things shouldn't be said to a woman unless she's his wife, so I'll leave it there."

Since she wasn't his wife, Kym cleared her head of naughty thoughts. Sitting at the kitchen table, Kym didn't want to stare and make the girl uncomfortable. Yet she yearned to make friends.

Chauncy snuck glances at Kym, and each time, she gave the girl a warm smile. When she didn't return it, Kym realized her mission wasn't going to be easy. Maybe the child was extremely shy. "So what's on the menu?" she asked Chaz.

"Green beans, meatloaf, and mashed potatoes for us," he said as he hovered over the stove. "For Chauncy, sweet potatoes and French toast."

"What?" Kym frowned. "Ah, Chaz, that's not very nutritious."

"I know that," he snapped, then apologized. "Sorry. I'm frustrated about that too. When Lana gave me a list of Chauncy's favorite foods, I had no idea that a lot of healthy ones were on the 'she will not eat' list. That's why corn kernels are still on the plate from earlier. She's been sampling since we've been home. Debra has been working with Chauncy on texture and gave her some at lunch today." He smiled at his granddaughter.

Despite Chaz being an excellent cook, Kym came to his side and rested her chin on his shoulder and asked anyway. "Need any help?"

"Nope. It's ready. Here." He pulled out a chair for her. "I've got two princesses." After taking his seat at the table, Chaz said grace. Kym took her first bite and glanced at his granddaughter. It felt odd to have another person in the room and not interact with them. Instead of eating, Chauncy rearranged her silverware more than once.

"Chauncy, eat." Chaz's command didn't faze the girl, as she stopped but didn't take a bite.

Kym tried to intervene in order to help. She spoke in a soft voice. "Chauncy, are you hungry? Your food will get cold."

The intervention failed because the girl slid off her chair and walked back into the living room.

Chaz sighed and stood, then followed his granddaughter. The scene repeated itself. Kym watched as Chaz retrieved Chauncy again. On the third attempt to get his granddaughter to eat, he scooted close to her. Chaz helped her pick up her fork, scoop up a portion of sweet potatoes, and guide it in her mouth. When she spit the food out, Chaz said she had enough and let her get down.

"Whew. That was exhausting," Kym said. "Why didn't you just feed her?"

"We want her to be independent, and feeding her makes her

dependent. She has snacks throughout the house to get nutrients in her. What I thought I knew about autism barely scratches the surface, and every day is an eye-opener." He yawned. "Despite any setbacks, my grandbaby will thrive, and I'm determined to help her achieve her dreams."

His conviction made her smile, but watching the exercise had been mentally exhausting. No wonder Chaz was tired. She got up and rubbed his shoulders a few times, then began to clean the kitchen. When she reached for Chauncy's plate, he said, "No, leave it, babe."

"Okay." Kym nodded and completed her task. Chaz kissed her cheek and went in search of Chauncy. Finished, Kym joined them in the living room where Chauncy was snuggled under her grandfather's arm. Kym sat next to the basket and pulled out the bear she and Judith had built. The stuffed animal had the works: a crown, wand, ballerina outfit, and more. It was adorable. If she had a niece, it would be the perfect gift.

As Kym handed it to Chauncy, Chaz shook his head as his granddaughter touched it, then threw it down and ran away into a bedroom.

Kym's eyes widened in shock. Not only had she paid good money, but she and Judith had created it with love. There was only so much rejection a person could take in one evening. "She doesn't like it," she whispered.

Chaz stood. "Sorry, she has a high sensitivity to texture." He gritted his teeth. "She doesn't like the feel of fur. That's why I shook my head."

"Another thing I didn't know," Kym mumbled. It seemed as if neither of them was faring well with Chauncy. How long would it take for Kym to pull the other goodies out of the basket to see whether the child would accept or reject them?

"It's okay. There's so much to learn."

"But I need a crash course." Kym gathered her things and stood to leave. Maybe she could salvage time on her project because she had struck out here.

Chapter 26

A wakeup call stirred Kym from her slumber the next morning. Chaz's husky morning voice didn't sound more alert than she felt. "Morning, baby."

She smiled. "Morning, handsome."

"I wanted you to have a good day. I know it didn't appear that Chauncy loved your gift, but she did. Long after you left and before her bedtime, curiosity got the best of her; she was fascinated with the jumbo jigsaw puzzle in the basket."

Whew. Finally, a breakthrough. That tidbit lifted her spirits and brought tears to her eyes. At least it wasn't a total rejection.

"I hope I made your day," Chaz said.

"You did. I love you," she whispered.

"If you promise not to stop, I'll do the same."

Before they disconnected, they prayed for each other and quoted 1 Corinthians 13:7: *Love bears all things, believes all things, hopes all things, and endures all things*. "Enjoy your weekend with your sisters."

"I will." She needed the rejuvenation, and her sisters were bound to get the job done.

Late that afternoon, Kym parked in the airport garage and walked inside to wait for the former Knicely sisters. She relaxed in her sisters' arms once they cleared the terminal. "I'm so happy you two are here." She sniffed.

"You look pretty. Don't cry, or you'll ruin your makeup. It's not like we weren't together on Christmas." Rachel fussed in her role as the hair, makeup, and fashion guru of the sisters.

"Yeah." Tabitha put her fist on her hip. "We were just together and trying to set you up, and here you are already set up and about to get married." She grunted.

"We're not there yet, but we've talked about it," Kym said, cautioning them, not ready for them to get wound up.

"Yes!" Rachel beamed and looped her arm through Kym's. Tabitha took the other side. In a leisurely strut, the trio followed the path to the baggage claim.

They accepted help retrieving their luggage from a nice-looking stranger, then Kym guided her sisters to where she'd parked her vehicle. "Don't take this wrong. Any reason for us to get together is a good one, but this wasn't an emergency trip. I needed to vent because I misunderstood Chaz's silence."

"If it wasn't for your 'venting,' we would still be in the dark. We're here for you, and it doesn't have to be because of something bad. The Lord knows we have had enough crises in our family for many years to come. We don't need a reason to leave our husbands—temporarily of course—to be with our big sister." Tabitha squeezed her arm.

"I've dated off and on, but I wanted to know if this was more than a couple of dates guy," Kym said, defending herself.

"Clearly, he is, because we're here. And for the record, I want to meet this man," Rachel mumbled from the back seat as she glanced out the window.

"Yeah, me too. I can't believe he was in St. Louis! We could've crossed paths. As far as I know, his family could live in my Pasadena Hills neighborhood. I wonder if there are any Bankses close by me?" Tabitha said in serious contemplation.

Once they were home, her sisters unpacked their bags, then gathered around the kitchen counter for some spaghetti made with Kym's homemade sauce.

"Mmm." Tabitha snacked her lips after they gave thanks and said grace. "This is so good." She didn't say another word as she and Rachel consumed the pasta lathered rich in spaghetti sauce. Kym nibbled at a small portion.

After Tabitha rested her fork, she crossed her arms. "Now, you've told us the story. If you love him as much as you're not telling us, what do you plan to do for the couple of months while he's caring for his granddaughter? How has Chauncy—that's her name, right?—how has she responded to you?"

"Not good. On my first visit, I thought maybe she was shy, and she needed time to warm up to me." Kym tsked. "She never did."

Rachel pouted. "I'm sorry."

Kym shrugged, then slipped another bite of pasta into her mouth and chewed. "The second time I visited, I came bearing gifts, but for some reason, what I was wearing spooked her or something."

"Huh?" Rachel squinted. "She's kinda young to be the fashion police," she said with an edge to her voice.

"No, Chaz says she doesn't like anything green—crayons, vegetables, and I guess clothes too, so there goes my color trend. I've got some sharp green outfits too."

"That's odd. She's forgiven, I guess," Rachel said in a calmer voice.

"Children are finicky," Tabitha chimed in. "I'm learning that from my son."

Kym dabbed her lips with a napkin. "Wait. That was strike one. I toted a basket full of goodies—books, puzzles, and a stuffed bear from Build-A-Bear. It was so cute. Judith and I had so much fun building that the bear, then dressing it."

"Ooh. It doesn't sound like you could go wrong with that." Tabitha wore a hopeful smile.

"But I did." Kym watched both her sisters groan. "Her senses are overstimulated evidently from sight, sound, and touch. She doesn't like certain textures…"

"Let me fill in the blanks—the furry bear," Tabitha said.

Kym shook her head in disappointment. "Yep. Even my bribe gift—as Judith called it—didn't help. I was offended, crushed, and mad, but at the end of the day, Chauncy's rejection hit me hard. Chaz told me not to take it personally. Easy for him to say."

Slumping her shoulders, Kym gritted her teeth to keep from screaming out her frustration, then balled her fists. "When I got home, I couldn't concentrate to write, so I prayed. I can't be a blessing to him if Chauncy won't interact with me. He's put his confidence in Debra, some autism spectrum disorder therapist, to work with her."

"Wait a minute now. You're not about to let another woman have inroads with your man because of her trade." Tabitha cleared her throat. "That could be remedied." As a pharmaceutical rep, Tabitha loved researching illnesses, drugs, and their interaction to improve the quality of life.

Kym huffed. She wasn't about to pile any more onto her plate to research. She had six years' worth of research to work with. "I really don't think this Debra woman is a threat to me. He knew her before he met me."

"Humph. Men are needy, and Chaz needs her. You *need* to nip that in the bud," Rachel said, doing snipping motions with her fingers.

Kym rolled her eyes. Something told her it was going to be a long weekend with those two plotting and strategizing over nothing. "Time out. Let's watch a movie."

Chapter 27

"I DON'T KNOW IF I SHOULD SAY 'WELCOME TO SOLID ROCK CHURCH' as a visitor, or welcome back, prodigal member. It's been a while, man." Zeke pulled Chaz aside after Sunday morning worship and slapped Chaz's shoulder.

"Funny." Chaz wasn't amused as he held on to Chauncy at his side. He rubbed the back of his neck in embarrassment. "Hasn't been that long. I had preferred attending early Sunday services with Kym. But Chauncy and I woke late last week—or rather, I did, and my time clock is off." He lowered his voice. "The repetition is a must for her, but it's testing my patience as I play along. Now, I'm trying to assimilate my granddaughter into a Sunday routine."

He had to call Lana to assist in coaxing her daughter to cooperate with Chaz. "You like church, Chauncy. But you're going with Grandpa."

Lana had sent her child's Bible, and he laid a dress on the bed to differentiate her play clothes. Finally, instead of giving her the yellow stress ball that Debra gave her to indicate the daily Monday through Friday therapy routine, Chaz used a white ball for the weekend that Debra had suggested.

Of course, Chauncy had to study the arrangements, then took off her play clothes and slipped on her dress. Chaz had scored a point, but they were still late for the give or take ninety-minute service, which was why Chaz had chosen a back pew when they arrived.

"Do that. And I'm praying with you, my friend." Zeke glanced away when a group of church members distracted them, then refocused his attention on Chaz.

"I've never been so tired." Chaz stifled a yawn to prove his point. "Forty-two is not the new twenty-seven, when I had the energy to keep up with two small boys. Whew. This little girl here"—Chaz shook his head and lifted his hand that was holding on to Chauncy's—"is opening my heart and mind to her world. She's the apple of PawPaw's eye." He winked at her. Her eyes gave no indication that she understood, but she could feel his love, which was most important. Where others might not understand his grandbaby's actions, or lack thereof, Chaz was determined to.

"Man, stop acting like you've just received your AARP card. I'm thirty-three, and you can hang with the best of us on a 5K run, a one-on-one game, and burn out a treadmill, so please. I'm not buying this old-man stuff." His friend folded his arms and leaned against the wall, as if he was patiently waiting to see if Chaz had other excuses.

Chaz had an exercise routine he didn't deviate from until now, but it was only temporary. In order to get back on the regimen, he needed rest, and at the moment, he couldn't get enough sleep.

Zeke squatted and smiled. "Hi, Chauncy, I'm Zeke." He extended his hand, and she shook it. He stood and grinned. "She likes me."

Chaz couldn't wait for her to react to Kym like that. His granddaughter's attraction to pink clothes reminded him of Kym's color binges. The two had that in common, but it was a struggle to get Chauncy out of her pink pajamas and into the pink dress she was wearing. There was no way he could reason with her that pajamas weren't appropriate outdoor attire. Why did every task seem like a tug-of-war and wills?

"Hello?" Zeke waved his hand in front of Chaz. "You just zoned out on me. I asked how's she responding to Kym."

"Put it this way, my lady hasn't gotten a handshake yet," he started. "Twice, she's been to my house to visit, and twice, Chauncy hasn't shown interest. I've been praying for a breakthrough, because Kym wants to visit more than she's able, when it's so close for her to submit the dissertation and defend her research. Her sisters were in town this weekend, so I hope their visit is giving her a boost."

Chauncy started to become fidgety and walk in circles, making Chaz dizzy from watching. "We're leaving soon, sweetheart." He reached for her hand and guided her closer. "When I met Kym," he exhaled, "that woman makes me feel like I had never been in love before." He smiled. "The way my heart swells, I haven't felt this much intensity before, not even with Valerie."

"So…when's the romantic evening and the proposal?" Zeke smirked.

"On hold." He leaned closer and lowered his voice. "Not anytime soon when I have to bring a four-year-old to a candlelight dinner. You know, I have to give kudos to parents whose children need one-on-one attention every waking hour. I don't see how my son and daughter-in-law have done it—no, they're doing it. I thought I knew. I didn't."

Zeke bobbed his head. "You're right about that. I'm not in your shoes, but if I ever find myself there, I'd hope the woman I love would support me too."

Chaz shifted on the wall and loosened his hold of Chauncy's hand. "Kym's love and support mean the world to me. I trust her. I've watched how my ex-wife and her husband, Kenneth, interact with…" He nodded toward his granddaughter.

He turned his head away so Chauncy couldn't hear him. "Valerie has been in denial, but she's slowly coming to grips with how autism is affecting our granddaughter. She's accepting Chauncy will never grow out of it. Her condition will stay with her throughout her life. We have to teach her how to navigate life with it. I don't think Kenneth has the patience to support her, although he acts like he does. Kym's heart is right. She went shoppin—"

"I know, with Judith. She told me." Zeke grinned and stuffed his hands in his pockets.

"You're blushing, man."

"And you think you didn't when you met Kym?" He barked out a laugh and apologized to church members passing by in the hall. Zeke squatted and said goodbye to Chauncy, who gave him side-eye. He stood again. "Now, got to go. I promised Judith a matinee."

Chaz nodded and lifted Chauncy in his arms, smothered her neck with kisses, and walked with Zeke to the parking lot, then they veered to their own vehicles.

After he strapped Chauncy in, Chaz sat there, tapping his fingers on the wheel. He wondered what Kym and her sisters were doing. He rubbed his chin. There were promises Chaz wanted to make to Kym. But he would have to bide his time. As he told Zeke, taking a child to a candlelight dinner wasn't romantic, even if he did propose.

Chapter 28

"I'm still mad I flew all the way to Baltimore and didn't get to meet Mr. Banks." Rachel feigned a pout the following Sunday during their weekly video chat.

As the oldest, Kym wasn't a pushover, even when Rachel tried her best to come up with every reason why she should meet Chaz. Kym smirked at her sister's theatrics, feeling victorious having not given in to Rachel's whims.

Rachel's free spirit and fun personality had finally returned post-cancer treatment. Kym credited that to Nicholas's unwavering prayers and spoiling his wife. *Would Chaz continue to pamper her?* Kym's mind drifted.

"So have you made a new friend in Chauncy yet?" Tabitha asked, forcing Kym back to the present.

Kym preferred her living in her daydream than answering. "Not yet. I'm torn between wanting to get to know Chauncy and giving my all on the project. The moment I leave for Chaz's house, my mind is scolding me that I need to practice my oral defense."

"A getaway will definitely improve your concentration. You still plan on coming to St. Louis for spring break, like you do every year?" Tabitha asked.

"Didn't we just see each other, what, a week ago?" Shaking her head, Kym squeezed her lips and readied herself to say no. "I planned to use the time here to concentrate."

"But it's tradition. Your nephew and brother-in-law are here. Plus, consider our impromptu trip to Baltimore as a wellness check to make sure you were okay," Tabitha stated. "So that doesn't count."

"Doesn't take much planning. Go online and book a ticket," Rachel said. "I'll even get away from work for a few days and fly there too."

"If your husband doesn't escort you." Kym snickered, reminiscing how Rachel's then boyfriend—now husband—escorted her on the plane to St. Louis for Thanksgiving when Rachel was still undergoing cancer treatments, to make sure she arrived okay, then took the next plane back to Nashville to be with his family. That was love.

"Yeah." Rachel grinned. "And he will, if I ask him."

"We know," Kym and Tabitha chimed in.

"Don't distract me," Rachel stated. "This is your time. You're the one who needs pampering and relaxation so you can pull those all-nighters."

Kym twisted her ponytail. "You're right. A change of environment might help. Okay, I'll book my flight."

"Cool. See you next weekend. Don't forget we're #TeamKym. Little Marcus can't wait to see his aunties."

Kym couldn't help but smile as they ended the video chat.

Chaz didn't know how he felt about Kym flying solo when she told him the news. She had stopped by his house to bring carryout dinner.

"Would you quit pouting, Mr. Banks? Although you look adorable." Kym attempted a straight face as they enjoyed the meal of Asian cuisine, but he knew her giggles would spill in three, two, one. She delivered.

His behavior was comical, so he chuckled too as he bobbed his head. "I traveled without you, so I guess we're even."

"It's not about being tit-for-tat." Their banter was lighthearted until they cleaned their plates, except for Chauncy, who ate a little pasta, then left the table.

If Chauncy didn't eat more, she would be skin and bones by the time he took her back home.

"You're not going to force her to eat any more on her plate?" Kym didn't hide her concern.

"I tried that one time and she threw it up." He scrunched his nose a couple of times. "Not a pleasant experience. That's why I give her snacks and don't remove her plate right away. I have found she likes chocolate milk—a lot—so at least she's getting her vitamin D," Chaz explained.

He surrendered to Chauncy's will on some days because he was too tired after work to skirmish with her and, on other days, to get the upper hand.

The pair straightened the kitchen, then Kym wanted to bond with his grandbaby in her bedroom. As Kym sat next to Chauncy on the floor, Chaz remained in the doorframe and folded his arms to study their interaction. He hoped today was the day Chauncy would give Kym a glimmer of hope that she liked her.

Kym had brought a bag of craft sticks, since Chaz had mentioned they seem to act as Chauncy's pacifier. She spilled them on the floor and began to build a square structure while talking softly to Chauncy. "I used to make these in art class when I was a little girl at school."

After about half hour with no response from Chauncy, he joined them on the floor and began to assist. "Babe, I've been thinking."

"And?" She gave him the side-eye.

"This will be the last time you fly to St. Louis without me. I don't like us apart. When I take Chauncy back home, I hope you'll be able to go with me."

"I like that idea." She stroked his jaw. She brushed her lips against his, and Chaz captured them in a brief kiss.

Kym giggled as she pulled back. "Not in front of the children—I mean child," she protested despite Chauncy's seeming lack of interest in them. As Kym motioned to stand, Chaz scrambled to his feet first, then helped her. "I guess that's my good-night kiss. I better get home." She glanced down at his granddaughter, who was still playing with the same craft sticks she already owned. "Goodbye, Chauncy."

"Bye," she said in a monotone voice without looking at Kym.

The awe on Kym's face was priceless as her eyes misted. It was the first time the girl had responded verbally to her. He praised God for the blessing and thanked Debra silently for the improvement. Chauncy's vocabulary was growing. Getting her to use it at appropriate times was still a work in progress.

"Let me know the time your flight takes off and I'll drive you. Be ready a little earlier because I won't know what the day will bring for Chauncy."

"I will." Kym placed a kiss on the top of his granddaughter's head and left.

Too soon, days later, Chaz dropped off Chauncy at the institute, then drove to Kym's to give her a ride to the airport. At her front door, he bestowed on her a lingering hug. "I'm going to miss you, knowing you're not near, but you deserve the break." He cupped her face and kissed her extra for all the dates they had missed. They smiled at each other as Kym wiped the lipstick off his lips. Next, he lifted both her suitcases and chuckled.

"What?" She frowned.

He laughed and shook his head. "My woman. All this for a week."

"Hey, I'm packing light this time." Kym humphed and jutted her chin.

Holding hands during the drive reminded him of what he missed with the one-on-one time with Kym. He wasn't rushing to send Chauncy home, but he couldn't wait until he and Kym were back on a regular dating schedule either.

At the airport, Chaz's heart pounded in protest as Kym checked her luggage. He pulled her aside and prayed for her safe travel. "Now, may the Lord watch between me and thee, while we're absent, one from the other…In Jesus's name." He stared into her eyes. "Remember, I love you. Chauncy and I will be here to pick you up."

"I can never forget how much you love me. I'll text you when I land," she said as she was about to walk away to join other passengers in the security line.

"No." Chaz stopped her. "Call me when you land. I want to hear your voice." Slipping his hands into his pants pockets, he didn't move as he watched Kym's steps until she disappeared inside the terminal. He exhaled, not realizing he had held his breath.

A few hours later at work, he got the call. Kym had landed safely in St. Louis. Chaz gave thanks. Now he could try another attempt at rereading the same article in his email. He yawned from his lack of sleep. Every morning, Lana called and asked if it was getting better. This was week three, and Chauncy had yet to fall into a pattern at home despite Debra's praising her progress at the institute.

Zeke popped his head into Chaz's office. "Hey. Should we celebrate?"

"Huh?" Chaz racked his brain. Did he forget an anniversary or something? "What's there to celebrate?"

His friend huffed and leaned against the doorframe. "Didn't you read the report? The state's HIV cases are at a record low. It's only taken about thirty years. Our efforts to educate the public about prevention is working. Maryland has finally reported under a thousand new cases. That's great news. One day, we'll get it under a hundred."

Zeke walked farther into the room and made himself comfortable in a chair. "You okay, man?"

Chaz rubbed the back of his neck and rolled the muscles in his back. "Sleep and rest deprived, but yeah. I think when my granddaughter senses my frustration, she rests her head on my chest as if to calm me down." *Now who was ministering the therapy?* he mused.

"Such a princess. Hey, you got a few minutes?"

"Sure." Chaz frowned and eyed his friend. "What's up? Everything okay?"

"Better than okay." Zeke clutched his hands together and displayed a goofy grin.

"What's going—wait a minute. Does this have to do with Judith?" Chaz had a suspicíon but would wait for Zeke to confirm it.

"I'm going to ask Judith to marry me."

"What?" Chaz stood in shock. When realization hit, he rounded his desk to pump Zeke's hand in congratulations. "Wow." He shook his head. "If I knew that you two were getting that serious, I'd have charged you a finder's fee."

Zeke grunted. "I'd gladly pay it. I love her, and she loves me." His phone alerted him to a text, and when he looked at it, Chaz guessed the sender.

"Go on, man. Talk to you later. Congrats." He patted Zeke on the shoulder as he walked out of Chaz's office without a backward glance.

Chaz stroked his chin. Marry? He exhaled. No children, no grandchildren, no ex-wife. No complications.

You don't have any either, a voice whispered, *unless you make things complicated.*

Chapter 29

"Welcome to the Whittington B&B," Tabitha said as she parked in her driveway, where colorful flower beds were swollen in bloom bordered each side. "You'll be sequestered in Aunt Tweet's old room for your privacy."

Closing her eyes, Kym inhaled deeply the fragrance of the flowers. "I love being here in the spring." She opened her eyes and stepped out. "I'm glad I didn't cancel."

She admired the snow-white Bradford pear trees that dotted the landscape with pops of wild plum dogwood trees mingled throughout. This was the cozy, historic neighborhood Kym grew up in as a child.

"See, told ya." Tabitha stuck out her tongue as she unstrapped and lifted Little Marcus out of his car seat. She kissed the top of his curly hair.

Kym grabbed her two suitcases. She sighed. "I miss Chaz already."

"You are banned from talking about him while you're here. He's a phantom boyfriend as far as I know, since since we haven't seen him."

"Would a phantom boyfriend give me this?" Kym lifted her necklace from Chaz.

Tabitha's eyes widened, and her lips formed an O, but no words came out right away. "Whoa. I saw you wearing that at Christmas and assumed you treated yourself." She bobbed her head in appreciation before turning around to insert the key into her door while shifting her son on a hip, then glanced back. "You said that Chauncy would be there for two months, right?"

Kym gave her sister the side-eye. "Now who's talking about him?"

"Nope, I asked about *his* granddaughter. There's a difference." Tabitha shrugged.

"According to my calculations, Chauncy has about five weeks left in Baltimore." Kym exhaled. "Two weeks after that, I hope to walk across the stage, if I get the dissertation done and it meets the committee's expectations."

"Number one, Rachel and I expect our big sister to strut across the stage. Next, you'll pass. That's why you're here. We'll be your impromptu board."

Right. Kym watched as Tabitha cuddled her son and Kym yearned to experience that as a mother. She had never found the perfect man who made her want that until now.

Once inside the house, Kym rested her things at the foot of the stairs and made her way to the kitchen. Her sister had stuffed the refrigerator with premade sandwiches, salads, wraps, and more. "What's all this?"

"Let the pampering begin. Food is fuel. Plus, you forgot, I have a husband with a hearty appetite and a brother-in-law, Demetrius, who consumes leftovers." The baby stirred in her arms but didn't wake. "I'm going to take this little fella up to his own bed to finish his nap. You might want to take a nap yourself so you can be more productive."

Kym yawned. "I think I will." Coming home had been the best decision. She would be taken care of physically and mentally.

"Rachel's flight gets in later," Tabitha said as she walked toward the stairwell. "We won't disturb you until you open the door. That will be our cue to storm your room." She grinned.

Hours later, Kym woke refreshed and ready to tackle her mission. She didn't move but stared at the ceiling. She'd rather daydream about Chaz or hear his voice, but that would be counterproductive.

Time to get busy. Her research question and proposal section drafts were done, so she had moved to the design and methodology chapter. After taking a deep breath, Kym climbed off the bed and situated her laptop on the desk near the front window overlooking the historic neighborhood that had charmed her as a child. She painstakingly began to compile all the research articles for her literature review section. Without realizing it, she had been at the task for hours.

After day one, Kym and her sisters fell into a routine. She would wake early and take a stroll through the neighborhood, which featured a park, pond, and fountain. It was serene, and the exercise cleared her head to work and ushered an atmosphere of quiet time to talk to Jesus before she FaceTimed Chaz.

"Morning, beautiful. I'm jealous, you're there and I'm here," he would often tease her. His lips curled into a handsome smile, but the sadness in his eyes conveyed he was half-serious.

Before they ended their brief morning chat, they would pray for each other's day and close out with reciting Genesis 31:49.

Late one evening, Kym hit a roadblock. The graphics chart on her spreadsheet that outlined the data in her analysis/discussion chapter wasn't working; the conversion came off as amateurish. Marcus overheard her frustration in a conversation with Tabitha, and he suggested a friend who was a computer whiz. She had nothing to lose, so she emailed him the information. Days later, the result was amazing.

"This guy does impressive work!" Kym was amazed. "How much do I owe him?"

"He owed me a favor." Marcus grinned, then disappeared into the kitchen to raid the refrigerator for dinner leftovers.

Each day, Kym tackled a portion of her project. Although she had started to compile all her sources, she had only accumulated twenty pages, a far cry from the finish line. There were at least ten more research studies she had to cite.

Kym had to step up her game. No longer could she put off finishing the literature review chapter. By the time she completed her dissertation, it would easily be a two-hundred page manuscript.

On the fourth day, Kym was locked in the zone and barely left her room. The intense concentration kept thoughts of Chaz at bay, wondering how he was faring and if Chauncy was having a good day. The only brief interruptions were her sisters bringing snacks and meals to her bedroom.

The next morning, Kym reappeared and announced she needed a distraction. "My head is going in circles from this intense focus." She exhaled.

"Sounds like spa day to me," Rachel suggested. "I've been waiting for a pedicure."

"I'll call my friend at Magnificent Nails to make an appointment for us to get the works," Tabitha said, and by the afternoon, the sisters had had facials and manicures and were enjoying pedicures with Kym in the middle.

"So you must be feeling confident about the project to take a break," Tabitha commented.

"I do." Kym nodded and gave them a brief overview of what she had done. "I need to get in some practice for feedback from my advisor to make sure I'll be ready to stand nervously before the committee and defend my research question on mobile tutoring."

"Hey." Rachel carefully shifted so as not to disturb the technician's task. "How about doing a dress rehearsal here and save me a trip to Baltimore to listen to your oral presentation? We can be your committee."

"Yeah, to make it more interesting, I'll ask Marcus to invite his brother and a couple of our neighbors over. I'll order food. We'll be an unbiased audience."

Since her sisters appeared eager to help, Kym gave it some thought. The downside was she needed professionals in academia to critique her. Laymen would only pacify her. But at the end of the day, practice was practice. "Okay, sounds like a plan."

Back at the house, Kym took a power nap and woke at the sound of Tabitha's doorbell. She smiled to herself. Mention food and the flock would come.

As if she were about to defend her research in front of the university board, Kym dressed as professionally as she could, borrowing one of Tabitha's many business suits. They weren't always the same size, but after Tabitha had Little Marcus, Kym welcomed her baby sister to the sistah hips society.

She scrutinized her appearance and smiled. "Dr. Knicely." She mimicked the greeting the board chairman gave as he welcomed candidates after the committee reached their decision. Kym grabbed her laptop and walked out of the room.

When she stepped off the last step in the foyer, Kym blinked at the audience awaiting her in the living room. It wasn't a couple of friendly neighbors. There was a cross section from teenagers to seniors. Some still had on suits, coming from work. Talk about pressure to impress these people; Kym was starting to feel it.

Tabitha winked, and Marcus wore an angelic expression, resembling his son, while Rachel gave her a thumbs-up. Demetrius, Marcus's brother, saluted her with his bottled water.

After releasing a deep breath, Kym set up her items. "Good evening. My name is Kym Knicely. I'm a doctoral candidate at Lewis Latimer University in Baltimore. For the past six years, two of them in the master's program, I have documented test scores from grade and middle school students in urban areas who don't have access to after-school tutoring. I'm here to defend my research question on mobile tutoring. The key is one-on-one, even if we have to go where the students are.

"The popularity and the success of pop-up businesses inspired my concept. They swoop into cities, sell their goods for a short time, then head out. Pop-up parties are the latest craze on social media. They draw a crowd in a matter of an hour or less. The Bomb Pop truck rings the bell, and children flock around the bus for goodies. Why not have tutors—grad students—pop up in neighborhoods and offer homework assistance? A young man wants to stay on the basketball team, but he's failing in math…"

To her amazement, Kym held their attention—even the teenagers perked up when she mentioned school activities. She would have to include that in her prepared introduction. "This deficit in learning is not limited to Baltimore." She cited other cities' statistics. "I believe my research answers the question of how to ensure our Black youths are prepared for higher education and beyond."

Once Kym concluded, she took a deep breath and smiled to brace for their comments, if they would give any. A few smiled back. Either they were bored or not impressed. Was her presentation weak? She refrained from gnawing on her lip because of her nerves. "Are there any questions?"

Many arms raised, to Kym's surprise, and she pointed to a teenager who sported a frohawk with gold ringlet highlights. Her makeup was flawless. She was stunning.

"Thank you, Miss Knicely, for working so hard to help people like us. I'm a junior at Normandy Senior High, and I'm struggling in chemistry. What if a student like me needs help with homework every day instead of a couple days a week?" Her thought-provoking question generated a couple of nods.

"The mobile tutoring concept isn't meant to replace programs that are already in place, such as homework help from the reference librarians or after-school tutoring. This program is to encourage and cultivate each student's strengths to master homework complexities and study skills to work independently. Thanks"—she paused and asked the girl's name—"thanks, Chelsea, for the question. The tutors are a springboard to push the students to thrive."

Kym's project received a more intense level of scrutiny than she had expected. Contentment filled her being, and she thanked God for it. An older gentleman who looked as if he should be retired yet wore a gray business suit raised his hand and leaned forward.

"Yes?" Kym nodded.

"Great presentation, young lady, but I'm curious about funding for the program. You mentioned two grants for this research. What about nonprofits and government funding?"

She was impressed her impromptu audience really listened. Kym asked the gentleman's name to respond.

"I'm Dr. Bradford Klines, chancellor emeritus at University of Missouri at St. Louis."

Kym swallowed. *Uh-oh.* Now she felt intimidated as she lifted a brow at Tabitha.

"Our neighbor." Marcus seemed pleased with himself as he squeezed his wife's shoulder.

That made sense, considering the Pasadena Hills neighborhood bordered the campus's property. "Thank you, Dr. Klines, for your presence. To answer your question, government intervention isn't always the solution to our problems. Making this program a part of college and university curricula will give our future educators one-on-one experience with students in struggling communities. My data represents lives, and every number has a name, face, and story. I want teachers to remember no two students' situations are the same, no matter how similar the zip code."

Dr. Kline seemed satisfied. When he clapped, the others followed. Kym was embarrassed and elated at the same time. She curtsied to hide her nervousness as she accepted accolades and well-wishes.

"This calls for a celebration!" Rachel said later after everyone was gone, and Tabitha agreed.

Marcus groaned. "Oh boy. Sounds like a shopping spree in the making." He lifted his son out of Tabitha's arms and kissed her cheek. "We're out of here."

Saturday morning, the trio hit the stores at West County Mall and the Galleria. "Let's stop at Jilly's for cupcakes," Tabitha suggested with a wide grin.

Rachel smacked her lips. "My mouth is watering for one of those twisted pink velvet cupcakes, but I might change my mind if their monthly special looks scrumptious."

"Still the sweet tooth." Kym shook her head. "This has been a good day. I'm glad I came home. I've been productive, practiced my presentation, got pampered, and now I'm about to indulge big time."

"Which you nailed, by the way!" With one hand on the wheel, Tabitha lifted her other hand up for a high five from Rachel, who was sitting in the back, while Kym had snagged the passenger seat up front.

"It's one of the reasons why we're celebrating. Woot! Woot!" Rachel giggled as they parked and strolled across the small parking lot to Jilly's Cupcake Bar & Café.

While Tabitha and Rachel perused the selections behind a glass counter, Kym ordered: "One Bee Sting please." Her mouth watered for the vanilla cake filled with honey lemon curd, but it was the cream cheese icing, toasted almonds, and other delicious secret toppings that made the supersized cupcake her favorite.

After her purchase, Kym chose a café table near a window, facing

Delmar Boulevard. They joined her with carryout boxes containing multiple cupcakes.

"What?" Rachel beamed with no shame. "One for now, one for later."

"I better not come home without a Jilly's cupcake for Marcus." Tabitha also brought scoops of ice cream. They gave thanks, then attacked their treats. "Thinking back to last evening, you commanded the crowd. I'm so proud of you. You fooled me saying you hadn't finished all parts of the dissertation. You were polished, knowledgeable, and engaging."

Kym couldn't stop smiling. "I had to bluff my way out of a few questions, but I made a mental note to address them before I present to the committee. Why didn't you tell me your neighbor was a chancellor emeritus?" She gave Tabitha the side-eye.

"Why spoil the fun? It made it more interesting." Tabitha chuckled.

"Since we're celebrating and all…" Rachel cleared her throat. "Nicholas and I are having a baby!" She grinned from ear to ear. Tears filled her eyes.

"What!" Kym and Tabitha screamed at the same time and scrambled to their feet. Their excitement startled other customers.

"Sorry. Our sister's having a baby!" Tabitha yelled, and some patrons clapped, others cheered and shouted their congratulations.

They took turns hugging Rachel as tears spilled from their eyes. "I am so thankful to the Lord Jesus for these blessings. So thankful," she repeated as they settled back in their seats.

"Y'all talking about me holding stuff. Please, I can't believe you kept this!" Kym fussed.

"Nope, this trip was all about you, Sis. Plus, I wanted to wait until the doctor confirmed it. Nicholas and I celebrated with a moment of praise, worship, and thanksgiving." Rachel shook her head. Awe radiated from her face. "Of course, my doctor says I'm high risk because I'm a cancer survivor and will have to be monitored closely. Hold on." Rachel pulled her phone out of her purse and tapped a number and put the call on speaker.

"Hey, baby," Nicholas's deep voice came over.

"Congratulations," Kym and Tabitha sang in unison.

Nicholas laughed. "You two are just finding out. I'm surprised my sweet little wife didn't explode before now. There are no words to describe our happiness. We already praised God for this blessing."

Kym reached across the table and grabbed her sisters' hands and squeezed. The moment was surreal as she happened to glance out the window and a familiar face came into focus. She watched the guy enter the café while her sisters finished chatting with Nicholas.

"Hey." Tabitha shoved her. "Nicholas said he's praying for you to ace your diss…" She followed the direction of Kym's eyes. "Whoa. Who's that? No wonder the cat's got your tongue."

Kym shushed Tabitha. "I think that's Chaz's son Geoffrey. They call him Gee. He's a carbon copy of his father." She squinted again. "I'm going to ask him." Her heart pumped faster, and the hairs on Kym's arms tingled as she got up and approached the tall, built man. He even stood erect like Chaz. "Excuse me." The young man turned around, and she stared at the mirror image of Chaz. "Gee?"

"Yes." He blinked and gave her a curious expression.

"I'm Kym Knicely, a friend of your father's."

Realization hit, and Gee's jaw dropped. His words were slow to expel, then it was rapid-fire, one question after another. "Wow. My dad has good taste. What are you doing here? He said you lived in Baltimore, where my daughter is. Have you met Chauncy? How is she?"

The composed man was flustered. "Hold on. Let me get my wife. She's supposed to be on bed rest, but she was craving Jilly's and came along for the ride. I'm sure she'll want to meet you." He hurried outside.

While he was gone, the sisters scooted to a larger table. Kym watched as Gee's swagger took him to a car where he opened the passenger door. He leaned in and must have given her a recap, then helped her out.

"She's pretty…and pregnant like me." Rachel's excitement blossomed. She might have ended the call without telling her husband goodbye.

Kym was really going to be outnumbered. "You are not very pregnant. She is."

"Yep, like father, like son, has good taste in women," Tabitha added.

Gee's wife looked uncomfortable with each step. Kym felt sorry for her. When she entered the café, her face lit when her eyes connected with Kym.

After the introductions were made, Gee made sure his wife was situated before going to place their order. They congratulated Lana, and the talk turned to babies—Tabitha showed pictures of Little Marcus, and Rachel whipped out her phone and showed her ultrasound at eight weeks, which prompted Lana to do the same from her recent doctor's visit a few days earlier.

Gee returned from the counter with Lana's desired cupcake. He grunted at the topic of discussion but smiled lovingly at Lana. Next, he snagged a nearby chair, straddled it, and joined them. "Have you met our baby?"

Kym lowered her head, embarrassed to tell them. "Yes…but she doesn't like me."

"She takes a little to make friends, so please, don't take it personal. Chauncy's so sweet, and we do a lot of fun activities to help her develop social skills. She has heightened sensitivity to touch and taste. I don't think she likes green things. Why green?" Lana shrugged. "We don't know."

"And I was rocking my green dress." Kym groaned.

Gee huffed. "My dad should have told you about Chauncy's uniqueness."

"Yes, Chaz should have told me a lot of things," Kym agreed, "but when I showed up wearing it, he could have at least given me a heads-up about Chauncy's possible reaction. My next misstep was that I came with an enormous basket of goodies, but she might as well have thrown it out the door. The Build-a—"

Lana gritted her teeth. "She doesn't like the feel of any rough material, like certain knits or fur."

Kym shook her head, not feeling as rejected as before. "It would be nice to have a dos and don'ts list," she stated. "Chaz told me afterward she liked the jigsaw puzzle."

"A perfect gift because she's obsessed with taking things apart and putting them back together over and over," Gee explained. "I wouldn't be surprised if my daughter grows up to be some kind of engineer."

"My specialty." Rachel lifted her hand and prompted Lana and Gee to do the same for a high five.

"Once Lana delivers the twins by the end of April, Chauncy will finally be coming back home. We miss her. I don't see how my wife has any room left for our sons to grow." Gee's expression reminded Kym so much of Chaz. "We better go so you can rest." He stood and helped his wife to her feet.

"They seem like a nice couple," Tabitha said after they left.

"Yes, they are. He's so attentive, reminds me of Chaz." Kym struggled with her thoughts. "I want to know more about Chauncy's condition, but honestly, I haven't had the time, preparing for my dissertation. It will be a shame for her to leave without her accepting me."

"I can overload you with anything you want to know about autism." Tabitha pulled her tablet from her oversize purse. "I'm sure there are a lot of successful people who have mastered their condition to achieve their goals in life."

Kym and Rachel exchanged knowing looks as their sister slipped into the pharmaceutical-rep zone.

"So far, the FDA has approved only one drug for children—Risperidone—but it's only effective with behavioral therapies."

"That's promising." Rachel nodded.

"Yeah..." Tabitha twisted her mouth in deliberation. "Chauncy has to be between five and sixteen years old."

Kym stuck her fist under her chin in thought. "She's only four. Hold all that info, Tab. Let me get through my oral presentation first."

"All right, but I still say you need to step up your game and don't let that therapist get the upper hand with your man's granddaughter," Rachel reminded her. "Food isn't the only way to a man's heart. So are his children, or in this case, his granddaughter."

"Noted. Now, let's go." Kym stood to lead the way to the door.

Chapter 30

"Hey, Dad. You'll never guess who I ran into today," Gee said over the phone. "Man, she was hot."

Although Chaz welcomed the call from his son, he didn't like hearing his son speak of another woman in those terms. He hoped Gee wasn't thinking about cheating. "Son, keep your eyes on your own wife and the mother of your children." His tone came out like a growl.

"But she was gorgeous, Pops—"

"Gee, I'm warning you," Chaz cut him off. "I'll disown you as my son if you step outside your marriage vows." He was seething until he heard Lana's chuckles. "Oh, you're in on this too, huh? Sorry, I'm too pooped to play after working with your daughter on her language exercises."

"Thanks, Pops, for having my back," Lana said in the background. "I told Gee not to joke, but he couldn't resist."

"Always. When you became my son's wife, you became my daughter."

"Well, we met your Kym Knicely this afternoon," Lana said in a teasing voice.

"Really?" Chaz perked up and relaxed. "Where did you see my lady love? How did you know it was her?"

"I didn't at first," Gee answered. "She walked up to me at Jilly's Cupcakes. Apparently she thinks you and I look alike."

That statement made Chaz puff out his chest. He couldn't be prouder of both of his sons.

"Nah, I think Pops is cuter." Lana fell into a fit of giggles until she cried out in pain.

The men reacted at the same time. "What's wrong?"

"Your sons kicked their mommy."

Gee and Chaz sighed in unison. "Can't wait to meet my boys."

Chaz's heart warmed. That was the son he reared, a loving and caring and faithful husband to his wife. Although Chaz and Valerie had divorced, infidelity didn't play a part. "Now, back to Kym."

"When she returns, do me and Lana a favor: give her more info about Chauncy, so she won't feel like she's always striking out with my daughter. I can tell her feelings were hurt, and I blame you, Dad."

"Excuse me?" Chaz didn't like Gee's tone. "Now, hold on, Son. How did I know what color she was going to wear or that she was going to bring a stuffed animal? I'm learning new things every day myself."

"Rearing Chauncy requires teamwork, and I think she wants to be part of the team, especially if you're serious about her, which I hope you are. Kym is intelligent, caring, and too gorgeous for my old man. We want you both to be happy."

He appreciated their support of his relationship, he mused as he craned his neck into Chauncy's room. She had mastered putting together the jigsaw puzzle Kym gave her and taking it apart. The best gift ever. Chaz paused. His son was right: Kym was the best gift God gave him since his divorce.

On Monday afternoon, Chaz left work an hour early to run errands before getting Chauncy. After speaking with Gee on Saturday, he was more than ready for Kym to come home. He was so ready to propose, but there was only one small problem. She was three and a half feet tall. Chauncy was thriving under Debra's therapy, but she hadn't stopped opening doors looking for her parents. It was a ritual repeated at least twice a week.

Chaz wanted to take Kym out to celebrate their love, her accomplishment, and their future together as husband and wife. He couldn't imagine a sitter, even one trained to care for a child with special needs, handling Chauncy if she acted out. Her environment was still too new. Maybe he was being overprotective.

"I can hold off a little longer," he told himself, but nothing would stop him from being in the room when Kym defended her research question and watching the committee bestow the coveted PhD after her name. That, he didn't plan to miss.

All the progress Debra had made with Chauncy on aggression at playtime had lapsed on Sunday. They missed church because his granddaughter refused to bathe. She kept pointing to the tub as if it were the enemy. A meltdown ensued, and Chaz didn't know how to remedy that as he tried a process of elimination concerning what could have caused her reaction.

Chaz was at wit's end to understand why she enjoyed bath time the day before but screamed today, then started kicking him when she saw the bathtub. "Lord, help me." It bugged him all night as he paced from room to room and always returned to the guest bathroom by where Chauncy slept.

Finally, he discovered the culprit was some grainy residue left in the bottom of the tub that was barely seen by the eye. He rinsed it again, but Chauncy hadn't forgotten, so since yesterday, she had only consented to a sponge bath. That threw off her nap time, playtime, and learning schedule.

He chided himself for counting the weeks until Chauncy left. This was his granddaughter—his only grandchild for the time being. If he didn't have patience for her disorder, how could he expect others to? He prayed and asked God for new mercies and patience to begin that workweek.

Chaz stretched as if he were warming up for yoga instruction. That didn't lessen his yearning for a nap, but he couldn't leave Chauncy unsupervised. He also craved spending time with Kym, who would return to Baltimore tomorrow—finally.

The next afternoon as he was about to knock on Debra's classroom door at the institute, he stepped back and watched his granddaughter's interaction with Debra and the other three children. She patiently repeated the rules of a game over and over. "When playing with a toy, we have to share." She demonstrated passing a soft toy from one child to another.

He folded his arms and observed. He repented for his thoughts about Chauncy leaving. Despite the adjustment, Chauncy had thrived in Baltimore with the one-on-one attention. Aside from Gee and Lana worrying about their firstborn, the couple was relaxing, waiting for their arrival of twin boys.

Debra looked over her shoulder and saw Chaz. She stood and waved him inside. As he walked farther into the room, he didn't take his eyes off Chauncy. He would never grow accustomed to the lack of emotions on her face. There was no hint for him to know whether she was happy to see him or sad because she had a bad day—no twinkle in her eyes or curl of her lips—just her blank expression.

"You're early." Debra smiled and clapped. "Chauncy had a great day. Actually, everybody in her group did. Social interaction has to make sense to them."

Chaz listened as he squatted before Chauncy and waited for her to greet him. She didn't disappoint.

"PawPaw."

He took her hand and gathered her jacket. "Let's go, sweetie pie."

Chapter 31

Kym had the best spring break ever. While away, she completed her dissertation and had a practice run with critical observers. She had been so excited, she called Chaz in tears.

It had scared him until she could form the words to explain it. He had been relieved but took her to task for adding more gray strands to his mustache. "I'm sorry, but this has been years in the making."

"I'm proud of you, and I'm sure your late aunt would be too."

Touched that he remembered Aunt Tweet, the only words that came to mind were how much she loved him. "See you in a few hours."

"And I hope your flight is early. You were gone too long." Chaz took her to task, but she relished hearing his frustration.

Next, she emailed her advisor and asked for a meeting to review her evidence and give another practice of her oral defense.

Soon, she and Rachel said their goodbyes before Marcus stored their luggage in his car. At Lambert airport, Rachel was about to check their bags, but Kym intervened and asked a skycap to assist. "You shouldn't be lifting anything. You're going to have a baby."

"You're making too much fuss. I'm healthy."

"I'll get Nicholas on speed dial if you give me any problems," she threatened and chuckled at her sister's sudden repentant expression.

Once the sisters cleared the security checkpoint, they scanned the board for the location of their gates, which were in opposite directions.

Kym's eyes filled with tears as she hugged Rachel and stepped back. "My heart is so full that God saw fit to spare your life. I can never tell the Lord thank You enough. Now, life is thriving within you, and I praise God for that. Please take it easy, Super Woman. Don't think I won't call Nicholas and put him in check if he doesn't put the brakes on you."

Rachel sniffed. "My bossy big sister. You just can't help giving me marching orders." They embraced again. "I'm so glad you accomplished your mission in school and that love found you. I'm going to sit out on traveling for the public presentation, but if the Lord wills, Nick and I will be there when you strut—remember the sassy strut Aunt Tweet taught us—across that stage."

"Of course." Kym rolled her eyes in jest. "Have a safe flight, and text me when you get home." As Rachel turned to leave, Kym squeezed both her hands to stop her. "Let's pray." Bowing her head, Kym closed her eyes and recited Genesis 31:49, the Scripture that had become synonymous with Chaz.

"Thanks, Sis." Rachel kissed Kym on both checks. They were reluctant to wave goodbye, but they did and continued toward their assigned gates.

Kym snagged a seat and sighed. *I love family*, she thought, reflecting on the time with her sisters, not realizing she had spoken aloud.

"Me too," a passenger mumbled next to her, which caused her to face him.

He grinned, and after a quick glance at her ring finger, he introduced himself. "Hi, I'm Trace Watkins. Are you flying to Baltimore?"

Kym groaned inwardly. "I am, but excuse me, I have to make a call." She FaceTimed Chaz.

His face lit up. "Hey, beautiful, please tell me you're not going to miss your flight." She shook her head. "That's what I want to hear. Chauncy and I will be there to pick you up."

"I miss you," she said, not meant for only his ears.

"Miss you too, baby. Have a safe flight, and don't talk to strangers!"

"I won't." She gave him a mock salute before she ended the call.

Trace cleared his throat. "Sorry, I meant no harm."

"Forgiven." Kym dismissed the stranger and reached for her tablet to read a novel.

As promised, Chaz and Chauncy were at the Thurgood Marshall airport, standing right outside the terminal. His eyes twinkled as he met her halfway with Chauncy beside him, holding balloons that were attached to a band around the girl's wrist. She also wore kiddie earphones.

Chauncy stayed close to his side as he engulfed Kym in a warm hug. A hug that said I missed you. A hug that conveyed how much he loved her. Chaz delivered a brief kiss before giving her the bouquet. "The next time you travel, I'm your escort."

"You'll get no protests from me." Kym blinked, then squatted. "Hi, Chauncy."

The child inched forward. "Hi," then scooted back.

Kym stood, shocked, and looked at Chaz. "I'm impressed."

"Debra has been working on her verbal skills, and I've been reenforcing them at home."

"That's wonderful." Now would be a good time for Kym to check out this Debra chick, but it would have to be *after* her dissertation presentation. In case there was drama, Kym didn't want any distraction to occupy her mind.

Kym had barely cleared her front door when Judith called her. "Are you back home yet?"

"Yep, Chaz just dropped me off." Kym kicked off her shoes and rested her keys on the table.

"It's taken you for-ev-er to get back."

"You too, huh?" Kym chuckled. "You sound like Chaz, but the trip was well worth it. I got my dissertation done! Praise the Lord." She pumped a fist in the air. Thinking about the accomplishment made her tear up again. "What's up?"

"I'm on my way over."

Kym's heart raced with worry. "Is everything okay?"

"I'll tell you when I get there." *Click.*

What is going on? What happened? Fearful thoughts invaded Kym's mind. Judith lived at least twenty minutes away without traffic. Gnawing on her lips, Kym began to pace the floor as she called Judith back and got her voicemail. *Grrr.* What could be so grave that Judith couldn't wait until she saw Kym at school in the morning?

"Lord, let everything be well with her," Kym prayed as she rebuttoned her blouse and slid her feet back into her shoes. She thought about calling Chaz, but she didn't want to worry him—like Judith was worrying her—without all the details.

She spied the clock in frustration and blamed the devil for stealing her joy. Kym had come home happy, and now something bad had happened. She closed her eyes and prayed. When her doorbell chimed, Kym practically leaped off the barstool and almost tripped over her own feet to answer.

Bracing herself for the unknown, she opened the door, expecting her friend to collapse with grief or to be in hysterics. Instead, her jaw dropped at the silly grin on Judith's face. She must have changed her brand of makeup, because she looked different, for lack of a better description.

Judith stuck out her hand, and Kym slapped it away. "What is wrong with you scaring me like someone died?"

A panicked expression flashed on Judith's face. "Someone died?"

"I don't know. You tell me." Kym shifted her stance and crossed her arms. "What's the 911 emergency?"

Harrumphing, Judith pushed past Kym and twirled around. "I came over here to show you my engagement ring, which you haven't even given it one glance, because you're too busy chewing me out."

"What? Engaged!" Kym slammed the door and grabbed Judith's hand. The diamond on her fourth finger was brilliant. She screamed and jumped up, almost lifting her friend off the ground. They squealed together and continued to bounce as if they were on a trampoline.

When Judith stopped shouting and started laughing, Kym screamed again. "Congratulations. When did this happen? How did it happen? Were you surprised?"

Kym's vision blurred with moisture. "Congratulations, sis. I'm so happy for you." She scrunched her nose playfully. "I leave for a week and a day, and you're practically a married woman. I had no idea you two had become that serious," she rambled on, not giving Judith time to answer. "It's only been, what, three months?"

"Three months and a week. We both knew what we wanted."

"Wow." Kym walked over to her chair and collapsed. "I never

imagined you and Zeke would beat me and Chaz. When my turn comes, hopefully soon, I'm going to pay you back and scare you silly." She patted her chest.

"It's not my fault you misinterpreted the excitement in my voice for doom and gloom. The two don't sound alike. Plus, you and Chaz's life experiences are different from mine and Zeke's. We're younger, don't have children, and we've never been married. With Chaz, you have the blended family scenario going on, so you two can't jump the broom so fast."

"Whatever, enough about that. Tell me every detail about how Zeke proposed. All the details you don't want me to know."

"I think we're going to need a cup of tea." Judith waved her hand in the air with a fake British accent.

Kym did her bidding, and minutes later, they were sitting at her counter, sipping an herbal blend. "Talk," she ordered.

"Zeke proposed to me Friday night. He said it was to celebrate the end of my spring break. We dressed up—"

"Okay, you're taking too long. Give me the highlights. The where and how, and were you surprised?"

Judith jutted her chin and gave a humph. "He took me to Dalesio's. Zeke has always been free with his compliments, but there was something about that night." She paused and smiled. "The intensity of his looks was like fire that warmed my soul. The words that poured from his heart were like a wet towel that he squeezed every drop of moisture from." She ran out of breath.

"Whew." Kym fanned. "Go on."

"I was mesmerized. Instead of waiting before the dessert to propose, like I've seen them do on TV, he got on one knee after we placed our orders. His words were so sweet as he asked me to be his wife for life. And he wanted me to wear my ring now, so he could imagine that we were out to dinner as a married couple."

"Wow-wow. All I got to say is Chaz better bring it." Kym laughed, hoping her day would come soon.

Chapter 32

This was it! The big day a week later, Kym woke before her alarm. Throughout her morning regimen, Kym's heart pounded as if she were running on a treadmill. She showered and dressed but was too anxious to eat as she sat in her kitchen and read her Bible to calm her nerves.

Tabitha's ringtone interrupted her. "You've got this," she said by way of a greeting. "Your impromptu presentation you did here was on point."

"Right." Kym took a deep breath, then grabbed her car keys to go. Her sister had pumped her up such that her heart danced to an imaginary salsa beat.

Then her doorbell rang. Opening the door to Chaz's presence with Chauncy at his side warmed her soul. "Morning, baby."

"Morning." She smiled. "What are you doing here?"

"I wanted to see you before you left for the university. No phone call, text, or FaceTime could do it for me today. I came by to tell you not only do I love you, but I'm your biggest fan as you defend your research question.

"Debra had to cancel Chauncy's therapy today for a family emergency, so if I'm not there, you'll know why. But my heart is with you, and so is God's presence." He reached into his pocket and pulled out a square box. "If you feel your confidence shifting during your presentation, I hope one look at this tennis bracelet will remind you that I believe in you."

Kym fingered the necklace he had given her for Christmas and now the bracelet. "Thank you."

"You're welcome." He leaned and kissed her. "I love you." He glanced down at Chauncy, whose eyes were on a sparrow in a nearby tree. "Sweetheart, can you wave goodbye to Miss Kym?"

Chauncy didn't as she focused on the bird as if it were her prey. Chaz shrugged and mouthed, *Sorry*, before he turned around and began to descend the stairs. Kym leaned against the doorjamb and watched him drive away.

A feel-good vibe stayed with her as she drove to work. Kym was minutes from the university when Rachel called and reenforced everything that Tabitha and Chaz had said.

On campus, Judith met her at her office with a card filled with inspiring words. Now, behind closed doors, Kym took a deep breath and rubbed the bracelet wrapped around her small wrist before gathering her tablet and papers. Her advisor had suggested Kym tweak a few things in her introduction, and she had.

Before leaving her office, she grabbed the handouts she'd asked one of the work-study students to print. She knew the drill: relax, stay focused, and only use her notes as backup. Kym had learned that by regularly attend other colleagues' dissertation defenses. The committee would judge Kym based on the clarity of her research and the confidence in her delivery style.

God, You brought me this far. Please don't leave me. In Jesus's name. Amen.

Judith appeared and ran down the list to double-check Kym's preparedness. "Are your PowerPoint slides in order?"

"Yep." Kym swallowed.

"Let's go." Judith matched her step, and the two walked to Devers Hall. The lecture room for the presentation had theater-style seating to hold up to seventy-three occupants.

When they reached their destination, Kym's heart rate accelerated. She wasn't expecting so many people in attendance. Yes, it was open to the public, but what if the committee rejected her presentation? And she had seen it happen. She would rather lick her wounds without so many witnesses.

Her advisor stood to greet her and gave her an assuring nod. Remaining focused, Kym powered up her laptop, then handed each member a hard copy of her dissertation.

After another short, whispered prayer, Kym began with the introduction. "Morning, everyone. I'm Kym Knicely, and the research question I will answer is the title of my dissertation: *Will Mobile Tutoring Close the Educational Gap for Minorities?* The stats show that students' confidence and grades improve when they are enrolled in after-school or community-led tutoring programs. As a graduate student in the masters' program, I received a grant to fund a pilot Teachers on Wheels program where I and other grad students traveled to inner city neighborhoods..."

Kym paced herself with each section. She directed them to the articles she had gathered to support her data. "A recently published study by Brandeis University shows children living in urban areas who lag behind in education will earn less income later in life." She directed the members to another article. "This one points to low student attendance."

She cited ten research studies from other universities and nonprofit agencies. Next, she outlined her method of driving the bus into the same neighborhood twice a week for two hours of tutoring. She pointed to the graphics that tracked each student's improvement as a result of their tutoring assistance. After the analysis, she opened the floor for questioning.

"I commend you for taking on a monumental task. However, I don't see how much impact mobile tutoring can have on a greater number of middle and high schoolers. Are you suggesting this should be a government-sponsored program, such as Parents as Teachers for young children, which has seen success?" Dr. McMillian asked, staring at Kym through wide-rimmed black glasses that reached high on his forehead. Kym's advisor had reiterated that he would be tough.

"This is a program that must be available on a consistent basis, and relying on government funding could be sketchy, although funding is welcomed. Baltimore has thirteen colleges and universities, plus two community colleges. My methodology is well documented so that any administrator in the education department can duplicate the program and introduce it into their curriculum."

She wrapped up her research with the conclusion. "I believe I've answered the research question why implementing mobile tutoring will make a difference." She exhaled and tried to gauge their thoughts from their expressions. Double poker faces—no, quadruple that. They looked downright scary.

"Very nice presentation, Miss Knicely," Dr. Sparrow said. "If you and our audience will take a brief intermission, we'll discuss our thoughts, after which we'll advise you of our decision."

"Of course." Kym nodded at Judith, and they walked out together. "What do you think?" she whispered, her confidence compromised.

"That you nailed it. You were so on point, and the authority of your research was impressive." Her friend rubbed Kym's back and encouraged her to breathe.

In the hall, some of her grad students who had been involved in the project approached and congratulated her on the presentation. There were other teachers from outside colleges in attendance too.

"If I can't persuade them of the validity of this program, then it will fall through the cracks." Kym frowned at the thought.

"You told them there wasn't time to waste, so hopefully that was enough." Judith rallied behind her.

"I guess. Sometimes, all the research available is never enough to convince folks." Kym dabbed at the beads of sweat on her brow.

Finally, Dr. Sparrow opened the door and invited everyone back inside. While observers took their seats, Kym stood before the board. Their faces and body language gave nothing away.

She blinked away the tears in the holding gate. Kym glanced down at her bracelet and exhaled. If the committee didn't agree that she'd answered the research question, she would be heartbroken and devastated for a moment, but she would bounce back eventually and keep pushing.

Was everyone holding their breaths like her as Dr. Sparrow cleared her throat? "Dr. Knicely, welcome…"

The screams in the room were deafening. Kym didn't hear another word as tears flowed. "Aunt Tweet, I did it," she whispered to the wind.

Chaz couldn't be prouder as he sat in on Kym's oral defense presentation. She was confident, convincing, and striking. While she wowed him by her appearance, Kym impressed the committee with her passion and intelligence around her years of research.

If only he could have stayed to let her know he was there, but Chauncy was getting restless. Once he was back to his office, he ordered express delivery of flowers with a note:

Congratulations on your presentation, Professor Dr. Knicely.

Kym seemed surprised when she called to thank him for the flowers hours later. "Chaz, I didn't know you were there! I'll never forget the first time you called me professor."

"Yes, at the airport. That day changed my life—our lives." He took a minute to reflect on seeing the woman again who had invaded his thoughts since he first saw her. "And yes, I was there. The day was too important to you for me not to be, although for a short time. You were magnificent, Dr. Knicely."

She giggled. "Thank you. I'm still in awe. It feels like a dream. I can't thank God enough for His blessing."

"I love you, baby. I love you," Chaz whispered. "I'm hoping you will let me make up all those dates I owe you soon. I can't wait to celebrate this accomplishment with you and so much more."

"Promises, promises. You better keep them," she said, teasing him.

"I plan to." When they ended the call, Chaz snickered. He couldn't wait.

Less than a week later, Chaz got an early morning wake-up call. "Pops, you have two new grandsons. Lana delivered a few hours ago."

"Yes! Congratulations, Son!" Chaz choked and asked about his daughter-in-law.

"She's happy that it's over, tired, and says she wants you to bring Chauncy home this weekend."

"You're kidding, right?" Chaz couldn't believe her request. "I have no problem bringing your little angel home, but Lana's still in the hospital. Why don't you wait until you two are settled, then I'll book the tickets?"

Gee sighed. "She's not going to like your answer, Pops."

"Well, you tell your wife that's an order from her dad." Chaz yawned.

"Now, kiss my grandsons"—he smiled—"for me. I need to get some rest. I'm on Chauncy's schedule, and no telling if she'll wake up before the alarm or not."

"A warning to my wise father. Lana isn't going to want to wait much longer," Gee advised.

"I'm sure. Night." Chaz rolled over.

The next morning, he noticed more gray hair in his mustache as he scrutinized his reflection in the mirror. How was Lana going to manage three children? His granddaughter was a handful just when he monitored her activities, when she was quiet or he was watching her rearrange things, like her socks or her utensils.

A few days later, before Chaz could call and check on the newborns, Gee called him. "Pops..." His voice was weak.

Chaz paused preparing breakfast for him and Chauncy. "What's wrong?"

"It's Lana. She's struggling mentally and physically." Gee sounded flustered. "The doctor thinks she might be experiencing postpartum stress or something like that."

"Oh no." Chaz's heart ached for Lana. "Is there anything I can do? Bringing Chauncy home now isn't an option. She's adjusting, although she still opens doors looking for her mommy and daddy. I've also seen progress with her therapy. She can stay with PawPaw a little longer. Let's take it week by week. I don't care if it's another month. I want to make sure Lana is okay. Plus, that'll give Kym more time to spend with Chauncy. You know she's a doctor now?"

"No. Tell her congratulations for me. Dad, if I haven't told you in a while, I love you and thank you for being the best Pops a son could ever ask for. If there was a grandfather-of-the-year competition, you would win that too."

Chaz wasn't expecting the accolades. It took a few minutes to compose his emotions. "Thanks, Gee. I couldn't ask for better sons, although I live in the same city with your brother and would like to see him more."

"Hey, cut him some slack. He's in residency, Pops. He's making you—us—proud."

Chaz nodded. "You're right. Debra told me he has stopped by the institute a couple of times to see his niece."

Since Chauncy was going to be with him indefinitely, Chaz didn't know how long he could wait to propose to Kym. He had a solid track record as a father with his sons. Chaz prayed he could hold that record with another set of children.

Chapter 33

Kym was ecstatic when Chaz called to say Lana had given birth to the twin boys but saddened days later to hear about her possible postpartum depression. Rachel came to mind. What complications would her sister experience? She had been through so much already.

"Lana wants me to bring Chauncy home on the next flight out of Baltimore."

"I can imagine." Kym twisted her lips in thought. "But do you think that's a good idea?"

"No, it's not. I understand they miss their daughter, but I suggested letting Chauncy stay longer until they can get settled," Chaz told her.

She had never met such a considerate man. "You, Chaz Banks, are the most selfless person I know."

"I'm trying to do what's best." He sounded frustrated. "So it's okay with you if Chauncy stays a while longer? I mean"—he rushed on—"I know we haven't had too much us time, and it's not fair to you."

"I don't have any say in your family matters, but thank you for asking." Kym fingered the necklace dangling from her neck. "I would do the same for my sisters if they needed help." She wanted to soothe his concerns all the while thinking about her sister again. "Maybe I'll go see Rachel."

"Is she sick?" Chaz didn't hide the concern in his voice.

"She's been having bouts of morning sickness going into her second trimester." As the big sister, Kym needed to step up to the plate. If her little sister gave her any pushback, Kym would get Nicholas on board. "Yeah, I think I'm going."

"All right, Professor Knicely. When you book your flight, let me know, and I'll take to you to the airport and wait impatiently for you to come back."

"Thank you. When I get back, we can go out to dinner with Chauncy. I want to include her." With more free time, Kym had started to read up on autism. After scanning one website after another, she had experienced information overload. *Whew.*

Once they said their goodbyes, Kym called Rachel. "Hey, Sis. How you feeling today?"

"Not any better than yesterday, but I know it will eventually pass. *Ugh.*" She groaned.

From the sound of it, Rachel probably hadn't left bed all day. Perfect timing for a sister visit to Nashville. "You need a babysitter, and I've decided to take a long weekend to come and babysit."

Rachel mustered a weak laugh. "Wrong city. The baby in the family is in St. Louis. Tab won't turn down a sitter."

"Not happening." Kym shook her head. "Tabitha has in-laws who would fly into town at a moment's notice for that."

"I have in-laws too, close you know, and we really like each other." That was an understatement. Nicholas's parents loved their daughters-in-love, as they referred to Rachel. "If I ask for anything, Mom Adams will be here faster than a pizza deliverywoman."

Kym twisted her lips. "Mm-hmm. You're not talking your way out of this. Tell your husband to have the spare bedroom ready for me."

"We just saw each other not long along. Plus, we'll see each other at your graduation," Rachel said weakly. "Will those excuses work?"

"Nope. Aunt Tweet left us with more inheritance than we could spend, so if I want to hop on a plane every weekend, you can't stop me. Where's Nicholas?"

"My beautiful wife is stubborn and doesn't want to bother anybody," her husband shouted in the background. "You're always welcome here, Sis."

"Ha! Thank you. You have just been checkmated, Rach." Kym giggled. She couldn't wait to experience the love of a husband who would overrule her when he felt it was best for her. *Pamper me!* "Thanks, Nicholas. I'll call you with my flight information. Love you guys."

"Fine," Rachel said in a stronger voice. "Since you two double-teamed me, Nicholas, I want a foot massage every night."

"You got it, babe," Kym heard him say tenderly.

"Isn't he sweet?" Rachel had more energy. "But you, Big Sister, should plan on staying for the rest of my pregnancy. Tabitha didn't give me fair warning about this part."

"Nope." Kym laughed. "I'm only staying three days. I'll fly out of Baltimore after my Thursday class and get back before my first class on Monday."

"That works…thanks, so much. Love you."

"Love you back. Bye." Kym ended the call, booked her flight, and started packing for nurse duty. The last time she had helped take care of Rachel was during her chemotherapy. Those were dark days, but God… only God. She shook her head to dismiss that uncertain time in their lives. Now, instead of fearing the death of her younger sister, Kym was rejoicing because of the new life growing inside Rachel.

On Thursday afternoon, Kym's plane landed at the Nashville airport. Nicholas was waiting with a bouquet. "Hey, Sis. The flowers are for you because my wife said I better not come to the airport empty-handed for one of her sisters." He snickered. "It was balloons or flowers."

Kym laughed as they exchanged a hug. "Sounds like she's feeling better."

Nicholas rocked his head from side to side. "She has her moments, from throwing up to wanting everything we don't have in the house. The clerks at the grocery store know me by name. Rachel won't be half as stubborn with you here. I can't say thank you enough for coming."

"That's what family is for," she said as they walked together toward baggage claim. Once at the house, Kym headed straight to the master bedroom where Rachel was sleeping. She looked too thin as far as Kym was concerned. "I'm going to fix one of Aunt Tweet's favorite recipes to fatten up this mommy-to-be."

A low birth weight was one of the risks for newborns of cancer survivors, and that stat was in the back of Kym's mind as she prepared chicken and wild rice soup. She was determined to get nourishment to Rachel's baby.

When her sister stirred from a nap, Kym was waiting with a food tray, which she situated comfortably in front of Rachel after they hugged. Kym stretched out on the lounger and monitored how much she ate while studying her. Her baby sister had grown up.

Between sips, Rachel chatted away. "It's surreal."

Kym frowned. "What do you mean?"

"A few years ago, I didn't know if any of this would be possible, but God stepped in, and now I'm beginning my twelfth week." She mustered up a smile. The first one Kym had seen since she arrived.

Kym's eyes misted. "God is awe. I'm putting my order in for a girl, so I can have a niece and a nephew."

"You can have your own daughters," Rachel suggested. "Little Marcus needs a playmate, but honestly, I don't care about the sex. I want a healthy baby." She rubbed her stomach. "Every night, Nicholas lays his hands on my tummy, and we pray. I think it's romantic."

Her brother-in-law might as well have Jesus on speed dial when he prayed, because the power was in the midst. "Oh, I think so too. Before Chaz or I fly out, we whisper a prayer together."

"A godly man is sexy, ain't he?" Rachel gave a soft laugh. "What's the latest on you and Chaz? How's Lana, his daughter-in-law, doing? Is Chauncy back home?" Rachel fired one question after another without giving Kym time to answer.

Kym didn't know how much of Lana's possible diagnosis of post-partum depression she wanted to share. She didn't want to give her sister one more thing to fret over. "Since Lana just gave birth to two babies, Chaz thought it best to give them time to adjust, so Chauncy's still with him."

"Doesn't sound very romantic between you and him." Rachel frowned.

"No candlelight dinners for sure, but"—Kym shrugged—"we have to work Chauncy into our plans, not exclude her. We're going out to dinner when I get back to see how she'll do. I signed up for these scenarios when I fell in love with him. According to Chaz, Chauncy's therapist is teaching her amazing skills."

Nicholas entered the room with his eyes focused on his wife. He bent down and kissed Rachel on the lips. "Hey, babe. How you feeling?" His words were tender, and he didn't hide the look of love or his patience in waiting for an answer as he stroked her hair.

"Better." Rachel smiled.

"Amen." He rewarded her with another kiss.

Kym cleared her throat and raised her hand to remind him she was there. "You have an audience, you two. Remember, Brother-in-Law, I'm here to keep my sister in line. Don't worry about her. I've got it."

"Yes, ma'am." Nicholas gave her a mock salute, then winked at Rachel, who beamed at her husband's attention before he turned to leave.

"Call her Dr. Knicely, honey. I like the sound of that. Aunt Tweet would be so proud. Can't wait to see my sister strut across the stage again, then I guess I'll finally get a chance to meet Chaz."

"Trust me. He won't miss the graduation, but you may if you don't eat to gain your strength."

Rachel twisted her lips. "All right. Can I have more soup, please?"

Kym burst out laughing, then stood. "Second helpings coming up."

Chapter 34

A MONTH LATER, THE MOMENT WAS SURREAL. CLOSING HER EYES, Kym inhaled and slowly exhaled. She opened them and whispered in awe, "I'll officially be addressed as Dr. Knicely." Kym brushed mascara on her lashes a few more times before turning around to face both of her sisters.

They and their husbands had flown in the previous night. The sisters had stayed up all night talking long after her brothers-in-law and nephew were in bed.

Tabitha danced in the doorway of Kym's master bath. "Finally, this is your big day!" Adoration flashed across her younger sister's face as Kym glanced at the reflection in her mirror.

Kym didn't need a holiday to be thankful with sisters like Rachel and Tabitha. She considered it a privilege to have been gifted two loving younger sisters…and they had both beaten her to the altar. "I always assumed *my* big day would be my wedding day, but today is life-changing."

"I'm sure it's coming." Tabitha gave her a knowing expression that reminded Kym of their beloved Aunt Tweet.

Feeling their great-aunt's presence, Kym shivered and smiled. "One big day at a time." She stared into the mirror again and dusted shimmery bronze powder on her cheeks, then admired the finished results.

Rachel said, rubbing her stomach, "Come on. Let's go, Professor Knicely. It's showtime. Your fan club needs to get good seats."

"Gotcha." In Aunt Tweet's absence, no doubt Chaz would be there with Chauncy, as he had mindlessly professed many months ago, as if knowing they would fall in love. "I'm ready."

Three hours. That was how much time Chaz gave himself to get ready for Kym's graduation. Surprisingly, Chauncy was in a compliant mood as she picked out a new pink dress.

As a favor, or rather after a desperate plea for help, Debra had offered to shampoo Chauncy's hair. Chaz had unbraided it after Lana had been horrified seeing her daughter's hair looking unkempt, despite the durability of the cornrows, while they FaceTimed. "Just take them down, Pops, and wash her hair. A ponytail will work for my poor baby."

Lana had made it sound easy. Nothing about his granddaughter's hair care looked painless. The plan had been, when Kym returned from seeing her sister, she would do Chauncy's hair, but as it got closer to the commencement, Kym must have forgotten.

He broached Chauncy's hair with Debra in hopes she would recommend a place, but his friend offered to do it herself. He had been so relieved until the time came. Chaz didn't know who had the worse experience, Chauncy or Debra.

What his white friend didn't expect was his granddaughter's long hair to swell into a dense mass of curls. The horror on Debra's face read *never again* as she tried her best to untangle Chauncy's natural hair for a ponytail. Of course, his granddaughter didn't make it easy. She protested Debra's methods of brushing hair into a ponytail that resembled more of a puff ball. It had been a lesson learned.

After that, Chaz subscribed to a YouTube hair channel for a step-by-step tutorial to tackle a girl child's hair. But *Hair Love*, an Oscar-winning short film about a dad conquering Black hair care, distracted him. The clip inspired him that he could manage the grooming with confidence. So now he spied Chauncy's hair and grinned proudly as they were ready to head out the door. The hairstyling only took him two hours.

Flowers—check. The card—check. The gift card—check. Then he reached for the most important item—his lifesaver—Chauncy's backpack that contained her favorite blanket, snack, earphones, and pieces from the jigsaw puzzle.

When he was about to pack her beloved craft sticks, Chauncy pushed his hand away. Was she weaning herself from them? He threw in a couple of stress balls anyway and a Rubik's Cube.

Recently, Chauncy's response to crowds had been tolerable. Even though Debra had worked with his granddaughter on social interaction, the child still preferred self-isolation. He didn't want to chance anything ruining Kym's well-deserved moment, so he prayed for Chauncy to either take a nap throughout the ceremony or be content with her toys.

During the drive to the campus, Chaz hummed one of his favorite gospel tunes, "How Great Thou Art." The day was perfect for an outdoor graduation with a few scattered clouds to keep the sun from beaming down directly.

Once they arrived in the courtyard for the ceremony, Chaz was torn between finding a seat as close to the graduates as possible or staying in the shadows in case the crowd overwhelmed Chauncy. He decided on the latter.

With the program booklet in one hand and an oversized bouquet in the other, he waited impatiently in his seat with Chauncy sitting quietly beside him. Headsets were a beautiful thing. Plus, the Rubik's Cube was her latest fascination. He doubted she would master it, but Debra advised him not to be surprised. His granddaughter might lag behind in one skill set but excel beyond belief in another.

The commencement began as university dignitaries in their academic robes paraded down the center aisle for the processional. Chaz recognized a few of them from alumni fundraisers and other events. The advanced degree candidates appeared second, and he locked eyes on Kym and tracked her until she disappeared into the sea of black robes.

He stood for the national anthem and alma mater song, then endured the speakers until it was time for graduate candidates to stand to receive their degrees.

It was sentimental for him that he had entered Kym's life in time to see her achieve this goal. He wanted to cheer, whistle, and whoop when her name was called, but he was concerned it might startle Chauncy. So in a reserved manner, he remained seated and clapped.

It was over in under seventy-five minutes and to LLU's credit;

the institution was dispatching 412 graduates into the workforce to change the world. It was a joyous moment, then he reflected on the amount of student debt many probably had incurred.

If only the graduates had a Black billionaire to pay off the graduating class's student loans, like Robert Smith had done for the Morehouse College Class of 2019. Chaz prayed they would find meaningful employment and reach their dreams.

Once the graduates began to disperse, Chaz coaxed his granddaughter to stand, then he lifted her in one arm and carried the flowers, card, and backpack in the other as he created a path to find Kym. He spotted her huddled in a small group. Her resemblance to the other two women was more evident in person than in photos. The men nearby must have been their husbands.

As if she could sense his presence, Kym glanced over her shoulder. Happiness shone from her eyes, mixed with tears as she smiled. His mind captured the moment of her pure bliss.

"You made it. I wasn't sure if you would." She maneuvered through her group to hug him. "Thank you."

"A posthumous promise to your aunt is a promise to you. I packed an arsenal of distractions—in case I needed them." He lifted the backpack and smiled at her.

"Thank you," she said, almost breathless, then glanced at his granddaughter.

"Hi, Chauncy."

"It's the headset," Chaz explained when the girl didn't respond. "These are for you." He handed Kym the flowers and card, then lowered his voice. "Congratulations, baby. Love you." He brushed a sweet kiss against her lips.

One of her sisters cleared her throat, reminding Chaz they had an audience. Since the woman was pregnant, she had to be Rachel. "You must be Chaz. Finally, we meet."

"Yes, finally." He turned on the charm to make a lasting impression, then he shook hands with the brothers-in-law.

Soon, he didn't know when, they would celebrate another occasion, and a kiss would symbolize something greater. Not long ago, Chaz hadn't expected to feel these emotions, but now all he knew was that life without Kym Knicely wasn't an option.

Chapter 35

Kym's heart was full. She didn't want to open her eyes from Chaz's soft kiss. If only she could enjoy the moment in slow motion. "Thank you for being a part of my day."

"Always." His nostrils flared with emotion. Reaching for her free hand, he massaged it.

The simple touch was making her weak, and she didn't want any spectators to witness how she swooned over this man. "We're going out to eat. Are you coming?" Her heart pounded with hope. It seemed like forever since they had spent time together.

"I've pushed the limits with Chauncy." He glanced at the girl, who was oblivious to the energy surrounding her. "I'd better get her home."

"Come and stay, even for a little while. I want you to be a part of this milestone with me." Kym tried to convince him.

"And I want to be, but..."

"Hey. If Chauncy becomes restless, I'll understand if you want to leave, but right now, she seems content. Plus, if Aunt Tweet were alive, she would expect any man who loves his woman to be by her side."

"Man, you might as well say yes." Marcus shook his head. "You ain't going to win against a Knicely sister. Trust me." Tabitha elbowed her husband. "Ouch."

"Just so you know, I do let you win sometimes."

Marcus wiggled an eyebrow at his wife in jest.

Chaz seemed unsure of a commitment but conceded. "I'll meet you there." He leaned forward and brushed a kiss against her cheek. It still tingled as she and her family drove to the restaurant.

Half an hour later, they arrived at Rusty Scupper Restaurant and Bar. Everyone patted their stomachs in anticipation of indulging in a seafood feast. As they were waiting to be seated, Kym experienced a bittersweet moment. Her aunt had given Kym the encouragement she needed to excel. In the absence of her loved one, God had placed a special someone in her life. She thanked God for that gift as Chaz walked up behind her and linked his fingers through hers and announced, "We're here."

Staring into his eyes, Kym's heart quivered with happiness. "Thank you for filling the void in my life." She doubted he understood the depth of her words.

"No, you were the missing piece in mine," he whispered with tenderness in his eyes. He bit his bottom lip as he gazed at hers. Yep, he wanted to kiss her. She could tell, and she didn't want to protest, but they weren't alone.

Once they were seated for their late lunch, Rachel addressed her, "Dr. Knicely."

"Yes, Dr. Knicely," Chaz repeated in a whisper.

Kym closed her eyes and let the words echo in her head, and she smiled broadly before answering. Chaz pampered her with looks of love, touches, and mouthed compliments until she blushed, all while not missing a beat with Chauncy. Nothing the child did got past him.

It was the perfect celebration as toasts were made in Kym's honor. In that moment, Kym was living her best life, and Chaz seemed amused by how she interacted with her sisters.

Rachel cleared her throat for what Kym thought was another toast. The table ceased activity except for Chauncy, who continued to manipulate the Rubik's Cube. "Chaz, our sister gave her version—finally—on how you two met. We want to hear your side of the story, so we can compare notes."

"And please don't leave out any details." Tabitha chimed in with a trademark Aunt Tweet mischievous smirk. "No matter how minuscule."

Getting comfortable in her seat, Kym folded her arms, listening in awe as emotions played on Chaz's face about his attraction, wooing, respect, and love for her.

Chaz weaved a web of tender memories as he recalled details of their first meeting, formal introduction, and dance in the rain. He pulled memories from the depth of his heart. To her surprise, he revealed some of his doubts that he wouldn't measure up to Kym's standards.

"I had no idea," she whispered and rubbed his hand.

He made her day complete. Kym enjoyed her sisters' *ooh*s and *aahs* as she relished the moment.

Although his presence captivated Kym, she discreetly kept an eye on Chauncy as she slipped from her chair and stepped to the next table. The girl stood there as if she were a pet waiting for a treat, then reached out to help herself, to the diners' gasps.

Since Kym was closer, she tried to steer Chauncy back to their table without drawing too much attention, but the girl avoided Kym's reach.

"Okay, take a deep breath," she coaxed herself as she could feel customers watching. "Chauncy, come sit with me." She stood to retrieve the girl. Bad move, as Chauncy let out a piercing scream that made the kitchen staff pause and investigate.

"I got her, babe." Chaz took swift action, scooped Chauncy in his arms, and walked outside the restaurant as the child's squalls grew louder.

How embarrassing. This was not how she envisioned celebrating the biggest day of her life. When she took her seat, her family was quiet and avoided eye contact. Nicholas encouraged everyone to join hands, then he bowed his head. She strained her ears to hear his whispered prayer for understanding. Kym closed her eyes to hide her humiliation and sorrow.

She sniffed as they whispered, "Amen."

Kym asked for the check but was advised that another patron had paid the tab. "Oh." Kym didn't know if that was out of generosity or bribe money to get them to leave, and their bill wasn't cheap. They gathered their things, and she grabbed Chauncy's backpack.

As her family made their way to the exit, Kym heard the comments, "that child should be disciplined," "people spoil their kids," "something's wrong with that little girl…" The customers didn't understand, just like Kym didn't—not really.

She didn't exhale until they were outside. She spied Chaz and his granddaughter sitting on a bench in a park across from the restaurant.

"Wait here," Kym said to her family. "Let me check on Chaz and Chauncy."

They nodded as she crossed the street. Still in shock, she didn't know what to say—what to do—as she stepped closer.

Chaz wouldn't look at her as Chauncy sat beside him whimpering. "I'm sorry, babe. We ruined your day."

"No one is to blame here. Not you or Chauncy. Maybe I shouldn't have touched her. I don't know, but I guess we'll figure this out."

He squeezed his lips and glanced past before mumbling, "Maybe."

Maybe? What kind of answer was that? If only this weren't her big day, Kym would have made herself comfortable and tried to talk through it. She couldn't, because it *was* her big day, and her family had come to town.

"I'm sorry again. I love you, but go spend time with your folks." He faced her and smiled.

Torn, Kym didn't budge right away. "All right, but I'll call you later." Rejoining her family, it was a quiet walk to their vehicles. Kym's steps were heavy amid their silence.

What just happened? Chaz wanted to know as Chauncy reached for the backpack Kym had set on the bench.

Her meltdown was over, but Chaz's unshed tears would remain hidden from view. He grieved for his granddaughter whose actions would be judged and for Kym who wanted to understand.

With Kym and her family long gone, he felt alone, desperately wanting and needing someone, anyone, to listen to him vent and reassure him that it was okay.

He had nothing. Who could empathize with how he felt at the moment? Under no circumstances would he let Gee and Lana know about this episode. That would only worry them. He thought about Debra. He needed to keep her on retainer as his therapist—mental and behavioral—for Chauncy.

A small voice tickled his ear, *Cast all your cares on Jesus, for He cares for you.*

That familiar Scripture in 1 Peter 5 made Chaz smile and bob his head. Yes, when no one else understood, God did.

"PawPaw. I want to go home." Chauncy patted his leg.

"Me too." He kissed her cheek and lifted her in one arm while swooping up her backpack. During the trek to his car, Chaz blocked everything from his mind—everything. To think too hard about the day would only bring on frustration.

When he got home, Chaz planned to read his Bible for other comforting Scriptures and go from there.

Chapter 36

Weeks after the commencement, Kym relaxed and breathed. With Chauncy's extended stay, Kym decided to use that time to interact with the child more. She didn't want a repeat of what happened at the restaurant. Instead of romantic dates, Kym suggested outings to include Chauncy. Kym also bribed Chauncy with more jigsaw puzzles that were a hit. A few times, the girl allowed Kym to play with her.

One Saturday afternoon, she and Chaz took Chauncy to the park for a picnic. Relaxing on a blanket, eating sandwiches, they kept an eye on her playing on a kiddie sliding board. "Babe, I can wash and comb her hair," Kym offered.

The show of relief on Chaz's face was priceless. It was also a natural way to bond. As a little girl, Kym felt contentment at her mother's knees while she straightened Kym's hair with the pressing comb. She would always cherish those memories. Kym wanted to establish a bond with Chauncy.

"If you have time, Dr. Knicely." He tugged on a loose strand. "And for the record, I like calling you Doctor."

"I like hearing it come from you too." She tapped his nose.

"Thank you for showing Chauncy love and accepting the unique person she is. You could've rejected her and our relationship, especially after her meltdown at your celebration dinner."

"I'll be honest, I never saw that coming with her shyness." Kym frowned. "Her actions were misunderstood by most people who haven't interacted directly with a child with special needs. I was embarrassed by the unwanted attention, at the same time sad for what Chauncy was experiencing. But she's precious in God's sight and mine. How can a person not love a sweet, innocent child?"

"I'm a blessed man." He gathered her hands in his and glanced in

Chauncy's direction. Kym did also. Other children had joined Chauncy on the playground. Chaz sucked in his breath. "Lord, please let her make friends today, not enemies…"

Kym prayed with him. "In Jesus's name. Amen."

He leaned closer and kissed her, but she pulled back first. "Chaz, we need to observe her interactions with the others and be ready to react if necessary."

Chaz smirked and nodded. "You sound like Debra," he said offhandedly, eyes on Chauncy.

No, he didn't compare me to another woman. "Sweetie. I sound like myself, Dr. Kym Knicely, not Debra or anyone else. My specialty is in urban education. Hers is autism. There are a lot of things I don't know, but while Chauncy is here, I plan to learn."

"Noted." Chaz studied her. "Did I say something wrong?"

She kissed him first before answering. "Women don't like to be compared to other women." She scrunched her nose. There was nothing playful about it. "I'm sure that won't slip again, right?"

"Right, baby, I didn't mean to insult or offend you." Frowning, Chaz shook his head. "There's only one Dr. Kym Knicely, and she's mine. No one can compare to you."

"I know how you feel about me," she said, trying to soothe him. Her sisters had said so more than once—it *was* time for Kym to check Debra out.

A few days later, Kym called Chaz and asked his permission to observe Chauncy at the Kennedy Krieger's Center for Autism and Related Disorders.

"Of course, babe. I'll call them now and let them know you're coming by. Ah, will I see you later?"

"Maybe." She was in a teasing mood.

"Should I be jealous that my lady is bestowing all her attention on the granddaughter instead of the grandfather?"

"Package deal. She's part of the package." She giggled and disconnected.

Kym didn't know what to expect when she walked in. When she thought about therapy, Kym had envisioned a doctor-type setting. The rooms were inviting with warm colors and set up like a playroom. The receptionist had her sign in, then escorted her to the room were Chauncy received her daily therapy.

While some children sat quietly, a few stood and were in their own worlds.

Kym was amazed to see how Debra worked with Chauncy in increasing her acceptance of different food choices. Mixed in with the carrots were green peas, which Kym had learned was Chauncy's least favorite food. *Uh-oh.* Kym braced herself for an unpleasant reaction from the child.

Debra was patient as Chauncy tried to grab carrots without touching the peas. It was an intense exercise until the girl lost interest. Debra took the carrot with the pea hidden and coaxed Chauncy to open her mouth for her favorite food. Even Kym was curious what Chauncy's reaction would be. After a few tries, the girl asked for more.

When the therapist noticed Kym, she stood and walked toward her with an outstretched hand. Kym accepted, then frowned. "How did you do that? I'm surprised she let the carrot touch the pea."

"We've been working on this since day one. Don't let her acceptance today fool you. Tomorrow she might not like it again. Progress takes patience and education, Dr. Knicely, which Chaz told me is your field of expertise."

Her heart warmed that Chaz had mentioned her, hopefully more often than Kym heard Debra's name. "Yes, my research focused on a mobile tutoring program where grad students go into inner-city neighborhoods to help youth who might be struggling with homework," Kym explained. "You have to meet students where they are and build on that."

"Exactly. However, there's a footnote with children with autism. Their response to situations might complicate matters when it's not appropriate. One needs to read the signals."

Kym listened and watched Debra's interactions with each child; she didn't have a one-size-fits-all approach. But Debra was big on rewards for correct answers and good behaviors. Contrary to the bug Rachel and

Tabitha had put in her ear, Kym sensed the woman was a professional and didn't pick up any vibes that she had a personal interest in Chaz.

She called him as she was leaving the institute. "I was impressed with the teaching and play style Debra uses."

"I think she's good too, so are you heading home?"

"No, since I'm not far from Inner Harbor, I thought I would enjoy the rest of the afternoon on the pier, then eventually stop in Barnes & Noble."

"Want some company? I can meet you there."

"Don't you have to pick up Chauncy?" She knew the answer.

"In a couple of hours."

The thrill of the two of them. Together.

Alone.

Take it.

"That gives me time to play hooky with you," he said in a husky tone that caused chills to race up her arms.

Kym wasn't about to talk him out of it. "Then I'll see you there." She ended the call and blushed. *Hooky was a good thing for teachers, right?*

After she parked her SUV, Kym strolled along the pier. The warmth of the sun dared her to stay out and play instead of going inside the bookstore to browse while waiting for Chaz, so she settled on a bench.

The wind teased her hair as her mind drifted to Aunt Tweet. She teared up at the many memories. Her great-aunt had introduced her nieces to the world of caregiving and service to others.

For Kym, she would forever cherish her turn to love on her aunt for six months before Tabitha took over the care. While staring out into the water, Kym racked her brain to see if Aunt Tweet's fingerprints could somehow be found on Chaz. Kym doubted Aunt Tweet and Chaz ever crossed paths.

Maybe it wasn't about the fingerprint but the seed her aunt had planted in Kym—a love for Black American history and HBCUs, which were created by the efforts of many Black churches, the American Missionary Association, and the Freedmen's Bureau.

Aunt Tweet made sure the Knicely sisters knew how the second

Morrill Act of 1890 set the foundation for Blacks to receive education despite white colleges and universities denying them admission.

The act mandated former Confederate states provide land grants for institutions that would admit and educate Blacks. Even though Kym knew the history, she was drawn to Temple University for undergrad, but Baltimore lured her to LLU because of its rich Black American history. Or maybe it was the Lord ordering her steps for the future. Otherwise, she might not ever have met Chaz.

And now, she was with a man who was essentially a caregiver. The tables had turned. He needed her.

"Thinking about me?" Chaz's deep voice broke into her reverie, startling Kym, but her heart settled quickly.

"You're somewhere up there in my thoughts." She angled her body and watched him walk from behind her and claim the spot beside her. He presented her with a red rose. She sniffed, and his cologne mingled with the floral fragrance. Instead of the wind, Chaz took possession of her hair and wrapped strands around his finger. She gazed into his eyes and flirted. "You always smell good."

He winked. "You smell better."

They chuckled as he reached for her hand and intertwined his strong fingers through hers. He scrutinized their hands, then slowly brought them to his lips for a kiss.

"You once thanked me for coming on the journey with you." Chaz shook his head. "No, thank you for saying yes to our first date and never saying no to the dates after that, even the ones that included my grandbaby."

"When we talked about the future and you quizzed me about would I be comfortable as a grandmother before being a mother…"

His body stiffened. He didn't blink or seem to breathe.

"Chaz, I learned something about myself." She frowned, accepting the truth. "Love is blind. I would love Chauncy whether she was your daughter or granddaughter…or your little sister." She giggled as Chaz began to tickle her.

"Little sister, really? You've got jokes, huh? I miss our downtime like this. But Chauncy will be leaving soon. Gee and Lana are getting anxious, and I want to see my new grandsons. You're going to fly back with us, right?"

"Of course." She snuggled closer and let the quietness lull them to contentment.

Chapter 37

Gee and Lana called Chaz constantly, demanding the return of their sweet angel. "We miss her, Pops," Lana whined. "Although Raymond and Rafael aren't sleeping through the night yet, I'm ready…"

The pleading did him in. The aching in Lana's voice tore at Chaz's heart. It was time. "How about the weekend after the Fourth of July? That will give me time to prep her and pack her things. Kym has taken Chauncy on shopping sprees." He marveled at how much stuff a little girl could possess.

"I like Kym. Not only is she pretty and nice, but I felt better knowing that she was in your and Chauncy's lives."

"Me too. She's hosting a barbecue for the Fourth. Her sisters and their families are coming to Baltimore to celebrate. I'd like to take Chauncy before I bring her back to St. Louis. Even Drake and Patrice are coming. Is that okay?" Chaz was excited that Kym's family gathering included his. This was one tradition he could see himself looking forward to every summer.

After a lengthy silence, Lana agreed. "How is Kym's sister? The one who is pregnant?"

"Rachel. She was at the graduation and looked good to me." He strained his brain. "I forgot how to calculate the pregnancy due date. All I know is she'll deliver in nine months and she's somewhere in between that."

"Pops." Lana chuckled. "If everything works out between you and Kym, you're going have to figure it out."

"Sure you're right about that. Thanks, sweetie. See you in about a week and a half." Once Kym had received her doctorate, she made caring for his granddaughter manageable—not less stressful but doable.

Her love had created a family atmosphere. He had stopped counting the weeks until Chauncy would return home. But now that was about to happen, Chaz was ready for the next phase in his life.

"I want everything to be perfect!" Kym was giddy as she, Chaz, and Chauncy strolled through the aisles at the grocery store for more meat to barbecue. "This is the first time my family is coming to Baltimore for the holidays."

"I get it, babe." Chaz's eyes twinkled. Her excitement was contagious. "You want to be the perfect host."

She nodded. "Exactly." Chaz winked while Chauncy gripped a bag of licorice as she swung her tiny legs from her seat in the shopping cart.

"You know I'm all in." He circled his arm around her waist and kissed her cheek. "Thanks for including Drake and his girlfriend."

"Of course!"

Back at her house, Chaz got Chauncy settled at the kiddie table that Kym had set up with jigsaw puzzles in the living room, within view.

When Chaz turned around, he folded his arms and stared at Kym in the kitchen. "You're amazing."

"What do you mean?" She didn't miss a beat as she put up groceries, then wrapped a colorful African apron around her skinny waist. She pulled a miniature one for Chauncy from the cabinet.

Chaz wasn't about to protest. "I'm a blessed man." There was so much more he could say, but this wasn't the moment as he noticed she had brushed up her hair into a long ponytail and her face was void of makeup. "Now, Dr. Knicely, I'm putting you out of your own kitchen, so you can finish preparing the guest bedrooms. I'll season the meat and prepare the other sides."

When Kym stomped her feet in an adult temper tantrum, Chaz leaned over and smacked a kiss on her pouty lips. "We can kiss all night, or you admit defeat and leave this kitchen to get ready for your sisters. Your call, sweetheart, because for every pout, my lips are on it." He laughed when she scurried away. "You're so easy to tease."

Chaz couldn't wait until the day he could chase her around the house—their house, his wife. He was so ready for a life with her in it permanently—so ready, he mused as he performed one task after another.

The next day, he and Chauncy returned to Kym's house later than he had hoped. It hadn't been a good morning at his place. For every piece of clothing he packed, Chauncy would unpack it. By the time they made it to Kym's, his granddaughter was highly annoyed. She wanted no part of the puzzles or craft sticks.

In Kym's living room, Chauncy twirled around until she became dizzy. When Chaz tried to coax her to sit now, his requests were ignored.

He jammed his fists at his sides, agitated. "We won't be able to stay if I can't get her to settle down."

Kym shrugged. "I'm just as clueless as to what to do, but you're not going anywhere. Maybe she can sense there's about to be a change because you were packing up her things. I don't know, but let's indulge her a few more minutes. Chaz, take her in the bedroom and give her some quiet space to see if that helps while I finish up."

"Okay." He huffed, closed his eyes, and rested his forehead on hers. "I just don't want to mess up your day." *Like at your graduation celebration dinner*, he thought but didn't dare voice. Was she thinking the same thing too?

"Your presence in my life has made my day." She smiled. "Now go."

The woman knew what to say to soothe his worries, and she was right. Chauncy did finally calm down and not a moment too soon. When Kym's sisters, their husbands, and the baby arrived, they were boisterous and ushered in high energy. He immediately dug into Chauncy's backpack for her kiddie headset.

Kym advised her family to give the child some space when they wanted to approach Chauncy with hugs and kisses. They conceded, maybe remembering Chauncy's meltdown, but they never said a word to him. Soon, Drake and Patrice arrived, and Chaz made the introductions.

Chaz kept Chauncy close as he enjoyed getting to know Patrice. She was smart, pretty, and her personality complemented his son's.

"Dad, I know I promised to catch up with you, but the residency program is kicking my behind."

"You're here now. That's all that matters." Chaz patted his son's shoulder.

In no time, Drake and Tabitha were talking shop about drugs and medicine while Patrice was fascinated with the toddler. Brothers-in-law Nicholas and Marcus caught up while Chaz multitasked between watching Chauncy and helping Kym play hostess.

"I think your guests are having a good time," he whispered.

"I'm glad." Kym's eyes shone bright with happiness.

After everyone ate, Drake grabbed a small ball from Chauncy's backpack, then he and Patrice played kickball to encourage Chauncy to join in the fun. It took a little coaxing, but eventually, she took the bait.

Chaz and Kym's brothers-in-law watched from their recliners on the deck.

"So everything been going good with you, Chauncy, and my sister-in-law?" Marcus asked after taking a swig from his bottled water.

"Kym looks happy," Nicholas added.

"We both are. Honestly, I didn't know how this was going to work out between us with Chauncy here. Talk about over my head, whew." Chaz patted his forehead for sweat. "I guess I was until Kym stepped in, and despite some of Chauncy's setbacks, she hasn't been deterred. What at times seemed like a mission impossible, my lady made possible. I love her."

"I hope enough to marry her sooner rather than later. She loves you too." Marcus looked over his shoulder before continuing. "She's not getting younger, and you, my brotha, are old."

The three roared with laughter. Chaz wasn't offended as he bit his bottom lip, bobbing his head in agreement.

"Don't let my age fool ya. I've got the stamina to hang with the best of y'all. My intentions have been delayed, not canceled. I did have doubts about starting a second family, but that's what Kym wants and deserves, and I happen to love her enough to give her what she wants—even four children."

"Four," Marcus repeated, gagging.

Nicholas's words seemed to have gotten stuck in his mouth.

The pair stared at him. "Whatever makes Kym happy," Chaz said.

After some silence, Nicholas spoke up. "Forgive my ignorance." He leaned forward after he glanced at Chauncy out in the yard. "So there's no cure for autism?"

Chaz shook his head. "No. Unless God moves to accelerate my granddaughter's brain development, she'll always lag behind. I don't care how much therapy she has. The best my family can do is to teach her to function as independently as possible. God will take care of the rest for her to achieve milestones."

Rachel opened the door and peeked her head outside. Nicholas turned and gave his wife his full attention.

"Babe, I'm a little tired. I'm going to lie down." She rubbed her belly as she glowed.

Chaz wondered if Kym would look just as beautiful when she carried their child.

Nicholas stood and took long strides to his wife and grabbed her hand. "That's my cue. Catch ya in a few hours, gentlemen. Got to tuck in the wife."

Marcus hooted. "You do know it's two in the afternoon, not ten at night."

Tabitha walked outside, carrying Little Marcus on her hip, and she playfully popped her husband on the head. "Leave him alone. I remember those days, and you should too. Here's your son. You can rock him to sleep." She handed the boy over and gave Marcus a loud kiss on the forehead, then walked back inside.

"Yep, I'm whupped too." Marcus grinned and squeezed his son tight. In minutes, Little Marcus was snoring in his dad's arms.

"I remember holding my boys and watching them sleep." Chaz chuckled to himself.

Marcus glanced in the direction of Chauncy, who stood not far away, dipping a stick into a bottle and blowing out bubbles. "How's her therapy coming?"

"There has been improvement, especially verbal and eating." He paused when Chauncy approached and blew bubbles into her grandfather's face, and as if to prove his point, she was a chatterbox in her monotone.

Chaz reached for the bottle, then blew bubbles into Chauncy's hands. He knew he had started something, but it was fun to watch Chauncy discover new things.

Marcus tilted his head. "She seems really enthralled. If Little Marcus were awake, he would get a kick out of the bubbles too."

"If she didn't like the feel, Chauncy would have shown her displeasure by blinking rapidly—it's called stimming—or running away. When she's fascinated about something, her focus is dead-on."

"I know that has to be challenging for you and her parents. I give thanks to the Lord every night and morning. I remember praying that our child—son—was born healthy and without any challenges."

Chaz, his son, and Lana thought so too when Chauncy was born, then her brain function reversed. Warning signs gradually surfaced until certain things couldn't be ignored. "Yes, and most parents of children with autism give thanks to Jesus for their gifts and pray for patience."

"Amen, brother." Marcus stood and kissed his sleepy son's forehead. "I better lay this fella down for his nap so he can grow up to be strong like his daddy."

Chaz nodded, then watched as Chauncy took the bottle of bubbles and scrambled down the stairs. The bubbles were forgotten, and she was twirling around. He smiled. "Lord, thank you for our precious gift." She had improved so much, to Debra's credit and the Lord's grace. Chauncy's stay had turned out to be a blessing for everyone, especially her.

Hours later, to his surprise, Zeke and Judith showed up, dressed alike in their denim attire. Chaz stood to greet them at the same time as Drake announced he and Patrice were leaving because he had a twelve-hour shift coming up. First, Drake and Zeke chatted a few minutes and promised to get together.

"Ha." Chaz chuckled. "Don't hold your breath."

Drake shrugged. "I know I've got a history of no-shows, but it won't be forever. Oh, I miss this camaraderie. It was good to spend time with family and friends. See you, old man." He gave his dad a hearty pat on the back with a bear hug.

There was nothing like family to build a relationship.

Kym sighed as Chaz whispered in her ear, "Success. Everyone had a good time."

She whirled around and wrapped her arms around his neck. "It was so much fun, playing hostess. I can't wait until next summer."

"I plan to be right by your side to play host." He loaded the glasses into the dishwasher. "I see why you look forward to your family gatherings. Plus, it was good to see Zeke and Judith."

"Yep, they do make a cute couple," she said in a whimsical voice as she watched him tidy up her kitchen.

"They aight." Chaz wiggled his mustache. "I think we're way cuter."

"You say exactly what I want to hear, Mr. Banks." She rewarded him with a sweet kiss, then slipped her arm through his and rested her head on his shoulder.

"I do my best." He rubbed her back. "Anything else you need?"

She stroked his jaw. "Babe, you've done enough. Plus, you look beat. Go home and get some rest and finish packing while Chauncy is asleep. My sisters and I can handle the rest."

Kym had observed Chauncy around her nephew. While her Little Marcus was hyperactive, Chauncy sat still in a corner and stared at a picture book as if she were memorizing the artwork on each page. "Don't pack things she's used to seeing yet. Some stuff you can probably ship."

"Yes, Doctor. I'm glad you're going with me to take her back."

"Me too."

Sunday morning, Kym's family attended Abundant Life Church with her. Chaz bowed out, citing the fact that Chauncy had a rough night and saying he would meet them at the airport later.

Pastor Harrison emphasized Christians having spiritual balance in their lives in his sermon from Psalm 27. "We have to build our faith in Christ, so when the trials come—and they will come—we can draw from our measure of faith that we've stored up to overcome fear, whose mission is to steal our peace."

She thought about Chauncy and considered that as an example not to be caught off guard when other unexpected situations knocked at the door. Chauncy had progressed so much, at times they had forgotten her special needs, which was a good thing.

A few hours later at the Thurgood Marshall Airport, Kym and Tabitha said their tearful goodbyes to Rachel and Nicholas, who were heading back to Nashville. Her sister looked healthy and happy with about four months to go.

On the plane, Chaz took the window with Chauncy sitting between them, and Kym claimed the end seat, so she could chat with Tabitha across the aisle.

When the group arrived in St. Louis, another reunion awaited them at the airport. Lana and Gee were there with the twins in strollers, Gee holding balloons.

Chaz mentioned he usually rented a vehicle so not to bother to get him from the airport. He chuckled. "I guess they just couldn't wait for me to bring Chauncy to them."

"I don't blame them." Kym admired the couple for the second time. Their faces glowed.

When Chauncy saw her parents, she took off for them. Gee scooped her up so she could hug them. The girl talked nonstop, to her parents' amazement.

Lana looked up at her father-in-law and mouthed, *Thank you*. "Wow, she's a chatterbox, Pops. And she's gotten bigger."

"She won't have to open any more doors to find her mommy and daddy," Kym mumbled to Tabitha and Marcus. After a few minutes, they approached to offer their congratulations and ooh and aah over the babies.

Kym watched as Chaz leaned over and picked up one grandson with great care. The look of awe on his face was heartwarming. He asked which one the baby was, then he cooed Rafael's name over and over. He glanced up into Kym's eyes. She saw love. He repeated the same steps with Raymond.

"Congratulations, PawPaw," Kym whispered before she turned to her family and hugged them goodbye. Kym was so ready for a family of her own, all her senses were on overdrive.

Chapter 38

Chauncy had been gone a week, and her absence created a void at outings with Kym. Chaz didn't mind sharing his granddaughter with Kym, but he would be a liar if he denied it felt good to have Kym all to himself again. He squeezed her hand after they left a Sunday matinee.

"I got an idea. How about we celebrate your love of museums with a visit to the Eubie Blake Cultural Center next Saturday? A young prodigy is performing."

Kym's eyes sparkled. "One of my coworkers was married in the Billie Holiday Garden. Despite the heat, it was a beautiful ceremony. Sounds like fun. I love you."

There was so much power behind those words; her declaration confirmed to Chaz he was blessed beyond measure. "I love you more." He brushed a kiss onto her freshly scented hair, ready to prove it.

A week later, Chaz stood on her porch, dressed in a suit and bow tie. Kym opened the door and spied his attire. "Wow. You told me to dress up, but wow. This young artist must really be talented."

"Oh, he is. Terrence Randall has been playing since he was four—the same age as Chauncy. He's twelve now."

He linked his fingers through hers during the short drive to Howard Street in Midtown Baltimore. A place that started off hosting an afterschool arts program for youth in the 1960s now bore the name of James Hubert "Eubie" Blake, native of Baltimore, who was a talented ragtime and jazz musician. He and his collaborator had penned *Shuffle Along*, one of the first Broadway musicals to hold the honor of being written and directed by African Americans.

Although the center was open to the public on Saturdays until five, Chaz had paid for the private event that was a couple of hours after that.

Kym stared at the four-story back building as she waited for him to come around.

He guided her up the steps to the entrance. A young woman with short, fluffy, coiled black hair greeted them.

"We're here for the recital," Chaz informed her.

Rita, according to the name on her badge, stepped aside and pointed. "Take the elevator to the fourth floor. Enjoy your event."

"We will." Chaz guided Kym along the marble floor.

Kym inhaled, then sighed. "Ah. I love the smell of old historic buildings."

The fourth floor was an open space with dozens of square tables for two, each draped with blue tablecloths. Centerpieces were blue cracked-glass globes with lit candles inside. In the front of the room, a piano and drum set stood slightly off-center, waiting for an audience.

Kym glanced around, seemingly curious. "There's no one here. I hate to be late, but I don't like to be the first one to show up either."

"Relax, babe." Chaz pressed a kiss against her cheek, then placed a hand on her back to guide her forward. They wormed their way through the tables until she picked one. "My lady," he said in a terrible British accent and pulled out a chair, then scooted her closer to the table.

Once he took his seat, a young man with a confident stride entered the room. "Good evening," he said as if there were a room filled with people. "My first selection for your enjoyment is Suzanne Ciani's 'The Velocity of Love.'" He slid onto the piano bench and drummed his fingers on the keys.

She leaned closer and whispered, "Talk about starting on time… People are going to miss him." She pouted.

"It's best if you close your eyes and listen," he said.

"I guess when I open them, the room will be packed." She lifted a brow.

"Shh, woman." He rested his hand on hers. "Velocity means the speed of an object. Love is an object, an intense feeling of affection." He watched as she sucked in her breath. Her pulse raced along her neck. "One look at you and the speed of my attraction was intense. At the airport, you were like a magnet that pulled all my senses to you. It was so profound, I couldn't explain the emotion. With you, and only with you, I want to explore life all over again."

When her long lashes didn't capture a tear, he caught it with his finger. "I was the first to say I love you, and I want to be the last man to profess it to you."

Her lips curled. "If you're proposing, my answer is yes, Chaz."

"Woman, would you let me finish? Terrence will play as long as I ask him to." He cleared his throat. "I want us to experience life together as husband and wife, a mom and dad of as many children as you want, and as helpmates to each other as God has ordained." He removed his hand and reached into his breast pocket for the heart-shaped diamond on a silver band. He stood and pushed back his chair, then knelt. "Kym Knicely, will you marry me?"

Now she was speechless. Chaz counted to three and repeated, "Kym, I would be honored to be your husband. Please marry me."

She nodded. "My answer is still yes."

He stood and helped her to her feet. He balled his hands into fists. "Yes!"

Immediately, Terrence played the "Wedding March" on the keyboard as Kym placed her soft hands on both sides of Chaz's face and sealed their fate with a kiss that promised the love to come. The rest of the evening, they were treated to a private concert.

The next day, Kym screamed at her sisters on the video call. "I'm engaged!!!" She fanned her ring in front of the monitor for both to see.

"'Bout time!" Tabitha said. "I'm so happy for you. Congrats."

"You're blinding us." Rachel jokingly shielded her face with both arms. "I knew something was up when you called us first. Congratulations, Sis." She turned and shouted, "Nicholas, Kym and Chaz are engaged!"

"Praise God," his voice echoed in the background.

Then Tabitha yelled for Marcus to come to the computer before telling him.

Marcus had a slow grin. "About time. I thought the brother was old and slow," he joked, and Tabitha elbowed him.

"Stop talking about my fiancé." Kym extended her hand and scrutinized the clusters of diamonds again. "It is beautiful."

"It's a private joke. Chaz will get it. Anyway, congratulations, Sis. He seems like a good guy who loves family and Jesus. That's the best combination." He nodded, then disappeared.

When they were alone again, Rachel folded her arms and leaned closer to the computer. "Okay. Details. How did he propose? Where? What were you wearing?"

"The evening was surreal." Kym retold the story with excitement. She paused because her cheeks started to ache from her grinning. "Did I say I love that man?" she asked as she finished.

"Yeah." Tabitha grinned. "We heard that, and after a couple of times, we started counting. You're up to seven. I've never seen you so happy. You were beaming on graduation day."

Her phone rang Chaz's ringtone. "Ooh. Got to go. That's my fiancé." Kym signed off without waiting for their goodbyes. She answered his call with a resounding proclamation: "I'm engaged!"

His chuckle was deep. "Hmm, I know. I put the ring on your finger. I happen to be the man who found favor with God to find a woman who is after my own heart. I'm glad you're happy. I just told my sons. They can't wait for you to become an official part of the Banks family. Thank you for saying yes," he said softly. "You have changed my life."

Kym stood from her table and padded across the floor to the living room, where she floated to the sofa, spun around before sitting, then closed her eyes. "You're the man I asked God for."

Chapter 39

"So you did it." Zeke slapped a handshake with Chaz as they passed each other on the walkway between their buildings. Both were coming from meetings. "This is the first time I've seen you as an engaged man. Congratulations."

"I know, both of us," Chaz said, boasting. "She's the one I couldn't let get away."

They stepped to the side, out of the path of foot traffic. "Do you think having Chauncy for a while put off your decision?"

Chaz grunted. "It was because of my grandbaby that Kym and I had clarity about what our future would look like. I wouldn't have changed anything."

Zeke gave him a fist thump. "Well, now that we're both engaged, I take back what I said about a double wedding. I'm not waiting on you and Kym. Judith and I will be married by the time you two set a date." He laughed.

"I may have been slow asking, but I want to marry Kym sooner rather than later. I'll keep you posted on the details." They did another handshake, then parted ways.

Chaz's meeting at the Bloomberg School of Public Health had lasted longer than expected. Since it had been rescheduled twice, attendance today had been mandatory.

He had joined a handful of physicians, nurses, and staffers in a conference room for an update on whether the community outreach on diabetes education was making a difference. Teams had been formed to implement a diabetes intervention program in partnership with local churches whose membership could be at high risk.

Susan King, the director, had circulated handouts at the table. "There are multiple factors in some communities: the lack of nutrition without access to neighborhood markets, medical care for those who don't drive, and the mistrust of the health care industry."

She paused to allow everyone to glance at the report she had compiled. "As you know, we had an ambitious goal of working with twelve congregations in twelve months. We are encouraged with the findings. Dr. Phillips can speak about the participants." She nodded to the physician.

Dr. Philips slipped on his glasses. "Of the five hundred and fifteen people in the study, one-third were surprised they tested positive for diabetes even though it was prominent in their family history."

Listening to the data, Chaz mentally crunched the numbers. Although the Centers for Disease Control and Prevention had been tracking cases for years, it couldn't account for people who hadn't been diagnosed by a physician.

The meeting adjourned with suggestions on how to reach out to schools in charge of selecting food vendors. Back in his office, his own stomach growled, but it was too late for lunch. For months while Chauncy stayed with him, lunch consisted of PB&J sandwiches, Jell-O, and apple juice every day with his granddaughter at noon at the institute. He suffered through the bare minimum nutrition to create a routine for her, then grabbed a hamburger on his way back to his office.

It had been a while since he made a surprise visit to LLU's campus to see Kym—now his fiancée. Chaz pulled out his phone and sent her a text. Hey, baby, how is your day going?

Kym responded not long after that. Great! God is blessing me! I can't wait to share some news! Dinner?

If the exclamation marks were any indication of her happiness, then Chaz was glad to have played a part in it. Pick you up at 7. Love you.

With new dinner plans, Chaz canceled out a late lunch. Yet he needed fuel. Chaz walked to the café for a chicken wrap or something to numb the hunger pains. At checkout, he noticed a small bouquet. *How convenient*, he thought and purchased it for Kym.

Since he had two hours before his last meeting of the day, Chaz detoured to the garage for his car, then made the twenty-minute drive to the campus, tearing into his food along the way. In her education building, Chaz stepped off the elevator. When he turned the corner, he slowed his gait as he spied Kym in the distance. He admired her strut alongside Judith as they made their way down the hall.

As if she sensed his presence, Kym happened to glance over her shoulder and graced him with a smile, then twirled around in a pose that was runway ready. Her eyes sparkled as he sped up to meet her. He nodded at Judith.

"For you." He handed over the flowers. Chaz wanted to add a kiss but held back because of their professional surroundings.

"Thank you." Kym blushed. "You could've waited until our dinner and saved a trip."

"No, I couldn't. I needed a love boost that I can only get from seeing you."

"Whew. How am I supposed to wait to plan a wedding a year off when you say things like that?"

He shook his head. "You're not, Dr. Knicely. Three hundred and sixty-five days is too long." Chaz lifted a brow as his nostrils flared. He winked and pivoted on his heel. This time, he made sure he added some swagger to his stride.

Kym's heart danced as she watched Chaz's frame fade down the hall toward the elevators. Judith cleared her throat. Kym turned around. Grinning, she fell back in step with her friend to their offices.

"Mm-hmm. I'm with Chaz on this one. I don't see you two holding out six months. That was few words but a lot of attraction. Your love has been in the making for a lifetime."

"Girl, don't I know it?" Kym exhaled as she entered her office with Judith on her trail. "Chaz said he would marry me on whatever day I chose." She paused. "However, he said if it wasn't soon enough, he wasn't going to make it easy on me. I love that man. I forgot to tell him about my tenure appointment." She waved her hands in the air.

Judith squinted. "I don't think that entered your mind at all with one look at your fiancé, but I'm sure you'll get around it, considering you've waited—"

"I've prayed and waited, prayed some more for the Lord's will in my life," Kym corrected. "And look what happened. God sent not just any man but the best man for me."

"Amen, sister Dr. Knicely. I'd better go and prepare for my fall classes. By the way, it's fun preparing for a wedding, isn't it? Maybe we can join forces, although mine is months away."

"I'll just copy your notes," Kym joked. "Anyway, I'm almost done with my syllabus for the two classes. Since I don't have any appointments, I'm heading out early so I can get ready for my dinner date with my fiancé."

Judith snickered, then playfully stuck out her tongue. "And just think, I was first to officially have a fiancé."

"Thanks to me." Kym laughed, trying to up her friend. "See you tomorrow."

At home, she stared at her color-coordinated clothes in her closet. She had been on a beige binge, but she wanted a color explosion to express her jubilant mood. She chose gold because she felt like a princess in it. She showered, reapplied her makeup, and dressed.

When she opened her front door to Chaz later, he was tongue-tied. His lips formed an O, and seconds ticked, then finally, "Wow" escaped.

"I was expecting some shade of brown, but you are stunning. Come here." He engulfed her in a hug, then whispered, "Whatever date you pick for our wedding won't be soon enough for me."

After smacking a few kisses on his lips, she stepped back and shook her head. "Uh-uh. I've prayed and waited a long time for this kind of happiness," Kym reasoned with him. "It's August now. The spring is the earliest, next fall the latest. That's all I can tell you now."

Stuffing his hands in his pockets, he resembled a sullen boy before mumbling, "I vote for *this* fall, but I'll pray for more patience."

"Amen, Mr. Banks."

On the way to dinner, Kym was content with the jazz music serenading them. She didn't need any conversation as she enjoyed the feel of Chaz's strong hand holding hers.

At SoBo Café, cuddled in a booth seat, Chaz's breath tickled Kym's ear without him saying a word. Instead of reviewing the menu, he flirted with her, making Kym blush until their server returned a second time for their order. *Behave, Chaz,* she mouthed with a straight face as she perused the selections.

"Why? I'm just admiring God's handiwork." He winked and picked up his menu.

"That works both ways," Kym said after they gave their orders. "I forgot to share my big, big news." She used her hands to demonstrate an expanding balloon. "Guess what happened to me today?"

Resting his elbows on the table, Chaz leaned forward and curled his lips into a faint smile. "Tell me. Don't make me guess."

"I was offered a tenure appointment at LLU!" Tears filled her eyes. "God has been faithful. Now I understand Malachi 3:10: the Lord has truly poured out blessings that there isn't room enough to receive them—professionally and personally. I'm so full of joy, I can't contain my happiness."

"Congratulations, baby. I'm happy and proud of you. You've worked hard for it." He smiled, but it didn't quite reach his eyes.

Maybe she was over-the-top with glee, so she tamed her enthusiasm. He said he was happy for her. The man had always been in her corner.

As expected, Chaz asked questions about the appointment and listened as she explained how big of a deal it was. Playing with her fingers, he coaxed her to meet him halfway for a kiss, then fingered the diamond on her finger. He snickered. "I put that there."

"Yes." Kym giggled. "You did."

When their food arrived, Chaz shared with her about takeaways from his meeting on the diabetes awareness campaign. After dessert, he reached for her hands again. When she saw him swallow, Kym frowned. What was wrong? Not Chauncy or the twins, she hoped.

"Do you trust me?" he asked.

What an odd question. "Of course. Otherwise, we would've been done a long time ago."

His eyes became intense. "I'm so glad we weren't." He exhaled. "I spoke with Gee and Lana last night."

Immediately, Kym's heart skipped a beat as she panicked. "Is everything okay?"

Chaz rested his hands on hers and rocked his head from side to side. "They're coping." She nodded for him to continue and make it faster. She didn't like how he was dragging it out. "Before you shared your news about your most deserving appointment, I had planned to ask your thoughts about relocating to St. Louis after we're married, to be closer to our family and help out Gee and Lana."

So many emotions ran through her head that Kym couldn't speak, only blink. Had she heard right? Leave Charm City. "Ah…" She was speechless.

It was as if he held his breath, waiting for her to fill in the blanks.

Choked with emotions, a tear fell from her eye until she began to sob. Immediately, he pulled her into his arms. He didn't care about any stares. "Baby, if you don't want to, tell me now, and I'll come up with a plan B."

Kym had no plans to move. She sniffed and took deep breaths. "Whew. I wasn't expecting that." Suddenly, she felt sick to her stomach. She looked at him through watery eyes. "You asked me if I trust you. What did you mean?"

He settled back into his seat. "Trust me to make you happy and not regret walking this journey with me. Just a thought, because it means I'd have to resign from my six-figure job and start over in St. Louis. But you would never go hungry," he was quick to add. "God will help me to supply all your—our—needs according to His will and riches in glory. As your husband, your well-being and happiness will be my number-one priority. Gee and his family will be second."

But your second priority is superseding your first, she wanted to say. Still, he deserved credit for sharing his thoughts. Kym respected him for not making the decision for her—them.

"I was hoping you would like to be near your sister, so when we started a family, Tabitha would be there to help. Like I said, I haven't mentioned this to anybody. If you say no, I'll regroup. If you say wait, then I will."

"Ha!" came out before she could catch it. "Chaz, you can't even wait to get married. How can you be willing to wait on my decision to move?" Kym didn't know how she felt. Confused, disappointed, definitely not the happiness that filled her when they'd first walked in. Yep, confusion topped the list.

Chaz nodded. "A fair question. All I ask is you think about it."

Kym rubbed her forehead. "This is a lot to take in. I envisioned us picking out a new house to live in in Baltimore, not moving across the country to buy a house. Not only will I think, but I'll pray about it too."

"That's the perfect answer." Chaz brought her hand to his lips. "Thank you."

Chapter 40

On campus the next morning, Judith peeked her head in Kym's doorway as she packed to move to a larger office reserved for instructors who held PhDs—finally.

"How was your evening, Dr. Knicely?" Her friend folded her arms. "*Ahhh*. I like saying that."

"I like hearing it, but I have to remember that people are addressing me." Kym chuckled when she really didn't feel it, not after the bombshell from last night. Chaz had tried to jump-start the carefree, easygoing, and playful nature between them. After dessert, she asked to go home, then a peck on the cheek was his good-night kiss.

Kym stopped separating books into two piles and looked up. "It was romantic, enjoyable, and…strange." She shrugged.

"Huh? You lost me on the strange part. What was strange about it?"

She looked up and stared at Judith. "He wants to move to St. Louis to be closer to his son and grandbabies. What do you think about that?"

Judith grinned. "Sounds like the honorable family man that he is."

Yeah, allegiance to family—check. Why did Kym have doubts about which one?

"When?" Judith pressed her.

"Oh." Kym sighed. "He didn't give me a timeline, but it sounds like sooner rather than later after we're married."

"Uh-oh." Judith blinked and gritted her teeth. "But you were just offered your tenure."

"I know," Kym groaned, then gnawed on her lips. "Why can't I have the love of a good godly man and the happiness of the perk position? Although he left the choice up to me, I'll feel guilty if I say no."

"But if you say yes?" Judith left the question hanging in the air.

"He'll resign from his job, and I'll have to start all over at a university and work my way up their food chain to be offered tenure again. Sounds simple on paper—no, I don't even like the sound of that on paper, because as you know, tenure isn't easy to achieve. I wondered if it was God's plan for me to move back to St. Louis."

"Big decisions." Judith stood. "I'll be praying with you to listen for the answer." She walked out of the office, leaving Kym to her own thoughts.

Chaz's ringtone interrupted her deliberation. "Hey, babe," he cooed. "I know the mood changed after I mentioned moving once we're married. I should have waited to say anything. I've been looking out for Gee and Lana so long, I don't know how to pull away."

Cut the cord, she wanted to say, but that would be selfish on her part, so she wouldn't dare. She was a big girl, and these were adult decisions they could make together. "Chaz, it's okay. I was hoping we would have some *us* time in our marriage first."

"I could sense that I had upset you, which is why I'm standing outside your office door. I wanted to make sure the coast was clear before I knocked."

"You're what?" Her spirits lifted, and she got to her feet to open the door. Chaz crossed the threshold with the ease of a salsa partner, guiding her back into her office. After he closed the door, Chaz wrapped his arms around her.

"Sorry about last night. While my heart wants to say yes to your idea, my head is whispering, 'what about me?'" She looked into his eyes.

Chaz released her and glanced away, gritting his teeth. He looked disgusted with himself. "I'm sorry I even asked that of you. I know my priorities will change once we have our children." He kissed her.

I hope so. "But will Gee and Lana understand that?" She quizzed him.

"They will." Chaz nodded. "They haven't asked for the help I've given them over the years." He cupped her chin in his hands. "You are the most important person in my life besides the Lord. Your happiness is my happiness. Again, congratulations on your tenure offer. I don't want to take away anything you've worked hard for."

Hearing him say that was the reason why she'd fallen in love with him. Again, she questioned whether she was being selfish when he was so giving. "It's just that you might be able to find another job right away, but that might not happen for me. I can't transfer a tenure offer, which is a minimum six-year hard-fought process at any university."

"I get it, babe," he said so easily that she wondered if he really did.

She dismissed her concern when Chaz delivered a few more pecks to her lips, then bid her goodbye.

Clearing her head of doubts, Kym smiled and resumed her task.

Sunday, during Kym's weekly family chat, she asked her sisters to weigh in on whether giving up a career that she worked for to follow the man she loved was a deal breaker. No surprise, their opinions were split.

"Chaz has good intentions," Tabitha said. "I had the same mindset as a caregiver. I started at a new company for less money to spend more time with Aunt Tweet. That was my sacrifice, and I have no regrets. But he backed down, right?"

"Well, he didn't rescind the plan, only put it on hold." Kym rubbed her temple. Was she overthinking this?

"From my research on autism, parents are overwhelmed and often feel isolated. After what we witnessed at your graduation dinner with Chauncy—whew." Tabitha grew quiet. "I exchanged numbers with Lana when I ran into her shopping, and I've even visited her once. She was surprised when I mentioned Chauncy's episode at your graduation dinner. Lana had no idea that happened." Tabitha rambled on.

"Chaz didn't tell her?" Kym said more to herself.

"Evidently not. Maybe he didn't want to worry her. She seemed horrified and embarrassed for you and apologized profusely. I felt so bad for her. I'm not trying to lay a guilt trip on you, Sis, but if you get closer to me, our children can have playmates. I'd say take the deal…because I can see she needs the help."

"Hold up, traitor." Rachel squinted at Tabitha. "Kym only has a ring on her finger. I've got a bun in the oven, so I thought my baby was going to be Little Marcus's buddy."

"He can have more than one," Tabitha assured their baby sister "Plus, you'll be first, since you're about to pop sometime next month."

Kym could always count on her sisters for distraction with their comic relief. "Okay, so what's your take, Rach?"

Rachel gnawed on her bottom lip. "I'm feeling you, Kym. I'm an engineer at a coveted firm in Nashville. It would be hard for me to walk away from what I have accomplished here, although I'm addicted to Minister Nicholas Adams and wouldn't say no to his requests. I have to know what God has to say about it, because I don't know if it's a good thing Chaz put that bug in your ear, or you're six months into the wedded bliss and he comes home from work and announces you're moving."

"You've got a point. I guess the Lord Jesus will have to be my tie-breaker," Kym heard herself say, but she wasn't convinced she would be happy with the outcome. Enough. She was an engaged woman and a professor; she wasn't supposed to be stressed, so she changed the subject. "So what is my nephew getting into?"

After a daily play-by-play of Little Marcus's antics, Rachel jumped in with her cravings. By the time they ended their video chat, Kym's stomach ached from laughing.

The following week, she stayed in God's presence through prayer and supplication, seeking His will. Jesus had remained silent, so she treaded carefully as she and Chaz agreed on a May 1 wedding. It was time to start the countdown.

Chapter 41

Chaz was living his best life. God was good. Gee and Lana were adjusting to their expanded family. Chauncy was thriving in her social and verbal skills, and Drake and Patrice were engaged. And after resolving to be a bachelor for life, Chaz had found his special someone.

He had never seen his fiancée so happy. The first time he married, Chaz was young and had no interest in the wedding planning process. With Kym, he wanted to be involved because it was his second chance at a happily ever after.

While they were snuggled together compiling their guest list, Gee and Lana FaceTimed them. Chauncy was a chatterbox at first before she lost interest. The twins were getting big, and Kym cooed at the boys.

She was the perfect fit in his life, and he would deny her nothing within his power.

"Well, Dad, we better go, but we wanted to check in on the lovebirds," Gee tee-heed.

"Yep." Lana giggled. "Kym, thank you again for making my Pops happy, and I'm so sorry about Chauncy ruining your graduation dinner. I'm glad that didn't chase you away."

"You know?" Chaz straightened his frame and squinted. He never meant for his daughter-in-law to find out. "Who told you?"

"Tabitha, when I ran into her a while back."

"Lana, your daughter"—Kym paused as if she was considering her response—"is a special little person who is navigating in our world. I was unprepared, but it's okay."

"You sure?" Lana asked.

"Yes." Kym beamed. "One thing I've learned about autism is it's a learning process for the child and the adult."

"God bless you. Whew." Lana's eyes were misty and Chaz's too. "Thank you."

After love-yous, waves, and blowing kisses, his family was gone.

"Chaz." Kym's tone was sweet but measured at the same time. "Why didn't you tell her?"

He shrugged. "I didn't think it was important. Besides, I didn't want to worry her." Evidently, that wasn't the right answer when she lifted a brow and twisted her pouty lips. "What?"

"Do you plan to keep things from me now and after we're married because you don't think something is important?" She did air quotes with her fingers. "Because I have a problem with that."

"No, dear." Chaz shook his head and folded his hands as obedient as a first-grader, hoping that was the right answer. It wasn't, because Kym folded her arms and stared. "What?" he pressed her.

"Chaz, don't keep things from me to spare my feelings. I need you to always be truthful with me. What happened at my graduation was unfortunate and did put a damper on my day. I wasn't prepared for or expecting a meltdown. It was horrific at first, then sad for Chauncy. I didn't know what I could have done to control the situation. But I want to know everything."

Chaz bobbed his head and exhaled. "I'm sorry, sweetheart. I have been properly chastened by the love of my life, and I appreciate it." He offered a faint smile as a peace offering and thought about a portion of Hebrews 12:6: "For whom the Lord loveth he chastens."

Kym wanted to include Chauncy in the wedding party, and Lana had been thrilled about the invitation but declined.

"Although Chauncy's verbal and social skills improved so much while in Baltimore, I don't want to chance her not following directions. Best to keep her on the sidelines."

Planning the nuptials together, Chaz had squeezed Kym's hand. "We understand, but dress her up as a flower girl for the pictures," Kym suggested.

Gee and Lana were sweet, which made Kym have empathy for them. Maybe, one day, St. Louis might be an option, not now.

That left only one child in the family who could be in the wedding party. Little Marcus was about to turn three, but he could be unpredictable too. "I'm striking out." She pouted. "Weddings are supposed to be a family affair, but all our babies are too young. Even Rachel's little boy, Nick Junior, is only eight months old."

The logistics had been exhausting, even with help from Rachel and Tabitha doing a lot of online shopping for flowers, invitations, the videographer, photographer, and other tasks.

Her bridal party included her sisters and Judith, who had tied the knot on Valentine's Day, and Drake's fiancée, Patrice. Chaz's groomsmen were his two sons, Zeke, and Marcus. Nicholas would assist in the officiating with Kym's pastor pronouncing the prayer.

The reception venue had to be 1840s Plaza because of her love of the Inner Harbor. Chaz secured the pianist who had serenaded them when he proposed to play the same selection for her procession to the altar. Together, they had checked off each detail. "We're done."

"Not quite, sweetheart. There is one more surprise I'll have for you on the wedding day," he whispered in a suspicious tone.

"What?"

He tapped the bridge of her nose. "My dear wife-to-be, you have to leave some wiggle room for surprises."

"Surprises at weddings are always scary." She eyed him with suspicion, and he kissed her worries away.

Chapter 42

The bliss of blended families. Kym wasn't under any illusions there would never be any disagreement, but deep down inside, she believed love did conquer all. On a sunny afternoon on the first Saturday of May, she scrutinized her reflection in the floor-length mirror in the dressing room of Abundant Life Church.

"Are you ready to do this?" Rachel asked as she fitted the bridal veil on Kym's head. "You look like a princess. For something old..." Rachel fastened Aunt Tweet's diamond bracelet about Kym's wrist. "She didn't live to make my wedding either, but this is a reminder she will always be a part of our lives."

"Amen." Kym choked on tears, staring at the bracelet that her aunt had worn when she attended high society events. Rachel wore it on her wedding day, and now Kym had that honor. "Thank you." She hugged her sister, then scrutinized her reflection again. The woman who stared back at her looked happy. She closed her eyes and took in the moment. "Yes to finally become Mrs. Charles 'Chaz' Banks."

Tabitha stood behind Kym. "I peeked through the doors to the sanctuary, and your husband-to-be looks happy but impatient... That's a good thing." They snickered together.

When the music echoed from the sanctuary, Judith, Lana, Tabitha, and Rachel stood on cue and graced her with a kiss on her cheek as they one by one left the dressing room.

She always imagined she would be nervous. She wasn't. Chaz had asked if she trusted him. She did and trusted God to guide them as a model Christian married couple.

There was a knock at the door, and Kym stood unsteadily as her legs trembled. Okay, maybe she was a little nervous because her heart was off rhythm as she picked up her bouquet, which Chaz had created with pearls and a dozen bits of diamond sprinkled in it. Closing her eyes, she smiled.

When the ushers opened the center doors, Kym locked eyes with Chaz at the altar. To say the man was handsome in his tux would be insulting. He was magnificent, and it was his love that beckoned her forward.

Wait a minute. She glanced at two boys no taller than four feet who stood beside him in tuxes, dark glasses, and holding what appeared to be black briefcases. This definitely wasn't part of their program.

Instead of Chaz meeting her halfway as planned, the pint-sized boys in black marched to her side in military precision. She looked at Chaz, clueless. The man's expression gave nothing away.

Matching her steps, they escorted her to the end of the aisle, where Chaz stood with an outstretched hand.

"You're under my protection," he whispered with all seriousness in his eyes. "They are carrying our rings."

Oh. Speechless, Kym operated on autopilot as he placed her shaky hand on his forearm and glided her closer to Pastor Harrison and Rachel's husband, Minister Nicholas Adams.

The pastor glanced at what Kym could only describe as ring bearers. "At ease, men." He chuckled, Kym mustered a smile. They were cute.

"Dearly beloved, we are gathered this afternoon to join Charles 'Chaz' Banks and Kym Knicely in holy matrimony. Holy because God ordained this institution…"

Kym stared into Chaz's eyes. She slowly exhaled as she listened to the vow she was about to make before God.

"Chaz, do you take this woman to be your lawful wedded wife, to live together in a holy union, to love her, to honor her, to comfort her, and to keep her in sickness and in health, forsaking all others, for as long as you both shall live?"

"I most certainly do," he said in a manner that made Kym feel as if it were only them.

Soon, all eyes were on her. "I, Kym, take you, Chaz, to be my lawful wedded husband…as long as we both shall live."

The moment was surreal as Chaz tapped a combination to open the briefcases and retrieve their rings. After he slipped the wedding band on her finger and she did the same, he cupped her shaky hands in his. The gesture was reassuring.

Pastor Harrison announced, "By virtue of the authority vested in me by the Lord Jesus Christ and the state of Maryland, I now pronounce you husband and wife."

As Chaz pulled her closer into his embrace, Nicholas intervened. "Not so fast. Let us pray. Father, in the name of Jesus, we stand before you, representing the first gift to man—a wife and helpmate. Sanctify their marriage and let no man or woman come to separate them, so their union may prosper. We ask for the Lord's blessings this day and forever. In Jesus's name. Amen."

Chaz squinted at Nicholas. "Now?"

"You may now salute your wife and my sister-in-law." Nicholas grinned.

Kym closed her eyes and enjoyed the first kiss as Mrs. Chaz Banks.

Epilogue

Kym and Chaz celebrated their first anniversary with a candlelight dinner at their favorite restaurant overlooking the Inner Harbor. "Is there a reason why neither one of your sons carry your first name?" she asked out of the blue.

He gave it some thought and shrugged. "Valerie wanted to name them, so I let her."

"Well, for the record, if our baby is a boy—" She drummed her fingers on the table and watched him.

"Wait. What?" he stuttered. "We're having a baby?" From the shakiness in his voice, it was as if Chaz had never heard "our baby" before.

"Or, if it's a girl, Chauncy will have a little playmate besides her brothers. Technically, she'll be her aunt, but yes, Hubby, I believe I'm pregnant, so I made an appointment with my doctor."

"I'm going too."

"You're the daddy, so why not, but if it's a boy, I want to name him Chaz Jr."

"If it's a girl, then I want bragging rights for naming my little princess."

"Fair enough as long as I like it." Kym jutted her chin.

Reaching for her hands across the table, he squeezed her fingers. "Thank you for being my wife and putting the brakes on moving to St. Louis. Although I'm there for them, I want to be here for you. Charge my misstep to my head, not my heart."

"Thank you for asking me to be your wife. I feel loved. Now"—she rubbed her imaginary bump—"your baby wants dessert."

Chaz released a hearty laugh. "Which one?"

"Both," she said with a saucy smile. Life couldn't get any better than this.

From a dark moment that shakes their faith,
to a profoundly happy ending,
check out Nicholas and Rachel's story in

here for you

Available now from Sourcebooks Casablanca

Dying? Rachel Knicely refused to accept that. Only three weeks ago, her great-aunt Priscilla "Aunt Tweet" Brownlee was the life of the party at the wedding reception. Her eyes had sparkled, her dance moves impressive for an eighty-five-year-old, and her childish giggles made the evening more festive, sometimes stealing the spotlight from the bride and groom. How could she be dying? *Nope, I won't accept that. I need her in my life.*

Closing her eyes, Rachel rubbed her face and tried to make sense of her aunt's rapid decline. The youngest of three daughters, Rachel had made an agreement with her two sisters to share Aunt Tweet's caregiving responsibilities six months at a time, first with the oldest, Kym, in Baltimore, next with Tabitha in St. Louis. Now it was Rachel's "tour of duty" to care for their beloved role model.

Life was suddenly becoming too short. *I'm not ready to lose my auntie yet.* Rachel yawned and stretched on the chaise longue. She had put the piece of furniture by the bed in the makeshift guest bedroom in the loft of her Nashville condo. She forced one eye open briefly to check on her aunt.

Rachel was drained and wasn't sure how she could be so tired. It was only 2:00 a.m., on a Saturday morning in a city known for its nightlife. Before Aunt Tweet's stay, Rachel would have been out on the town with her best friend, Jacqui Rice, at one of the many "must-attend" events around Music City after a long work week.

She had tweaked her social calendar until June 1, when Kym would begin her second rotation as Aunt Tweet's caregiver and would relocate their aunt to Baltimore again.

Over the past months, Rachel had learned being a caregiver wasn't a nine-to-five shift. She did what it took to make her aunt comfortable, and her late nights were now spent watching over her loved one, even more so since the dementia symptoms caused by Alzheimer's had her aunt acting out of character.

Rachel had had no concept of the term *sundown* until Aunt Tweet began to wake in the middle of the night and wander through her condo, trying to get out. Her loving aunt had been downright mean and combative toward Rachel for more than a month. Aunt Tweet's behavior had crushed Rachel to the core.

A trip to St. Louis last month for Tabitha and Marcus's wedding had seemed to give her aunt a second wind, then after a few days back in Nashville, her aunt had slipped into another personality again.

Aunt Tweet stopped eating for two days. *Two days!* Rachel had freaked out and called her sisters, who in turn had a conference call with the doctor—the third one since Aunt Tweet was initially diagnosed more than a year ago. After moving Aunt Tweet from her home in Philly, she had a specialist in Baltimore with Kym, one in St. Louis with Tabitha, and now Dr. Allison Watkins here in Nashville.

"The kind of symptoms you're describing become severe as the patient transitions into the last stages of Alzheimer's," Dr. Watkins had said, too casually in Rachel's opinion, as her heart shattered. Was it fair that her designated time with Aunt Tweet was marred with worry that, at any time, her aunt would slip away?

"Aunt Tweet's doctor in Philly said a patient with dementia can live up to twenty years," Rachel pointed out.

"Yes," the doctor confirmed, "with no other contributing factors, but the average life span is usually four to eight years after diagnosis. Changes in the brain begin before any signs manifest."

"That's the preclinical period of Alzheimer's," Tabitha, the second oldest and a pharmaceutical rep, whispered.

"Yes, also called the mild stage, which allows her to remain active socially. Stages can overlap, so I suspect Miss Brownlee might have moderate to advanced Alzheimer's. It is usually the longest stage and can last for many years."

"Living longer is good news, but not with her condition worsening. My aunt is the sweetest person on earth." All Rachel wanted was more bonding time with Aunt Tweet so she could tell her over and over again how much she loved her, admired her, and would live up to the expectations Aunt Tweet had for her three nieces.

"Based on these new symptoms, let me see her in my office to determine if she has progressed to the next stage."

"Which is?" Kym, the oldest, asked, but Rachel wasn't sure she wanted to know.

"The late stage," Dr. Watkins said matter-of-factly. "Unfortunately, the last stage of Alzheimer's is the most severe. Without warning, she can lose the ability to respond to her surroundings, control movements, or she may stop walking, sitting, and eventually swallowing."

When the call ended, Rachel had been numb. The conversation had both depressed her and upset her stomach. Dr. Watkins's speculation was one thing, but taking Aunt Tweet into the office to confirm the inevitable was disheartening. Had her aunt stopped eating because she couldn't swallow?

The next day, Aunt Tweet woke with a voracious appetite. Relieved, Rachel cried like a baby with a wet diaper. This was proof that Aunt Tweet had not progressed to another stage. She had bounced back. "Thank you, God," she whispered and considered canceling the doctor appointment.

Kym was the first one to veto the idea. "Go, Rach, or I'll fly down there and take her myself," she threatened.

"All right!" Rachel reluctantly agreed.

On second thought, Rachel wondered if all three of them going to the doctor with Aunt Tweet wasn't such a bad idea. Depending on what the doctor had to say, they may need to hold each other's hands.

Unfortunately, one week later, Rachel was on her own as she escorted Aunt Tweet to the appointment. She didn't care what it looked like to others in the waiting room, Rachel held her aunt's hand as if she were a little lost girl, not a twenty-nine-year-old engineer who was at the top of her game.

After the preliminaries, Dr. Watkins gave Rachel the heartbreaking news. "From my assessment and everything you shared on the phone, your aunt has indeed transitioned to the last stage." She was quick to add, "Don't give up hope yet. It's not over. This stage can last from several weeks to several years. It's not the quantity of time but the memories you have with her that will give you comfort."

Rachel nodded but didn't feel any comfort in her words. It was the memories of Aunt Tweet's laugh, unfiltered conversations about life, and her attention to a meticulous appearance that was fading too fast, being replaced by a shell of a woman whose independence had been stolen.

"It's important that you keep a sharp eye on her for signs of pain, since her level of communication may become more limited."

Oftentimes, that meant Rachel sitting at her bedside throughout the night, reminiscing about happy times as a child, unsure if Aunt Tweet remembered or understood, but it was therapy for Rachel.

The influence Aunt Tweet had on the Knicely sisters—especially Rachel's life—was astonishing. Their aunt was all about confidence and character building, plus detailed attention to a woman's personal appearance.

As the oldest sibling, Kym inherited Aunt Tweet's wisdom. Tabitha's features were almost identical to a younger Aunt Tweet, as if their parents, Thomas and Rita Knicely, had no say in their daughter's DNA. As the baby girl, Rachel had a special bond with her great-aunt.

Aunt Tweet seemed to infuse Rachel with more of her personality: a flair for fashion, which included showstopping hair, nails, and makeup at all times and a thirst to achieve a high level of intellect with education being the primary goal. Then there were the many life lessons, including on how to act like a lady, and the most important was philanthropy. There was nothing wrong with enjoying the finer things in life, but one had to remember others less fortunate and help them climb to success.

Rachel sighed. There were so many life lessons learned courtesy of Aunt Tweet. The only topic her aunt didn't bring up much was living happily ever after with the love of your life.

Wednesday morning, Nicholas Adams was on his way home from his overnight shift when he received a call from his church. He was a project manager at the Nissan plant in Smyrna, about half an hour from downtown Nashville. However, he was never off duty as a minister for God. His pastor assigned him and several other ministers to visit church members who were sick, homebound, or hospitalized.

"Hello, Minister Adams," Mrs. Eloise Emerson greeted him when he answered. "I know it's early, but we received a call over the weekend from a Tabitha Whittington with an urgent prayer request. She's a member at one of our sister churches in St. Louis."

"It's okay, Mrs. Emerson," he reassured the elderly church secretary.

"Good, I'll send you the information," she said in a quiet voice. "Miss Whittington would like someone to visit her great-aunt, Miss Priscilla Brownlee, who is staying here in Nashville. I'm sure she'd appreciate your visit—the sooner the better, the note says."

Nicholas nodded to himself. If someone needed healing or comfort, it was his job to pray with them. As soon as he said, "I'm on it," Nicholas glanced in his rearview mirror and groaned. He had planned to get to the barber before heading home. His hair demanded a cut that was a week delayed.

His phone chimed as he took off. At a stoplight, he stifled a yawn as he glanced at the address Mrs. Emerson had texted him for Miss Brownlee. It was in Midtown, not far from Vanderbilt University, but a good half-hour drive during morning rush hour. It was also a bit early for a house call. Going home wasn't an option either. If he closed his eyes, Nicholas would be down for the count for a good seven hours. Not good in this case.

He rubbed his hair again and made a decision: a pit stop at Hats

Off Barbershop in Antioch, which was in the direction of downtown. Hopefully, he could get in and out.

When he arrived at the place, he counted seven heads before him, or maybe his eyes had crossed. Nicholas resolved that he would have to wait longer than he had hoped. Making himself comfortable in an empty folding chair, he mumbled a prayer for Priscilla Brownlee before he dozed off. A few times, someone nudged him to pull him into a conversation about sports or to give his opinion about a world event from a "preacher's viewpoint," because his barber always addressed him as preacher.

Two hours later, he walked out a tired man with a fade cut to his wavy hair, a trimmed mustache, and a five o'clock shadow outlining his jaw. At least he had gone into the restroom to rinse his face with cold water and pop a breath mint. He slipped on his shades after squinting at the sunlight that seemed to have brightened while he'd been inside. Now he felt presentable enough to perform his task.

Once in his car, he confirmed the address again. It was after ten, so surely someone would be awake by now. He tapped the address to activate the navigation app and headed westbound on I-24.

The West End Avenue area was a trendy part of Nashville that attracted grad students and young professionals drawn to the surrounding downtown nightlife, Lower Broadway, or East Nashville.

Rumor had it that Midtown was so pricey the rent there was comparable to the mortgage of a custom-built house. Personally, Nicholas enjoyed being a homeowner in a quiet Smyrna neighborhood with a spacious ranch house that was close to his job. To him, that was preferable to living in the midst of a constant bustle of people.

Since the traffic flowed, he arrived in less than half an hour and parked around the corner. He grabbed his Bible from the back seat and headed to the building's grand entrance with a maroon awning and street-level retail shops lining the front windows. He strolled inside. Whoever lived in this place had money with a capital *M*.

The interior resembled a hotel lobby with marble floors and expensive decor. Voices above him made him take notice of a mezzanine. *Wow* was the only way to describe the Westchester. A middle-aged gentleman stood from behind a sleek desk in an office with see-through walls and strolled around to greet him.

He asked for Nicholas's ID, which he looked at carefully. "Who are you here to see?"

"Miss Priscilla Brownlee who is staying with her niece Rachel Knicely in 1402."

"Of course." He returned Nicholas's license and pushed a button to open the elevator doors.

Nicholas nodded his thanks and walked inside, where spotless mirrors, brass trim, and accent lighting surrounded him as the doors closed. He had never visited a residence with this type of security, but it was close to a busy area, so maybe that justified it.

On the ride up to the fourteenth floor, soft music entertained Nicholas until the bell chimed and the doors opened. The decor screamed elegance from the floor to the overhead mini chandeliers that lit the path. Should he remove his shoes to walk on the plush carpet? He didn't and continued to 1402, where an artistically carved wood front door rivaled the one at his house.

After he pushed the doorbell, Nicholas dusted any stray hairs from his shoulders. When he made first-time house calls, he liked to portray an image of a respectable, serious, and clean-cut man.

Respect, at times, was based on perception—what people thought a minister should look like and how elegantly he spoke. Nicholas didn't think that should matter. His attire wasn't dress slacks and a collared shirt. Instead, it was his Nissan polo work shirt and jeans.

He was about to ring the bell again when a woman answered. They blinked at each other. It was a toss-up whether Nicholas had wakened her or she didn't care about her appearance. Either way, her beauty wasn't dimmed, even with messy hair, wrinkled clothes, and one missing big hoop earring. Nicholas had seen worse. He offered a smile.

She looked at him as if she was in a daze. "Yes?"

"I'm Minister Nicholas Adams, from Believers Temple Church. I'm here to see Miss Brownlee."

The woman's eyes widened with fear, and she slammed the door in his face.

What? I don't have time for this. Nicholas was sleep deprived and hungry. Maybe his eyes were bloodshot and she thought he was drunk or high on drugs or something. Unfortunately, there were instances when he was met with hostility from families who weren't Christians and resented his presence.

Nicholas tried not to take their rudeness personally. This was his godly calling, and he was going in to see Miss Brownlee. He gritted his teeth and was about to knock again when the woman slowly opened the door with a sheepish expression. "Sorry. I wasn't expecting you."

Clearly. He kept that to himself, then relaxed. He smiled again to ease the tension, and she returned his smile, although hesitantly. "Your sister in St. Louis called our church office."

"Tabitha," she mumbled, then squeezed her lips together.

That somewhat explained her reaction. "Since I'm here, do you mind if I visit with Miss Brownlee?"

"She was alert a few days ago, but she's shut down again. I'm not sure if she'll know you're here." Rachel grunted. "I'm not even sure if she knows I'm here." The look of hurt didn't go unnoticed.

"I'm sure she feels your presence," he said, trying to console her. "You're Miss Knicely?"

"Yes, I'm Rachel Knicely," she confirmed.

"Nice to meet you. Again, I'm Nicholas Adams."

Before his eyes, Rachel's sluggish demeanor disappeared, replaced with alertness as she leaned on the doorjamb, crossing her arms. "First, may I see your ID?" As he reached into his back pocket for his wallet, she added, "I have a photographic memory."

Nicholas contained his amusement at her personality swing from fear to fierceness.

A Yorkie and a cocker spaniel appeared at her side, barking and wagging their tails, undecided if Nicholas was a friend or foe. He kept a straight face, trying not to show his amusement at their veiled threat as guard dogs.

Back to Rachel. He wasn't offended by her request. Despite the tight security to get to her door, a woman could never be too careful, whether a man was carrying a Bible or not. He only had a younger brother, Karl, but if he'd had any sisters, he would have taught them the same precautions.

He handed over his license. She glanced at it, squinted at him again, then handed it back, reciting his license number, height, weight, and eye color to prove she wasn't kidding. Did she say his weight? Seriously, hey, he had lost ten pounds since that was taken. He was lean and all muscle. She didn't need to know that, but he decided to tell her anyway. The woman had some serious skills. "Just so you know, I was ten pounds heavier then," he said in defense.

"And you had a bad haircut," she sassed back and stepped aside for him to enter. He couldn't tell if she was joking about his hair then or now. He refrained from asking and sized her up as well—about five feet four or five inches to his six feet two, messy dark brown hair—wig or weave—tired brown eyes, curly lashes, and a face that probably could use a morning wash. All in all, she was cute—very.

He stepped in and noticed the richness of her hardwood floors; they looked as if no one had ever walked across them, much less pets. He admired her living space, which was an open design with the dining room/eating area and kitchen on one side.

Nicholas followed her along a hallway that turned a corner as the dogs trailed behind them. They stepped down into a spacious living room with a nice decor and floor-to-ceiling windows. The sunlight was streaming through.

They climbed a few steps to a loft overlooking the living room, offering little privacy, except for a trifold room divider. Massive bedroom furniture held court. The dogs had beaten them and scrambled to a spot at the foot of the bed. "Nice place," Nicholas said, and he meant it.

"Thank you," she said without looking at him. Her attention was on the woman in the bed. "Aunt Tweet," she called softly. "Nicholas Adams is here to see you. He's a minister."

Her loved one didn't respond. The slight rise and fall of the cover was proof she was still alive. *Whew.* Nicholas had never witnessed someone taking their last few breaths. He didn't want to see it today.

Chapter 2

How embarrassing. Rachel couldn't believe she had slammed the door in a man's face—and a minister at that. The doorbell had rescued her from the vortex of a nightmare about a Death Angel trying to get inside her house.

She could thank her best friend, Jacqui, for putting that image in her subconscious. She had mentioned her family called a priest to administer the last rites to her grandfather, then minutes later, Mr. Rice died. Her mother said it was as if the priest had summoned the angel of death.

Still shaken from the dream, Rachel remained leery about whether the minister was there to give Aunt Tweet her last rites, despite not being a priest. She watched Nicholas from the doorway as he perched on the chaise that she had slept on for many nights. Leaning closer, he rested his hand on Aunt Tweet's forehead and softly called her name. "Miss Brownlee, I'm here to pray for you."

God, please let his prayer make a difference. The moment was tranquil, and she noted his gentle manner. Something she wouldn't expect from a man who had a handsome face with a fierce expression and the physique of a bodybuilder. His tenderness was endearing.

Aunt Tweet moved slightly but didn't open her eyes. Excitement, hope, and anticipation swirled in Rachel at her response. Next, Nicholas opened his worn leather-bound Bible. The pages seemed to part without a bookmark, as if they knew the passage he wanted.

As he began to read from Psalm 23, the softness of his voice deepened to a rich baritone. The sound was like a sweet melody. Rachel closed her eyes, drifting into serenity as she listened.

"'He makes me to lie down in green pastures: he leads me beside the still waters,'" Nicholas continued. "'He restores my soul…though I walk through the valley of the shadow of death, I will fear no evil…'"

Death. Wait a minute! Rachel's eyes opened in horror. Her aunt was very much alive, and she was hoping his prayer would keep it that way. Was the minister summoning death for Aunt Tweet? This was too much talk about death—the doctor, her sister, her friend, and now this minister.

The thought ignited a sob from somewhere deep within her, and Rachel couldn't stop the floodgate. She felt weak in the knees.

"Are you all right?" Nicholas looked at her and asked in a concerned tone.

She shook her head, unable to answer. He coaxed her to sit on the ottoman. She felt the seat shift as he sat next to her. When she inhaled, the faint scent of his cologne acted as smelling salts and revitalized her. It was a familiar brand that some of her colleagues and male acquaintances wore. The distraction was only temporary.

"Can I get you some water?"

"Yes," she choked out, as if he knew the layout of her kitchen. *Let him find his way.* She opened her eyes in a daze and glanced at Aunt Tweet. She was still alive, and Rachel exhaled in relief.

He returned quickly with ice water in a crystal glass. Her best dishes were reserved for entertaining, but she didn't care as she accepted the glass with trembling hands. Nicholas's hands steadied hers so she could drink. Rachel gulped down the water as if she'd been parched for days. "Thank you."

Nicholas took the seat next to her again. "Are you okay?"

"I don't know." She turned and stared into his eyes and noticed their unusual shade of brown. They weren't light or dark but almost sun-kissed, as if sunlight was drawn to them. "I lost it when I heard you say 'death.'"

Nicholas nodded his head, but she doubted he understood what a blow Aunt Tweet's passing would be, losing the last connection to her father's side of the family. "Death is part of life," he told her, then stood. "If you're all right, do you mind if I pray for both of you before I leave?"

"Sure."

Returning to the bedside, he smiled at Rachel, then at Aunt Tweet, who appeared to be resting quietly. Reaching inside his jacket, Nicholas pulled out a tiny bottle no bigger than a sample size of perfume or scented oil. Unscrewing the top, he placed a dab of oil on Aunt Tweet's forehead, then looked at Rachel inquiringly. "It's anointed oil."

She declined to take part in the anointing but joined him at the bedside. Closing her eyes, Rachel bowed her head and waited for the prayer.

"Lord Jesus, let this household feel Your presence and be at peace. All power is in Your hands, and nothing can be done without Your permission…" His short prayer was as soft as his reading voice, which had lulled even her cocker spaniel, Shelby, and Aunt Tweet's Yorkie, Sweet Pepper, to sleep, and finished with, "Amen."

"Amen," Rachel repeated, then exhaled.

Nicholas faced her. "If you'd like another ministerial visit, don't hesitate to call the church office."

You mean if my aunt is still alive, Rachel thought fearfully. Since that dream, she was having a hard time shaking this death thing.

"If you promise not to slam the door in my face," he added with mirth dancing in those brown eyes, breaking through her reverie. When he smiled, his dimples peeked out from his beard.

So he had a sense of humor. She returned his smile. "You spooked me." Rachel had only seen a woman slam the door in a man's face in the movies. That had been a first for her. She looked away in embarrassment before she tilted her head in a challenge. "You're not going to let me forget that, are you?"

"Consider it forgotten." He gathered his Bible and waited for her to show him to the door. He offered a slight wave, then walked down the hall to the elevator.

After closing the door, Rachel leaned against it and sighed. Of course, death was a part of life, but she didn't want it to happen on her watch. She needed more time with Aunt Tweet—just like her sisters had created recent memories with their great-aunt, Rachel had that right. She might not get her full six months with Aunt Tweet, but if God could give her a couple more weeks…

She sighed. "I'll be so thankful."

Yawning, she pushed off the door and headed back to Aunt Tweet's room. Passing by the hall mirror, she backtracked, then screamed at the haunting image staring back at her. Her curls were a matted mess, her face needed attention, and her lounge clothes were wrinkled. She'd taken unkempt to the next level.

If Aunt Tweet were alert, she would take Rachel to task about her appearance. "A woman should always get a man's attention, whether she wants to or not. Honey, take it as long as your beauty lasts" was Aunt Tweet's mantra.

Before Nicholas had arrived, Rachel had pushed all thoughts of men and the dating world aside to focus on caring for her auntie. How Nicholas Adams had broken through her resistance was a mystery.

Maybe it was because he was a man a woman could not easily dismiss, including Rachel. She had appreciated the eye candy for about thirty seconds—no, make that twenty-nine—but he was a minister. She doubted Nicholas had given her a second glance.

Back in the bedroom, Rachel checked on Aunt Tweet, who hadn't stirred. Neither had the two dogs. She had adopted her cocker spaniel from a shelter less than a week after she'd moved into her condo, and her pet had taken to Aunt Tweet the moment she'd arrived but not to Aunt Tweet's dog, Sweet Pepper. Then, oddly, a few weeks ago, the two made some sort of dog truce to live in harmony at her side.

Rachel bent and brushed a kiss against her aunt's cheek. For an eighty-five-year-old, Aunt Tweet retained her natural beauty. Flawless dark skin complemented her silver-and-white hair. She was a classy lady with a larger-than-life personality and the right of amount of sass to make a stranger crave to be counted among her circle of friends.

"I hope God answers this prayer. Love you, Aunt Tweet," Rachel whispered and descended the loft. She would shower, then prepare a light breakfast in case Aunt Tweet opened her eyes and was famished again.

Three times a week, Rachel employed a home health aide to assist with Aunt Tweet's care, so Rachel could go to the firm in the afternoons. The other two days, she worked from home to be close by.

Rachel had come to depend on Clara Rodgers on Mondays,

Wednesdays, and Fridays, not only to do light housekeeping and patient assist but also to guide Rachel as a caregiver—even if that meant Clara had to endure Rachel venting her frustrations. Besides Clara, there was her best friend, Jacqui, who always had a listening ear, and her sisters were only a phone call or flight away.

Initially, it wasn't the Knicely sisters' plan to have outside help. They thought the three of them could handle Aunt Tweet's care on their own. Kym had sailed through her six months, but Tabitha's six months had been an eye-opener. No medical textbook could have prepared her for the practicum. Rachel expected a less mobile aunt but instead got living a nightmare with whispers of death. None of them were prepared for the dementia symptoms that plagued Aunt Tweet.

When Rachel's sister Tabitha had cried out for help, her friend and neighbor, Marcus Whittington, had answered. The two of them felt a home health aide would relieve some stress. At first, Rachel and Kym had been incensed about Tabitha leaving Aunt Tweet in the care of a stranger, but the woman turned out to be attentive and trustworthy, so Rachel hadn't thought twice about getting help when she'd brought Aunt Tweet to Nashville.

Since Rachel hadn't set her alarm, the minister's visit had been a lifesaver. She pinched the bridge of her nose. That sounded too much like a pun, but she needed to prepare updates on a project that was almost complete. She couldn't ask for a better boss and company, both allowing her work flexibility during her brief tenure as caregiver.

It was after two when Rachel breezed through the doors of Gersham-Smith, one of the oldest and most successful engineering firms in Nashville. Rachel was respected among her peers and management.

She could probably credit Aunt Tweet for inspiring her to study math and science in high school and college before the STEM curriculum—science, technology, engineering, and mathematics—became popular. The subjects were so easy, and as a teenager, she had often been one of the few Black girls in a class.

Aunt Tweet was Rachel's "shero", instilling her with confidence so she wouldn't be intimidated by men in the workplace. She preferred to impress with her brains, wit, and beauty—in that order—so she didn't believe in leaving the house without being polished from head to toe, not even to walk the dogs. She wanted her appearance to be as exquisite as her intellect. She was fashion-forward and could manage complex projects as though they were building blocks or simple puzzles.

Her boss, Harlan Goode, appeared as she stepped out of the elevator. "Afternoon, Rachel. How's your aunt?"

He was an older man with thinning hair on the crown of his head and a thick mustache. His father had started Gresham-Smith, and Harlan had expanded the firm to include offices in fourteen states and two overseas. The firm had drawn big-name clients to its roster with cutting-edge designs, including winning the bid to design a deep pump station project for the Metropolitan St. Louis Sewer District.

As a St. Louis native, Rachel took personal pride in handcrafting the design for the sump, dry wells, and other components for a structure that would be 180 feet belowground. It had been an honor to give back to her childhood city in the form of jobs and better living conditions.

The company stressed work-life balance, which Rachel had never fully appreciated until she became Aunt Tweet's caregiver. The past four months had been a roller-coaster ride, and it didn't look like the next few months would be any better, considering Aunt Tweet's deteriorating condition.

"About the same." She mustered a smile. Rachel believed in keeping a professional demeanor with her colleagues and tucked away the meltdowns until she was at home, behind closed doors. "My sister had a local minister come to pray with her."

"Good. They say prayer changes things," he said, then continued to his office for the afternoon briefing.

She believed prayer changed things—if only she could see a change with her aunt. Although Rachel was hopeful, she was realistic. The body required food and water to thrive, and Aunt Tweet needed to be alert in order to receive both.

Once in her office, Rachel had to force her mind to focus as she switched to job mode. Her team had been assigned to find solutions to ease Music City's congestion and reduce travel time for the ever-growing population and tourists. Millennials wanted no part of long commutes. They were attracted to communities where residents could work, live, and play, like she had been. One politician suggested adding more highway infrastructure. That would be a quick fix but wouldn't solve long-term problems.

Although Rachel was licensed as a civil engineer, her area of specialty was structural. While the client wanted to preserve some historical aspects in the area, Rachel wasn't convinced their request to build a tunnel for a walkway was sound. She and her team had a brainstorming session to determine whether the addition was possible and within budget.

After the meeting, Rachel delved into her RISA-3D program to analyze the structures. It was impossible to cram eight-plus hours of work into a five-hour shift, but she had to get home to Aunt Tweet so Clara could go to hers. The aide was a nursing student and single mother of an eight-year-old girl.

With only a short commute, Rachel slipped behind the steering wheel in her car, and a craving hit. Although she practiced healthy eating, a serving of Monell's skillet fried chicken was her guilty pleasure. It wasn't far, but it would close in twenty minutes.

She called Clara. "I know you're off within an hour, but my senses got a tracker on some of Monell's skillet fried—"

"Chicken." Clara smacked her lips and laughed. "Bring me some and all is forgiven."

"Got it, and I'll get some extra in case Aunt Tweet ever gets an appetite again. Any change?"

"Sorry, no, there hasn't been, but her vitals are stable."

Rachel's reality was her aunt's failing health. Suddenly, her appetite dulled, but she'd practically promised Clara, so she turned north on Second Avenue for the short drive to Bransford Avenue.

She arrived ten minutes before they closed. While she waited for her order, Rachel's mind drifted to her loved one. "You've got to bounce back, Aunt Tweet," she mumbled. "You've got to."

With her order in hand, Rachel returned to her condo and gave

Clara her sack of food plus a twenty-dollar tip, then she ate alone. She didn't make a habit of arriving late, mindful that Clara had a life too, and on the occasions when Rachel did, she always gave Clara something extra as a reminder that the woman's services were appreciated. Aunt Tweet wouldn't have wanted it any other way.

Her aunt had set up a monthly stipend of $5,000 for her care. She had stipulated that if the time came when she had to reside at a nursing facility, it had to be top tier.

Rachel had hoped the chicken's aroma would tease Aunt Tweet's senses, but the only thing that stirred in her aunt's bedroom was Shelby and Sweet Pepper, yet they didn't leave Aunt Tweet's side.

Rachel checked on Aunt Tweet again, then changed into her pajamas. Next, she grabbed her laptop and headed for her balcony. The nighttime view of the downtown skyline was worth the price she paid to live there. The antennas on top of the AT&T building resembled Batman, so she always pretended she lived in Gotham City and Batman was keeping her safe.

She loved Nashville, but not because it was the state capital. It boasted a large African American population. The city had a rich black history of struggle, determination, and empowerment that was seamless: before and after the Civil War and during the civil rights movement.

Her mind wandered as she booted up her laptop. There were so many unsung heroes during slavery besides Harriet Tubman. The Harding family was one of the largest enslavers in Tennessee, and they invested heavily in thoroughbred horses. Who would have guessed one of the most famous horse jockeys in the 1800s was an African American man named Isaac Murphy who was enslaved at the Belle Meade Plantation?

Fast-forward to post-Emancipation Proclamation and education was a priority for freedmen and women. Nashville fed the hunger of eager pupils with four historically black colleges and universities among the city's thirty-two.

Add other contributions to music and a thriving social scene, and it was a no-brainer why Rachel made the Athens of the South her home after her college graduation. There was never a weekend without an event to attend, and she and Jacqui hit the circuit.

Just like her hometown of St. Louis was more than the Gateway Arch, Nashville was more than the Grand Ole Opry, even though it was also nicknamed Music City and NashVegas.

Rachel caught herself from further drifting and took a deep breath. Reclining on her balcony was akin to a spa visit. Day or night, it was the perfect place to relax her mind and ease stress from her body. However, she hadn't been productive, so she stood, waved good night to Batman, and walked back inside. She padded across her living room floor and up the stairs to the loft-converted bedroom.

She settled in the chaise next to Aunt Tweet's bed with her laptop and prepared for a long evening of working and watching Aunt Tweet.

Rachel didn't realize she had dozed off until Aunt Tweet's mumbling woke her. Startled, she caught her laptop before it tumbled to the floor. Her aunt's aging brown eyes were watching her.

"Aunt Tweet!" She pushed everything aside and shooed the dogs out of the way and climbed into the bed. Rachel hugged Aunt Tweet as tight as she could without crushing her. "You've got to stop scaring me. Hungry? I got you some Monell's. But you're probably thirsty." She scrambled off the bed more than ready to do her aunt's bidding, then realized she hadn't yet thanked God for answering her prayers.

Shaking her head, Aunt Tweet pointed to the flat screen where Rachel had played countless movies for them to watch together, but her aunt had a fascination with one video. It was a keepsake of her niece's nuptials. The wedding video had captured raw emotion on Tabitha's and Marcus's faces that would make a skeptic believe in love.

Rachel had a bargaining chip. She rested her hands on her hips and shook her head. "Only if you drink and eat something—please." After a few rounds of stubbornness on both sides, Aunt Tweet consented in a weak voice to bottled water and toast.

She propped Aunt Tweet up so she was sitting in the bed and fed her. When her aunt became combative about the wedding tape, Rachel conceded. She had force-fed Aunt Tweet enough—half the bottled water and one of two pieces of toast.

If Aunt Tweet stayed awake, Rachel would give her a small snack in a little while. Rachel made herself comfortable, then started the video. Holding Aunt Tweet's hand, they watched in silence as if they had never before seen Marcus dabbing at one of Tabitha's tears in an emotional moment, or Marcus's brother, Demetrius, handing Marcus a hankie to wipe the sweat off his forehead, or Aunt Tweet yelling, "That's a whopper," in response to the bride and groom's passionate first kiss.

Somehow, the reruns of Tabitha's wedding sparked a happy place within Aunt Tweet that she had never shared with her nieces. They did know Aunt Tweet was briefly married, then divorced before the Knicely girls were born. Her aunt seemed content without a significant other in her life, but her love for watching the one-hour-and-twelve-minute video seemed to challenge that.

A mystery man's name always surfaced on her aunt's lips, Randolph, and sadness would wash over her face. The longing was unmistakable, and Rachel wondered if her aunt had missed out in love despite men's attraction to Aunt Tweet like flowers to the sun.

Not only did Rachel inherit Aunt Tweet's sass, fashion sense, and other mannerisms, she knew she had the physical assets to capture a man's eye too. To date, none had captured her heart, at least not the way her brother-in-law had her sister Tabitha's.

Despite the revolving door of men she allowed into her life, briefly including Demetrius, Marcus's older brother, Rachel never trusted a man to want her beyond her looks, so she had resolved herself not to expect it.

"Listen to me." Her aunt called her by name and pulled Rachel out of her reverie.

Some days, Aunt Tweet seemed unsure of Rachel's identity, but when she heard her name, her heart warmed. She gave Aunt Tweet her full attention.

"Make sure you don't let love pass you by, you hear?" She waggled her finger as if Rachel were a little girl again.

"Yes, ma'am." Rachel grinned. The nourishment, although very little, had given her aunt renewed energy.

"A good man isn't always the best looking. He's got to have a good heart too."

"Okay." Rachel agreed, but waking up to an ugly man every morning would be a test in any marriage.

Aunt Tweet seemed to become more sentimental after each viewing of the wedding video.

"Make sure he holds your hand…prays for you…feeds you…loves you." Her voice drifted off. Oh no, her aunt needed to eat some more, but right before her eyes, Aunt Tweet dozed off, and within seconds, Rachel heard a light snore. Not good at all.

The next morning, Rachel woke and stretched. From her place on the chaise, she glanced at Aunt Tweet, who seemed to be in the same position as yesterday. Had Rachel dreamed their conversation, or had it really taken place? She spied the remote on the bed and knew it hadn't been a dream.

Was there a subliminal message in that wedding tape? If her aunt was hinting that Rachel would be next, then Aunt Tweet would be disappointed. Rachel had no prospects, time, or desire to be anybody's wife. She was only twenty-nine. Maybe at thirty-five, she would look at her options. Until then, it was business as usual.

Chapter 3

Fear. Nicholas had sensed it yesterday from Rachel. He hoped that praying together on her aunt's behalf provided the niece comfort.

As he drove home Thursday morning from his overnight shift, Nicholas wondered if Rachel would request another prayer visit, which would be more for her own peace. Priscilla Brownlee was in God's hands whether Nicholas returned or not. He had never witnessed life leaving a person before, but from the looks of the woman in the bed, he doubted she could stay in that state much longer.

Why was that home visit still on Nicholas's mind twenty-four hours later? Maybe he had never seen a disheveled woman look so beautiful.

Attraction was far from Rachel's mind and for good reason. Her aunt was dying, and ironically, as a man who ministered to countless families, Nicholas had no personal experience with that within his own close-knit family. He was grateful the Adams family had been free of tragedy. *Thank you, Jesus.*

There was more to Miss Knicely than what he saw on the surface, because he couldn't stop thinking about the aunt and her niece during the short drive home from the Nissan Smyrna plant to his brick ranch house on Nautical Street. He pulled into the two-car garage where his other car, a Nissan Infiniti QX60, was parked.

The upside of living four miles away from his job was it was a great community, a good investment, and a time-saver when he worked overnight. The downside was he lived a good half hour from the Believers Temple Church in Brentwood and twenty minutes from his parents and his brother's family in Antioch.

He yawned as he strolled through the garage door to the kitchen and disarmed his alarm. He glanced around his humble dwelling—not bad for a bachelor. It wasn't pristine like Rachel's condo, but it was comfortable, with a spacious master bedroom, another one reserved for when his twin nephews visited, and a third bedroom that was part home gym/storage room/computer room/whatever he needed it to be at the time.

He had done enough thinking for one morning, so he grabbed a bottled juice, then headed for his bedroom to get some rest. He prayed, then slid under the covers, sighed, and closed his eyes, ready to succumb to blissful sleep.

Nicholas felt a nudge that stirred him from his sleep. He strained to open his eyes as his body protested the interruption. Did someone touch him? Nicholas scooted up and glanced around the room before blinking at the clock to bring the time into focus: 11:00 a.m. What? His body demanded five more hours.

Pray for Rachel. The thought came unbidden. Nicholas blinked and immediately became alert. *She's going to need comfort. Be there for her.*

His heart sank. Was Rachel's Aunt Tweet passing so soon? There was no question the two had been on his mind. He swallowed his sorrow for them and slid to his knees to pray. Almost an hour later, Nicholas climbed back into bed, but this time, sleep didn't come so easily.

Rachel couldn't wait to tell her sisters the latest on Aunt Tweet's condition during a Skype call. "All this talk about death got in my head. My friend Jacqui had mentioned about a family priest giving the last rites for a relative, then my dear sister"—she squinted at Tabitha—"summoned a minister to my doorstep without giving me forewarning, not to mention Aunt Tweet's doctor discussing the symptoms of the latter stage of Alzheimer's. It was too much." She shivered.

"I know, Sis, I know," Kym said. "Anything encouraging going on?"

"Well, yeah." Rachel nodded. "Aunt Tweet woke last night wanting to see the wedding video again."

Tabitha rocked her head from side to side, blushing. "It was romantic. Did she eat?"

Rachel's shoulders slumped. "Not much. I fed her some water and toast. I feel so cheated."

"Why?" Tabitha and Kym asked in unison.

"My quality time with her isn't what I had hoped for or expected when we agreed to the caregivers pact."

"None of us knew what to expect," Kym explained.

"Well, I'm not trying to be a drama queen..."

"But you usually are." Kym lifted a brow and laughed, and so did Tabitha.

"Okay, you got me." Rachel chuckled, then sobered. "You experienced the Aunt Tweet we knew and loved during your six months as a caregiver. Tabitha, you shared Aunt Tweet with Marcus to create memories..." She patted her chest. "Me? Aunt Tweet has been either combative or withdrawn. It hurts. I had imagined us bonding during long walks and her sharing life lessons like she used to. Last night, she mumbled something about prayer and hand-holding. I want to do more for her," she admitted in frustration, "and with her. What's my purpose in her life now?"

"Maybe it's just to hold her hand," Kym said and shrugged.

"You know, she said something like that to me," Tabitha said. "'You never know whose hand will give you that last piece of bread.'" She shivered. "Whenever she talked like that, it scared me."

Rachel crossed her arms against her chest. "I don't want it to be *my* hand that feeds her her last meal or my eyes that watch her take her last breath. We agreed to take care of Aunt Tweet, not watch her die." She started tugging on her hair until she tangled it in a curl. "Even the doctor said she could live a long time in this stage. I just need to get her healthy."

"Sis, prayer strengthened her. Maybe that's what she wants now. Why don't you ask Minister Adams to add her to a rotation for prayer?" Tabitha suggested. "You need it too. Prayer brings about peace."

Rachel was silent. The fact that Aunt Tweet asked for prayer troubled her spirit. She couldn't get the priest and the last rites thing out of her head. "I don't have his number."

"Let me give you the number to the church," Tabitha said, then repeated it slowly, waiting as Rachel tapped the number into her phone.

"Okay, I'll call," she agreed hesitantly. "At least this time, I'll be expecting him and won't look a hot mess."

"You?" Tabitha screamed and laughed. "Since when are you a hot mess? Even going to bed, you dress up in pajamas and head wraps as if you're about to do a photo shoot for lingerie."

"Not as a caregiver. Flannel pj's and socks have been my sleepwear. My nightly beauty regimen is on hold. Thank you very much."

"And what would Aunt Tweet say about a disheveled appearance in front of a gentleman? I'm just trying to lighten up the mood here." Kym joked, but Rachel didn't laugh. "A gentleman like Minister Adams. Was he old, young, a big guy?"

Rachel didn't want to think about a man, not at the moment, but her mind had other plans. Nicholas Adams was very attractive. It had been a while since she had seen a man look that handsome. He reminded her of actor Daniel Sunjata, but she wasn't going to tell her sisters that. "My mood is tentative. It will change to upbeat if I can get Aunt Tweet to eat more."

"Hey, Marcus is making too much noise in the kitchen. Got to go. Remember to call the church!" Tabitha said and ended the call.

"I'll talk to you later too. Love you, Sis. Give Auntie a kiss for me," Kym said and was gone too.

Rachel's emotions remained unsettled. Was she ready for a repeat of yesterday? Aunt Tweet mumbled, "Prayer," so Rachel had no choice but to do her aunt's bidding. She would make the call, but first she had to take another look at a client's requested change so she could email her team. Whether she was at home or at the firm, it was still a workday.

While Aunt Tweet rested, Rachel powered up her work laptop and switched to work mode. She bounced back from her 3-D program, trying to create a visual and input math formulas in the STAAD.Pro program for analysis. She had been so focused on the project that she had forgotten to eat lunch. Going into the kitchen, Rachel made a veggie sandwich, checked on Aunt Tweet, then called the number Tabitha gave her.

"Good afternoon, Believers Temple Church. This is Mrs. Eloise Emerson."

Rachel cleared her throat and explained the reason for her call. "Hi, this is Rachel Whittington. Is it possible for Minister Adams to come and pray with my aunt, Miss Priscilla Brownlee, again? I know it's too late for today, but hopefully tomorrow, Friday morning. The sooner, the better."

"I'll get this message to him," the woman said.

"Thank you." At least this time when he arrived, she would be awake and presentable.

That night, Rachel played Tabitha's wedding video, hoping it would coax Aunt Tweet to awaken. It didn't, so after a few minutes, Rachel turned it off and opened her laptop. She was determined to give the client what they wanted, but as a structural engineer, her focus was on ensuring the design and construction of any walkway tunnel was sound and not subject to collapse. She had to review documents before she scheduled an early morning conference call.

She was starting to feel the pressure of being on top of her game at work and an attentive caregiver. *If only I could be cloned*, she thought as she drifted off to sleep.

Seven a.m. came too soon when Rachel was operating on five hours of sleep. She stood and studied Aunt Tweet. She moaned a little as if she was about to wake, but her eyes never opened.

Rachel didn't know if she could describe her current feelings: flustered, discouraged, scared. Every night, she prayed, but to be honest, she didn't have confidence in her prayers. At least she looked forward to Nicholas's visit to pray. She liked the sound of his soothing voice. His prayer had changed things. Rachel had no timeframe for when he would come, so she hurried to her bedroom to shower, noting the time for the conference call was within forty minutes. If he came during her conference call, at least she would be presentable.

After the shower, she dressed in slacks and a sweater, then combed her long hair into one braid and twisted it on the top of her head. Her beauty enhancement was pink lip gloss.

"Sorry, Aunt Tweet, this is the best I can do," Rachel whispered to her reflection. In the kitchen, she prepared a bowl of fruit and oatmeal, gave thanks, and nibbled. If she had time between the conference call and Nicholas's visit, she would freshen up Aunt Tweet and her bed, even though it was Friday and Clara would come to do those tasks.

With a few minutes to spare, Rachel set her laptop on the dining room table with her handwritten notes on one side. She had several windows open on her computer. By 8:00 a.m., she was patched into the conference call with her boss, two team members, and the client.

"Good morning, Mr. Thomas," Rachel began. "We've had a chance to review the addition you requested for the common ground play area. Although the tunnel might enhance the overall appearance, the area is prone to flooding, and that would compromise the physical integrity of any walkway tunnel."

She listened as her colleagues offered suggestions as they emailed design options. An hour and thirty minutes later, the call ended with a plan to review building codes and sewer locations. The easy way out was to tell the client no, he had agreed on the plans, but her company didn't do business by telling clients no.

Rachel tugged strands of hair out of the braid—a childhood habit she still did when she was baffled about a problem or situation. Her doorbell rang. Nicholas. She had momentarily forgotten he was coming.

She opened the door with a cordial smile, then blinked. The person standing before her wasn't Minister Nicholas Adams. The woman was as thick as the huge Bible she carried and was dressed in white from her bonnet to her stockings and shoes. Did Tabitha call for a hospice nurse? Did the agency send a different home health aide besides Clara? Who was this stranger?

"May I help you?"

The woman lifted her chin. "You called the church for a prayer warrior, and I'm here. Mother Jenkins, sugar. May I come in?"

Rachel frowned and stepped back. "I…I was expecting Minister Adams."

"Mm-hmm," she mumbled, "they all do." Then, with a no-nonsense expression, she asked, "Now, where is Mother Brownlee?"

What does that mean? Rachel wondered as she closed the door and led the way to the loft. Where Nicholas's tone was soft and smooth, this

Mother Jenkins's voice boomed as if she were about to sing a song loud enough to raise the dead. Rachel cringed at the pun, but in this case, if it would prevent her aunt from dying, Rachel welcomed it. "She's my aunt, not a moth—"

"Oh, praise God," Mother Jenkins said when she saw Aunt Tweet, then she glanced over her shoulder and held her hand out to Rachel. "Aren't you going to join us for prayer?" The side-eye she gave Rachel conveyed that there would be no opting out.

She came to the bedside, and Mother Jenkins clutched her hand. The woman had such a strong grip that when she yelled, "Jesus," she practically crushed Rachel's fingers.

Rachel cringed and bit her lip to keep from crying out in pain.

"Lord, we come boldly to Your grace, where we may obtain mercy and favor for our dear sister here, Mother Brownlee..."

Rachel picked her battles. She wasn't about to attempt to correct her again that Priscilla Brownlee was an aunt and never a mother. However, the woman's body language took "hold your peace" to a whole new level.

"In Matthew 8, we know that if You speak Your word and we believe Your word, Mother Brownlee can be healed, according to Your will... This is all about You, Jesus!" Mother Jenkins prayed with such power, Rachel trembled as she whispered her requests. Soon, the prayer ceased, and silence filled the room.

Rachel opened her eyes to see Aunt Tweet smiling. Rachel sniffed. It wasn't as if she didn't believe in prayer, but to see instant results was amazing. Yes, Tabitha was right: adding Aunt Tweet to a prayer rotation schedule was much needed, whether it was Nicholas or Mother Jenkins. "Thank you," she whispered.

"Thank God." She patted Aunt Tweet's arm, then looked at Rachel. "My job here is done. Keep praying and praising God, and everything will be all right."

After walking the woman to the door, Rachel thanked her, then returned to see Aunt Tweet smacking her lips. "I can't remember the last time I ate."

"It's been a while." Rachel chuckled. "I'll get you something, then freshen you up."

The doorbell rang while Rachel was preparing soup. Why was she disappointed to see Clara? Rachel smiled at the home health aide while chastening her own thoughts. Did she really think it would be Nicholas after Mother Jenkins had already visited?

Whatever tug-of-war was going on inside her, Rachel had to stop it. Her sister's wedding tape was starting to play with her head.

"How's Miss Brownlee?" Clara asked, staring at her.

"Oh." Rachel jumped and closed the door. "She's having a good day. Go on back."

Clearly, Nicholas had moved on to the next sick church member. Rachel doubted she would see him again, which was fine. Mother Jenkins was a good replacement.

Chapter 4

Dead. Nicholas didn't realize his phone's battery had died overnight at work, and he didn't have his charger. Once at home, he powered up right away. He didn't expect the first call he received would be from Mother Jenkins, who could be long-winded. He withheld his groan as he answered, craving sleep.

"I tell you, Minister Adams, you need backup when you visit these women. They're all jezebels."

"Now, Mother Jenkins—" Nicholas tried to interrupt politely. She was called Mother Jenkins instead of Minister Jenkins because of her no-nonsense manner that dared anyone to cross her. The older woman was not only a powerful prayer warrior, but she had also appointed herself Nicholas's protector from all women—church ladies didn't get a free pass either.

"You should have seen that woman in those skinny jeans and top—Mother Brownlee's niece. Showed too much curvature, then those lashes were too long to be real. She was disappointed when I showed up outside her door instead of you…"

Really? Nicholas no longer tried to interrupt. So Rachel had been expecting him? It was a toss-up whether that tidbit amused or flattered him. Placing his call with Mother Jenkins on speaker mode, he checked his phone log, and sure enough, he viewed three missed messages, two from Mrs. Emerson at the church. This explained Mother Jenkins's call.

His heart pounded. What was going on—not with Rachel but with her aunt? What happened to cause Rachel to call the church—or maybe it was her sister again. Nicholas needed to ask, but he had become too distracted with Mother Jenkins's description of Rachel's assets. He was glad she hadn't slammed the door in Mother Jenkins's face. That would not have been good.

"Excuse me, Mother Jenkins, how was Miss Brownlee?" He held his breath.

"The way God wanted her—alive and well," she stated as if he should know.

Nicholas exhaled. "I'm sure they were both glad you visited."

"Mm-hmm, but remember what I said, Minister Adams. That girl is too cute for her own good. I'm ready to go in with you, into the lion's den, when these women are trying to dig their claws into you."

He nodded as if she could see. "I'll take your offer under advisement." When Mother Jenkins paused to take a breath, Nicholas used that space to say goodbye. Besides the calls from Mrs. Emerson, the other one was from his brother. He listened to Karl's message first.

Just as Nicholas had suspected. His brother needed a babysitter for his five-year-old twins because he and his wife had been invited to speak at a church. Again? The two were a "spiritual power couple" who fed the hungry, ministered to the sick, taught seminars, and more.

Whenever Karl and Ava were out of town, Uncle Nick was the default.

Both Adams brothers were ministers. There wasn't much sibling rivalry between them, but how did his younger brother by four years beat him to the altar? It would be nice to have a special someone besides his family to share his life with.

If his chances were left up to Mother Jenkins, that wouldn't happen in his lifetime, but she did have a point. Many of the women were fascinated that he was a minister. What they didn't understand was that being a minister wasn't glamorous. Nicholas wanted a woman to love who could be a wife, a mother, and a helpmate, like Ava was to his brother. In essence, Nicholas craved a Proverbs 31 woman.

At thirty-six years old, he was still waiting for that woman. Ladies always said they were waiting on their husbands. Men were no different. "We're waiting too," he mumbled. Reining his thoughts in, he texted his brother that he was available to watch his nephews. Without a social life, of course he was available. He stifled a yawn.

Although his weekend began Friday morning, all Nicholas wanted was sleep. First, he slid to his knees to pray for Rachel and Miss Brownlee. Next, he petitioned the Lord Jesus for the well-being of the elderly everywhere, for the homeless, for fatherless children, and more until he realized an hour had passed.

In bed, his body was ready to succumb, but his thoughts were still on Rachel and her aunt; then their images faded as he turned over and fell asleep. He didn't wake up again until an hour or so before the twins were set to arrive and turn his house upside down.

He grudgingly climbed out of bed and headed for the bathroom. He showered, dressed, then padded across the house to the kitchen. As he munched on a bowl of cereal, his thoughts turned to Rachel—again—and he thought about whether he should personally check on her. He noted the time and wondered if the church secretary was still in her office on a Friday evening at five thirty.

Mother Jenkins's warning, which was warranted around single women, rang in his head, but he called the church office anyway. Surprisingly, the secretary answered cheerfully.

Yes! "Hello, Mrs. Emerson. I'm sorry I got your message late about seeing Priscilla Brownlee. Mother Jenkins said her visit went well."

"Good. The niece, Rachel Knicely, called and wanted you, but I left a message and never heard back, so Mother Jenkins was the next contact."

He nodded. Yes, protocol was to go down the list of ministers until one could be reached. "Did Miss Knicely leave a number?"

After a brief hold, she returned to the line. "Yes, she did." She proceeded to give it to him.

After thanking Mrs. Emerson, Nicholas immediately called Rachel. She sounded like she was on the same sleep schedule as him. "Did I wake you?" he asked.

"Who's calling?" Rachel's voice was soft.

"I'm sorry for not identifying myself. This is Minister Adams—Nicholas."

"Oh, hi." She cleared her throat. "Yes, you did, but I've learned to catch a nap whenever I can."

"I called to apologize that I didn't get your message in time. It wasn't Mrs. Emerson's fault. My phone died, and I didn't have my charger."

"And I thought you were standing me up."

Was that a tease, or was she serious? Either way, he was interested. "Never. I understand Mother Jenkins ministered to your aunt. How is she doing?"

When she was slow to answer, he braced for the worst.

"Why don't you come and see her for yourself?"

What? Nicholas wasn't expecting an invitation. Was his mind playing games with him, or was Mother Jenkins's warning ringing true? "Thanks, but I'm babysitting this evening. Can I visit tomorrow?" His heart stopped, waiting for her answer.

"A minister who babysits." She chuckled and he smiled, liking the sound of her laughter. He was honored to contribute to any of her happiness at this time in her life.

"They are my nephews, Kory and Rory, and I'm their favorite uncle."

"Let me guess, you're their only uncle, right?"

Nicholas grinned. "Yep." He enjoyed talking to her when she wasn't stressed out, but he had to go and prepare snacks for the twins. "Sorry to disturb you. If the Lord wills, I'll see you tomorrow. Is noon too early?"

"See you then, Uncle Nick." She laughed and ended the call.

Reading Group Guide

1. Talk about Chaz's involvement in his son Gee and daughter-in-law's life.

2. Do you know someone with autism spectrum disorder?

3. Kym wanted children. Discuss whether that should have been a deal breaker in her relationship with Chaz.

4. Discuss Chaz's request to relocate and Kym's response. Whose side would you be on?

5. Has the story informed your views so you could differentiate between a child's temper tantrum and autistic behavior?

Acknowledgments

It takes a village to create a story with such depth and emotions. The following exceptional friends helped me breathe life into my characters. Thank you for giving me access to your lives and sharing your knowledge.

Cousin Sherry, Deacon Earl Bingham, and Jovan
Minister Darlene Martin and Erica
Former KMOV-TV colleague and friend Terry Cancila and Keegan
Former KMOV-TV news anchor and HBCU instructor Vickie Newton
Sister Dr. Kim L. Eastern
Sister-in-Christ Dr. Jackie Hoskins
Longtime editor and friend Chandra Sparks Splond
Sourcebooks editing and marketing staff
Author assistant Jackie Roberts
Beta reader Stacy Jefferson
Fellow author Rhonda McKnight
Represented by Evan Marshall Literary Agency

About the Author

Pat Simmons is a multipublished author with more than thirty-five titles. She is a self-proclaimed genealogy sleuth who is passionate about researching her ancestors and then casting them in starring roles in her novels. She is a three-time recipient of the Romance Slam Jam Emma Rodgers Award for Best Inspirational Romance.

Pat's first inspirational women's fiction with Sourcebooks, *Lean on Me*, was the February/March Together We Read Digital Book Club pick for the national library system. *Here for You* and *Stand by Me* are also part of the Family Is Forever series. Her holiday indie release, *Christmas Dinner*, and *Here for You* were featured in *Woman's World*, a national magazine. She contributed an article, "I'm Listening," to *Chicken Soup for the Soul: I'm Speaking Now* (2021).

Pat holds a BS in mass communications from Emerson College in Boston, Massachusetts. She has worked in various positions in radio, television, and print media for more than twenty years. She oversaw media publicity for the annual RT Booklovers Conventions for fourteen years. In addition to researching her roots and sewing, she has been a featured speaker and workshop presenter at various venues across the country.

Pat has converted her sofa-strapped, sports-fanatic husband into an amateur travel agent, untrained bodyguard, GPS-guided chauffeur, and administrative assistant who is constantly on probation. They have a son and a daughter.

Read more about Pat on her website: patsimmons.net.

FAMILY IS FOREVER

Explore love through the eyes of a caregiver in this poignant romantic women's fiction series from Pat Simmons, award-winning and national bestselling author

Lean on Me

When her neighbor Marcus Whittington accuses Tabitha Knicely of elder neglect, he doesn't realize how hard Tabitha is fighting to keep everything together. But the more she leans on him, the happier he is to share her burdens.

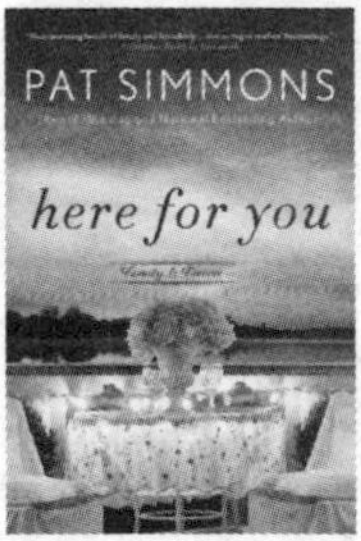

Here for You

Nicholas Adams's ministry is bringing comfort to those who are sick and homebound. He responds to a request for help for an ailing woman with dementia, but when he meets the Knicelys, he realizes that youngest sister Rachel is the one who needs support the most.

Stand by Me

Until she met Charles "Chaz" Banks, Kym Knicely didn't realize how much caregiving can vary. She was a caregiver for her elderly aunt, while Chaz helps look after his seven-year-old granddaughter, Chauncy, who has autism. Although Kym's attraction to Chaz is strong, she has to decide whether a romantic relationship can thrive between two people at different stages in life.

"Pat Simmons pulls at the heartstrings by focusing on love, faith, and family."

—Naleighna Kai, *USA Today* bestselling author, for *Here for You*

For more info about Sourcebooks's books and authors, visit:

sourcebooks.com

WINNER TAKES ALL

Bestselling and beloved author Sandra Kitt is
back with The Millionaires Club series!

Jean Travis has the job of announcing the latest lottery winner on TV and is stunned to find that Patrick Bennett, her teenage crush, is the top mega winner. They haven't seen each other in years, and Patrick is thrilled to renew their acquaintance. Jean, not so much. After all, a lot has changed since they used to study together and Jean worked so hard to hide her feelings. Now that he's won so much money, Patrick faces a whole new world of demands from family, friends, coworkers, strangers. The only person he knows for sure he can trust, is Jean…

"Sandra Kitt writes beautiful stories... *Winner Takes All* is romantic, tender, emotional, and compelling."

—RaeAnne Thayne, *New York Times* bestselling author

For more info about Sourcebooks's books and authors, visit:

sourcebooks.com